TINY MIRACLES

*Two best friends find love, happiness
—and little bundles of joy!*

Friends Fran and Kellie have been through
thick and thin together since childhood,
and now both are facing the fact that their dreams
of motherhood might never happen.

Follow the two women's stories as they fall in love
with two gorgeous Greeks, and find happiness
beyond their wildest dreams, as well as the little
longed-for miracles they never thought possible…

Dear Reader,

Along Came Twins is the second book in my series TINY MIRACLES. In my first book, *Baby out of the Blue,* the heroine had to deal with the problem of never being able to give birth to a baby. In this second book the heroine must go through artificial insemination in order to try and get pregnant—but all seems hopeless.

In real life, one of my dear sisters and her husband adopted two precious babies. Then lo and behold, maybe ten years later, she found herself pregnant— and a year later was pregnant again. They now have four precious children. Our family considers *those* babies miracles!

I'd like to dedicate this book to my sister Heather and all those would-be mothers waiting for their own miracles to happen.

Enjoy!

Rebecca Winters

ALONG CAME TWINS...

BY
REBECCA WINTERS

First published in Great Britain 2013
by Mills & Boon, an imprint of Harlequin (UK) Limited,
Eton House, 18-24 Paradise Road, Richmond, Surrey TW9 1SR

© Rebecca Winters 2013

ISBN: 978 0 263 90107 8
ebook ISBN: 978 1 472 00475 8

23-0513

Harlequin (UK) policy is to use papers that are natural, renewable and recyclable products and made from wood grown in sustainable forests. The logging and manufacturing processes conform to the legal environmental regulations of the country of origin.

Printed and bound in Spain
by Blackprint CPI, Barcelona

Rebecca Winters, whose family of four children has now swelled to include five beautiful grandchildren, lives in Salt Lake City, Utah, in the land of the Rocky Mountains. With canyons and high alpine meadows full of wildflowers, she never runs out of places to explore. As well as her favorite vacation spots in Europe, they often end up as background for her romance novels, because writing is her passion, along with her family and church.

Rebecca loves to hear from readers. If you wish to email her, please visit her website, www.cleanromances.com.

CHAPTER ONE

"DR. SAVAKIS? Thank you for seeing me at the end of your busy day. When Dr. Creer, my doctor in Philadelphia, told me I was pregnant with twins, no one could have been more surprised than I was. You wouldn't know that since my last visit to you before I left Athens, I filed for divorce. It will be final in a few days."

Her fertility doctor shook his balding head. "After such a joyous outcome, what a pity, Mrs. Petralia. I remember how excited you both were to know your allergy problem didn't have to interfere with your ability to conceive. Now that you're pregnant, I'm extremely sorry to hear this news."

No one could be sorrier than she was, but she didn't want to discuss it. "I still need to tell my husband, but it isn't the kind of thing he should hear over the phone. That's why I'm here in Greece for a few days."

"I see."

"I wanted to pay you a visit to let you know the procedure worked. After all we went through together, naturally I wanted to give you my personal thanks." Her voice caught. "It's been a dream of mine to have a baby. Despite my failed marriage, I'm ecstatic over this pregnancy. Leandros will be thrilled, too. As you know, his first wife died carrying their unborn child, and he lost them both. Without your help, this miracle would never have happened."

She should have gone to Leandros first with the news, but decided that by coming to their doctor to tell him her marriage was over, it would make the divorce more real somehow and help her to face Leandros.

Dr. Savakis eyed her soberly through his bifocals. "I'm glad for you and pleased you phoned to see me. How are you feeling?"

"Since the doctor prescribed pills that help my nausea, I'm much better."

He smiled. "Good. You'll need to take extra care of yourself now."

"I know. I plan to, believe me."

"As long as you're here, I have information that might interest you at some later date."

"What is it?"

"More medical research has been done on your condition. Did your doctor tell you?"

"No. I've only seen him once."

"He'll no doubt discuss this with you during one of your appointments with him."

Kellie thought about all the anguish she'd been through hoping to get pregnant. "It doesn't matter now. I'm going to have my hands full raising my twins."

"Nothing could make me happier in that regard. But you need to keep in mind what I'm telling you for the future. You're only twenty-eight. In time you could find yourself remarried and wanting another child."

She shook her head. "No, Dr. Savakis. That part of my life is over." Though they hadn't been able to make their marriage work, Leandros had spoiled her for other men. He'd been the great love of her life. There would never be another.

"You say that now, but one never knows what the future will bring."

"I—I appreciate that," she stammered, "but I can't think about anything else except raising my children."

"I understand," he said kindly. "If you have any problems while you're here in Athens, call me. There's a Dr. Hanno on staff here who's an OB and works with high-risk patients. If you're going to be in Greece for any length of time, I'd advise you to call him and make an appointment for a checkup. Tell him I referred you. And don't forget. I'm always at your disposal."

"Thank you, Dr. Savakis. You've been wonderful. I want you to know I'll always be grateful."

Kellie left his office in the medical building attached to the hospital and took a taxi back to the Civitel Olympic Hotel in central Athens. She was exhausted and hungry. Tomorrow morning she'd approach her soon-to-be ex-husband, wherever he happened to be. Her breath caught just thinking about seeing him again. It was better for her mind not to go there.

Once she had dinner in her room, she'd phone her aunt and uncle to let them know she'd arrived safely.

It was after eleven at night when the door connecting Leandros's office with his private secretary's opened. Everyone had gone home six hours go. It was probably one of the security guards, but he still resented the interruption. He looked up to discover his sister-in-law on her way in with a tray of food in hand.

A scowl broke out on his face. "What are you doing here, Karmela?"

"Mrs. Kostas told me you'd be working through the night to get ready for your mysterious trip. Is it true you're leaving in the morning?"

"That's not your concern."

"I thought you'd like a cup of coffee and some sandwiches to help you stay awake." She put it on his desk.

"You should have gone home with everyone else. I'm not hungry and need total quiet to work through these specs."

"Well, I'm here now." She grabbed a sandwich and sank into one of the chairs near his desk to eat. "Don't be grumpy. I worry about you. So do Mom and Dad. They've tried to get you to come to dinner, but you keep turning them down."

"I've been busy."

"Where are you going on your vacation?"

"That's confidential."

"I'm family, remember? I like to do things for you."

"You need to lead your own life. I appreciate the coffee, but now you have to go."

She didn't budge. "You shouldn't have married Kellie. She wasn't good enough for you, you know."

His hands curled into fists. Before Kellie had shut the door on him in Philadelphia, she'd expressed the same sentiment to him. He'd been crushed that she would even think such a thing, let alone say it to his face.

But for Karmela to dare speak her mind like this made him furious. She was never one to worry about boundaries. His first wife, Petra, had warned him about it and had asked him to overlook that flaw in her sister.

Unfortunately, tonight Karmela had stepped over a line he couldn't forgive. Something wasn't right with his sister-in-law. He recalled the times Kellie had made a quiet comment about Karmela's familiarity with him. *And how many times did you brush it off as unimportant, Petralia?*

He fought to control his temper, but it was wearing thin. "You've said enough."

"Ooh. You really are upset." She got up from the chair. "The only reason I came in here was to help you." Tears filled her eyes. "You used to let me when Petra was alive." *Only because Petra asked me to be kind to you.* "I miss her and know you do, too."

He'd had all he could tolerate. "Leave *now*!"

"Okay. I'm going."

"Take the tray with you." He kept the coffee.

At the door she turned to him. "How long will you be gone?"

"I have no idea. In any event, it's no one's business but mine."

"Why are you being so hurtful?"

"Why do you continually go where angels fear to tread?" he retorted without looking at her. "Good night. Lock the door on your way out."

Relieved when the sound of her footsteps faded, he got back to work. In the morning he'd call Frato and go over the most important items before he took off. His eyes fastened on the picture of Kellie that sat on his desk. He was living to see his golden-blond wife again. Though they'd both hurt each other, he'd do whatever it took to get her back.

When Kellie awakened the next morning, she was so nervous to see Leandros again, she decided it was a mistake to have come to Athens. The talk with Dr. Savakis had opened up thoughts and feelings she'd been trying to suppress.

Soon after their wedding she'd been diagnosed with a semen allergy, but the doctor had said he saw no reason why they couldn't get pregnant. She and Leandros went to their first artificial insemination appointment with such high hopes. Kellie wanted a baby with him desperately. He was eager for it, too, and had made certain his business matters didn't interfere while they went through the steps necessary for conception to work.

Leandros had been so sweet and tender with her about their situation. Like any happily married couple wanting to start a family, they'd waited for the signs that meant she had conceived. Two months into their marriage, her period came. Leandros had kissed her and loved her out of her disappointment.

"Next month," he'd whispered.

Knowing he was disappointed, too, she'd loved him back with all the energy in her, wanting to show him she wouldn't allow this to dampen her spirits. Once again they went back to the hospital, for another try, only to be disappointed the following month.

So many tries full of expectations, but each waiting period had seemed harder than the last, contributing to the problems that had slowly crept into their marriage. What bittersweet irony that now they were divorcing, she was pregnant.

After she showered and got dressed, she phoned for a breakfast tray. Halfway through her meal she panicked. What she ought to do was go right back to Pennsylvania and phone him when there were thousands of miles between them. But it would be the cowardly thing to do. Her aunt and uncle never said as much, but she knew they'd be disappointed in her if she left it to a phone call.

You have to tell him.

You can't leave it up to anyone else.

Whatever is ultimately decided about the children, he has the right to hear it from you in person.

All the voices speaking in Kellie's head finally drove her to follow through with her agenda.

She asked the front desk to phone for a taxi. In a few minutes she found herself being driven along Kifissias Avenue toward the Petralia Corporation office building in downtown Athens. When it pulled up in front, she paid the driver and got out.

After taking a deep breath, she squared her shoulders and opened the doors, where Giorgios, looking like a well-dressed prizefighter, sat at the security desk near the entry. When he saw her, he shot to his feet in surprise.

"*Kyria Petralia*—"

Her chocolate-brown eyes fastened on him. He was one of Leandros's bodyguards and fiercely loyal to him. "Good morning, Giorgios. It's nice to see you. Is my husband on the premises?"

"He arrived an hour ago."

The news relieved her, since she hadn't relished the thought of trying to hunt Leandros down. He could have been out of the city doing business right now. Then again, he could have been at his apartment here in Athens, or at his villa on the family estate on Andros.

"If you still want a job with him, you won't let him or Christos know I'm here," she said in fluent Greek.

His expression turned to shock before Kellie walked

around his desk to the elevator located behind him. Unless Leandros made a helicopter landing on the roof after his flight from Andros Island, the elevator existed for his exclusive use when he entered or left the building from the street. For convenience sake it opened to the foyer of his private inner sanctum on the top floor. Giorgios had orders to guard it with his life.

She pressed her hand to the glass by the door, wondering if it would still recognize her code. For all she knew, Leandros had deleted it. But no, the door opened. She entered, still feeling Giorgios's stunned gaze on her before it closed.

A little over a month ago she'd left Greece, vowing never to return. But a week ago nausea had driven her to make an appointment with her doctor in Philadelphia. When he told her what was wrong with her, a transformation had taken place inside Kellie. It transcended the anguish and pain of the past year and gave her the spine she needed to face Leandros one more time.

Their divorce would soon be final. She intended for nothing to change in that regard, but since this totally unexpected contingency had arisen, it required an alteration in the documents their two lawyers had drawn up. Twenty-four hours should give Leandros's attorney enough time to take care of the necessary changes.

Kellie was desperate to catch her husband off guard; it was the only way to get through this final ordeal with him. She dreaded it, knew it would hurt, but had no other choice. For that reason she hadn't even told her best friend, Fran Meyers, she was coming.

Fran was now married to Nikolos Angelis, a good friend of Leandros's. They lived here in Athens with Nik's baby niece, Demi, soon-to-be their adopted daughter. If Nik knew of her arrival, he'd have phoned Leandros. Among the legal papers in her purse was evidence of the restraining order she'd placed on Leandros to call off her bodyguard. Yannis had been her shadow for the two years she'd been married to Leandros. But when she'd demanded a divorce, she'd drawn the line at the retired secret service agent following her to the States. Leandros had been forced to comply, with the result that he had no prior knowledge she'd flown to Athens yesterday.

As the elevator carried her skyward, Kellie planned to take care of business as quickly as possible. She knew she'd soon be on her way back home to Philadelphia, where she'd been living with her aunt and uncle for the last month. But that was about to change.

By next week she'd move her aunt and uncle from their small apartment into a lovely four-bedroom brick row home in Parkwood with her. It was a charming residential neighborhood in the far northeast corner of Philadelphia, perfect for children. She'd already put down a deposit. A new life awaited her, but first things first.

When the elevator stopped and the door opened, Kellie took a deep breath and headed through the foyer. She walked past Christos, her husband's chief bodyguard. He started to reach for his phone to warn Leandros, but she put a finger to her lips and smiled. He nodded and sat down again.

A few more steps and she reached the entrance to her husband's private suite, which was also protected by a security code. As CEO of the Petralia Corporation, which built resorts all over Greece, he was one of the most successful businessmen in the country and had been a target for crazies long before Kellie had met him.

She had no idea what she might be interrupting, but that wasn't her concern anymore. It had been on her wedding day, two years ago, when Kellie realized she had an enemy in Karmela Paulos. Karmela was the sister of Petra, Leandros's first wife, who'd been pregnant when she'd died in a plane crash. At Kellie's wedding to Leandros, the beautiful, fashionable Karmela would willingly have scratched Kellie's eyes out if she could have gotten away with it.

Fran had been Kellie's matron of honor and had witnessed the obvious fact that Karmela had hoped to become the next Mrs. Leandros Petralia. But it didn't happen, so his sister-in-law had done the next best thing by becoming indispensable to Leandros, first as a confidante to the grieving widower, who was family, and later as a secretary in his inner office, under Mrs. Kostas. With cunning, Karmela had worked her way to the top floor, where she had daily contact with him.

Combined with the stress Kellie had been under because she couldn't conceive, plus her struggle with feelings of inadequacy, the situation had grown intolerable for her. After much thought and soul-searching, she'd told Leandros she wanted a separation, and had left on a trip with Fran. But because of disastrous circumstances, it came to an abrupt end, with her friend staying in Athens to be with Nik. At that point Kellie had left for Philadelphia.

On the night before she was due to fly back, she'd had a fainting spell and Leandros had taken her to the ER. When the doctor could find nothing wrong, she was sent home with the warning to eat, so it wouldn't happen again. They'd just returned when Karmela, whose hand was obviously recognized by the security entry, slipped into their apartment, as she'd done when Petra still lived there.

The fact that Leandros said nothing about his sister-in-law letting herself in unannounced had led Kellie to worry that he had more than brotherly feelings for Karmela. After all, she did resemble Petra. Perhaps, as Kellie had confided to Fran earlier, Karmela had become his pillow friend?

Evidently his brazen sister-in-law figured she had free reign with Leandros now that Kellie was leaving him. Her smiling, catlike eyes stared boldly at Kellie as she explained she'd brought some work for Leandros that needed his attention. Before she slipped out the door again, she'd wished Kellie a safe flight back to the States. No doubt she thought she'd seen the last of her. Kellie knew that her presence would knock the daylights out of Karmela, but this wasn't about her. It was about them—Leandros and Kellie—and their babies.

She put her palm against the glass next to the door. She suspected Karmela's manipulative smile would falter when Kellie walked into the office and word eventually circulated about the miraculous news. Everyone close to Leandros knew he'd mourned the loss of his first wife and unborn child, who would have been a girl.

Despite Kellie's impending divorce from Leandros, for him to learn he was going to be a father again would come as a tremendous thrill. But it would deal a near fatal blow to his sister-in-law's plans to have him for her own.

Kellie knew in her heart that Karmela was waiting for her chance to provide him with a living heir. At least that's what Frato Petralia had confided to Kellie at the wedding, after having too much to drink.

Frato was Leandros's good-looking first cousin and closest friend in the family. Still single, he was one of the vice presidents of the corporation, and enjoyed the company of several beautiful women, which didn't surprise Kellie at all. That evening he'd said quite a few things she didn't take seriously in the beginning, but over time she realized he'd spoken the truth.

On the day Leandros mentioned in passing about hiring Karmela to work under Mrs. Kostas, she'd tried not to let it affect her. But her first impression of Petra's sister at the wedding wouldn't leave her alone. She'd seen the way Karmela had behaved and talked to him. Karmela was no impartial bystander. Two years later the younger woman had insinuated herself into Leandros's office life, and who knew how much more. But it was all history now.

The elevator door opened silently along the wall away from his desk. Leandros sat in his swivel chair, half turned from her while engaged in an intense business discussion with Frato on the speakerphone. She recognized his voice.

At first glance she realized Leandros needed a haircut and a shave. There were wavy tendrils of dark hair, a shade away from being true black, clinging to his bronzed nape. It looked as if he'd been running his hands through it. The sleeves of the white shirt he wore had been pushed up to the elbows. Given his condition, and the accumulation of coffee cups on the desk, she could imagine he might have spent the night here.

She'd never seen him like this before. He was thirty-four, yet he looked five years older right now. Her normally fastidious, temperate husband was nowhere to be found. Kellie had seen him truly out of control only

once before. It was the night she'd told him she wanted
a divorce. In a way, this was worse—different, even—
because there was a savage air about him. For a second
she feared she'd done the wrong thing by coming here
without his knowledge. But with so much riding on this,
she couldn't run from him now. Too much was at stake.

Finding her courage, she called out softly to him.
"Leandros?"

She knew he'd heard her voice, because his hard,
lean body seemed to freeze in place before he slowly
swung around to face her.

He'd lost weight. A pronounced white ring encircled
his taut mouth, testifying to his incredulity at seeing
her here. It stood out almost as much as his gray eyes,
which had gone black as pitch at the moment. Their
color reminded her of the dark sky before the tornado
had struck the Petralia resort near Thessalonika five
weeks ago, killing little Demi's parents.

Frato was on the other end of the phone line, still
talking. Leandros muttered something she couldn't understand, before he hung up. His haunted look sent a
shiver of alarm through her body. She sensed he was
ready to spring from his chair.

"Don't get up," she urged, and walked over to one
of the chairs in front of his desk to sit down. Not only
had her legs turned to mush at the sight of him, she
couldn't handle him touching her. He was still the most
gorgeous man she'd ever known. In that regard, nothing had changed.

Kellie heard his sharp intake of breath. "What in the
name of all that's holy brings you back to Greece?" His
deep voice sounded so shaken, she hardly recognized
it. His overarching look of disbelief sent a fresh shock

wave of despair through her. The month apart had done the rest of the damage to their marriage, crushing the rubble to microscopic bits.

Suddenly there was a tap on the door and Karmela started to enter. "Not now!" Leandros snapped. Kellie had to admit she'd never seen Leandros this upset with an employee. Maybe he hadn't even realized it was Karmela.

Kellie was shocked by the other woman's sangfroid before she did Leandros's bidding. She was tall enough to wear the attractive black-and-white dress skimming her figure. With her hair falling like a silky black curtain, she was extraordinarily beautiful and would cause a traffic jam when she walked down the street.

Since she and Petra shared such a strong resemblance, Kellie could well imagine how his former wife had turned the sought-after bachelor into a married man. Karmela's hourglass figure was so different from Kellie's rounded curves.

The younger woman closed the door, but not before she shot Kellie a venomous glance. That reaction alone vindicated Kellie's belief that Karmela planned to win Leandros one way or another, if she hadn't already.

"Karmela still works for you, I see. And is still dropping in unannounced. As I recall, the last time we thought we were alone, Karmela dropped by with some papers for you. Though she didn't find us making love, she certainly *could* have if we hadn't been on the verge of divorce."

That was the first time Kellie had truly feared Leandros had been unfaithful to her with Karmela. Before that time, she'd only worried about the other woman's behavior.

"She was wrong to have done that, Kellie."

"It certainly was wrong, but you didn't say so at the time. I was so hurt when you let her come to work for you, and I told you as much, but you kept her on. We're almost divorced, yet she *still* works for you. As I've told you many times, your sister-in-law always had a habit of insinuating herself around you.

"Even a little while ago she walked in without as much as a tap on the door, but it's all right with you because *she's family.*"

Why did she sound so bitter? Kellie wondered. It was no longer her concern what Karmela did with Leandros. They were getting divorced. But the thought that he'd replaced her so soon hurt more than she could ever admit.

His beautiful olive complexion darkened with lines. "It's never been all right with me and I *am* going to do something about it. I'll ask you again. Why are you here?" He seemed to have lost some color.

Clearing her throat, she said, "I have news that demanded I come here in person." She was in possession of certain facts that would alter his world forever.

His hooded gaze pierced hers. "Has something happened to your aunt or uncle?"

Kellie could understand why he'd asked that question. He'd been wonderful to them from the moment he'd first met them. "This has nothing to do with them. They're fine." She moistened her lips nervously. "A week ago I was so nauseated, I went to the doctor in Philadelphia to find out what was wrong. I learned that I'm…pregnant."

His dark head reared back in complete shock. "*What* did you say?" She heard excitement exploding inside him before he'd even had time to assimilate the news. Though he'd never given up hope they would get pregnant, Kellie had stopped believing such a miracle would happen to them.

She breathed in deeply. "I'm more amazed than you. It seems that the last artificial insemination procedure I underwent *worked*. Impossible as it sounds, Dr. Creer says I'm already seven weeks pregnant."

A triumphant cry escaped Leandros. He leaped out of his chair, charged with an energy that transformed him before her eyes. Her pulse raced, because she'd known this would be his reaction. "The doctor said it's the reason I fainted the night before I left Athens. My periods have never been normal, so I never suspected anything."

Leandros came around and hunkered down in front of her, like a knight kneeling before his lady. When he grasped her hands, she could feel him trembling. Emotion had taken the blackness from his eyes, filling the gray irises with pinpoints of light. "We're going to have a baby?" There was awe in his voice as he kissed her fingertips. The news had started to sink in, but he didn't know all of it yet.

"There's more, Leandros."

Fear immediately marred his striking features and his hands gripped hers tighter. "Did the doctor tell you you're a high-risk pregnancy? Is something wrong?"

"No," she rushed to assure him. After he'd lost his first wife and unborn child, she didn't want to put him through such anxiety again. He didn't deserve any more trauma in that regard.

His expressive black brows furrowed. "Then what *do* you mean?"

Averting her eyes, she said, "The doctor ordered an ultrasound."

"And?" His voice shook.

"The technician detected two heartbeats."

"Two?" His explosion of joy reverberated off the walls of his office. "We're going to have twins?"

She nodded. "They're due March 12."

"Kellie—"

The next thing she knew he'd picked her up and wrapped her in his strong arms, burying his face in her neck. She felt moisture against her skin as he crushed her against him. He'd been at the hospital with her to do his part while they'd gone through procedure after procedure. Every time it turned out she hadn't gotten pregnant, he'd been there to comfort her and promise her it would happen next time. He never gave up, and now they were going to be parents. But it was too late for them. The situation had put too much strain on both of them.

His reaction to the news was all she could have wanted if they'd been happily married, but that was the excruciating point. Their marriage was over and had been for months.

Soon they'd be divorced. Having his babies wouldn't solve what was wrong between them. When he lifted his head to kiss her, she put her hands against his chest to separate them, but he wasn't having any of it.

"Don't push me away, *agapi mou*. Not now," he cried. Before she could move, he drew her back into his arms and lowered his mouth to hers, kissing her with startling hunger. She could taste the salt from his tears. Her mind and body reeled from the passion only he could arouse.

For a moment she responded, because it had been
so long since she'd known his touch, and because she
simply couldn't help herself. But when he moaned and
deepened their kiss, she remembered why she was here.

Since he was physically powerful, her only weapon
was to refrain from kissing him back until he got the
message. He went on kissing every inch of her face
and hair till it slowly dawned on him she was no longer participating.

A tremor shook his tall, hard-muscled body before he
released her with reluctance. Dazed by his passion, she
sank down in the chair behind her. His eyes searched
her features, trying to read her. "Are you still suffering
from morning sickness?"

"No," she answered honestly. Though she'd love to
use it as an excuse, she couldn't. From here on out, everything she told him would be the whole truth and
out in the open.

Dr. Creer was very worried about her going through
a divorce right now. He'd warned her that since she
didn't want to burden her aunt and uncle with her problems, then she needed to find an outlet to deal with all
her emotions. Keeping them bottled up inside was the
worst thing for her at a time like this. She could tell Dr.
Savakis had been worried about her, too.

After being alone with her thoughts for the last
month, she realized the doctor was right. She'd gone
about things wrong in her marriage. She was sick of
trying to protect herself, Leandros and everyone else.
But no longer. No more mistakes if she could help it.
That's why she'd come all this way. "The doctor has
given me medication for it."

His hands went to his hips, as if he needed to do

something with them. Unfortunately, he stood too close to her, affecting her breathing. "This pregnancy puts a different slant on our impending divorce."

"I know. That's one of the reasons I'm here."

"You do realize that a great deal of our pain came from trying to get pregnant without results," he reminded her grimly.

"So now that I'm carrying your child, you think that erases everything?"

"No," he murmured, "but you've just brought me news I'm still trying to assimilate. One moonlit night on the sailboat, after we'd been disappointed a second time, you lifted tear-filled eyes to me and asked me if it was asking too much to reach for the stars. I told you we'd keep reaching for the stars and the moon. Now you've just told me we've been given *both*!"

"I remember." She averted her eyes. "Please sit down so we can talk."

Studying her through veiled eyes, he hitched himself on a corner of his desk. It still wasn't far enough away from her, but that was as much room as he was willing to give her. "I have a better idea. We'll go to our suite at the hotel, where we won't be disturbed."

He was referring to the Cassandra, the main Petralia five-star hotel in Athens, where he kept an elegant, permanent suite. It was like a small house, really, with three bedrooms, a dining and living room and kitchen facilities.

When she'd stayed at the hotel with her aunt and uncle on their first trip to Greece, that's where she'd met him. Some of her happiest memories of their life together were associated with the Cassandra before they were married. It would be painful to go there.

"Why do we have to go to the hotel? Why not the apartment?"

He moved off the corner of the desk. "We can't go to the apartment because I sold it to Frato three weeks ago. I'm living at the hotel."

CHAPTER TWO

LEANDROS HAD SOLD his fabulous penthouse to his cousin? Kellie couldn't believe it. Stunned by the news, she said, "What's to stop Karmela from hurrying over to the hotel with something important for you before the day is out?"

He breathed in sharply. "It'll never happen again."

Kellie blinked. "That sounded final. She must have received quite a shock to see me in here with you a few minutes ago, but no worries. I won't be in Athens much longer."

In the tangible silence that followed, Kellie lowered her eyes and opened her purse. Inside was the paper her attorney had drawn up. "If you'll please read through this and consult with your attorney, then we'll sign it and our divorce can go through as scheduled."

Leandros made no move to take it. She should have known this was going to be a battle to the end. "That's all right. I'll read it to you.

"Point One. If and when one or both children are born, the mother will retain custody at her address in Parkwood, Pennsylvania."

"Why *if*?" he demanded in an anxious voice. "Is there something you haven't told me?"

"No. My attorney simply wanted to cover every contingency."

Shadows darkened his features.

"Point Two. Liberal visitation rights will be offered to the father.

"Point Three. Both mother and father will discuss times when the mother will bring said child or children to Athens for visitation, and when the father will travel to Parkwood for visitation.

"Point Four. The mother asks for no additional money. The father can decide what monies he will afford for the child or children's upbringing."

She looked up at him. "It's all very simple and straightforward."

His eyes glittered a frostbite gray. "If you think I'm going to agree to that, then you never knew me." The words seemed to come from a cavern miles underground.

"You're wrong, Leandros. After being married for a while, I discovered the *real* you. That's why we've reached this impasse." Heartbroken, she stood up and left the paper on his desk.

With a grimace, he immediately wadded it in his fist before pocketing it. "When did you fly in?"

"Yesterday morning. I'm staying at the Civitel Olympic near the north park. You can reach me there after you've talked with your attorney."

Leandros moved like lightning, preventing her from leaving the room. Standing in front of the door, he talked into his cell phone and rapped out instructions. When he clicked off, he said, "You won't be going back to the Civitel. I'll send Yannis for your personal belongings and have him bring them to you. We're flying to Andros right now."

Where else would he take her? It was his favorite place on earth. *Hers, too, except...* "You mean where Karmela and her family drop in on a regular basis to visit your family whenever you're in residence there?"

His eyes narrowed to slits. "They come to visit my parents in their villa. As for my family, they've already left for the yearly reunion in Stenies village and will be gone overnight, so no one will be around. In any case, we'll be staying in my villa. Shall we go?"

So much had happened in the last month, Kellie's mind was spinning. Since he'd dictated the location for the conversation they needed to have, she was left with no choice but to go along with him.

After grabbing his briefcase, he opened the door that led to the elevator, and stepped in behind her. Their bodies brushed, sending darts of awareness through her as they rode to the roof, where the helicopter blades were already rotating.

She smiled at his pilot, Stefon, before climbing in the back to join Christos. Kellie had done this so often in the past, she strapped herself in before Leandros could do it. She watched him take the copilot's seat and put on the earphones. Soon they were airborne for the short flight to Andros, an hour and a half from Athens by car and ferry. There was no airport, but with a helicopter, Leandros could be where he wanted in no time at all.

That pang of familiarity attacked her in waves as they left Athens and headed for the fertile green island in the Cyclades that Leandros called home. It was a contrast of craggy mountains, woods, valleys and streams rising out of the blue Aegean.

The Petralia estate was located on the eastern slope of a hillside with its share of vineyards, lemon and walnut groves near Gialia beach. To Kellie, the island was glorious beyond description.

Close by was the picturesque stone village of Stenies, with its paved streets. The cluster of villas on the estate had been built in the same traditional stone architecture of the region. Parents, grandparents, uncles and aunts, cousins...all lived in the vicinity.

Leandros loved it because tourism hadn't been developed in this quieter area, thus preserving the whole place's authentic character. After their wedding, at the church in Chora, Kellie had thought she'd found paradise on her honeymoon here, until she learned the Paulos family, among other wealthy families, lived on the same part of the island. The two families had enjoyed a warm relationship over the last fifty years.

Once she'd realized this was where Leandros had fallen in love with Petra, Kellie never felt as excited when they flew over on the weekends he didn't have a business commitment elsewhere. To her growing discomfort, she'd often discovered Karmela and her parents were there visiting Leandros's family at his parents' villa. They would always call Leandros and ask him to join them. Their presence had to be a reminder of what he'd lost.

Since his feelings for home were intertwined with his memories of Petra, Kellie imagined he was a prisoner of both. To fight her pain, she'd preferred they stay at the apartment in Athens when she wasn't traveling with him on business.

Now there was no apartment, but none of that mattered at this point. Wherever Leandros took her so they could talk, nothing would change the fact that they were getting a divorce, children or no children. There were some things they just couldn't overcome, no matter how much her heart broke at the thought.

She'd done the right thing by coming to him with the news of his impending fatherhood. It was his God-given right. If he found a way to prevent the divorce from happening as soon as she'd anticipated, she would still go back to Pennsylvania day after tomorrow, and let her attorney deal with it.

While she was deep in thought, Stefon flew them over the capital town of Chora, where the tourists came in throngs to see its charming Venetian architecture. Farther on she spotted the seventeenth century tower of Bisti-Mouvela and the nearby church of Agios Georgios. Soon they were passing over the Petralia estate. It was a wonderful place with an old olive press building, all part of Leandros's idyllic childhood and an intrinsic part of who he was.

The first time Kellie ever saw his romantic stone farmhouse with its flat roof, she'd fallen instantly in love with it. When she stayed there with him, she enjoyed the many terraces planted with fruit and nut trees that flourished in the climate, as well as shrubs, flowers and kitchen gardens. Hidden in the foliage was a small swimming pool.

One of her favorite features was the kitchen with its open fireplace. They could eat on two of the terraces, one alcoved between the kitchen and living room, the other above the master bedroom with its own garden and a view of the beach just steps away. Farther along the beach was the private boat dock housing various watercraft, including the sailboat he'd given her. One thing she'd learned early: Leandros loved the water and swam like a fish.

She thought about the babies growing inside her. After they were born, they'd enjoy this legacy from their father. When they came on visitation, they'd become water babies, too. But their roots would be firmly planted in Philadelphia.

There couldn't be two places on earth more unalike. Almost as unalike as the way she and Leandros viewed their marriage and what was wrong with it. Kellie couldn't bear to look back at what had happened to destroy their happiness, and fought tears as Stefon set them down on the east side of his parents' villa.

Leandros was already removing his headset. Now that she was pregnant, she had to expect that he would watch over her with meticulous care for the short time she was back in Greece. He didn't know any other way. That was one of the reasons she loved him so much.

Too much.

As he helped her down from the helicopter, his pulse raced to see moisture glazing those velvety brown eyes that used to beg him to make love to her. Until this minute, Leandros hadn't seen a sign of emotion from his normally loving, vivacious wife.

Since Kellie had first told him she wanted a separation, she'd turned into an ice princess, erecting walls he couldn't penetrate. For the last month they were together, he hadn't been able to get through to her on any level. The hurt he'd felt had turned to anger.

During the months when she'd gone through one procedure after another to get pregnant, and been so brave about it, they'd both felt the strain. Every time

her period came, they both suffered depression and had
to fight their way out of it.

Sometimes the strain made them short with each
other. Other times there were periods of silence over
several days. The emotional turmoil took its toll. By the
last month, he didn't feel he knew his wife anymore.
His disillusionment was so total, he'd been devastated.

Only the pregnancy could have caused her to ven-
ture back here. Though he was euphoric to learn he
was going to be a father, his world would never be right
again if the divorce went through without one more attempt to try and heal their wounds.

That's why he'd planned to leave today, with a prop-
osition to save their marriage before it became final.
For her to have flown here with news of their babies
had saved him from flying to Philadelphia. Leandros
couldn't have asked for a greater gift than her presence right now.

While the men disappeared to the guest cottage, she
walked ahead of him, strolling down the flower-lined
path to his villa in her pale orange sundress and jacket.
His eyes followed the feminine lines of her hips and
legs as she moved. In the summery outfit, his wife took
his breath away.

Once upon a time they'd paused and kissed as they
made their way along the ancient paths. But he had to
push those rapturous memories to the background of his
mind and start over with her again in a brand-new way.

Kellie waited for him to unlock the door, then
stepped past him into the beamed living room with
its simple white walls and hand-carved furniture. Her
arm brushed against his, triggering a surge of desire for

her with an intensity that caught him off guard. They'd been apart too long.

He set down his briefcase. "Why don't you rest on the couch by the window and I'll get us something cold to drink."

"Thank you."

When he returned a minute later with an icy lemon fruit drink for her, he found her seated on one end of the sofa, staring out at the beach. He handed her the glass. "Wouldn't you like to put your legs up? Since we're having twins, I'm sure the doctor told you to stay off your feet after your long flight from Philadelphia."

"You're right, but I had a good night's sleep at the hotel and ate breakfast in bed before I took a taxi to your office." She sipped her drink. "It's a hot day and this tastes wonderful. Thank you." Her controlled civility was anathema to him.

"You're welcome. When you're hungry, I'll fix us some sandwiches."

"I'm fine for now, but you go ahead."

He frowned. "I haven't had an appetite lately, but I can't claim the excuse of pregnancy." It wasn't meant to be a joke and she didn't take it that way. "How are you feeling physically?"

She avoided looking at him. "Dr. Creer says I'm in great shape. No problems in sight so far, but twins require special monitoring and I intend following his advice."

"That's good. Are you taking any other medicine besides your antinausea medication?"

"Just prenatal vitamins."

He drank part of his drink, then got to his feet, too

restless to sit there. "When you walked in my office, I was on the phone with Frato."

"I know. I recognized his voice."

Leandros stared at her moodily. "He's taking over for me while I'm gone."

That statement caused her to lift startled eyes to him. "Where are you going?"

"I told him I needed a vacation, but no one knows my plans."

"You're taking another one?"

It didn't surprise him she'd ask that question. A month ago he'd taken time off to fly her back to Philadelphia. He was pleased to detect a note of concern in her voice before she smoothed her hands over her knees in what he recognized was a nervous gesture. "That's right."

"For how long this time?"

"For as long as it takes."

She stared at him. "I don't understand."

Leandros rubbed the back of his neck. "I was going to take my jet and fly to Philadelphia today to talk to you about giving us another chance. If you hadn't come to the office this morning, we would have missed each other."

Her eyes widened, then grew shuttered, and her lovely features hardened. "It's too late. Our divorce will be final soon. The fact that I'm pregnant changes nothing."

"I get that, Kellie, but I'd like you to hear me out first."

"What more is there to say?" The bleakness in her question crushed him. "I only came to discuss future visitation for our children and get it in writing."

He had to weigh his words carefully. "Our babies haven't arrived yet. Until they do, we have a lot to talk about that impacts our lives right this minute. What I need you to know is that I *did* listen to what you said to me before I flew home from Philadelphia a month ago. To my shame, it took me until last week to come to terms with it. I can't lose you, so I've made a decision that will affect both of us."

A troubled expression entered her eyes. "That sounds ominous."

He sucked in his breath. "I'm willing to do as you asked and go to marriage counseling with you."

Looking dumbstruck, she put her glass on the coffee table. "I thought you didn't believe in it. I brought up the subject a year ago, but you were adamantly against it."

He scowled in self-deprecation. "It's my nature to believe only in myself, but after being apart from you this last month, I recognize how arrogant that was of me. Since you suggested counseling as a last resort, I'm willing to try anything to save our marriage."

Besides her inability to get pregnant, which had tested them to the breaking point, there'd been other side issues throughout their marriage to exacerbate what was already wrong. One of them was Kellie's insistence that Karmela had a crush on him. Whenever she'd brought it up, he'd dismissed it, telling her Petra's sister was simply a clingy girl who needed lots of attention. Her behavior didn't mean anything. In fact, Petra had asked him to be extra kind to her.

But, he remembered, when Karmela had said last night that Kellie wasn't good enough for him, something in him had snapped. Mostly because in trying to do as Petra had asked, he hadn't taken Kellie's concerns seriously enough, he realized.

She got to her feet, as if on the verge of running away.

"I realize it will have to be someone you trust," he added, "so I want you to pick the therapist." Leandros knew this was a drastic departure from his former attitude, but he was desperate. Seeing her again proved to him he couldn't live without her. "We can do it here in Athens, or we can fly to Philadelphia and find someone there. It's your choice."

Without saying anything, she moved over to the French doors and opened them to walk out on the patio. He followed her, inhaling her flowery fragrance and the scent of the lemon trees close by. Incredible to think that inside her beautiful body, their babies were already seven weeks old and growing.

"Are you too embittered at this stage to even consider it, Kellie? I wouldn't blame you if you were...but I'm begging you."

She clung to the railing. Still no words came.

"I've spent the last week doing research on the best therapists in the city and came up with a list of six names recommended to me. Four men and two women. Let me show you."

He went back inside and reached for his briefcase. After pulling out his laptop, he set it up on the coffee table and turned it on. Kellie came back in and watched as he clicked to the file so she could see it.

"I was going to give you this list when I flew over to see you, but you can look at it now if you want. All the information I've gathered is here. But if this doesn't interest you, I'll fly you back to Philadelphia tomorrow and we'll search for a therapist there."

She shot him a startled glance. "You can't just go back and forth from Greece between sessions. Therapy takes time."

"I can do whatever I want. Frato will be running the company for as long as necessary. He knows the business the same as I do. With both our fathers still alive to advise him, along with other family members on the board, the company will function seamlessly. If you and I decide to do therapy in Philadelphia, then I'll live there and do business. With your help, of course."

"*My* help?"

"Yes. You once asked me if you could work for me. I told you I'd rather you didn't, but I was wrong about that and a host of other things. We can be a team and scout out a property for the first Petralia resort in Pennsylvania. But since you're pregnant, we'll have to proceed as your health dictates."

"You're not serious," she whispered.

"Try me and find out." He fired back the response. "We'll buy or build a house in Philadelphia near your aunt and uncle, if that's what you desire."

She shook her head. "And take you away from your family and responsibilities?"

"*You're* my family. No one else is more important. If we decide to live there, I'll step down as CEO."

"I wouldn't want or expect you to do that. Never!"

He stared into her eyes. "Why not? Don't you realize no place is home to me without you? I'll do anything, Kellie," he vowed. "I know we can make this work. It's not too late. For the sake of our unborn babies, I'm pleading with you to reconsider. If counseling will help us, then it will be worth it for all our sakes. We'll post-pone our divorce while we're in therapy."

If Leandros had said these things to her a month ago…

But he's saying them to you now, Kellie.

For a proud man like her husband to be willing to undergo therapy told her how far he'd come. She moved closer to the coffee table, where she could see the list of names on his laptop. He'd done all this without prior knowledge that they were expecting twins? She couldn't believe it.

After supplying her this kind of proof that he was serious, she *had* to believe he'd planned to fly to Phila-delphia today. But for Leandros to submit to marriage counseling… It just wasn't like him.

He was a dynamic wonder in the business world and a law unto himself. He'd probably last one session and that would be it. She couldn't imagine therapy work-ing on him. But since she'd been the one to suggest it in the first place, how would it look if she told him no?

Kellie knew exactly what he'd think. During one of their arguments he'd told her she was inflexible, un-reasonable and didn't really mean what she'd said. He would have every right to accuse her now of not put-ting their children first.

The more she thought about it, the more she real-ized the wisest thing to do would be to try out one of these therapists in Athens. When the counseling didn't work, then she'd fly back to Philadelphia and the di-vorce could go through. She'd have to let her aunt and uncle know. The news would be welcome to them, be-cause they adored Leandros and were crushed by the news that he and Kellie were getting a divorce.

He watched as she sat down and scrolled through the list of names. All seemed to have impressive credentials. She was glad he'd included some women. She preferred their therapist to be a female, who would understand Kellie's point of view about things. Leandros probably wouldn't like it, but he'd said this was her choice.

She looked at their ages. The first woman was forty-eight, younger than Kellie's aunt. The other therapist was seventy-six. That sounded pretty old, but she did have a long record of running a practice. At that age she'd probably seen thousands of couples, with every type of problem, enter her office. To still be in business meant she'd enjoyed a certain amount of success.

"Today is a workday." Leandros's deep male voice permeated to Kellie's insides. "Is there a name on the list you'd like to call now?"

He stood behind the couch, more or less looking over her shoulder. Though he'd sounded in control just now, she sensed his impatience for their therapy to get started. Actually, she was anxious, too. The sooner they met with someone and discovered counseling wouldn't help, the sooner she could go home and start getting over Leandros once and for all.

"I'm rather impressed with this older woman, Olympia Lasko." She glanced back at him. "The notes say she's been in practice forty-five years. That's longer than any of the other therapists' histories. I think it speaks quite highly of her."

"I couldn't agree more. Go ahead and phone her."

Leandros didn't act the least upset with Kellie's choice. If he was, he'd learned how to hide his true feelings. That ability made him the shrewd genius who'd become one of the leading business figures in Greece.

She reached in her purse for her cell phone and made the call. It rang several times before a woman answered. "This is Olympia Lasko."

"Oh—" Kellie's voice caught. "I guess I expected a receptionist." She spoke in Greek.

"I've never used one. Your name, please."

"Kellie Petralia."

"What can I do for you?"

"M-my husband and I are on the verge of getting a divorce and need marriage counseling," she stammered. "Could I see you soon to discuss our situation, or are you too booked up?"

"Both of you come to my house tomorrow morning at ten o'clock."

"Both?" Kellie had planned to talk to her first and explain things.

"I never see you individually. It's together or nothing."

"I see." She bit her lip. "Then we'll both be there."

"What's your husband's name?"

"Leandros Petralia."

"Thank you. When you enter the driveway, keep going until you reach the side door. Just walk in."

The other woman rang off without making a remark about Kellie's husband. Ninety-nine percent of the time, people couldn't refrain from commenting on him and the famous Petralia name. Kellie sat there blinking in surprise.

Leandros walked around to look at her. "When can she see us?"

"Tomorrow at ten. We're to go to her house. She must work out of her home."

"Would that we all could do that," he murmured.

"I can't believe she had an opening this fast."

"My dentist always leaves the first hour free for emergencies. It sounds like she operates the same way. I'm impressed already."

Kellie got up from the couch, unnerved by the prospect of talking to Mrs. Lasko in front of Leandros without any private time first. "She's very different than I'd supposed." No chitchat of any kind.

"Let's keep the appointment. If we decide she's not the one for us, then we'll try someone else."

Leandros was being so supportive, just as he'd always been during their visits to the hospital, that Kellie felt like screaming. But not at him. She was frightened, and nervous of being alone with him. "I think I'm hungry now."

"Why don't we drive to Chora and have an early dinner." He was reading her mind. She needed to be around other people and he knew it. "Do you have any particular cravings at this stage in your pregnancy?"

"Not yet."

"Let's try a restaurant you haven't been to. The Circe is on the far side of Chora. It's cozy and the cuisine is basically traditional Andriot." He'd probably been there with Petra. *Of course he had, you fool.* If the therapy didn't work out, Kellie would have to take part of the blame, because she couldn't rid herself of her demons. "You'll love their seafood mezes and froutalia."

"I've forgotten what froutalia is."

"A sensational omelet with sausage and other kinds of meat."

"Oh, yes. That sounds delicious."

"Good. Why don't you freshen up first. I'll meet you at the car parked around the side of the house."

"I'll hurry."

"There's no need. We have all the time in the world. By the time we get back, Yannis will have arrived with your luggage. You can have an early night in the guest bedroom."

Her heart ached as she realized how far apart they'd grown. No sleeping in the same bed for the past two months. Most likely never again...

When Kellie went outside a few minutes later, he was waiting for her, and helped her in the passenger side. She glanced at his striking profile as he started the engine. Whether immaculately groomed or disheveled with a five-o'clock shadow as he was now, Leandros's male beauty stood apart from other men's.

Her heart thudded ferociously. A month ago she'd never dreamed she'd be on the island with him again, going to a romantic spot for dinner.

During the six-mile drive to town, she stared out the window at the fruit trees dotting the ancient landscape. When she couldn't stand the silence any longer, she turned to him. "Have you seen Fran and Nik?"

He nodded. "They invited me to their apartment last week for dinner. Demi is thriving and has started to say words even I can understand." Kellie smiled. "I've never seen two people so happy."

Guilt washed over Kellie for the part she'd played in trying to influence Fran to stay away from the gorgeous Nik Angelis, Leandros's good friend. The press had labeled him Greece's number one playboy. Like Leandros, Nik was the head of his family's multimillion-dollar business and could have any woman he wanted.

In Kellie's zeal to protect her divorced friend's wounded heart, she'd done everything she could to get her away from Nik. She'd been convinced he would only use Fran. But it turned out Kellie was wrong. Ultimately, he'd proved to be the perfect man for her, and had married her on the spot. Since he couldn't give her children and she couldn't conceive, they were adopting Demi, who'd lost her parents in a tornado. In time they planned to adopt more.

"I'm so happy for them," Kellie said aloud.

"Me, too."

To Leandros's credit, he didn't rub it in about Kellie's behavior with her best friend before they'd flown to Philadelphia on his private jet. "I'll phone her while I'm here."

"She'll be delighted. Being a mother has turned a light on inside her."

You mean unlike me, who's pregnant but still wants the divorce?

Kellie wouldn't blame Leandros for thinking it, but again, he kept his thoughts to himself. That was the trouble between them. They were both festering in their own private way from behaviors that had driven them apart.

The therapist would have to perform a miracle for them to put their marriage back together. How ironic that Kellie had been the one who'd brought up the idea of counseling. Yet now that Leandros had finally agreed to it, she was only going through the motions. Deep inside she had no real hope of success.

There'd been too much damage done during those

months of planning each hospital visit like clockwork. Everything had to be gauged down to the second— the temperature taking, the preparation, Leandros's time off from work…. All of it had affected the natural rhythm of married life.

If he suggested they skip a month of going to the hospital, and give things a rest, she was afraid he was losing interest in her. Maybe he didn't want a baby as badly as she did. When she asked him if he would still love her if she couldn't give him a child, he'd acted incensed, which in turn made her afraid to approach him again about it.

There were times when she'd feared he needed a break from her, and would tell him to enjoy a night out with friends or go visit his family. If he took her up on the suggestion, she cried herself to sleep. If he insisted on staying home with her, she feared it was out of a sense of duty. The spontaneity of their lives had vanished.

Aside from making sure she'd prepared a good meal for him at night, Kellie found herself spending more and more time playing tennis at Leandros's club with friends, or studying Greek with the tutor he'd hired for her at the university.

With the gulf so wide and deep between them because of what they'd gone through to have a baby, they were different people now. Her heart ached, because she couldn't imagine how they could find their way back to the people they'd once been.

CHAPTER THREE

EARLY THE NEXT MORNING Stefon flew the two of them to the Cassandra in Athens. After eating breakfast in their room, Leandros called for his car and drove them to the Pangrati neighborhood, where Olympia Lasko saw her clients.

Silence filled the Mercedes, as it had last evening on their way home from dinner. Kellie had hardly talked to him and went straight to bed once they'd returned to the villa. If she'd gotten on the phone with Fran or her aunt and uncle, he knew nothing about it.

To his relief she'd eaten a healthy meal this morning and shown more appetite than he had. Leandros didn't know about Kellie, but he'd slept poorly. Not only was he concerned over the process they were about to undergo, he feared Kellie's reaction. Though it had been her idea, this was new territory for both of them.

After he'd dismissed the idea of counseling in the beginning, he was thankful that she was still willing to try it. When they'd reached Andros yesterday, he'd been terrified out of his mind she would tell him it was too late, and fly right back to Pennsylvania.

Before long, he turned the corner and spotted the Lasko home. It was a moderate-size, gray-and-white two-story house, typical of the settled, comfortable looking residences along the street in the quiet neighborhood. Leandros pulled in the driveway and stopped at the side entrance.

He eyed his wife, who, thankfully, was still his wife. He'd already contacted his attorney to get in touch with her attorney and put off the divorce. The only thing left was to follow through with counseling and pray for a breakthrough. "Shall we go in?"

She nodded and started to get out of the car. He hurried around to help her. Together they walked beneath the portico to the porch. "Mrs. Lasko said to just go in. She must be a very trusting person," Kellie murmured.

"Even so, she'll have had cameras installed, as well as an electronic lock." He reached past her and opened the door. They stepped right into an office with a desk and several leather chairs placed in front of it. At a glance he saw shelves with family photos, grandchildren. On one wall was a large oil painting of flowers.

As he closed the door, he heard the click. A few moments later a connecting door into the house opened. A small, attractive woman with streaks of silver in her black hair, worn in a bun, entered the room. She looked on the frail side.

"Thank you for being on time. I'm Olympia. Please call me that. You must be Kellie."

"Yes. It's very nice to meet you. Thank you for making time for us so quickly. I'd like to introduce you to my husband, Leandros."

"How do you do." They all shook hands. "Please sit down."

While the therapist took her seat in a comfortable padded chair behind the desk, Leandros helped Kellie.

With her hair falling like spun gold to her shoulders from a side part, she looked particularly stunning. She was wearing an aquamarine, two-piece summer suit with short sleeves he hadn't seen before. He loved the color on her.

"We'll discuss the fee after I've decided I can help you. As I told you on the phone, I only counsel you as a couple, not individually."

"You mean you never have private sessions with your clients?" Kellie asked.

"Never, and I never record conversations. Once you start down that road, it doesn't work. To remove suspicion, everything must be said in front of each other in my hearing. Otherwise we're wasting each other's time."

Kellie's face crumpled. He wasn't too thrilled about the rules himself. This counselor drove a hard bargain, reminding him of his own business practices. But in all honesty it made the most sense, and his regard for the older woman went up several notches.

Olympia put on her bifocals. "How long have you been married?"

Leandros decided to let Kellie do the talking.

"Two years and one month."

"Which one of you felt the need for counseling?"

"I did," his wife answered.

"What matters is that you're both here. I'll go out of the room for a few minutes. If you're in agreement with my method, then let me know when I come back in, and we'll get started." She disappeared, leaving them alone. His wife sat there, hunched over.

"What do you think, Kellie?"

Slowly she lifted her head and glanced at him with

mournful eyes. "She's the most direct woman I ever met. I think this could be very painful."

He inhaled sharply. "More painful than what we've already been through?"

"Yes," she said without hesitation.

He'd had to ask the question, even though he'd known what her answer would be. Yet upon hearing it, he felt as if she'd just delivered a crippling blow to his midsection. Their problems were like the tip of an iceberg, with nine-tenths lying beneath the surface of the water. Without therapy, they'd be left unexplored, and the prognosis for a happy marriage was anything but good.

Unfortunately, he knew that once they got into deep therapy, the things they found out about each other could bring more pain. It would be a treacherous journey, but they had to make it if they hoped for a resolution that would preserve their marriage. No matter what he'd be forced to go through, he'd do it if he could have back the adorable woman he'd married.

"I want to do it, Kellie."

Her brown eyes swam with tears. "If you really mean it."

His temper flared, but he fought to control it. "I wouldn't have said so otherwise."

Olympia came back into the room. This time Leandros spoke first. "We'd like to go ahead with the therapy. Since we're expecting twins next March, any fee you charge will be worth it if we can fix what's wrong."

Her dark eyes studied them without revealing her thoughts. "That's courageous on both your parts." She took her place at the desk and named her fee. "I'd prefer to see you twice a week for the first month. The sessions will last an hour. When the month is out, it might not be necessary to see you more than once a month or even at all. My only opening left is at eleven in the mornings, Tuesdays and Thursdays."

Leandros didn't need to confer with Kellie. They both wanted the same thing. "We'll be here."

"Good. Then let's get started." The older woman sat back in her chair with her palms pressed together in front of her. "We'll begin with you, Kellie. Why did you marry your husband?"

Bands constricted his lungs while Leandros waited for her answer.

Kellie wouldn't look at him. "Because I fell painfully in love with him."

"Why painfully?"

"Because I didn't want to love a man who'd been married before, let alone one who'd been madly in love. Her name was Petra. Everyone told me they had the perfect marriage."

Leandros stifled a groan. She couldn't have been more wrong.

"Who's everyone?"

"All the people I met before our wedding. His family and friends. I was terrified I would never measure up to the woman who'd died."

"Why would you want to do that? He married *you*."

Kellie looked confounded. "I—I don't know," she stammered.

"Think about that and we'll discuss it at one of your next sessions. For the moment I'd like to know if you had been in love before you met your husband."

"Not like that. Never like that," she whispered.

Her fervency thrilled Leandros.

"But there was someone else?"

"Yes. One of my college friends had wealthy parents who belonged to a club where there was a tennis pro named Rod Silvers. Since I'd played tennis since my junior high days, she often invited me to play with her. That's where I met Rod, and we started dating.

"He was from a prominent Philadelphia family. I was attracted and flattered. But after a month of seeing each other pretty constantly, he stopped calling me. When I broke down and told my friend, she said his family already had someone from the Philadelphia society register picked out for him to marry."

Kellie had mentioned she'd once dated a tennis pro, but this was the first Leandros knew about his background.

"I see," Mrs. Lasko said. "Now I'd like hear when you first suspected all was not well in your marriage."

A few seconds passed before Kellie said, "At our wedding."

"Our *wedding*?" Leandros blurted. Her quiet response stunned him, because he'd noticed a difference in her after they'd gone to his villa to begin their honeymoon. But he'd never suspected she thought anything was wrong.

"I can see this has surprised your husband, Kellie."

Olympia possessed an unflappable demeanor that reminded him of his maternal grandmother. While his heart thundered in his chest from his wife's revelation, the woman went on talking to Kellie with a calm he could only envy.

"How long did you know him before you were married?"

"Three months."

"Was there an official period of engagement?"

"No."

"What happened at the wedding?"

"That's when I became aware I had competition for my husband's affection."

"You mean besides the memory of his dead wife."

"Yes."

"Did it come from another man? Or was it a woman?"

Leandros shot out of the chair, infuriated by the question. "Neither!"

Olympia glanced at him. "That sounded final. Did you hear him, Kellie?"

"Yes," she answered in a muffled voice.

"Go on."

He sat down again, feeling like a ten-year-old child who'd acted out in class and had just been dismissed by his teacher.

"It was a woman."

"Someone he'd known before he met you?"

"Yes."

"Her name is Karmela Paulos," Leandros broke in, completely frustrated because he'd known Kellie would bring her up. "She's the sister of my deceased wife, Petra."

"Karmela is very beautiful and resembles Petra," Kellie continued. "She's smart like her, too. They were only a year apart."

"What did she do that threatened you?"

Upset and curious to hear what Kellie would tell Olympia, Leandros extended his long legs and folded his arms to hold himself in check while he waited for the answer.

"After our wedding at the church on Andros, his

family held a reception at their nearby villa. Everyone invited came up to congratulate us. When Karmela appeared with her family, she cupped his face in her hands and gave him a long kiss on the lips. As her eyes slid to mine, I saw an angry flash no woman could mistake for anything other than pure jealousy."

Leandros sat there, stunned. He'd been so excited to make Kellie his wife, he didn't remember that moment. In fact, the events of the reception were a big blur.

"After kissing my husband, she kissed me on the cheek and murmured, 'Good luck in holding on to him.'"

He straightened in the chair, aghast by what he'd just heard. Karmela's childish, petulant behavior was out of bounds at times, but he hadn't known she'd subjected Kellie to it as early as their wedding reception.

"My best friend, Fran, was standing a little distance off. When she came over to congratulate us, she whispered that she'd noticed Karmela had fixated on my husband throughout the day. In her words, 'By no stretch of the imagination could that kiss be construed as platonic.'"

While Leandros was still digesting information that stuck in his throat, Kellie said, "My friend isn't the kind of person who looks for trouble or thinks the worst of anyone. Her opinion wasn't the only one I heard that night on the subject of Karmela."

He furrowed his brows, wondering what else in blazes she was about to reveal that he knew nothing about.

"At the wedding, my husband's best man, Frato, took me aside to congratulate me. He happens to be his first cousin and is very close to him. After he kissed my cheek, he said that he had something to tell me in confidence, but didn't want it getting back to Leandros."

What in the hell?

"Frato confided he was worried about me because Karmela had had a thing for Leandros even before her sister's marriage to him. After the plane crash that killed Petra and their unborn baby, Karmela confided to him that she planned to be the next Mrs. Petralia and give him the child he wanted so desperately."

What?

"Frato said that since I'd beaten Karmela to the altar, he wanted to warn me to watch out for her, because she didn't care who she hurt. He was afraid Leandros had a blind spot when it came to Karmela, so I had my work cut out."

Leandros's blood pressure spiked through the ceiling.

"I could smell alcohol on Frato's breath and feared he'd had too much to drink, but on the heels of Karmela's kiss and my friend's observations, I couldn't completely ignore what he'd told me. Especially when I found out that the Paulos family were neighbors of the Petralia family on Andros and the children had grown up together. But considering it was my first day of marriage, I chose to push it all to the back of my mind."

Incredulous over what he'd heard, Leandros clenched his hands into fists. He couldn't sit here much longer without exploding. The news about Frato had knocked him sideways.

"Why did you keep your husband in the dark about this?"

"B-because I was trying to be the kind of wife who trusted my new husband completely. Since it was his good friend and cousin who'd asked me not to say anything, I just couldn't betray his confidence. But a little over two months ago, Leandros brought Karmela into his office to be one his secretaries."

That hadn't been Leandros's doing, but he wanted to hear the rest before he interrupted her again.

"For my husband to do that meant he'd had talks with Karmela I didn't know about."

You're wrong, Kellie. So wrong I'm sickened by what I'm hearing.

"That's when I feared what Frato had told me was coming true. In response to the news, I asked Leandros if he'd let me come to work at his office, find me a position."

Good grief. That's why she'd asked him for a job? The pain in her voice stung him.

"What did you hope to accomplish?"

"In case Karmela was still infatuated with my husband, I wanted to be closer to him, so he wouldn't turn to her. With hindsight I can see it was very childish of me. When I broached the subject of my being at the office, Leandros dismissed the idea. Naturally I thought the reason he wouldn't want me there is because it would interfere with his interactions with Karmela."

Leandros flew out of his chair a second time, hot with rage over these new revelations about Karmela's behavior. "I told you why I didn't want you at work, Kellie. I preferred to get business and everything associated with it out of the way, so I could come home to my loving wife every night."

Kellie gave him a pained look, reminding him that their relationship had deteriorated severely over those last months. "I told him I wanted a divorce," she went on, talking to Olympia. "The night before I was going to leave for the States, Karmela walked into our apartment from the private elevator, *unannounced*, to bring Leandros some papers."

Just as she'd done the night before last!

"The two of them disappeared into his den for a little while. After she left, I asked him if he needed further proof of her infatuation with him. He denied any knowledge of expecting her, and swore he had no feelings for her. But I'm afraid I couldn't believe him this time, not when he hadn't even deleted her code from the elevator entrance."

Leandros was afraid he'd jump out of his skin. "Once you and I were married, I never gave the code a thought, Kellie. Only the night Karmela let herself in did I remember. You have to believe she came uninvited." He could have strangled his sister-in-law that night. As for the other night…

"None of it matters anymore, Leandros. All I knew was that I had to get out of our marriage."

"All right," Olympia stated. "I've heard enough to understand where suspicions of infidelity, whether warranted or not, put a pall over your marriage from day one. Let's turn to you, Leandros." She eyed him directly. "Why don't you sit down and try to relax."

Relax being the operative word.

Wild with fury over Karmela's behavior, he raked a hand through his hair before doing her bidding.

"If I understand correctly, you and your first wife knew each other for years prior to your marriage."

The change of subject threw him off for a minute. "Yes, but I went out with various girlfriends and had no romantic interest in Petra. Not until she was living in an apartment in Athens with her sister, who worked for an accounting firm. Both sets of parents asked me to look in on them as a favor, which I did from time to time.

"Petra was an excellent businesswoman who was hired by a local textile company. I admired her drive and intelligence. One thing led to another."

"Did you have an official engagement?"

"Yes. Six months. We were married a year and a half when she was killed."

"You were a widower how long?"

"Two years before I met Kellie."

"Considering you knew your first wife for years and went through a six-month engagement period, your second marriage happened fast. Twelve small weeks, in fact." Olympia scrutinized him. "Why did you ask her to marry you?"

His gaze swerved to his wife. Her wan countenance put him in fresh turmoil. "She thrilled me from the first moment I met her. With the fire lit, that feeling only grew stronger, and I knew I couldn't let her go back to Pennsylvania."

"Tell me, Leandros. When did *you* first know your marriage to Kellie was in trouble?"

Letting out a sigh of frustration, he clasped his hands between his knees. "On our wedding night." His admission brought Kellie's head around in surprise. "When I took her back to the villa, she went through all the motions of being in love with me, but something had changed. I felt she was holding back from me emotionally somehow, and I couldn't figure it out."

He glanced at Kellie. "Now I know why, but at the time I thought it was because she hadn't been married before and everything was still new. I believed that by the time morning came, she'd be the Kellie I'd fallen in love with, but that woman didn't emerge. She was sweet and affectionate as always, but the passion I'd felt from her before the marriage wasn't the same.

"To make things even more complicated, she came down with a rash and hives so severe on the second day of our honeymoon, we had to go to the doctor. We learned she had an allergy to me. Since that meant using protection all the time, it made it impossible for us to get pregnant by normal means."

"How did that make you feel?"

"I won't pretend. It was hard for both of us to hear. We spent the rest of our honeymoon discussing options, and decided we'd try artificial insemination. After the first procedure was done, I took her traveling with me while I looked for new properties. I loved being with her.

"In the beginning, we went everywhere together and spent the odd weekend on Andros. But over the last eight months, she preferred to stay at the apartment in Athens if we weren't going out of town. I assumed maybe she was worrying too much, and wanted to stay close to her doctor. When I asked her about it, she told me nothing was wrong. I could tell she didn't want to discuss it, but I knew the stress of waiting to see if we were pregnant seemed to overtake our lives.

"Two months ago I asked her to go to Rhodes with me. She told me no, that she wanted a separation."

Kellie jerked around, white faced, to look at him. "At the family dinner party a few nights before, Dionne mentioned that Karmela would be accompanying you there on business."

"Then my cousin lied to you, Kellie! I would never

take Karmela with me anywhere under any circumstances."

"Why would Dionne do that?"

Leandros studied her pinched features. "I don't know, but I'm going to find out."

Olympia sat forward. "Let's leave the subject of your cousins and sister-in-law for our session on Thursday. Did you go to Rhodes without your wife?"

"I had no choice, because of business arrangements that couldn't be changed. Then unbeknownst to me, I found out she'd made plans for her best friend, Fran, to come to Greece."

"Best friend, as in Frato has been *your* best friend?"

"Yes." Kellie spoke up before he could. "She's been like the sister I never had."

A grimace marred his features. "They were going to take a two-week trip together while I was away on business. After making that announcement, she moved to the guest bedroom. It meant we'd be missing our next appointment with the doctor."

"Since our marriage had failed, I couldn't see the point."

Olympia eyed the two of them. "Artificial insemination is an arduous process even when a couple is totally committed."

"I was prepared to do anything to have a baby," Kellie cried softly.

"No more than I." And now, miracle of miracles, they were expecting twins just before their divorce.

Kellie glanced at him briefly, then turned away. He drew in a fortifying breath. "Even though things were bad between us, when I flew Kellie back to Philadelphia, I told her I didn't want a divorce. That's when she challenged me to go to counseling with her.

"In my anger and bewilderment, I told her I didn't believe in it, and I returned to Athens. But after our separation, I realized I couldn't bear to lose her, so I agreed to it."

"Did you fly back to Pennsylvania to tell her that in person?"

"I didn't have to. She flew here two days ago with the news that she was pregnant. That's when I told her I'd been doing research to find some good therapists here in Athens. If she didn't want to get therapy here, then we'd do it in Philadelphia. After thinking about it, she chose you to help us because of your long record."

That brought the first sign of mirth from Olympia. "I'm an old fossil, all right. When did the subject of getting pregnant first come up?"

"Before we married, I told her I'd love to have children with her. She told me she couldn't wait to have a baby. Unless I'm wrong, it was a mutual decision before we took our vows."

"You aren't wrong," Kellie blurted in a wounded voice.

Olympia's gaze fell on both of them. "I'd say on that score you've communicated brilliantly. Artificial insemination is not an easy route to go, but you did it—otherwise you wouldn't be expecting twins in the near future. As for the rest, you can see you're poles apart for a married couple who hope to stay together.

"Surely today's revelations have given you your first inkling of where to dig to start finding understanding. You'll have to be brutally honest, open up and listen to each other. You'll be forced to wade through perceptions, whether false or accurate, and no matter how painful, arrive at the truth. I'll see you on Thursday."

Kellie nodded, filling him with relief that she was in agreement. He'd been afraid that when they got out to the car, she would tell him she'd changed her mind, and would refuse to go through with this after all.

While his mind was on the conversation he intended to have with Frato, whether his cousin wanted it or not, Leandros watched Olympia get up from her desk and enter her house through the connecting door. Kellie beat him to the outside door and hurried out to the car, strapping herself in.

He got behind the wheel and backed out to the street. A disturbing silence enveloped them. After heading for the main artery, he turned to her, anxious to fill the rest of their day with something constructive. "Where would you like to go for lunch? Or would you rather eat back at the hotel?"

"The hotel, if that's all right with you."

"Of course. You can rest there for a while."

She recrossed her shapely legs, a sign she was agitated. "Please don't assume I'm always tired."

"I'm sorry."

A heavy sigh escaped her lips. "Forgive me for being cranky."

"After that session, neither of us is at our best." He put on his sunglasses. "You're restless, Kellie. Instead of keeping it all inside until you reach the breaking point, let's take Olympia's advice and start really talking to each other."

"I—I'm afraid…." Her voice faltered.

"Of me?" he demanded.

"Yes—no—I don't know."

"Try me. I swear I won't erupt like I did in her office."

After a long pause, Kellie said, "I have a lot of questions. For one, I don't understand why you sold the penthouse."

Olympia's words still rang in his ears. *Surely today has given you your first inkling of where to dig to start finding understanding. You'll have to be brutally honest, open up and listen to each other. You'll be forced to wade through perceptions, whether false or accurate, and no matter how painful, to arrive at the truth.*

He cast his wife a covert glance before throwing the truth at her. "Pure and simple, I couldn't stand living there without you. That was the only reason. When I got back from Pennsylvania and walked into the living room, it hit me you wouldn't be coming home again. I couldn't take it, and phoned Frato. He'd coveted the penthouse and had said as much many times."

Through the gold curtain of hair, her lovely profile was partially visible, yet her expression hidden. "But I know you missed Petra horribly after she died. Why didn't you sell it then?"

If they hadn't been in therapy today, Leandros could see Kellie would never have had the temerity to ask that question. Now that she had, she deserved all the honesty he could give her.

"As you know, I'd rather live on Andros, and would have always lived there and commuted. But Petra wanted to live in Athens, and kept looking for a place for us. She met with a Realtor who knew the penthouse and its furnishings were up for sale if someone could pay the right price for it. She fell in love with it and wanted nothing else.

"To be honest, I didn't want to move in there, but I bought it to please her. Only two things about it appealed to me. The private elevator and the helicopter landing pad. I figured I could wing back to Andros without fuss when I wanted, but the penthouse never felt like home.

"Petra was a working woman who traveled a lot and kept late hours, like me. She wasn't there that much and hated to cook. That's because she threw all her creativity into her job. We ate out ninety percent of the time. When we entertained, she had the food catered. Once we found out she was expecting, it didn't stop her from working. When the plane went down, she'd been returning from a business trip."

"How awful that period was for you." Kellie's voice shook.

"It was, but you need to understand she never turned the apartment into a haven. *You're* the one who did that for us. Every day I found myself watching the clock, waiting to get home to you and make love. Half the time I cut my work short so we could have more time together in the evenings.

"Without you there, the memories tortured me. You know how it was with us. When I traveled, I had to have you with me—otherwise I couldn't have stood the separations. When you stopped going with me, it was torture."

She'd gone stone-cold quiet.

"Are you upset I sold it?"

He heard a sharp intake of breath. "If you'd asked me that question before we got married, I would have told you I was overjoyed."

CHAPTER FOUR

"WHAT?" LEANDROS'S THOUGHTS reeled, trying to keep up with Kellie.

"Since I'd never been married before, I wanted to start out our life together without memories of Petra. In my mind, that penthouse was her home with you. On our honeymoon, when you told me you had a special wedding present for me, I assumed you were selling it and had plans to find a place in Athens for the two of us.

"Truthfully, I never liked the penthouse. I guess I wanted a real home on the ground, one you and I picked out together."

Leandros groaned. "That small sailboat I bought you hardly qualified, did it?"

"I *love* that boat. It's been one of my great joys."

His hand tightened on the steering wheel. "Why in heaven's name didn't you tell me you didn't want to live at the penthouse?"

"And have you think I was a scheming woman who married you for your money and was already rearranging your life and your assets?" she cried out.

Her reaction astonished him. "Where's all this coming from, Kellie?"

"It doesn't matter now."

"The hell it doesn't. Tell me!"

She smoothed some golden strands away from her temple. "When I resigned from my job at the advertising agency, my boss, Brandon Howard, said, 'Now that you're marrying a man as rich as Croesus, you'll be able to buy anything you want, and become the paparazzo's favorite target.

"But if you think you're the only woman in his life, because of all the toys the great Leandros Petralia gives you, you're even more naive than I thought. Have you ever known a wealthy Greek playboy to be faithful to one woman all his life? You can't name one! It's a fairy tale, Kellie. Wake up and get out of it before it's too late.'"

A gush of adrenaline attacked Leandros's body. "Now I'm beginning to understand some of your initial concerns about Fran getting involved with Nik. It's all making sense. But don't you know that was your employer's jealousy talking, because you would never go out with him?"

"I realize that now, but at the time he made it sound so ugly, I determined never to be the creature he was talking about. No matter how much I might have wanted to ask you to sell your penthouse for my sake, it wasn't something I could have found the nerve to do.

"It would have given your family and friends more ammunition to find fault with me, and start saying that I was trying to change you to get more gifts out of you."

"My family loves you!"

"In your eyes, Leandros, because you see what you want to see. But I heard your cousins Dionne and Zera talking with Karmela at your grandmother's birthday six months after we were married. They didn't know

I'd picked up enough Greek to understand what they were saying. It was quite illuminating to learn all the ways I didn't come close to matching Petra's virtues.

"They saw a foreigner who would never fit in, who couldn't speak Greek in the beginning or get pregnant, who put you through one artificial insemination procedure after another."

"But you never heard my parents say such a thing!"

"That's true," she admitted quietly. "I'm sorry. Your parents are wonderful."

"They love you, Kellie. Just remember that Dionne and Zera are close friends with Karmela. That would explain the damaging conversation." His gut twisted. "You should have told me. You've suffered in silence all this time."

"I married you, not them, Leandros. Families will gossip. That I understand and forgive."

"Your generous nature should make them ashamed."

"I wish I hadn't said anything. As for the penthouse, I would hardly call living there a penance."

"But it took an emotional toll," he muttered grimly. Everything had taken a toll....

By this time they'd arrived at the hotel. He drove into his underground parking space and helped her out of the car to the elevator. After they'd reached his suite, he asked her what she'd like to eat, and called for room service. But when they sat down at the table to eat, he wasn't hungry.

"Kellie? Would you answer me something honestly?"

"What else do we have if we don't have that?"

He leaned forward. "The last thing you said to me before I left Philadelphia was that I shouldn't have married you, because you weren't good enough for me. I never understood where that came from until today, when you told Olympia about Rod's background. For you to clump his family with mine is—"

"His rejection made me feel inferior," she interrupted. "It hurt my pride, nothing more."

"Maybe that feeling was linked to Petra," he theorized. "Why didn't you talk to me about it?"

"I suppose I didn't want to bring her up if it would be painful for you. I realize now that isn't the case. I shouldn't have said I wasn't good enough for you. It was a foolish remark. You and your family are nothing like that. In my pain I've said a lot of things I regret."

"That works both ways. I should never have shut you down when you asked if I'd go to counseling with you."

For the next few minutes they ate in silence.

"I have another confession to make, Leandros."

He put down his coffee cup.

"When you wanted to keep trying the procedure—even though we weren't getting along—I couldn't believe you weren't discouraged," Kellie murmured. "I'm afraid I started thinking that the only reason you married me was to replace the child you'd lost."

He eyed her soulfully. "If that were true, I would have suggested we adopt a baby and save ourselves all the angst we went through. But I loved you and knew how much *you* wanted the experience of being pregnant. I'd already been through that part with Petra."

"I know," she whispered, "and I was secretly envious of her. Years ago, when Fran told me she could never have a baby, I felt terrible for her, but I didn't begin to understand the depth of her pain until the doctor explained how hard you and I would have to work to conceive. You just take it for granted that you'll grow up, get married and have a baby. But it doesn't always play out like that."

"I'll admit I wasn't prepared to find out you were allergic to me. If you want to know the truth, I thought your hives were a physical manifestation that you'd regretted marrying me."

Her eyes teared. "You're kidding me."

"No. Not at all. My heart almost failed me to think the woman I'd married was no longer enamored in the same way. It hurt *my* pride. I know there were times when we couldn't communicate because I couldn't handle it. That didn't help us at a time when we needed to be totally supportive and confident of our love."

"Oh, Leandros...I had no idea."

He took a steadying breath. "This morning's session has opened my eyes to many things, not the least of which is the part Frato has played in our lives. Before we do anything else, I want to sit down with him in person."

Kellie rested her fork on the salad plate. "Because you don't believe I told the truth about him?"

Leandros's hurt and anger were simmering beneath the surface. "I believe you, Kellie. What I didn't know until a few hours ago was that he's not the friend I thought he was. Apparently blood *isn't* thicker than water."

Her brown eyes filled with more pain. "Don't say that, Leandros. He's your cousin, and was only trying to put me in the picture."

Leandros wiped the corner of his mouth with the napkin. "I'll reserve judgment until we've talked to him."

"We?"

"Yes. We're going to take a leaf out of Olympia's book and face him together, where there's no squirming room. He'll be at the office. I'm going to call him now and tell him to meet us at the villa on Andros after he's through work today. I'll put it in terms that won't allow him to avoid the summons."

She pushed herself away from the table. "Well, if you're going to do that, I'm going to phone Fran. She's left several messages over the last few days and has no idea I'm in Athens. I need to respond. Excuse me."

Encouraged that, since their therapy session, they weren't at each other's throats, and she felt like talking to Fran, Leandros pulled out his cell to call his cousin on his private line. Frato answered on the third ring.

"Hey, Leandros—missing the job already?" he teased.

His affection for Frato made this difficult for him. "Actually, something of vital importance has come up. No matter what you've got planned for this evening, I need to talk to you in private and want you to fly out to Andros. How soon can I expect you?"

After a period of quiet his cousin said, "This sounds serious."

"Make no mistake. It is."

"I'm in Volos, doing a walk-through of the construction for the new resort. Those specs you worked up really helped. I should be finished by two-thirty at the latest, then I'll fly straight to Andros."

"I'll be waiting."

"Leandros? What's wrong?"

"I can't talk now. See you later." He purposely hung

up, for fear his anger would overtake any good judgment or magnanimity he had left.

Next he phoned Stefon and told him to get the helicopter ready.

"Kellie? I'm so thrilled it's you! I told Nik that if I didn't hear from you soon, I was going to call your aunt."

"Sorry I didn't get back to you before now, but a lot has been going on. Is this a bad time?" She sank onto the edge of the bed in the guest bedroom to talk.

"Not at all. I just put Demi down for her nap. The next time you see her, you won't believe how much she has grown. I sent you pictures, but you have to see her in person. She's so sweet and beautiful, Kellie. Gorgeous like Nik. I love them both so much I can hardly stand it, but forgive me for rattling on."

The happiness in her voice caused Kellie's eyes to fill with tears. "That's the kind of news I long to hear. After warning you against Nik, I feel so terrible."

"You're my best friend. Don't you know I understood why? Please promise me you won't bring it up again. It's all in the past. So how soon do you take possession of the house in Parkwood? We're going to fly over and help you and your aunt and uncle move in."

"I love you for offering, but I've had to put my plans for the house on hold." In fact, she needed to call her Realtor after she hung up with Fran.

"Why? Was there a snag in the negotiations?"

"N-no," she stammered.

"Kellie...I can tell by that hesitant sound in your voice something's wrong. What is it?"

"Are you sitting down?"

"Do I need to?" she cried in alarm.

"No. I'm sorry. It's good news."

"Thank heaven."

"This week I found out I'm seven weeks pregnant with twins."

"Twins?" Fran squealed with joy.

"Can you believe it?" Kellie half laughed through the tears. "After all my angst?"

"It's another miracle! Oh, wait till I tell Nik! How are you feeling?"

"Dr. Creer gave me medicine for the nausea. I'm doing fine."

"Forgive me for the next question, but I have to ask. How soon are you going to tell Leandros? I have to say, he's so devastated by what's happened, I hardly recognize him."

Kellie had hardly recognized him at the office. She'd been waiting for Fran's question. "He already knows. I flew here day before yesterday."

Another cry came over the phone line, almost bursting her eardrum. "You're in Athens?"

"Yes. There's so much to tell you, I hardly know where to start. Unfortunately, I can't stay on the phone right now because we're flying to Andros the minute I get off. But I promise I'll call you tomorrow. Maybe we can meet for a late lunch on Thursday. Leandros and I will be back in town for the next session with our marriage counselor."

She heard another gasp. "Leandros Petralia, *the* Leandros Petralia, finally agreed to go to counseling?"

"Yes. I flew to Athens to tell him I was pregnant. That's when he told me he wants another chance to save our marriage. I don't know if it will work, but I'll tell you all about it tomorrow. Give that baby and Nik a big kiss from me. *Au revoir*, for now," she said. It was a habit she'd picked up since their boarding school days in France. Aware Leandros would be waiting for her, she clicked off before Fran could say anything else.

After leaving a message for her Realtor to call her back, Kellie freshened up. But before she joined her husband, she ran her hands over her stomach.

"My precious little babies," she whispered. "You deserve a mother and father who love each other desperately and have no secrets."

She might have known Leandros would insist on talking to his cousin ASAP. It was his way to swoop in and take care of whatever needed doing, but this wasn't a business transaction. They would need to tread carefully to find common ground, in order to deal with their problems. Today was a start, but what if this didn't work?

Kellie put her head back. Refusing to think negative thoughts at this early stage, she walked through to the sitting room. He'd changed out of his suit into jeans and a burgundy polo shirt. She averted her eyes to keep from staring at his well-defined physique.

Kellie had always been wildly attracted to him, but in the end even such a strong attraction hadn't been able to overcome her distrust and pain. She could scarcely credit that he was willing to go to counseling with her. However, she needed to remember this was only the first day of therapy. A frisson of fear ran through her because she knew anything could go wrong in the weeks ahead.

"Were you able to reach Frato?"

His haunted gray eyes swerved to hers. "He'll be arriving later this afternoon. How's Fran?"

"She sounds happier than I've ever known her to be."

"Did you tell her about the twins?"

"Yes. She's elated for us. I told her I'd see her on Thursday after our therapy session."

"Good." Leandros's gaze swept over Kellie. "Is there anything you'd like to do before we leave for Andros?"

"No."

"Then let's go."

Except for the kiss at his office, they'd had no contact or relations in over two months. He didn't try to touch her again except to help her get in and out of the car or the helicopter. In those early months, they'd never been able to stay out of each other's arms. Even though Leandros had admitted in therapy he'd felt a change in her since the wedding, he seemed to have brushed his fears to the back of his mind, with the result that she was convinced he thought all was well.

Somehow she needed to learn how to shut off her memories of what it used to be like with them. Otherwise she wouldn't be able to get through this experiment. But it was so hard when they slept under the same roof at night. He went to his room, she went to hers, where she died a little each time without him.

Once more Kellie had to fight the desire that shot through her when he grasped her arm to assist her into the helicopter. His touch always played havoc with her senses. Christos couldn't help but notice.

With her heart still pounding, they were carried over the Parthenon of the three-thousand-year-old city to the island where she'd known joy, accompanied by doubts and fears she'd never been able to shake.

Now she was facing a new fear. She'd seen the wintry look in Leandros's eyes when she'd told him what

Frato had said to her at the wedding. Her husband was a wonderful man, but when crossed he made an even more wonderful adversary. Kellie had it in her heart to feel sorry for Frato, who had no idea what was waiting for him.

It wounded her that there might be trouble between the cousins, who'd always been so close. That was one of the reasons she'd never told Leandros anything. But therapy had forced her to open up if they hoped to save their marriage. It was too late to beg her husband to call off this meeting. In any case, she didn't want to.

For Leandros to hear from his cousin's lips that he had a blind spot where Karmela was concerned would give credence to what she'd told him. Her husband would have to take her fears seriously. She was so deep in thought, she didn't realize they'd landed until Leandros called to her.

"Kellie?" He looked worried. "Are you all right?"

"Yes. Of course." She unstrapped herself and got out of the helicopter with his help. This time she felt his hand slide down her arm like a caress, as if reluctant to let her go. Her breath caught before she moved away to thank Stefon for another safe flight.

Leandros was right behind her as she hurried down the path to his villa. With each step she wondered how many times he and his first wife had rushed into his house to be alone and shut out the world.

When Kellie reached the door, she waited for him to unlock it, but he stood there instead, staring at her with penetrating eyes. "After the many revelations during our therapy session, I realize you have more questions about Petra and me. I wish you'd asked me long ago. I would have told you anything."

He seemed to be reading her mind. "I should have, but I wanted to pretend you didn't have a past. That was another mistake on my part."

"Kellie," he said in a tone of exasperation. "Let's not talk about the mistakes we made. Before we go inside, I want you to know something important."

She gripped her handbag a little tighter.

"Petra agreed to our wedding taking place at the church in Stenies, but after the ceremony, we spent the night aboard her father's yacht with all the amenities. It's moored in a bay two miles from here. The next day we flew to New York for our honeymoon."

Kellie couldn't believe they'd chosen New York when they could have stayed here.

"She was never happy on Andros. It was too steeped in the past for her. She craved life in the big city. We rarely spent time here. On the few times we did come, it was to see her parents. At her insistence, we always spent the night at her parents' villa."

"But what about *your* wishes?"

"I came home when she was away overnight on business." Leandros searched Kellie's eyes. "I'm telling you all this to let you know we never slept in my villa. No woman has ever stayed overnight here except you."

While that piece of news sank in, he turned and unlocked the door. After opening it, he suddenly picked her up like a bride. "I want to carry you over the threshold again. This time you can have the sure knowledge that every memory inside these walls since we met is associated with you and no one else."

She didn't doubt he was telling her the truth. His sincerity reached that vulnerable spot inside her.

"Leand—" She'd started to say his name, but it got

muffled as his hungry mouth came down on hers. He began kissing her with growing urgency, as he'd done on their wedding night. For a moment it was déjà vu. Without effort he swung her around and carried her to his bedroom. Before she knew it they were tangled in each other's arms on top of the bed, and she found herself clinging helplessly to him.

"I love you, Kellie. More than you can imagine. Let me love you. I need you, *agapi mou*."

Here she was again, succumbing to her needs and his. Though he'd relieved her of her false assumptions to do with Petra, there was still so much to deal with, she didn't dare let this go any further. She knew herself too well. To allow herself to be blinded by passion and make love with him might satisfy the ache inside her for the moment. But it wouldn't solve the things that were still wrong outside this bed.

When he lifted his head so she could breathe, Kellie took advantage and rolled away. She got to her feet, wobbling horribly. He lay there looking devastated. "Why have you pulled away from me?"

She held on to his dresser for support. "I'm glad you told me about Petra. It has helped a lot. I *do* love you, Leandros. That will never change, but—"

"But Karmela is still the big impediment." His eyes flashed a gunmetal-gray as he got off the bed.

Kellie took a deep breath. "It isn't just Karmela. I think that until we've finished with therapy, we should concentrate on our problems and not sleep together. I can't forget that Frato will be here in a little while, and I have to admit I'm frightened."

"Why?" he demanded. "Because you haven't told me the truth? Or is it because you finally divulged a secret he asked you not to tell me, and you fear repercussions?"

She clasped her hands together. "I would never lie to you. I'm just afraid of what it might do to your friendship after he's confronted. A rift between the two of you could hurt your family in ways that make me ill to contemplate."

"Because you're afraid they'll blame you?"

"Deep down I suppose I am."

Leandros's eyes glittered in pain. "No rift could be more deadly than the one between you and me. I'll go to any lengths to fix it." She believed him—otherwise he wouldn't be going to therapy with her. "If it alienates my cousin and me, or my family, so be it. I'm going down to the beach for a swim. Do you want to come with me?"

"Yes," she said, making a snap decision that seemed to surprise him. "I'll go in the other bedroom and change into my suit."

Over the past few months, before she'd gone back to Philadelphia, he'd become used to her turning him down. But as Olympia had pointed out, there was a lot Kellie had kept from Leandros. She realized now she'd done so out of fear. Unfortunately, it had combined with his hurt pride to help contribute to the serious problems in their marriage. His determination to put it back together at any cost made her cognizant that she needed to play an equal part in this.

Throwing a wrap over the white bikini he'd given her on her twenty-eighth birthday, four months ago, she joined him at the front door and they walked down the steps to the beach.

"Ooh, this sand is almost hot."

Leandros eyed her up and down after she removed her wrap. His gaze focused on her stomach, which was getting thicker, but so far wasn't protruding. "Then let's get you in the water quick."

"Oh no, you don't!" she cried, and started running toward it, barely escaping his arms, which would have picked up her again. Kellie was a good swimmer and took off, not worried about the depth, since it was fairly shallow for about a hundred feet. He came after her like a torpedo and circled her, preventing her from going out any farther.

"You need to be careful now that our little unborn babies are starting to make their presence known."

Kellie treaded water. "You noticed?" she teased, feeling playful in a brand-new way, because therapy had opened up a dialogue, and she no longer felt threatened by Petra's specter.

His white smile turned her heart over. "You're no longer concave. I love your new shape."

"I'll hold you to that when I need to be carted around in a wheelbarrow at seven months." After the words flew out of her mouth, she realized her mistake. They might not be together in seven months, or even in one more month.

He moved closer, catching her around the hips. The next thing she knew he'd turned her body so her back was against his chest. A voluptuous warmth filled her as moved his hands over her stomach, exploring her until her senses leaped. "I've got the world in my arms," he whispered, kissing her on the side of her neck.

Kellie was so filled with chaotic emotions, she couldn't talk.

"When you told me you were expecting twins, you

made me the happiest man alive, not only for me, but for you. I'm here for you in every way."

"I'm happy for you, too, Leandros. No man ever tried harder to become a father. You never let me give up. For that you have my undying gratitude." His touch had reduced her to pulp, so she was slow to realize she could hear a helicopter coming close to the estate. "That will be Frato!"

"So it is, but we'll beat him. Let's keep our personal business to ourselves."

"I agree."

Leandros pulled her with him to shore, then picked her up again and carried her up the steps into the villa, without taking an extra breath. "I'll meet the helicopter and walk him down here. That should give you enough time to change."

He lowered a hard kiss to her mouth before he took off out the front door to greet his cousin. She pressed fingers to her lips, which still tingled as she watched him leave. He wore black swim trunks that rode low on his hips.

He looked magnificent.

CHAPTER FIVE

LEANDROS WANTED A LOT MORE than his wife's gratitude as he approached the pilot's side of the helicopter. He waited until Frato started to climb out before he told Stefon to stay put. "My cousin will be needing a ride back to Athens, but I don't know the time. You go ahead and use the guest cottage. He'll ring you later."

After the pilot nodded, Leandros walked around the other side. Six feet tall, his cousin was still in a business suit. His dark curly hair and brown eyes proclaimed him a Petralia. Leandros's coloring differed because he'd inherited his mother's gray eyes.

"You made good time, Frato. Thanks for dropping everything to get here so fast. As you can see, I was taking a swim."

"Your phone call made me nervous, so I came as soon as I could. I didn't know you were going to vacation at home."

"My plans are subject to change from moment to moment."

Frato stopped walking long enough to look at him. "That sounded cryptic. What's going on?"

"That's what I want to know. But let's go in the house

first. You need to get out of this heat and shed your jacket."

"If I didn't know better, I'd think you were setting me up," he said with a nervous laugh.

His cousin was a quick study. "If I didn't know better, I'd think maybe that was a guilty conscience talking," Leandros replied.

Frato stopped at the front door. "You *are* setting me up!"

When it unexpectedly opened, revealing Kellie, his jaw went slack. She'd arranged her damp, golden hair in a loose knot and changed into jeans and a summery, blouson-type top in a delicious shade of ice-blue. Pregnancy had made her radiant. "Hello, Frato." She kissed him on both cheeks. "Come in and let me fix you something cool while Leandros gets dressed."

"You're back!" His cousin more or less staggered into the living room. "I had no idea."

She nodded. "Do you want a fruit drink or something stronger?"

"Nothing for me." He removed his jacket and tossed it over one of the chairs.

"Then please sit down. It's good to see you."

"I'll be right back." Leandros disappeared to get dressed. In under a minute he returned, wearing shorts and a sport shirt he was still buttoning. "You're sure you won't have a drink?"

Frato shook his head. "I know you when you've got something important on your mind. Why don't we just get to the point."

Leandros stood in front of his cousin, who'd taken a seat on one end of the couch. Kellie sat on the other.

The moisture on Frato's upper lip wasn't all due to the heat. Leandros detected nervous tension.

"Today I learned of a confidence you shared with Kellie at our wedding. You told her not to tell me. Do you recall what I'm talking about?"

His cousin looked mystified. "I'm afraid I don't. If you say this happened the night of your nuptials, I remember doing more drinking than usual."

"I could smell the alcohol." Kellie spoke up. "You took me aside to congratulate me. Then you told me some things that were very disturbing, before you asked me to keep it to myself. I honored your wishes until this morning, Frato, but I have two regrets. One, that you ever told me anything, and two, that I kept it from Leandros for so long."

"Refresh my memory." Frato could be obstinate when he wanted.

Leandros listened as she repeated verbatim what she'd told Olympia. The room went an unearthly quiet after she'd finished. Frato got a sick look and moved off the couch to gaze out the window with his back toward them.

"Has it all jelled yet?" Leandros asked in a quiet voice.

His cousin continued to say nothing. Leandros moved closer. "So it's true what you told Kellie?"

Frato finally wheeled around with a tormented look in his eyes. "I meant no harm, Leandros. I swear it."

Anger raged inside him. "How would you know if Karmela had feelings for me before I married Petra?"

"Because she told me!" he blurted.

"How intriguing. Why would she tell *you*?"

"Because I've always been crazy about Karmela."

That was news to Leandros. "There've been a few things in our lives I haven't told you. Especially after she refused to go out with me. When I pressed her for a reason, she said she'd been in love with you since she was a teenager on the island."

"Then it was a fantasy of her own infantile imagination."

"Several girls had a crush on you. But unlike them, she never got over it."

After Karmela's performance the other night, Leandros knew it was true. "Then what purpose did you think it would serve to run to my brand-new wife and alarm her?"

Frato's head reared back. "Because you were so oblivious. I was in love with her, but it did no good while she had her heart set on you. When she found out you were marrying Kellie, she told me that one way or another, she was going to get pregnant with your baby. In her mind she assumed that when it happened, you'd have to get a divorce and marry her."

"Surely you could see she was delusional then," Leandros exclaimed. After her appearance at the office, he realized Petra's sister had a problem that had needed a psychiatrist a long time ago. He was appalled at his own lack of vision, but Kellie had seen it. *She'd* been the one hurt by Karmela at the very beginning of their marriage.

"All I saw was a woman who'd had to live in Petra's shadow. I figured that if I bided my time, she would eventually turn to me. But when I saw how she kissed you at the wedding, I couldn't take it and started drinking."

So Frato had noticed that kiss, too. Leandros hadn't remembered anything but his love for Kellie.

His cousin turned to her. "I felt I had to warn you about what was going on. It was because I liked you and was afraid for you."

"Afraid for my wife?" Leandros bit out.

"Yes." He turned back to Leandros. "Karmela always seemed to have you wrapped around her little finger. It looked like she could do no wrong in your eyes. From my vantage point you let her get away with whatever she wanted."

"So you assumed I'd welcome my own sister-in-law into my bed?" Leandros was livid.

Frato's brow rose. "I didn't know, did I?"

"Good grief! What's happened to you? Where's the cousin I grew up with?"

"You got the woman you wanted! Life was easier for you."

Leandros couldn't believe what he was hearing. "I was going to wait to tell Kellie everything until I'd talked to you. But now this can't wait. Though you don't deserve an explanation, I'm going to give you one.

"When Petra and I started seeing each other, she asked me to be kind to her sister. She worried that Karmela would start feeling abandoned and alone after we got married. Now that I have certain information I didn't have two years ago, I'm convinced Petra knew her sister was very disturbed, but she was afraid to tell me.

"As a favor to her, because she was so concerned, I agreed we would let Karmela come and go from the penthouse like she was part of the family. But I never liked it."

Frato gesticulated with his arms. "Then you understand it was an act she put on for Petra, to win her sympathy and get closer to you."

"I agree and I'm convinced." It was all making an ugly kind of sense. "Now I need the answer to another question. If you were so worried I might take advantage of the situation, then perhaps you'd like to tell me and Kellie a couple of things. Why did you beg me to let her come to work under Mrs. Kostas? And why didn't you want anyone to know it was your doing?"

Kellie's shocked cry was music to Leandros's ears. He prayed his wife was taking all this in.

"Because that favor was for *me*," his cousin insisted. "Karmela never left me alone about coming to work for the company, but I wanted it to look aboveboard, and that meant the decision had to come from you."

A scowl broke out on Leandros's face. "I thought you said she wasn't interested in you."

"In the beginning that was true. But I'm not a quitter. It had been a long time since your wedding to Kellie. About eight months ago we started seeing each other and one thing led to another. Since she came to work in your office, things have been really good behind the scenes," he admitted.

"What happened to Anya?"

"I only see her from time to time, but that's all over now."

Leandros wondered if he'd ever really known his cousin.

"I have more news and might as well let you in on it, since it's going to get out pretty soon," Frato continued. "Karmela and I are going to get married."

"You *what*?"

"Shocking to you, isn't it," he muttered. "Don't you know that's why I took you up on your offer and bought the penthouse? In five years I'll have it completely paid off. She loves it there because it feels like home to her."

Kellie's stunned gaze flew to Leandros. By now she'd gotten to her feet. "There's something you need to know before you make a mistake that could ruin your life, Frato," she said.

"What do you mean?"

"The night before Leandros flew me back to Philadelphia, a month ago, Karmela came to the penthouse *uninvited*. You see, she'd heard the gossip about us getting a divorce, and thought I'd already left for the States.

"What she didn't know was that I'd been sick that night and had to go to the E.R. Leandros brought me back to the penthouse. While we were there, Karmela walked in as if she lived there. I could tell she was shocked to see me, but she covered it well and said she'd brought papers from the office for Leandros to look over and sign.

"Did she tell you about that visit? I can give you the exact date and time. Before you marry her, you'd better find out the truth!"

Frato got that bewildered look on his face, one Leandros had seen many times in their childhood. "Since Petra died, I've never given Karmela permission to come to the penthouse," Leandros told him. "If I were you, I'd ask her about that night. If she can satisfy you that she had a legitimate right to use my private elevator and walk in on me unannounced and unexpected, then it appears you're the one living in an oblivious state."

His cousin got off the couch again and started pacing.

"Frato," Kellie said in a kindly voice. "I'm very

sorry, but it's clear to me Karmela has been using you all this time to get to Leandros. That's why she wanted to come to work at his office. She hasn't given up on this fantasy of hers, and needs professional help. If you marry her, you're in for so much pain, you can't imagine."

While his cousin digested everything, Leandros made a decision. "Why don't you stay overnight on the island with your family? If Karmela is expecting you at the penthouse, tell her you had business that kept you longer than planned. Tomorrow you need to call her into the office and tell her you have to let her go."

Frato hung his head. "I can't fire her."

"Then you want me to do it? I'd rather it came from you."

His cousin looked terrified. "I can't. Leandros—if you insist on this, I'll lose her!"

"We don't have a choice here. Though this is going to be painful for you, I have more news. Do you know where she was at eleven two nights ago?"

"Yes. She said she had to work late, and didn't get back to the apartment until midnight."

"She told you a lie, Frato. While I was working at my desk, she came into my office with a tray of food."

"I don't understand."

It was now or never if Leandros was going to get through to him. "I have no idea how long she'd been in the building, but everyone else had gone home at quitting time. I asked her to leave, but she seemed to think it was some sort of game."

"What do you mean?"

"She acted like a rebellious teenager, wanting to know my business. First she cast disparaging remarks about Kellie. Then she pulled tears about how much she knew I missed Petra, and that she wanted to help me. I believe she's ill, as ill as she was at my wedding to Kellie, but I didn't realize it then. She's gotten sicker with time. I came close to removing her physically from my office before she finally left."

His cousin paled. Who would have guessed that Karmela would turn out to be Frato's Achilles' heel?

Kellie shook her head. "She needs to be let go, Frato. If you lose her because of it, then it will prove she was never really yours to lose. Don't you see this is the only way, for the good of the company and our personal lives? How could anyone hope to function with all that subterfuge going on?"

Perspiration broke out on his forehead. "She'll turn her family against ours and everyone will blame me."

Leandros's jaw hardened. "That will be nothing compared to the fact that she's already created enough trouble between Kellie and me to bring us to the brink of divorce!"

"But they're your in-laws! Out of respect for Petra, how can you do that?"

With that remark, Leandros realized his cousin wasn't capable of viewing the situation rationally right now. Maybe never.

"How can I not? You've missed the point, Frato. I have no doubt her parents have been worried about Karmela for years. When this gets out, it's possible they'll be able to find her the help she needs. While they're doing that, you can move on. Don't forget I'm on vacation until further notice and need you to run the company."

Frato reached for his jacket and headed for the door. "I've got to get back to Athens, where I can think."

"It's your life. But if you're tempted to tell Karmela anything before we meet tomorrow, at nine in the morning, then word could get back to the board through her. You'll be lucky if they only give you a forced leave of absence from the company until you come to your senses."

His cousin wasn't listening. No sooner had he disappeared than Leandros's cell phone rang. It was his mother, who explained she'd just returned from town, and saw the helicopter. "I didn't know you were here."

"Frato and I were having a meeting, but he's leaving now."

"Then come up for dinner."

"I can't tonight, *Mana*."

"Leandros...your papa and I hardly see you these days."

"I know, but I'll make it up to you." He wanted Kellie with him when they told his parents about the twins, but they needed to have another session of therapy before he felt they could inform his family of what was happening. "Right now I'm in the middle of delicate negotiations and don't have the time." It was the truth.

"I've been concerned about you. The last time I saw you, you looked too thin. Since Kellie left, you haven't been taking good enough care of yourself."

"Don't worry about me. I'll call you very soon, I promise."

He rang off and went in search of his wife, who'd gone into the kitchen. When he found her, she was eating a peach. He'd like to eat one of those and then start on her, but that was an activity he had to put on hold for the time being.

"How's your mother?"

"Being motherish."

Kellie flashed him a sad smile. "My aunt gets like that, too."

"Let's drive somewhere along the coast for dinner. I'm starving, as well."

"That sounds good. I'll grab my purse."

As they walked out the front door, the helicopter flew overhead, taking Frato back to Athens. Leandros was thankful he'd gone.

Once they got in the car and were on the road, she turned to him. "Do you think he'll tell Karmela?"

Leandros slanted her a veiled glance. "There was a time when I thought I knew my cousin, but no longer. It's anyone's guess what we'll find when we arrive at the office tomorrow."

She glanced at the shimmering blue water. "I've always liked Frato. It's so sad that he's been enamored of someone who never loved him. My heart aches for him."

"It's possible this intervention will shake the scales from his eyes. I care deeply for my cousin and would like to see him work this out with as few repercussions as possible."

"Do you know one of your great traits is your charitable attitude about people, even under the worst of circumstances?" Her comment warmed him.

They drove in silence another five miles to a fishing village before she spoke her mind. "I—I wish you'd told me it was Frato's idea to bring her into the office...."

Kellie's voice faltered. "Why didn't you tell me she walked in on you two nights ago?"

"I could have, but I was waiting to hear what Frato had to say first before I laid every card on the table." Leandros flicked her a glance. "For that matter, I wish you'd told me what he'd said the night of our wedding. As we've both found out, my cousin knows how to wear you down until you end up doing what he wants."

"I—I never wanted to believe you were interested in Karmela," she admitted.

"The idea was so ludicrous, I couldn't understand your suspicions. I was blind in the beginning, because I was so in love with you. But between Fran's and Frato's observations, it's no wonder the bloom was off our wedding night. Frato can be a valuable asset to the company when he's out doing business. But in our case, he's helped the enemy within."

"I remember that quote from Marcus Cicero. 'A nation can survive its fools, and even the ambitious. But it can't survive treason from within.'"

"Exactly. Years ago my father made me memorize it when I started working for the company."

"How does the rest of it go? I'm positive you know it."

He flashed her a smile, because for a few minutes it felt as if they were really communicating again. "'An enemy at the gates is less formidable, for he is known and carries his banner openly. But the traitor moves amongst those within the gate freely. He speaks in accents familiar to his victims, but works secretly in the night to undermine the pillars of the city.'"

After he'd spoken, Leandros felt the shudder that ran through her body even though they weren't touching. "He could have been describing what's happened to us," she murmured

"When you think about it, those words could apply to your former boss, too. Once you told him you were getting married, he couldn't leave it alone and planted doubts in your mind, all in the name of wanting to keep you for himself."

"He never had me." Kellie rested her forehead in her hand. "His assumptions were so hurtful and angered me so much, you'll never know. But looking back, I realize I did worse. In my zeal to protect Fran from getting hurt after her painful divorce, I made a lot of assumptions about Nik that weren't the truth. You have no idea how ashamed I am. He must think I'm horrible." Tears ran down her cheeks.

Leandros pulled into the parking area of one of their favorite seaside restaurants. To his sorrow they hadn't been here for at least six months. He shut off the engine and turned to her. "You're wrong, Kellie." He wiped the moisture from her cheeks with his thumb. "Nik wasn't as completely open as he should have been with Fran about the real reasons he'd never married, thus arousing your suspicions. He regrets that."

She looked away from him. "You're just being diplomatic, but that's another thing about you I admire. I happen to know my aspersions about him hurt you. The breakdown of our marriage turned me into someone I didn't like."

"I didn't like myself, either, Kellie. By the end, I was jealous of their ability to get past their fertility issues. With us, it was the other way around. The more we tried to get pregnant, the more we got bogged down in our insecurities and became alienated. My frustration over not being the man you thought you were marrying turned into anger. You weren't the only one who threw up a wall between us."

"Leandros…" she said, sounding distressed. "If you don't mind, let's go inside. One thing I'm noticing about this pregnancy. I have to eat on time or I get famished."

He kissed the tip of her nose before getting out of the car to help her. He was famished, too, for *her*. But for the moment he had to be satisfied with this amount of detente, including the compliments she'd been paying him. Before she'd shown up in his office two days ago, he couldn't have imagined this much progress. Unfortunately, when they faced Karmela in the morning, there could be a setback that might undermine any progress they'd made.

At ten to nine the next morning, Kellie got out of the helicopter with Leandros's help and rode the elevator down to his office suite with him. She hadn't slept well during the night and had gotten up early to shower and wash her hair. After blow drying it so it fell in natural curls around her shoulders, she'd gone into the kitchen to take her pills and fix breakfast for the two of them.

After the fabulous seafood dinner with him the night before, she couldn't believe she was hungry again. Eating for three was no joke, but at this rate she'd have to start watching her weight. Already her clothes were fitting tighter. Pretty soon she'd need maternity outfits.

In order to feel comfortable, she'd put on a cream-colored blouse with a khaki skirt that tied loosely around the waist. On her feet she wore bone-colored leather sandals. The doctor had warned her high heels weren't a good idea.

The way Leandros's eyes lingered on her while they ate on the terrace raised her temperature. His appeal was so potent, she was in danger of forgetting her own rule to keep her distance with him. But knowing they'd been through only one session of therapy, not to mention that they'd be confronting Karmela in a few hours, Kellie made certain she didn't succumb to him out of weakness. Instead, she got up and did the dishes before announcing she was ready to go.

No one was in Leandros's office when they entered on the dot of nine. She really hadn't thought Frato would be here, and was sure Leandros hadn't counted on it, either.

"Leandros? I'd rather wait outside the door with Christos while you speak to Karmela. I don't want her to feel like she's being attacked."

He caressed her cheek. "You're an amazingly kind person, Kellie. Tell you what. I'll record everything that goes on so you'll know exactly what was said. No more secrets, remember?"

She nodded and sat down next to his bodyguard to wait. Before Leandros disappeared into his office, she noticed how fabulous he looked in a tan suit and tie that accidentally matched her outfit. He was the picture of the successful CEO in charge of his domain.

There were times, like now, when she wondered how she'd been the one to catch his eye after Petra died. No woman was immune to him. Kellie's heart rate sped up as she imagined what was about to happen.

Leandros closed the door and went around his desk to buzz Mrs. Kostas. "Would you please send in Karmela?"

"Mr. Petralia! I thought you'd gone on vacation."

He smiled to himself. "I thought so, too. Where's Frato?"

"I haven't seen him yet. I'll send Karmela right in."

"Thank you." Leandros sat back in the swivel chair. "Good morning, Karmela," he said as she opened the door. "Come all the way in and sit down."

Karmela walked straight up to him. "Frato told me about your conversation at the villa yesterday. I understand you want my resignation. But let me give you warning. So far he thinks he's the father of my baby. I'll go on letting him believe it as long as I can keep my job. If I can't, then we'll see how well you handle public opinion when news leaks to the press that you're the daddy."

What more proof did anyone need to know she was ill?

"If you're putting on this performance for me, it isn't necessary, Karmela. I have no idea if you're pregnant or not, but a pregnancy test demanded by a court order can clear that up in a matter of minutes. If you're pregnant, it couldn't possibly be my baby. A DNA test will provide the evidence, but surely you don't want to put Frato through that."

Leandros had seen that catlike smile on her face before. "Frato's more gullible than you. Why do you think the company made you CEO at your age? I'll tell him you and I were lovers during the times Petra was away on business. My family's yacht provided the perfect place away from everyone.

"Before you went to Rhodes on your new project, we got together. That was the time I conceived our baby.

Three nights ago we were in this office alone for hours. All he has to do is check with Christos to believe me."

Leandros got to his feet. "I feel sorry for you and Frato. You need help to get over this obsession. It's tragic you've dragged my cousin into it. There's no more job for you here. If you'd like, I'll have your belongings sent to your parents' home."

When she made no move to leave, he paged Christos and asked him to come in.

"You wanted me?"

"Yes. Please follow Ms. Paulos to her desk so she can get her purse. Then escort her out of the building and put her in a taxi."

Her cat's eyes glimmered. She glared at Leandros. "You have no idea what you've done."

"On the contrary. It's the best decision for everyone concerned. Goodbye, Karmela."

As if nothing was wrong, she strode to the door and walked out, with Christos trailing her. The minute they left, Leandros rushed out into the hall to get Kellie and lead her inside.

She eyed him as he spoke to Mrs. Kostas over the phone. "I'm officially on vacation, but I'll be staying in Athens at the Cassandra. If you can't reach Frato, feel free to call me. Karmela will no longer be working for us. See that her final paycheck goes to her parents' home on Andros Island. I'll be out of the office for the rest of the day."

"Yes, sir."

He shut off the speakerphone. "Before we leave, I'll play the recording so you'll know exactly what was said."

Kellie sat down to listen. When it ended, she looked

up at him. "I don't believe for a moment she's pregnant with your baby, or even pregnant. She's like a defiant little girl. What a shame."

"I agree. All I can say is, thank heaven this is over." Leandros called for his car to be brought around the side of the building, his eyes blazing a hot silvery gray as they pierced Kellie's. "Let's get out of here. I want to take us for a drive around the residential neighborhoods in Athens. Maybe we'll see the house you'd hoped I would buy for your wedding present."

"Leandros..." Her voice shook. "After this scene with Karmela, how can you even think about anything else?"

"Very easily. Whatever she chooses to do or not do, we're through with her."

"I'd like to go back to the hotel."

His eyes scrutinized her. "I thought this confrontation meant we'd put Karmela to rest forever."

She shook her head. "I'm still reacting to what she said. Don't you understand? Even though it's not true, she has threatened to go to the media."

His mouth thinned to a white line. "*Even?* That means you're still not sure about me."

"Of course I am, but after her threat, I can't concentrate on anything else right now."

Leandros ushered Kellie inside the elevator and pushed the button. "If you can't, *I* can. With the twins coming, I want to get settled in the right place to raise them. If you've made up your mind to leave me no matter what, I still have to provide for them, and don't want them living in a hotel when it's my turn for visitation."

"I didn't say that!" She felt ill, especially after he'd done everything in his power to deal with Karmela and Frato since they'd left Mrs. Lasko's house. "Please give me some time, Leandros. Don't you realize how worried I am about the damage she could do to *you*?"

"That's not what's bothering you. A part of you is still worried about Karmela," he said in a wintry tone.

Silence reigned during their swift descent to the ground floor. He'd turned into his forbidding self, the side of him she'd seen toward the end of their marriage. It made it impossible for her to reach him. They walked to the car and he helped her in. When they drove out to the street, he said, "I'll drop you off at the hotel."

"No, Leandros. I've changed my mind and want to come with you."

"Why, since you won't be living with me? I'm going to use the rest of the day to look at houses with a Realtor. It could get too tiring for you. I may not find what I'm looking for today or tomorrow, but I can begin my search. If nothing suits, I'll buy a piece of property and hire an architect."

The Cassandra wasn't that far from his office. He pulled up in front and got out to help her inside the front doors, where people were coming and going. "I'll see you later." A nerve throbbed at the corner of his hard mouth. "Promise you'll call me if there's any kind of emergency."

"Leandros…"

"You may be carrying our children, but don't forget I helped put them there, and love them as much as you do."

Fighting tears, she grabbed his arm. "As if I could forget."

But he wasn't listening. "You already have a home

picked out in Philadelphia. I need to find one for our children when they're with me."

I know.

His eyes were mere slits as he helped her to the elevator in the hall. He pinned her with an undecipherable glance before wheeling away. There was no extra squeeze or caress on the cheek. Why would there be when she was still behaving like the woman who'd insisted on leaving him?

Once he'd driven off, Kellie went up to their suite with a heart so heavy she wanted to die. Without hesitation she ran to her room and pulled the phone out of her purse to call Fran. It rang four times. *Please pick up.*

"Kellie? I've been hoping you'd call soon."

"Thank goodness you're there!"

"Hey…you sound frantic."

"I am. Nothing changes, does it?"

"Yes, it does. You're pregnant with twins! That makes three miracles for us."

Tears filled Kellie's eyes. "I know, but I'm still the same mess I've been for months. Can you talk?"

"Yes. My little miracle from out of the blue is in her swing, listening to the songs. I won't be feeding her for another half hour. Now's the time to tell me what's going on. You left me hanging yesterday. That wasn't fair."

"I'm sorry." Kellie kicked off her shoes and flung herself across the bed before she remembered she needed to be more careful. Slowly she turned over on her back and tucked a pillow under her head. Once she got started talking with her best friend, everything came tumbling out, until Fran was completely caught up.

"Deep down I always thought she was unstable, but I never dreamed Frato was involved."

"It's very sad."

"Hey, Kellie? What's going on? Please tell me you didn't believe Karmela's claim that she's carrying your husband's child!"

She shuddered. "No, but you never heard such a convincing performance in your life."

"Oh, Kellie... After everything that's happened, did you tell Leandros you still believe her?"

"I told him just the opposite!"

"But you left him in doubt by not going house hunting with him."

"I couldn't right then," she said defensively as tears scalded her cheeks.

"Then it sounds like she's won and you've lost the greatest man you'll ever meet on this earth. They don't come any finer than Leandros. I love you, Kellie, but I'm sorry for you."

Fran's comment was like a stab through the heart. "I'm going to hang up now."

"Don't do that! Talk to me! Surely learning about Frato's involvement with her explains everything. It should have made a new woman out of you! What's going on with you?"

"Honestly, it *has* removed every doubt I ever had, but I'm terrified of what she's going to do to him. The second Karmela left his office with Christos, Leandros acted like nothing traumatic had happened. After what she'd vowed to do, I couldn't imagine going anywhere."

"That's your husband, Kellie. He seizes the moment, then moves on. It's part of his brilliance."

"But Karmela is going to come after him! It will

cause terrible trouble in their families, just as Frato predicted. I know it."

"Obviously Leandros isn't worried about it. I'd say he's much more concerned about where the four of you are going to live."

"We're not officially back together. We still have other issues to work through. After the way I left him earlier, I don't know when he'll speak to me again."

"Just have faith that he will! You're the one who wanted counseling and agreed to do it here in Athens. Since he gave up his apartment, it's only natural he's anxious to find a place for the new family coming. Hotel living gets old in a hurry, even in one as posh as the Cassandra."

"I realize that, but I'm still reeling from what went on his office with Karmela. I don't know how he puts one foot in front of the other. Oh, Fran, I know I've hurt him again. He probably won't come back to the hotel until I'm asleep tonight."

"Maybe that's not a bad thing. It will give him time to cool off. Just remember he's a big boy and will get over it. You can discuss it with him in front of Mrs. Lasko at your session tomorrow. That's what marriage counseling is all about. What time do you have to be there?"

Kellie could hear little Demi making noises in the background. "At eleven. I think your daughter is getting hungry. I'll hang up so you can feed her."

"Okay. But before you go, you have no idea how thrilled I am that you're going to be in Athens for your therapy. I've missed you."

Kellie closed her eyes tightly. "Same here."

"Why don't we leave plans open for tomorrow? I'd

love to have lunch with you, but depending on how things go at therapy, maybe the four of us could get together for a barbecue here at the apartment on the patio toward evening. Nik and I are dying to be with the two of you again. He told me to ask you to come over."

"I'll talk to Leandros and let you know. That is, if he's still speaking to me."

"Don't be ridiculous."

"Give Demi a kiss from me. Goodbye for now."

Kellie clicked off and rolled onto her stomach. The day's events had drained her. Unfortunately, the relief of knowing the truth about Karmela was overshadowed by the ugliness of her threats.

Kellie was afraid Leandros wasn't taking this seriously enough. Tomorrow she'd discuss this latest fear in front of their therapist. He would be forced to listen. If anything happened to him...

Tears crept out of the corners of her eyes before she knew nothing more.

CHAPTER SIX

AFTER SEEING KELLIE safely inside the hotel, Leandros drove over to his former apartment, feeling like a shellshocked victim. If his wife still harbored any doubts about him where Karmela was concerned, then their marriage truly was over. But until he calmed down, he wanted another talk with Frato.

Leandros didn't know what to expect, but he knew his cousin was in deep trouble and needed help. In order not to embarrass Frato further, this was one visit he needed to make without Kellie.

En route, he contacted a Realtor he knew well and asked him to come up with some houses to show him and Kellie later on. After he'd finished that call, Leandros phoned his attorney and brought him up to speed about the situation with Frato and Karmela. "I want you prepared for anything that might happen in the next few hours or days. Let's get some private detectives to put her under surveillance."

With that accomplished, he drove into the underground parking. He spotted Frato's BMW, but it didn't necessarily mean he was there. As for Karmela, she could be anywhere, drumming up trouble. She was impulsive, disturbed and furious. Leandros didn't know what to expect.

The second the elevator door opened to the penthouse, he saw Frato dressed in a robe, sprawled on the couch in the living room. He had one foot on the floor and had been drinking. His cousin had been doing more and more of that over the past few years.

"Frato? Where's Karmela?"

He squinted up at Leandros. "It's a cinch she's not here with me. I haven't seen her since all hell broke loose after I got back from Andros yesterday."

"For your information, more broke loose in the office this morning after I let her go. She threw out some expected and unexpected threats before I asked Christos to escort her off the premises."

At that news, Frato struggled to his feet with a groan. "You went in to work?"

"Someone needs to be running the Petralia Corporation, don't you think? Don't worry. I covered for you and told Mrs. Kostas I was still on vacation. We're family, Frato, and we have to stick together. The last thing I'm going to do is fire you, but I need you sober. Go take a shower and get dressed for work while I fix you some coffee so we can talk."

While he waited, he phoned his electronics technician and asked him to come over and remove all codes except Frato's from the elevator security system. As Leandros clicked off, Frato reappeared. His cousin had done his best to disguise the fact that he was hungover.

"Who was that?"

"Not Karmela." After telling him he'd called the security technician to come, Leandros handed him a mug of coffee. "I'll explain why in a minute. Tell me the truth. Is Karmela pregnant with your baby? Is that why the rush to get married?"

The shocked look on Frato's face was all the explanation Leandros needed. With that question answered, he pulled out his cell phone. "I recorded everything the second Karmela walked through the door to my office." He turned it on and they both listened.

By the time they'd heard the door close behind Christos, Frato's tanned complexion had faded several degrees. With a trembling hand, he set down his empty mug.

Leandros switched off the recording. "I'm sorry you had to hear that, but it was necessary. She's got a serious problem, Frato. For a long time she's been using our weaknesses to play all of us against each other.

"You need to know I've already alerted my attorney. If you and I join forces, then whatever she tries to do to discredit us to the media or the families, we'll be a step ahead of her until she gets the help she needs."

He had never seen his cousin's brown eyes water like that before. "I can't believe what I just heard." Frato sank down on one of the bar stools. "What a damn fool I've been all these years."

Leandros patted him on the shoulder. "You don't want to hear what a damn fool I've been since I listened to Petra and gave Karmela carte blanche to do what she wanted. In my desire to placate Petra, I enabled Karmela in a way that has brought my marriage to Kellie to the brink of disaster. But we've started marriage counseling to try to save us."

"You're kidding…."

"No. Naturally it was Kellie's idea, because I've been too impossible to deal with."

"So that's what brought her back?"

Leandros shook his head. "She flew here to tell me in person that we're expecting twins next March."

Frato let out a long whistle that reverberated throughout the penthouse. "Twins? I'm beyond happy for you, Leandros."

His cousin sounded so genuine, it brought a lump to Leandros's throat. "I'm ecstatic myself. Kellie said I deserved to hear the news in person, but she still expected the divorce to go through. I told her I'd just made arrangements with you so I could fly to Pennsylvania, where we could go to counseling. After talking it over, we decided to do our counseling here. We've had one session already, with another one scheduled for tomorrow."

Frato's head jerked back. "Does Karmela know about this?"

"Not her or anyone. I want to keep it that way for the time being."

"Understood. Do you want the penthouse back?"

"It's yours, Frato, with my blessing. I found out Kellie never wanted to live here."

"Why not?"

"Because Petra lived here with me. Kellie wanted a place of our own, but I was too caught up in my desires to ask her what she wanted. Right now we're looking for a house."

"Incredible."

"Are you with me?"

"*Yes!*"

"Good. Together we can withstand any storm. When the families start calling you, pretend you know nothing. I suggest you get to the office so no one will suspect anything's wrong. Mrs. Kostas knows Karmela has been fired. She'll send her final check to her parents. While you dig into work, I'm going to enjoy my vacation."

Frato nodded. "I'm leaving now."

"One more thing. The technician is on his way over to delete Karmela's code from the elevator. When she calls because it's on the blink, tell her to find herself a good attorney, and assure her you'll have her things shipped to her parents."

As Leandros started to leave, Frato grabbed him and gave him a bear hug, the kind they used to share before their lives got complicated. "I swear I'm going to do better."

"I'll make you the same promise." He knew his cousin would hurt for a long time, but at least Frato's blinders had come off for good.

With everything taken care of for the time being, Leandros felt an enormous weight had been lifted. He left for the hotel, eager to talk to Kellie and explain why he'd thought it was wise she remain there until he got back. His Realtor had called and left the message that he had some wonderful prospects for them, whenever they wanted to see them.

It was midafternoon when Leandros found her in her bedroom, sound asleep on top of the bed, resting on her side. She was still dressed in the skirt and top she'd worn to the office. Her shimmering gold hair was splayed across the pillow. There was no sign that she'd eaten lunch.

He stood in the doorway while his eyes devoured the sight lying before him. She was his whole world. Inside her delectable body their children were growing.

They had a glorious future ahead of them. As badly as he wanted to lie down on that bed with her, he didn't dare. For once in his life he needed to practice patience and restraint in order to win back her trust.

"Leandros?" she murmured, after he'd turned to walk down the hall. "Is that you?"

He came back. "Who else?"

She sat up, trying to arrange her disheveled hair. His wife reminded him of a tantalizing mermaid. "When did you get back?"

"Just now."

"It's four o'clock. I can't believe I slept this long."

"Jet lag has finally caught up with you. Did you eat in the restaurant?"

"No." She slid off the bed, causing her skirt to ride up her thighs before she stood. Kellie had no idea how desirable she was to him. "After I got off the phone with Fran, I fell asleep. Have you eaten?"

"Not yet."

"Then you must be starving, too. I'll order something from the kitchen for both of us."

"While you do that, I'll check my voice mail." He went into the sitting room, curious to see if there were any developments that needed immediate attention.

Dionne and Zera had both called. No surprise there. They wanted to know why Karmela had been fired. He moved on to the next call, from his Realtor.

"I've got a property in Mets. It's a taste of old Athens, with a tiled roof and a charming courtyard. Lots of flowering trees and shrubs of jasmine and bougainvillea. It's in one of the most beautiful neighborhoods and won't stay on the market long. If you're interested,

I'll show it to you this evening, along with a couple of others."

Nothing could have pleased Leandros more. The last message came from his father, asking him to call him as soon as possible. As he clicked off, Kellie joined him. "Anything important?"

"I'll let you be the judge. From here on out, you and I are going to do everything together, so there won't be any more misunderstandings that could start another war." He replayed the messages for her.

Kellie looked shattered by his cousins' calls. "Karmela didn't waste any time, did she? It appears her family has already gotten to your father."

"I'll call him back after I've heard from my attorney. That might not be for another day or two. I want to be in possession of more facts before I touch base with him. He'll know how to calm down my mother."

"He's good at that."

A knock on the door alerted them that their dinner had arrived. Once the waiter had come and gone, they sat down to eat. "Shall I let the Realtor know we'd like to see those houses he phoned about?"

"Yes," she said unexpectedly. "This is a lovely hotel, but it's not a home. I'm sure you're anxious to get settled in something permanent."

Meaning she wasn't?

Her response left him feeling raw, but for once he wasn't going to erupt. Instead, he pulled out his phone and made arrangements with the Realtor that would keep them occupied for the evening.

Tomorrow would be their second therapy session. It couldn't come soon enough for him.

* * *

Olympia was already in her chair when Kellie walked into the room with Leandros at eleven. "Good morning, Mrs. Lasko."

"Good morning to you. Thank you for being on time."

Kellie gave the credit to Leandros, who had seemed equally anxious to get on with the therapy once breakfast was over. After they'd looked at four different houses the evening before—all of which she found had something wrong with them—he was up early on the phone with the Realtor, getting another list of houses for them to look at after their session.

"Please sit down."

Leandros helped her into the chair before he took his seat.

"Anything to report since our last session, before we get started?"

"Quite a lot, actually," Kellie blurted. She looked at Leandros. "Shall I tell her?"

"Go ahead."

Kellie explained about their meetings with Karmela and Frato. When she'd finished, Olympia eyed her in surprise. "I had no idea the results of our first session would produce anything as dramatic as what you've just described. Indeed, Karmela Paulos needs professional help.

"What's more important is that you've taken steps to remove the hornets' nest from your lives. It's an impressive start. I wish all my clients had results like yours within a forty-eight-hour period. Are you prepared to face what might come if she goes to the media in her rage?"

"My attorney is already working on it," Leandros stated with his usual confidence.

"In that case, why don't we begin with you. I'd like you to give me a picture of your life growing up on Andros. The mention of cousins came up in the last session. What part do they play in the family dynamic that has brought grief and makes them stand out?"

Since Olympia wrote no notes and didn't use a tape recorder, Kellie marveled at her photographic memory.

"We're a big family and all work in the Petralia Corporation. I have two living grandparents, but they've long since retired. My parents are semiretired. Though I'm an only child, I have five uncles and aunts, all married with children. I also have two great-uncles and aunts still alive with family.

"Of all the cousins, I'm closest to Frato. He's acting as CEO in my place while I'm on vacation right now. I have five boy cousins and six girl cousins, some older, some younger, two of whom have always been friendly with Karmela Paulos."

"So the joining of the Petralia and Paulos families at the time of your first wedding brought you all together even more intimately."

"Yes."

"All are well married, wealthy?"

"Yes."

"Including the Paulos family?"

"Yes."

"Except for Karmela, who's still single and delusional."

"Yes."

The older woman's gaze swerved to Kellie. "Now I want to hear about *your* upbringing." Olympia moved from subject to subject with a swiftness that made it hard to keep up.

Kellie cleared her throat. "My parents died when I was a baby, so I was raised by my mother's sister and her husband in Philadelphia. They weren't blessed with children, so it was the three of us. They're still alive."

"What does your uncle do for a living?"

"Before retirement, he was an insurance salesman who worked very hard. My aunt helped him. They were wonderful to me. As soon as I could, I got jobs while I went to school. My last year of high school, Fran and I went to school in France for an adventure. I paid for half of it, my uncle the other half.

"With student loans I made it through college, and continued to live with them in order to help them out. That's because my uncle suffered a stroke that put him in a wheelchair. It affected his legs, but not his mind. Once I graduated, I obtained a good position at an advertising agency. After working there for a year, the three of us decided to take our first trip to Europe.

"That was about two and a half years ago. When we flew here to Athens, we stayed at the Cassandra. One day while I was trying to get his wheelchair into the elevator, Leandros happened to be walking by, and helped me. That accidental meeting changed my life." Kellie couldn't prevent her voice from trembling.

"It changed both our lives," he declared with unmistakable fervency.

Olympia put her palms on the table. "I hope you've been listening to each other, really listening, because I want both of you to put yourselves in my role as a therapist. Imagine you're sitting in front of this husband and wife who've come to you. Their nationality, upbringing, social, economic and emotional standings are entirely different.

"The husband's parents are living. He comes from a big family with many tentacles, whose name is known throughout Greece. He's been married before to a socialite, but lost her and their unborn child in a tragic accident.

"The second wife has never been married, has never known her own parents and has committed herself to helping the aunt and uncle who raised her on a modest income without any other family around. She's in a country whose language and customs are unfamiliar to her.

"Kellie? Look at your husband and tell him the second emotion that came to mind when you told him you'd marry him. We already know the first one, that you were painfully in love with him."

Her mouth went dry, and her heart was thudding so hard she didn't know if she could get the words out. She turned and lifted her eyes to him. "I was terrified because I felt so completely inadequate in every way."

Leandros started to say something, but Olympia waved her thin index finger at him. "Your wife has just given you the key to understanding her. Do you remember the statement she made on Tuesday, about fearing she would never measure up to your first wife?"

"Yes."

"Now you can understand it was her feelings of inadequacy that made her feel intimidated. Before you override her comment with your well-meaning protests, sit back for a minute and let it sink in while I ask you a question."

His expression sobered.

"After she said yes to your proposal, what emotion drove you?"

In the quiet that followed, Kellie couldn't imagine what his answer would be.

"It's hard to put into words," his deep voice grated.

"Why?"

His gray eyes sought Kellie's. "Because I felt so many things."

"Name the dominant one."

She heard him take a fortifying breath. "Joy."

Kellie had felt joy, too. In fact, it had been overpowering.

"What manner did it take?"

His black brows furrowed. "I'm not sure I understand."

Olympia sat forward. "How did you manifest your joy?"

"I guess I wanted to give her the world."

Following his answer, Kellie started to tell him the world was the last thing she wanted, but Olympia stopped her with another warning finger. "It's your turn to sit back and think about what he just said, because it's the key to *his* personality."

Silence filled the room once more. Olympia eyed both of them. "There's no wrong or right here. What I see before me are two perfectly wonderful people who want the same thing. But you must follow what I'm saying.

"Leandros? Your problem is that you *can* give her the world, financially. You want to remove every obstacle from your wife's path and make her life easier. Being the confident male you are, with few insecurities, you sweep in and take over for the worthiest of reasons. But it makes you a poor listener and blind to certain facts sitting in front of you. In the end you come off seeming cold and insensitive."

He looked thunderstruck.

"Kellie? You have a different problem. You never knew your mother and father and had no siblings. Strictly speaking, Leandros was Petra's husband before he was yours. You couldn't get pregnant in what we consider the normal way. You're tired of not being able to claim anything of your very own. Not even the children growing inside you are strictly yours. All this has made you angry, with the result that your insecurity makes you distrustful and less than sympathetic."

A gasp escaped Kellie's throat. Olympia had hit the nail so squarely on the head, she was astounded.

"It's no wonder that when insensitivity met up with distrust, you two reached an impasse in your marriage."

Kellie darted Leandros a glance and discovered him studying her intently through shuttered eyes. With Mrs. Lasko's help, it all seemed so clear what was wrong.

"Now let's analyze the positive. Though Kellie's insecurity caused her to ask for a divorce, Leandros, she threw you a lifeline by suggesting you go to marriage counseling. That's because she's a problem solver. She's had to be to make it through life this far. Consider that when she found out Karmela was working in your office, she asked if she could work there, too."

"In all honesty, my friend Fran gave me the idea," Kellie exclaimed.

Leandros darted her a shocked glance. "I didn't know that."

Olympia's brows rose. "The point is, you acted on it."

He got up from the chair with a bleak expression on

his hard-boned features. "But I was too blind to understand what was happening, and turned you down."

"Your blindness was temporary," Olympia asserted.
"You've been a winner all your life and aren't used to
losing. Once separated from your wife without being
able to do anything about it, you were humbled enough
to realize that money and power couldn't help you ob-
tain the one thing you wanted above all else. In your
vulnerable state—a condition in which you've rarely
found yourself—you grabbed the lifeline she tossed
you, and agreed to go to counseling."

Kellie felt his penetrating gaze before he said, "It's
a miracle you didn't tell me it was too late."

While a flood of emotions swept through her, Mrs.
Lasko got to her feet, signaling the end of the session.
"Before you leave, I have homework for you. Leandros? I want you to explore how you really feel about
Kellie's best friend, Fran. I sensed resentment of her
at our first session, but I want you to consider the fact
that resentment masks jealousy."

"Jealousy?" he exclaimed.

"That's right. Why does she bring out that emotion
in you?"

Kellie was so surprised by Olympia's comment, she
didn't realize the therapist was now addressing her.

"As for you, Kellie, you not only feel guilt over your
aunt and uncle's sacrifice, you feel as if you abandoned
them when you married your husband, and are torn between two worlds. These issues need to be resolved in
order to stabilize your marriage."

Hearing those words, Kellie bowed her head. How
did Olympia understand so much?

"The more you dig, the more you'll begin to achieve

that joy you first felt when you decided to make a life together. I'll see you on Tuesday. Goodbye."

On unsteady legs, Kellie got up from the chair and headed for the door. Leandros reached it first and opened it for her. He must have noticed she was shaken, because he cupped her elbow as he walked her out to the car, parked in the hot sun.

Before he put the key in the ignition he turned to her with a grim look on his striking Greek features. "Would you find me too insensitive if I told you I'd like to put off our plans for dinner with Fran and Nik this evening?"

Kellie drew in a deep breath. "I would have suggested it if you hadn't. What I'd really like to do is forget everything, including house hunting, and fly to Andros."

A light flashed in the recesses of those somber gray eyes. "You mean it?"

"Yes. We have so much to talk about, I hardly know where to begin. I'll call Fran right now and cancel."

"Do you think she'll be offended?"

"Disappointed, certainly, but not offended. It'll be fine." With Olympia's startling observations still spinning in her head, Kellie needed to show her husband that she put him first.

While he started the engine and they backed out to the street, she reached into her purse for her cell and pressed the speed dial. When Fran answered, Kellie turned on the speakerphone so Leandros could hear their conversation while they drove. *Everything out in the open*. Olympia's mantra.

"Kellie!" Fran sounded excited to hear from her. "How did the therapy go?"

She swallowed hard. "In all honesty, it was so heavy-duty this morning, I'm still reeling. Do you mind terribly if Leandros and I take a rain check for this evening?"

"You know better than to ask me that."

"Thanks for being so understanding." Kellie had almost said *thanks for being my best friend*. It was what she always said to her, oftentimes in Leandros's hearing. When she really thought about it, Kellie realized Fran had figured heavily in her life whether on or off stage. Not until this moment did it occur to her that Leandros needed to know *he* was her best friend.

The therapist had picked up on it, while Kellie had been oblivious. Was it possible that in some nebulous way, Leandros felt he came in second in her affections? Before the four of them spent any more time together, this was an area they needed to talk about.

"Fran? I'll call you on Monday."

"Take all the time you need. I'm not going anywhere. *Au revoir.*"

After she clicked off, Leandros turned to her. "If you're hungry for lunch, we can eat at the hotel before we leave for Andros."

She shook her head. "I'm still full from breakfast, but please don't let that keep you from ordering something."

"I'd rather wait until we reach the villa. I'll alert the housekeeper to get things ready for us."

In truth, Kellie had lost her appetite by the end of the session, and sensed Leandros wasn't any better off.

Without more talk, they returned to the hotel to grab a few things and board the helicopter. The presence of his bodyguard further inhibited conversation.

During the flight her mind kept harking back to the conversation at their first therapy session with Olympia.

"Did you go to Rhodes without your wife?"

"Yes. Unbeknownst to me, she'd made arrangements for her best friend, Fran, to come to Greece."

"Best friend, as in Frato has been your best friend?"

"She's been like the sister I never had."

"They were going to take a two-week trip together while I was away on business. After making that announcement, she moved to the guest bedroom."

Kellie recalled the bleak tone in Leandros's voice, but she'd been too upset at the time to give it any real thought. It had taken this second session with the therapist for her to remember it, and it sent a stabbing pain of guilt through her.

Once they reached the villa and were finally alone, she followed him into the kitchen. He'd gone over to the sink and drank from the tap for a long time.

"Leandros?"

He slowly turned around, revealing a wounded expression. She took a step closer. "I'm so sorry."

Lines bracketed his hard mouth. "For what?"

"For making travel plans with Fran behind your back at the height of our marital troubles. It was cruel of me and made it impossible for you and me to communicate. But at the time I was too consumed with pain to realize what a selfish person I'd turned into."

She could hear her voice throbbing. The tears had started. She couldn't stop them. "I—I wouldn't blame you if you never forgave me for what I've done."

Heartsick, she hurried into the guest bedroom and lay down on her side, clutching one of the pillows to her while she sobbed.

"Kellie?" When she looked up, she saw him standing at the side of the bed. "There's nothing to forgive."

With tears dripping down her cheeks, she raised herself up on one elbow. "How can you say that? I used Fran to put a buffer between you and me."

"That was the only time I've ever been hurt by your friendship with her. Olympia caught it because she's good at what she does."

"You're not just saying that to make me feel better?"

"Why would I do that?"

"Because it's your nature to be kind." Kellie wiped her eyes with the back of her arm. "Olympia's a genius. She has me so figured out it's frightening."

His hands went to his hips. "Frightening?"

"Yes. She was right about my always having wanted something of my very own. When I met you, my heart and soul claimed you on some level I wasn't even aware of. After a lifelong search, finding you answered the question of my existence. But knowing you had a history with Petra tortured me."

"Kellie..."

"It's true," she cried. "I grew too possessive of you. You were my best friend and lover. But instead of running to you with my fears, I held them in and became a shrew of a wife. Olympia's right. I *have* been angry, but the fault has lain with me. I'm so ashamed."

Convulsed in fresh tears, she buried her face in the pillow. Within seconds the mattress dipped and Leandros pulled her into his arms.

"I don't know how you can even stand to touch me," she moaned.

His answer was to pull her close. He felt so wonderful and substantial that she relaxed against him, having no desire to push him away as she'd done a few days ago. While in this halcyon state she heard familiar voices calling to Leandros.

Her eyelids flew open in surprise. "Your parents—"

Leandros kissed her temple before rolling away from her. "For them to walk in without phoning first, it means they're either tired of being ignored or they've heard the news about Karmela." As Kellie slid off the bed, he grabbed her hand. "Come on. Let's go talk to them."

"My skirt and blouse are wrinkled."

"I don't see anything wrong."

"Well, I should at least brush my hair."

"No. I love your mussed look."

Leandros. Her heart skittered all over the place.

They found his parents in the living room. Thea hurried toward Kellie and kissed her on both cheeks. "Forgive us for barging in, but we saw you arrive in the helicopter, and it's been too long," his mother cried. She was a beauty in her own right, a stylish and elegant brunette. "We've missed you, Kellie."

"Indeed we have." Leandros's father, an aristocratic-looking man with salt-and-pepper hair, held out his arms to her.

"Vlassius…" She gave him a hug. "It's so good to see both of you."

He held on to her hands. "We retain Christos and Giorgios to keep our son safe. They were so happy to see you back in Athens, they let us know the moment you arrived at the office. You're a sight for sore eyes."

Kellie laughed. "I might have known they couldn't

keep a secret, but at least they let me surprise Leandros in his own lair."

That brought more laughter.

CHAPTER SEVEN

"My lair?" Leandros teased.

When he thought about it, he realized her remark was entirely apropos. After the desolate month he'd spent alone, her presence had been a surprise, all right. While he'd been hiding out in his office like a wounded animal licking his wounds, he'd suddenly heard her voice and seen his gorgeous blonde wife standing there like a vision. For a moment he'd thought he was hallucinating.

"Why don't you two join us out on the patio? We haven't eaten since breakfast," he said.

"Oh, no!" his mother exclaimed. "Let me help."

"We have it covered, *Mana*. Would you like to eat with us?"

"I don't think so. We only finished lunch a while ago."

In a minute he and Kellie took plates of salad and rolls out to the wrought-iron table. The housekeeper had also prepared iced tea. They could all enjoy that.

After devouring a third roll, Leandros eyed his parents frankly. "Before you explode from curiosity, Kellie and I have a few things to tell you. Our divorce has been put on hold while we undergo marriage counseling."

Their eyes widened, but they didn't comment. He admired their restraint.

"It was Kellie's idea. I fought it at first, because you know me, I think I know everything."

His mother laughed. "I never thought I'd live to see the day when you admitted it."

"It takes a big man," his father interjected.

"Yes, it does," Thea joked, staring at her husband.

Leandros thought Kellie had to be enjoying this.

"As soon as I came back from the States alone, I realized I couldn't live without her, and finally agreed to it. But remember, we're not together." He eyed Kellie. "As our therapist says, we're a work in progress."

"Bravo," his mother exclaimed. But there was no bravo about it if Kellie believed Karmela's lie.

"I apologize for not having returned your phone call yet, but there've been reasons," Leandros went on. "As I informed you a few days ago, I'm on vacation. That's why I asked Frato to take over for me at the office. For your information, Kellie and I had our second session this morning."

Leandros darted his wife a glance. "We probably would have walked up to the villa to visit you later today." Kellie's nod confirmed it.

His mother clasped her hands together and let out a happy cry. His father smiled in obvious satisfaction. Their reactions had to have reassured his wife that they loved her. They'd been crushed when he'd told them Kellie was leaving him.

Leandros sent his wife another glance. If she wanted to tell them their other news, he was leaving it up to her. A hushed silence fell over the room. When it became deafening, he started to bring up another subject, but Kellie suddenly put her glass down and said, "Last week I went to my doctor in Philadelphia for a checkup and found out…we're expecting twins."

"Twins?" His mother was so ecstatic, she jumped up from the table and ran around to hug him and Kellie again.

With tears in his eyes, his father followed suit. "This is a great day, a miraculous day!"

Thea's face was wreathed in a huge smile. "Two grandbabies to love. I can't believe it! Thank heaven for modern medicine."

"I can hardly believe the artificial insemination worked," Kellie admitted. "But the thought of taking care of *two* babies at once is pretty overwhelming."

"We'll all help," his mother assured her. "Your aunt and uncle must be thrilled. When are you due?"

"March seventh. They're nearly eight weeks old. The doctor said they're as big as blueberries, with tiny hands and feet emerging."

His parents laughed and cried. Inside, Leandros was thrilled, but until he knew unequivocally that Kellie believed in him, he couldn't celebrate the way he wanted. As for therapy, they still had a long way to go. The only thing helping him right now was that she'd let him hold her a little while ago. She'd even seemed to welcome his arms around her.

He waited until his parents sat down again before asking if there was another reason they'd walked down to his villa unannounced. They shook their heads, clearly mystified by his question.

It meant Karmela still hadn't played her trump card. That's why he hadn't heard from his attorney. He was hoping that not hearing anything yet meant she might be backing down on her threats. If that was the case, then things couldn't be working out better.

"The therapy we've been undergoing has opened my eyes to a dangerous situation that was brewing long before we took our vows. Though we have other issues to work on, this has been one of the big ones threatening to undermine our marriage."

Both his parents frowned, but it was his father who demanded clarity. "Be explicit."

"As Kellie and I discussed earlier, there's been an enemy within our walls. Not only has she done everything in her power to come between Kellie and me, she's been doing an expert job of destroying Frato in the process."

"She?" his mother questioned, patently bewildered.

Leandros nodded grimly. "My former sister-in-law, Karmela."

The shock on his parents' faces convinced him they would never have suspected Petra's sister of any wrongdoing. They'd been completely in the dark about her.

"Kellie? Tell them what you told the therapist about the night of our wedding reception. My parents need to hear from you to understand what we've been up against. Don't leave anything out."

Once his wife began her tale, he watched their reactions. By the time she'd finished, he knew they were horrified.

"There's more," he said, pulling out his cell phone. "Once you hear this conversation between me and Karmela at my office, you'll realize what our family could be up against. Kellie has already listened to it." He switched on the recording.

While his parents sat there in shock, he eyed Kellie. He could tell she was worried about their reaction. When it had played out, he shut the device off.

"The girl's clearly unwell," his father declared.

His mother nodded. She looked ill. "What are you going to do, Leandros?"

"After I took Kellie back to the Cassandra, I went to the penthouse and had a serious talk with Frato. He's been in love with Karmela for a long time, but when he listened to this recording, it forced him to wake up. Frato's finished with her. If she tries to get into his penthouse, she won't be able to."

"Who would have dreamed she had such problems?"

"Maybe her parents *do* know, but haven't been able to help her. It's anyone's guess how far she's willing to take this. Dionne and Zera phoned to find out why I fired her, so she has revealed that much to those in the family who are sympathetic to her. But at this point, anything could be going on. Rest assured I've got her under surveillance and have alerted my attorney."

That didn't seem to mollify his father. "Has Frato told my brother all this?"

"I don't think so, Papa, but I could be wrong. They've always been close, but this business with Karmela is something Frato has kept hidden for years. I've advised him to go on doing his job at the office and say nothing."

"Well, there's something I can do!" His father pushed himself away from the table and stood up. "Let's go, Thea. We're about to pay a visit to Karmela's family right now. Let me have your phone, Leandros. They need to hear this so they can take their daughter in hand."

Leandros shook his head. "Though you know the

facts, I don't want you getting involved. You've been friends for too many years. I'm the one who fired Karmela, and she knows why. If anyone's going to talk to her parents, I'll be the person to do it. But it may not come to that. Should they contact you about this, then direct them to me. I want your promise on that."

His mother got up. "But if she should call one of the newspapers…"

Kellie darted Leandros a worried glance. "That's what I'm concerned about, Thea. Today's so-called journalists don't check their sources. Even if it's all lies, and your attorney forces them to print a retraction, the public goes on believing the lies. This could destroy your reputation and Frato's. The whole family could be hurt, including Karmela's."

"She's right," his father muttered. "With you two expecting twins, I don't like this at all. Does Karmela know about your miraculous news?"

"No. Besides you and her doctor, the only people aware are Kellie's aunt and uncle, our therapist, Frato, and Nik and Fran. For the time being, we'd prefer the rest of the family doesn't know about this."

"Understood. Come on, Thea. We're going to leave, to give you some privacy."

The four of them gravitated to the front door. After more hugs, his father said, "Even if you've got people watching Karmela, you need the security on you doubled."

"I've already taken care of it." Leandros eyed him solemnly. "I promise to keep you informed."

"See that you do. We're in this together. How long do you think you'll be staying on Andros?"

Leandros glanced at his wife. "We don't know yet."

His mother cupped Kellie's cheeks. "Whatever you do, wherever you go, you have to take extra special care of yourself now."

"I agree."

"I had two miscarriages before Leandros was born," Thea confessed. "After that, I was never able to get pregnant again." Her eyes misted. "Those babies you're carrying are extra precious."

"I know. Thank you for caring so much." Kellie kissed his mother again before his parents started walking away.

When Leandros couldn't see them anymore, he closed the door. Kellie had already gone out to the patio to clear the dishes. He had an idea she was trying to hide her emotions. Once he joined her, they got everything cleaned and put away in no time.

"Leandros?" She turned, resting her back against the kitchen counter. His body was on alert for any change of mood in her.

"What is it?"

"Would you like to go for a walk along the beach with me? I feel like stretching my legs."

This was the first time since she'd flown back from the States that she was the one asking him to do something with her. Excitement flooded through him.

He almost said, "I was about to suggest it, if you weren't too tired." But he'd learned his lesson. Because of therapy, he'd discovered she didn't like him hovering, let alone sweeping in and taking over. "I could use some exercise myself. Give me a minute to put on a pair of shorts."

Kellie didn't want to change out of her wraparound skirt. It was the most comfortable piece of clothing in her wardrobe. First thing tomorrow she would go shopping. She needed some loose fitting tops and maternity jeans. Dr. Creer had warned her she'd grow bigger fast.

She went into the bathroom and brushed her hair before fastening it in a ponytail with one of her bands. Though it was late afternoon, the sun was still hot. After applying sunscreen and lipstick, Kellie went in search of Leandros. She found him in the kitchen on the phone, in his bare feet.

He'd changed into a short-sleeved, white cotton shirt left partially unbuttoned. In it and his navy shorts he looked better than any statue of a Greek god. Without her volition, a surge of desire for him welled up inside her.

Glancing up, he finally noticed her, and turned on the speakerphone so she could hear. The conversation with a man she didn't recognize ended soon enough. "That was the private investigator. Karmela's been staying at the Athenian Inn and hasn't left her room all day. He'll continue to keep me apprised."

"Leandros... Since we started therapy, you've let me listen in on every phone conversation. I know why you've been doing it, and I appreciate it. But it isn't natural or necessary. I trust you, and I believe that when you have something important to share with me, you will."

Some of the worry lines on his arresting face relaxed. "That works both ways." He put a couple of water bottles into a pack he fastened around his hips. "I don't want you to get dehydrated."

"Thank you for being so thoughtful." He was being so polite. *Too polite.* She knew why.

"You're welcome," he answered in his low, vibrant voice.

"Before we go, there's something I need to tell you."

"I know what it is."

"No, you don't," Kellie countered. "Petra was revered by everyone in your family. You wouldn't have fallen in love with her if she hadn't been a wonderful person. Unconsciously, I endowed Karmela with the same qualities.

"When she was in your office and declared she was pregnant with your baby, I honestly didn't believe her, but I was in shock to realize I was looking at a truly disturbed woman who isn't anything like her sister. That's why it took me getting out of there and going back to the hotel to see everything for what it is. I hope you can believe me when I tell you my doubts about her are gone. I do trust you. Completely."

"Thank heaven," he answered emotionally. "What do you say we take advantage of the sun?" Her husband never revisited a problem once it was over. He was such a remarkable man.

They left the villa. When they reached the sand, she removed her sandals and dangled them from her fingers while they walked in the opposite direction from the private pier. Kellie saw several boats in the distance. The light breeze was enough to fill their sails, so they skimmed along the shimmering blue water.

Paradise.

She had a lot on her mind and knew Leandros did, too, but neither of them spoke. Slowly they made their way around an outcropping of rocks. It led to a much smaller, sheltered cove where the hillside was filled with wildflowers. No villas had been built here so there were no people around. They had the thin stretch of beach to themselves.

"Leandros," she said tentatively, "I'd like to talk to you about something important."

"There are things I want to discuss with you, too."

"Then let's sit for a little while."

His brows furrowed. "You don't mind getting sandy in that skirt?"

"Not at all."

After she sank down, Leandros handed her a bottle of water. While she took sips, he put his own bottle to his lips and quenched his thirst. When he'd drained it, he stretched out on the sand and leaned back on his elbows. His dark wavy hair gleamed in the sun while he stared out at the water. Kellie got a suffocating feeling in her chest just looking at him.

"Leandros?" she whispered.

He turned on his side toward her. With his jaw set and his eyes shuttered against the sun's slanting rays, she couldn't read his expression, but sensed his emotions were raw. "What's on your mind?"

"Something Olympia hit on about my guilt over my aunt and uncle really touched a nerve with me. I was the luckiest girl in the world to be raised by them. When I married you, there was a part of me that felt like I was abandoning them. Because of that I suffered guilt, and didn't realize it could do so much damage."

His dark brows furrowed. "What do you mean?"

"If on our honeymoon I wasn't the same woman you'd fallen in love with, I'm afraid it was because I couldn't enjoy it completely, knowing they'd gone back to Philadelphia alone. The business with Frato's and

Fran's observations about Karmela were only a small part of my inability to be myself with you.

"All this time I thought I'd hidden it from you, but when you told Olympia you knew something was wrong on our honeymoon, it really threw me. Hindsight is a wonderful thing, but in our case it has come too late."

Kellie felt his body stiffen. "Go on."

"I just want to explain why I didn't like any of the houses we looked at earlier. I know you liked the one with the tiled roof and the courtyard. I liked it, too, but—"

"But what?" He broke in tersely. "Just say what you have to say, Kellie."

"Do you remember when you were talking to me about the penthouse?"

His eyes, dark with emotion, played over her face. "How could I forget?"

"You said," she stammered, "you said that you would always have lived on Andros and commuted if Petra hadn't wanted to live in Athens."

"That's right," he muttered.

"Do you still feel that way? Please be honest."

"Kellie…I'm discovering we can't always have everything we want."

"In other words, you *would* prefer living on Andros if everything else lined up the right way?"

In a sudden move, he got to his feet and stared down at her with a black expression. "What's this about? Are you trying to work up the courage to tell me you're going back to Philadelphia, so I can do what I want?"

"No!" she cried, and hurriedly stood up, shaking the sand from her skirt. "It's too soon to talk about anything like that. You're deliberately misunderstanding me."

"What else am I supposed to think?"

She put a hand on his arm. His body had gone rigid. "Why did you say we can't always have everything we want? Tell me."

He eased his arm away, as if her touch burned him. "Surely you know why. I'm aware of how crazy you are about Athens."

"I am. With all its history and monuments, it's a magnificent city. But I loved your home on Andros the first time you brought me here. When we were looking at houses with the Realtor, I kept thinking about your villa. No place else in the world could possibly compare. It's no wonder you love it so much. To buy or build a home in Athens is ludicrous when this is the only home where the children should live and be raised."

"You honestly mean that?" She heard a tremor in his voice.

"Yes. Their heritage is here with their grandparents and relatives."

Kellie heard him struggle for breath. "Their heritage is in Pennsylvania, too. Don't think I don't know how torn you've been over being separated from your aunt and uncle. I always wanted them to move to Greece, but you said no. I didn't need to hear Olympia's thoughts on the subject to realize how hard it's been for you."

"That's because I know my aunt. She's afraid my uncle wouldn't want to leave their friends. There's also the issue of his health care companion, and whether my uncle could adapt to a new environment. Unfortunately, my thinking has been foggy because of all my hang-ups. But therapy has made me see I've been a fool. I've missed them terribly and realize they've missed me, too. Naturally, I've been their whole world since my parents died. Nothing else has been as important to them."

"I'm glad you finally understand that."

She nodded. "Leandros…if we make the decision to stay together, I want to live here year-round."

He looked thunderstruck. "You love it that much?"

"I might not have been born here, but I love it probably as much as you do. Olympia was right about me. I do crave something of my very own. Since you told me Petra had never lived in the villa with you, that changed everything for me. I know now there was no third party on our honeymoon. I feel like we could start a new life here, built on a firm foundation. But—"

"But you couldn't do it without your aunt and uncle living here, too," he finished for her.

"Yes."

"I've always been aware of that. We need them with us. So will our children. Otherwise we'll never be completely happy. Come on. On our way back to the villa, we'll take a detour. I want to show you something."

After putting their water bottles in his pack, he grasped her hand and held it tightly. Kellie could feel her husband's excitement. He came alive as they retraced their steps around the point to the next cove. When they reached the path leading away from the beach, she slipped her sandals back on. They followed it until it diverged. He took the trail to the right until they came to a small stone villa.

"Wasn't this your great-uncle Manny's house?"

"That's right. His wife died while I was in college. They never had children. Since his death a year ago, it has stood empty." Leandros reached for a key left above the lintel, and let them in the side door. It led into the kitchen.

"I remember being in here before. It's very cozy and charming."

"With some renovations, I believe your aunt and uncle would be very happy here. It's all on one floor and would accommodate his wheelchair. We'd hire a housekeeper to take care of them so they could maintain their independence."

"Oh, if I thought this were possible..."

"Of course it is. If there's a drawback, it's that they'd be surrounded by my relatives. But we'd provide them with a car, so they could drive to the different villages, or go visiting whenever they wanted company."

Kellie's eyelids prickled with salty tears. "This would be a perfect place, but I'm sure your family would have something to say about it."

Leandros grasped her upper arms, bringing her close to his hard-muscled body. "Dozens of people with a lot of money have coveted this villa, sitting on the most prime property of the island. My father and uncles have had dozens of offers to buy it, for many times what it's worth. But they haven't wanted anyone who wasn't family to live here on the estate."

"I can understand that."

"They'd rejoice if your aunt and uncle made this their home. You're family, after all. My extended family will celebrate, anyway, when they hear we're expecting twins."

"You're g-generous beyond belief, Leandros." Her voice caught. "I've never known anyone like you."

She felt his gaze narrow on her mouth, but he held back from kissing her. For once she wished he would

devour her the way he used to do, but she'd changed
all the rules when she'd asked for a divorce. He was
much more careful now. Kellie sensed he was waiting
for her to initiate any intimacy between them, because
he didn't want to make more mistakes.

Neither did she.

Afraid she'd killed something inside him, she turned
away with an ache in her heart, and started for the door.
On the way back to the villa, he suggested they drive
to one of the other villages to eat dinner. He said it so
airily, the tension-filled moment in the kitchen, when
she'd wanted to pull his head down to hers and give in
to her desire, might never have happened.

On impulse, she said, "I have another idea. Why
don't you start up the grill on the patio and I'll make
us some lamb kabobs." He loved them. "I'll be able to
marinate them for only a few minutes, but they'll still
taste good. We'll finish off the salad and rolls, too."

"You really want to cook tonight?" He sounded
eager, yet once again she noticed he was careful not to
ask her if she was too tired. What had she done to him?

"Absolutely."

I want to do something for you.

Kellie hadn't made a meal for him in over two
months. A Greek man loved his food. Leandros had
always liked finding her in the kitchen while she cooked
up a storm. When he'd claimed in front of Olympia that
he'd loved coming home to Kellie after work, she knew
he hadn't been lying about that. Because of therapy, she
realized he'd never lied to her about anything.

"Make a lot of them," he called out before disap-
pearing into the house.

She smiled, remembering the dozens of times he'd

said the same thing to her when he'd phoned her from work, telling her he was coming home.

After washing her hands, she got busy. As she assembled the ingredients, it occurred to her she hadn't ever been this happy before. This was her kitchen. She was making dinner for her husband. They were pregnant with twin babies. He'd just told her they would move her aunt and uncle to the estate. Except for news about Karmela's next move still hanging over them, Kellie had more joy than any one woman deserved or could hope for in this life.

She was in the middle of her preparations when Leandros came back into the kitchen with his phone in hand. Judging by the lines bracketing his eyes and mouth, the news was bad.

"Who just called you?"

"The private detective."

"Did Karmela elude him and get to the press, anyway?"

Leandros inhaled sharply. "No. She managed to fix it so they got to *her*."

"What do you mean?"

"She's even more devious than I realized. After overdosing on some pills at the hotel, for the sake of theatrics, she called the police so they'd be certain to find her before she could do any real damage. The private detective was out in the hall when the paramedics arrived. He followed them to the hospital, where her stomach was pumped.

"He spoke to one of the officers who heard her statement. She said I ended our affair after finding out she was pregnant with our baby, and fired her from the Petralia Corporation. The news will leak out. It always does."

Somehow Kellie wasn't surprised. "Even if it makes the ten o'clock news, it won't matter," she declared. "Anyone who knows you will realize she's a very sick girl who needs a psychiatrist. Let's get to the hospital. Call your parents so they can fly to Athens with us. It'll be better if we're all together when we talk to her parents. I'll phone Frato. He'll want to meet us there."

Leandros's eyes pierced hers. "You're willing to come with me?" he asked in a grating voice.

She knew what he was asking. Besides everything else, they might have to face a barrage of reporters. If ever they needed to present a united front, it was now. "Yes. I'm your wife. We do everything together."

"Kellie..." For once he forgot the rules and crushed her in his arms. She clung to him before he was forced to let her go and alert Stefon to get the helicopter ready. While Leandros changed clothes and made the call to his parents, she phoned Frato. To her relief, he picked up fast.

"Kellie?"

"Yes. Please listen. Where are you?"

"I'm at the penthouse."

"Then you don't know about Karmela yet."

"What's happened?"

Once she'd explained, he said, "I'll phone Father, then head on over to the hospital and meet you there."

"Good. If we're all together, it'll be the best statement we could make."

"Agreed."

After they hung up, she made a couple of sandwiches for them to eat on the helicopter and put the uncooked food in the fridge. Leandros appeared in the kitchen wearing a gray suit and tie. "Ready?"

"Almost." She wrapped the sandwiches. "Here, take these." While he found a sack and added some apples, she went to the bathroom to freshen up. Moments later they hurried out of the villa. She didn't worry about the coals in the grill. They would burn down.

Her thoughts were on a real fire burning out of control at the hospital in Athens. Kellie loved her husband desperately, but never more than at this moment, when his life and reputation were at the mercy of Karmela.

CHAPTER EIGHT

LEANDROS TOLD STEFON to land at the hotel. From there, he drove the four of them to the hospital. There was a delivery entrance on the south side of the building. Hoping to avoid the paparazzi, he called for permission to park there, and a security guard allowed them to enter the building.

Frato had just phoned and told Leandros to go to the psychiatric unit on the third floor, west wing. He'd be waiting for them in the lounge off the hallway. To his knowledge, the police had notified Karmela's parents, who were still inside the locked area with the doctor.

Kellie held on to Leandros's arm, the way she'd done in the early days of their marriage. He hardly recognized her as the same woman he'd brought to this hospital five weeks ago, after she'd fainted. That woman wouldn't let him touch her.

He wanted to believe she was aching for the intimacy they'd once shared, and that's why she was clinging to him. If this show of solidarity in front of everyone didn't extend beyond this hour of crisis, he didn't think he could bear it.

"Leandros…"

Frato's parents had just appeared, but he'd been too

deep in his torturous thoughts to realize it. Kellie got up first to greet them. Soon Leandros's parents had gathered around. While they were huddled together discussing Karmela's sorry state, the door opened and her parents emerged, white-faced. Leandros thought they'd aged ten years.

Kellie was right with him as they walked over to embrace them. "How is she, Leda?"

"Sedated. We can't see her again until tomorrow morning." Karmela's mother lifted tear-filled eyes to him. "She's always been crazy about you, Leandros, but we hoped and prayed she'd get over it after you married Kellie. If anything, it made her worse, but we had no idea she would try to kill herself."

Leandros's heart went out to them. "Just remember one thing. She called the police so they'd be sure to find her in time."

Nestor nodded. "The doctor said it was a call for help. She didn't want to die. She did it to get your attention. We're so sorry for the grief she has caused you and Kellie...and Frato." He eyed Leandros's cousin with compassion before looking at Leandros again. "Are you two back together?"

He sucked in his breath. "We're working on it. I can tell you with conviction that with enough love and therapy, she'll get through this."

"You really believe that?" Leda's voice trembled.

"We do," Kellie interjected. "We're going to counseling right now. It's been a liberating experience for both of us. I'm sure it will be for Karmela, too."

Leda hugged Kellie. "You deserve all the happiness in the world."

"So does Karmela."

"You can say that after everything's she's done? What we heard her tell the doctor horrified us. But a pregnancy test was done. She's not pregnant."

"We didn't think she was. From what I've learned, she's been in pain for years, Leda. The doctor will help her understand that pain, and then she'll get well."

"Bless you." Leda hugged Kellie again.

Nestor eyed all of them. "The second the police called, I asked them to do all they could to prevent this from leaking to the press."

Leandros patted him on the shoulder. "Don't worry. If there's fallout, we can handle it. One thing you could do is put the record straight to Dionne and Zera. They love Karmela. She'll need their friendship more than ever now."

Leda nodded. "We'll call them before we go to bed."

In an automatic move, Leandros put his arm around his wife's shoulders. "Since there's nothing more we can do here, we'll go. Keep in close touch with us. You know we'll do whatever we can to help."

After more hugs, they said good-night to Frato and his parents, then the four of them left and drove back to the hotel. It was decided his parents would stay the night. Tomorrow they'd fly back to Andros.

Once ensconced in the suite, Kellie made coffee and ordered more food from the kitchen. They all needed time to settle down and relax before they could think about bed. It was better this way.

Leandros was on fire for his wife, but until she showed him she wanted him, body and soul, he wasn't about to push anything. In fact, this would be a good time to broach the subject foremost on his mind, now that Karmela was finally getting the help she needed.

He sat back in the chair, eyeing his parents over the rim of his coffee cup. "Kellie and I have been doing a lot of talking. Since our wedding, she's suffered over missing her aunt and uncle. We've flown to Philadelphia when we could, but traveling there every few months hasn't been enough. It's been harder for them to come here, because he's in a wheelchair.

"Yesterday, while we were out walking, I made a decision." Kellie's head jerked toward him in surprise. "If we agree to stay together, it will depend on her aunt and uncle where we live permanently."

The room went perfectly still.

"Kellie has been worried, with good reason, about uprooting them to live in Greece. They've built a lifetime of memories and friends in Philadelphia, and the move might be too hard on them. This last month she put down earnest money on a house big enough for them and our children. We would all live there."

His mother shook her head in consternation. "But what would you do?"

"I could still work for the corporation long distance. Naturally, I'd step down as CEO."

"And then you'd come and visit us every few months...." His mother's mournful voice trailed off.

"Nothing's written in stone yet, *Mana*. If Kellie and I decide to stay together, and if by some miracle they'd be willing to move here, then we'd live on Andros permanently."

"Permanently?" A squeal of joy escaped his mother's lips before she got up from the couch. "Then we'll make that miracle happen! Your aunt and uncle will be so welcome here, they won't have time to miss peo-

ple. Think how busy we'll all be when the children are born!"

She flew across the expanse to hug him. "I hated it when you moved to that penthouse in Athens."

"I did it for Petra."

"We know you did, but nothing's been the same since." She moved to Kellie, seated in the other chair. "You really want to live on Andros?"

"It's my favorite place in the world. The children will thrive there." Kellie's heartfelt response made its way inside his heart and convinced his parents. His mother squeezed her.

"Did you hear that, Vlassius?"

His father's eyes had glazed over with happy tears. "I heard. I'm still trying to take it all in."

"So what can we do to get your aunt and uncle to come, Kellie?"

Leandros sat forward. "On our way up from the beach yesterday, we stopped to look at Uncle Manny's villa. How do you think the family would fee—"

"It would be perfect for them!" his mother cried out, before he could finish his thought.

His father nodded. "I go fishing every morning on the boat. Jim will come with me."

"And Sybil will come shopping with me!" his mother exclaimed.

"Family should be together and that place shouldn't go empty any longer," his father declared. "With twins on the way, I think it's the best idea you've ever had."

"You're the most generous people on earth," Kellie declared in a tremulous voice. "I guess you realize your son takes after you."

Leandros liked the sound of that. "Though it seems

like a perfect arrangement to us, everyone in the family would have to be in agreement. The villa needs work. I'd want to make improvements to the bathroom."

"I can tell you right now the family will welcome the idea without reservation."

"Thanks, Papa. However, if there is a problem, then there's still room on my piece of the property to build a new villa for them. But until Kellie talks to them about moving to Greece, it's a moot point, considering we're still in the middle of therapy."

His father stood up. "Come on, Thea. Let's go to bed and plot."

Kellie laughed out loud. It was the full-bodied kind he'd missed hearing all these months.

He eyed his parents. "That's a good idea. I'm suddenly exhausted and crave sleep. Everything you need should be in the guest bedroom. We'll see you at breakfast."

Taking a leaf out of their book, he got up and walked over to Kellie. "Get a good night's sleep." He kissed her on the cheek. "See you in the morning."

His heart leaped to see the look of disappointment in those chocolate eyes before he headed for his room. But he was doing better at disciplining himself where his wife was concerned. He wanted her to come to him, day or night, of her own free will. No holding back.

The apartment had gone quiet. Feeling wide-awake, Kellie carried the coffee mugs to the kitchen. She was still in shock that Leandros had gone to bed so fast. After what had happened today, there was so much she wanted to talk to him about, but by leaving the living room with his parents, he'd made any more conversation tonight impossible.

She knew she could always go to his room, but he would take that to mean she wanted to be with him in every sense of the word. Of course, she wanted that more than anything in the world. But when the moment came that they decided to recommit to each other, she preferred to be strictly alone with him on Andros.

Since arriving in Greece, Kellie had done so much sharing with her husband, she hardly recognized the person she'd become. Without him being available, her normal impulse would have been to phone Fran and talk to her about everything, disregarding the lateness of the hour. But that was before the therapy sessions. The revelations they'd uncovered had changed Kellie's life. She was turning into a different person.

When she really thought about it, her only real concern at this point was her aunt and uncle. If they could have seen and heard the reaction of Leandros's parents tonight, it would have warmed their hearts to know how much they wanted them to move to Greece.

Kellie checked her watch. It would be afternoon in Philadelphia. Now would be the best time to call them and have a long talk. After getting ready for bed, she climbed under the covers and picked up the receiver on the bedside table.

"Aunt Sybil?"

"Honey…"

"Have I caught you at an inconvenient time?"

"Heavens, no! I'm just putting the raspberry jam I made into the freezer. You know how much Jim loves it. We were just talking about you at lunch, wondering how the therapy is coming along. Are you still suffering nausea?"

"No. The medicine Dr. Creer prescribed has really helped. Listen, there's something very important I need to talk to you about."

There was a small silence before she said, "You sound excited."

"It's more than that, Aunt Sybil. Could you get Uncle Jim to pick up the extension in your bedroom?" They were one couple she knew who didn't use cell phones.

"Just a minute. He's out on the terrace. I'll wheel him into the bedroom. Hold on."

Kellie's heart was pounding so hard, she feared it couldn't be good for her, but there wasn't anything she could do to slow it down.

"Is that you, Tink?" Her loving uncle had called her his golden Tinker Bell from her childhood. "How's the therapy going? Are you making any progress with this Mrs. Lasko?"

Tears filled Kellie's eyes. She loved them so much. "To make a long story short, Leandros and I are finding our way back to each other."

Sounds of pure joy reached her ears.

"I'm going to tell you everything that's happened. Then I need to ask you a question, and you have to answer it honestly, because I love you more than anything in the world and want you to be as happy as you've made me all these years."

The silence that followed let her know she'd captured their attention. Getting in a more comfortable position, she began her tale. Leaving out their biggest problem, which had to do with artificial insemination and their struggle to get pregnant, she got into the ins and outs regarding Karmela and Frato.

Next she told them about Leandros's relationship with his first wife, and the many misconceptions Kellie had drawn throughout their marriage. Finally she explained why Karmela was now in the hospital, hopefully getting the kind of help she needed.

"That brings me to the one of the issues in our marriage we still haven't resolved."

"You mean there's more?" her aunt asked in a quiet voice.

"Yes, and it has to do with the two of you."

"What do you mean?"

"Leandros loves you and wants all of us to be together on a permanent basis. If you feel you could never leave home, then he's ready to step down as CEO of the company and move to Philadelphia."

She heard her aunt's gasp.

"I've told him about the house in Parkwood. I already have earnest money down on it. Since you've seen it, you know the place is big enough to accommodate the six of us after the children are born. We'll turn one of the upstairs rooms into a study for Leandros. He'll do business for the corporation from there."

"But—"

"Don't say anything yet, Uncle Jim. Let me finish. Here goes. We've decided that if you're willing to move to Greece, we'll make our permanent home at his villa on Andros Island and commute to Athens by helicopter."

"Honey—"

"I'm not through yet, Aunt Sybil. There's a small, vacant villa only a two-minute walk from his. It belonged to his uncle Manny until he died last year. Thea and Vlassius live only a three-minute walk from the villa in the other direction. We'd all be together! With the babies coming, it would be heaven."

She heard sniffing, but didn't know if it was a good or bad sign.

"Leandros has already talked to his parents about the renovations we'll have done to make you two as comfortable as possible. It's a darling, cozy house with the most glorious garden and fruit trees. The beach is only steps away."

"Tink—"

"We'll hire a person to help you," she talked over him. "It won't be Frank unless he's willing to relocate with you. If not, we'll find someone equally wonderful. There's a small swimming pool on the side of the villa where you can do therapy. The temperature of the air and the water is perfect. Vlassius will be thrilled to take you fishing every morning on his boat, Uncle Jim. Now he'll have someone to go with him."

Her uncle made a croaking sound.

"You'll have your own car, Aunt Sybil. You and Thea can go shopping all the time. We'll take you to visit all the sites and museums. You can browse to your heart's content in all the little villages. And something else about Thea. She's a homebody like you who loves to cook and have family around. There are a bunch of Petralia family members living on the estate. You'll love all of them.

"In fact, I think you'd be shocked how much you have in common with them. We'll get you started learning Greek. By the time the babies are born, you'll be able to converse and understand almost everything. We'll become a bilingual household."

"Kellie," her aunt interrupted her. "You've convinced us it all sounds like a dream come true, but you don't need to go to these lengths because we're perfectly content here."

That was her aunt's stubborn side talking. "If that's your final answer, then I won't say any more about it. But since I'll never be truly content away from you, then Leandros and I will be moving to Philadelphia."

"Then *his* parents will be alone—" her uncle blurted.

"In terms of his being their only child, that's true. But they have brothers and sisters living on the island. They're not in your situation where you've never had family to call on. Of course, they'll fly to the States to visit us whenever possible. Leandros is determined to make this work, because he loves you."

Kellie heard her uncle clear his throat. "We love him…. Sybil? We can't expect Leandros to move here. He's an important man with a job to do." His words caused Kellie's heart to run away with her again.

"I know. I'm only thinking of you, Jim." Her aunt's voice trembled.

"Fiddle faddle. Moving to Greece will be a new adventure for us. Before my stroke, we'd planned to spend a lot of time traveling."

"You can still travel, Uncle Jim. The helicopter will take us everywhere. You can invite your friends to visit."

"Well, that settles it for me. If you want to know the truth, Sybil, I don't want to miss a day of watching our grandbabies grow up. Do you?"

Her aunt had broken down crying. "No."

By now Kellie was dissolved in tears herself. "You two don't have any idea how happy you've made me. Throughout our marriage, Leandros has worried continually about you, but no longer. I can't wait to tell him."

"Do you have any idea how different you sound?"

"All I know is how I feel, Aunt Sybil. I'm so deeply happy on every level, I'm afraid I'm going to burst."

"We don't want you to do that. It's awfully late for you to still be up, honey. You need to take care of yourself and get to bed."

"I will. The next time I call, I'll put Leandros on the phone and we'll start making moving arrangements. In the meantime, decide what you want to bring to your new house. Love you. Good night."

After hanging up, Kellie turned on her side. Oblivion took over while she was imagining when and how she would tell Leandros. It had to be the perfect time and place.

Leandros had just finished shaving when he had a call from his attorney. "Turn on your TV to the nine o'clock *Athenian Morning Show.* I've heard they're doing the story on you this morning despite my attempt to quash anything about you. Call me when it's over and we'll plan a damage strategy."

There was no such animal. Karmela had always been one step ahead and hadn't missed a trick. On a burst of adrenaline, Leandros reached for the TV remote and got in on the last of the weather forecast. Hot and sunny.

"Welcome, everyone. Thanks for tuning in to the *Athenian Morning Show.* Once again the Petralia Corporation is in the news. Five weeks ago a tornado swept through Greece, taking lives and destroying part of the Persephone, their newest resort outside Thessalonika.

"Today we bring you our top story involving the attractive thirty-five-year-old CEO himself, Leandros Petralia, who's been involved in a scandal that has rocked the country. He's been unavailable for comment since the news broke that his striking sister-in-law, Karmela Paulos of the Paulos Manufacturing Company, and one of the secretaries at the Petralia Corporation, is carrying his child.

"Frato Petralia, a cousin who's vice president of operations, has been installed as acting CEO of the corporation while they attempt to weather this crisis. A reliable source has informed the station that his second marriage, of two years duration to Kellie Petralia, his American-born wife, fell apart because of the affair.

"She's divorcing him for an undisclosed amount of money. If you remember, his first wife, prominent beauty Petra Paulos, who'd been working for Halkias Textiles, died four years ago in a tragic plane accident along with their unborn baby. More on this story and pending lawsuits will be reported in tonight's news.

"Moving on to another scandal involving one of Greece's major banks..."

Furious for what this could do to Kellie, Leandros shut off the TV and got dressed. He was on his way out of the room when his phone rang again. Seeing the caller ID, he picked up eagerly. "Nik?"

"I'm glad you answered. It's good to hear your voice. I'm just sorry to learn about your precarious circumstances. My brothers both phoned to tell me about the horrendous lies put out on the morning news. How can Fran and I help? She's beside herself for the two of you.

Frankly, so am I. You don't need this while you're both still in counseling. Karmela's form of sabotage leaves a taint no matter how you try to squelch it."

"It's ugly, all right, but Kellie and I are far enough along in our therapy to have surmounted most of our difficulties, and we know the truth."

"Thank heaven for that."

"Tell Fran not to worry. My wife will be calling her shortly to explain. I'm afraid we're just going to have to ride this storm out. Talk to you later. Thanks for your support, Nik. It means everything."

Leandros hurried out of the bedroom and down the hall. Kellie's door was still closed. It could mean she was still asleep, or maybe she was already on the phone to Fran. Practicing patience wasn't his forte, but once more he held back from joining her, and headed for the living area. He found his parents enjoying breakfast at the dining room table.

His father looked up. "Did you catch the news on TV this morning?"

"Afraid so."

"It's pure tripe."

Nerves twisted his insides. "Have you seen Kellie yet?"

"I'm right behind you."

He wheeled around to discover his wife dressed in the same blouse and skirt she'd worn here last evening. His heart raced at the sight of her beautiful face and body.

She eyed him intently. "I watched the news, too. You have to hand it to Karmela. With her smarts and energy channeled in the right direction, she could do wonders with anything she set her hand to."

His spirits plunged. "I wish you hadn't seen it."

Her smile disarmed him. "Leandros… We knew she'd do her worst. She wove just enough truth into the lies to make it sound authentic. You and your attorney probably have a plan to deny the allegations. But if you want my opinion, I think we should just leave it alone and go on living our lives."

"Oh, I agree!" his mother declared.

His father followed with a "Bravo!"

Leandros drew in a fortifying breath, relieved by his wife's response. "Then the four of us are on the same page."

Those brown eyes shone with a new light. "I've given up on the news stations doing their research and getting documented proof about anything anymore. People who want to believe the worst always will. If you lose business, you wouldn't want them for clients under any circumstances. In time even *they* will realize the story had no substance to it. Unless you have other plans, I'd like to fly back to Andros."

"Not without breakfast, you don't," his mother exclaimed. "Sit down. There's plenty here for both of you."

Suddenly his appetite had come back. He helped Kellie into the chair, tantalized by her alluring fragrance. "You look rested. I take it you got a good sleep."

"The best I've had in months. How about you?"

As he took his place next to her, a prickling sensation broke out on the back of his neck. Something was different about her. He glanced at his parents. "Do you want to fly back with us?"

"No. We're going to stay here until tomorrow," his

father stated. "We'll be meeting up with some of the family later. You two go on."

Anxious to get away from the paparazzi who'd spring at them at every opportunity, he phoned Stefon to get the helicopter ready. Thankfully, he'd doubled the security on Andros to keep them off his property.

Within ten minutes they'd kissed his parents goodbye and were on their way. En route he phoned his attorney and told him there was nothing to be done for now. After thanking him, he made a call to Frato, who'd insulated himself with extra security so he could get his work done.

His cousin seemed to be in surprisingly good spirits considering his pain over Karmela's betrayal. Frato wasn't taking any calls except from his family and Leandros. He did want to know when Leandros planned to return to work.

There was no way to answer that question. If he and Kellie got back together—and that was still an if—then there was a distinct possibility they'd be living in the States. But he was afraid to speculate that far ahead. Though he knew they were making progress in terms of understanding their conflicts and doing something about them, he didn't know if she could bring herself to live with him again. That's what this was all about.

The history they'd been through might have been too painful for her to allow herself to be open and vulnerable to married life once more. That he'd been too blind in certain areas and too inflexible on occasion had done a lot of damage. To live with him on faith, hoping he'd catch himself when he was in danger of falling into old habits, was a lot to ask of her. Maybe too much.

Until further notice he'd remain on vacation. Next

week was their third counseling session with Mrs. Lasko. A month ago he'd fought the idea of allowing anyone to get into his private thoughts, let alone be willing to listen to any constructive criticism. He found it amazing that in just a few visits, he welcomed any insights their therapist offered that would help in bringing him and Kellie back together.

When the helicopter touched down and they'd made their way to the villa, Kellie turned to him. "Do you think it would be all right if we drove into Chora? I realize there'll be reporters lurking, but I'd like to buy some maternity clothes. This skirt is the only thing that feels comfortable. My jeans are too tight."

Her request sent a burst of excitement through him. For once he'd been caught off guard and ran a possessive eye over her curvaceous figure, when he'd promised himself he wouldn't. As a result he almost didn't answer her question. "I've hired enough extra security to make certain we're not bothered."

"You wouldn't mind going with me?"

It thrilled him, because it sounded as if she really wanted him to come. "To buy some outfits for my expectant wife? I've been looking forward to this moment since the day we married."

She bit her lip. "Me, too. There's a darling maternity shop I remember passing."

If he knew his wife, throughout their marriage she'd probably gone in it to look around while they'd both been waiting for the news that she was pregnant. She'd been so brave over all these months, submitting to the procedure. As disappointed as he was each time they found out she wasn't pregnant, it was her pain that had killed him. He'd felt so helpless knowing there were no words to bring her the comfort she needed.

"Let's do it. We'll eat lunch afterward."

"I was hoping you'd say that. Maybe there's something wrong with me that I'm always so hungry."

He frowned. "I'm sure there isn't, but to be wise, let's make an appointment for you to see your doctor in Athens on Tuesday, after our counseling session. If a problem did come up, he needs to know you are pregnant and living in Greece for an undetermined period."

Leandros was getting good at tempering his words so he wouldn't come across as harassing her for a commitment she wasn't ready to give.

"Actually, I saw him the day I flew in."

That came as a surprise.

"I wanted to thank him and let him know the procedure finally worked. I'm sure it made him happy."

"Did you tell him we were getting divorced?"

"Yes. I heard the sadness when he said he was very sorry. He told me to call him anytime...." Her voice trailed off, as if she had something else on her mind. "Give me a minute to change my blouse and freshen up."

"Take your time. I'll meet you at the car."

CHAPTER NINE

AFTER A SHOPPING SPREE that resulted in taking home a couple of loose fitting sundresses, plus three new tops and jeans that allowed for growth, Leandros put the purchases in the car and treated Kellie to a delicious lunch.

When she couldn't eat another bite, she lifted her eyes to her husband. "I ate too much, but it tasted so good."

His white smile turned her heart over. "Do you know this vacation is putting weight back on me?"

She studied his handsome features. "It's done it to both of us." He'd looked gaunt when she'd surprised him in his office last week, but with regular meals and rest, he'd started filling out. No man was more gorgeous than Leandros.

"Do you want to go home, or would you like to stretch your legs for a while longer?"

"There's a cute children's shop down on the other corner. If you don't mind, I'd like to pick up an outfit for Demi before we go back to the villa. Fran says she's growing fast. I imagine she needs the nine-to-twelve-months' size."

"I'm ready when you are." He put some bills on the table and they left the restaurant.

Kellie walked alongside her husband, realizing she had absolutely nothing to complain about. He was his affable, charming self, and he went along with everything she suggested, but a vital spark was missing from his normally vibrant personality.

Every day since her return to Greece, she'd been more and more aware of it. She felt as if she was living with a whitewashed version of the dynamic lover she'd married. All the color seemed to have gone out of him.

That's your *fault, Kellie.*

Over the last few days she felt as if they'd unearthed every major problem and now possessed the tools to keep the lines of communication open. But somewhere in the process he'd changed.

Fear clutched at her to think that the problems in their marriage had done something irreparable to him. She knew he loved her. She knew he loved their unborn babies. But he might not feel the same desire for her anymore. Except for cupping her elbow, or steadying her as she got out of the car, he didn't try to touch her or make overtures as a prelude to making love.

She thought back to the first time she'd met him. It had taken only twenty-four hours from the time he'd helped her get her uncle wheeled into the elevator before he'd kissed her senseless. Kellie would never forget what he told her after he'd finally lifted his head so they could breathe.

"I want you so much, I wish I could bite the heart out of your body. But then I'd never be able to have that experience again, so we need to get married as soon as possible. Don't tell me you don't want the same thing. I've got you in my arms and can feel your heart leaping to reach mine."

"I'm not denying it." She'd half gasped the words while she tried to catch her breath.

"Not everyone experiences the intense desire we feel for each other. It's a precious gift we don't dare lose, Kellie, or neither of us will ever be happy again."

A tremor shook her body when she remembered that incredible night and her passionate response.

Yet the month before she'd left him, she'd been too distrustful and angry to turn to him for the intimacy she'd always craved. It seemed it had been years since they'd made love. The more he'd tried to love her physically, the more she'd pushed him away.

What if he'd done the same thing to her?

But he hadn't! No matter how bad things had gotten, he'd always reached for her in bed. *She* was the one who'd moved into the guest bedroom and had made plans to vacation with Fran.

Rejection like that could be too painful to forget. Leandros was the total opposite of a spiteful person, but if he didn't crave her affection in the same way anymore, it was because she'd killed something inside him.

Last night he'd gone to bed when his parents did. Their presence had never inhibited him before if he'd wanted to be alone with her. Since her return, he'd had every opportunity to come into her bedroom, whether they were at the Cassandra or on Andros.

All these thoughts were torturing her as they shopped for Demi's gift. The whole time they were in there, he didn't suggest they pick out something for their babies. Her old husband would have bought out the store for them by now.

As the clerk wrapped their gift of an adorable pink top and shorts, Kellie felt a blackness descend. This was how all the pain and suffering had started before. She'd let her fears develop into giant problems without sharing them with Leandros.

What was the expression about not learning lessons from the past, or mankind was destined to repeat the mistakes? Suddenly Mrs. Lasko's warning filled her mind.

"Surely today has given you your first inkling of where to dig to start finding understanding. You'll have to be brutally honest, open up and listen to each other. You'll be forced to wade through perceptions, whether false or accurate, and no matter how painful, arrive at the truth."

It came to Kellie that the problems of trying to get pregnant and the disappointment each time it didn't happen had blown up all the other problems until there was no more communication. Now she was dealing with another inner conflict, one she had to step up and face.

What if she girded up her courage and asked him outright how he felt right now?

Why was it so hard?

What was her greatest fear?

That he'll tell you the truth, that his desire for you has waned.

Was she brave enough to hear the truth from his lips? If she wasn't, then she'd learned nothing from therapy.

They left the shop and went back to the car. As they were leaving the town, they passed the church where they'd been married. On impulse, she turned to him. "Leandros? Would you pull over to the curb for a minute?"

He shot her a concerned glance and immediately

found a parking space. "What's wrong? You went quiet on me in the shop. Aren't you feeling well?"

"That's not it," she assured him. "I feel fine, but I realize I haven't been in the church since we took our vows. I only want to go inside for a moment."

A puzzled look broke out on his face. "Why?"

"It's one of my whims. Will you humor me? I've been getting them a lot lately. Do you know, while we were planning our wedding, one of your family members mentioned you and Petra had been married on Andros and—"

"And you assumed this was the church." He ground out the words.

"Yes. I'm sorry to have to admit it was another one of my false assumptions."

He shut off the engine. "Do you want me to go in with you?"

Yes, yes, yes. "If you'd like to."

"I would have brought you here whenever you wanted, but you never expressed a desire. If I'd had my wits about me, I would have asked you to tell me why."

She shook her head. "I wouldn't have told you the real reason. Not then. As for now, I'd like to see it again, knowing you didn't marry Petra in here. Let's face it. I had more than one veil over my eyes on our wedding day."

"I was blinded by the wonder of you."

Leandros.

He came around and helped her out of the car. They walked across the cobblestones to the entrance. The beautiful white church with the latticelike windows had two of the Cycladic, blue-topped spires.

A few people were inside as they entered the nave.

Kellie looked around, marveling over the paintings on the walls and ceiling. He escorted her past columns to the front, where they'd stood before an icon of the Virgin to become man and wife.

His gray eyes searched hers for a heart stopping moment. "What do you remember about that day?" he whispered.

"Being terrified I'd make a mistake in front of all your family and friends," she whispered back. "What about you?"

His features sobered. "I couldn't believe you'd agreed to become my wife. Throughout the ceremony, which I confess was mostly a blur to me, I prayed you wouldn't back out at the last minute."

"You truly worried about that?" She couldn't fathom it. Not Leandros of all people.

"I chased you from the moment we met. You were such an elusive creature, you'll never know the relief I felt when the priest finally made you mine."

Kellie was bemused by his answer. "So I was yours, eh?" she teased.

"Yes," he declared savagely.

Emotion almost closed her throat. "I was so in love with you, I feared you couldn't possibly love me the same way. What had I done to earn such a man's love?"

"Don't you think I asked the same question about you? How come this wonderful, beautiful American woman had agreed to marry me?"

"All I know is I got my heart's desire." Her pulse rate sped up before she grasped his hands. "Two years have gone by and with them a lot of history. Now it seems the tables have turned and I'm the one chasing you."

At first she didn't think he'd gotten the full import

of her words. Not until she saw his chest rise and fall, and felt his fingers tighten around hers.

"We're standing before God. If you lie to me, He'll know it and so will I. So I'm going to ask you a question. Leandros Roussos Petralia—do you still want me in all the ways a man wants a woman? You know what I mean."

A sound like ripping silk came out of him.

"Cat got your tongue? Remember, you're under oath."

He looked tortured. "Kellie…what's going on?"

"If you think about it hard enough, it should come to you."

Removing her hands gently from his, she walked out of the church to the car without looking back.

Leandros grabbed hold of the last pew to steady himself. He didn't know what to think. Kellie was the kind of passionate lover a man would kill for, but she'd never taken the initiative with him in their marriage, not verbally or physically. It had always rested on him.

Therapy had taught him she'd been too insecure all her life to say the words and reach out to him first, of her own accord. But if he'd read her correctly just now, she'd done something unprecedented by letting him know with words she *wanted* him. They hadn't even been to their next therapy session.

Maybe it had taken being in this holy place, with no associations of Petra, for her to find the courage. He was blown away to realize she wanted to sleep with him again. But this didn't necessarily mean she was ready for the final step to get back together.

In a sense he felt fragmented. Part of him couldn't

wait to get her home alone. Yet another part feared that once he'd made love to her again, and then she decided she couldn't live with him, after all, he wouldn't be able to handle the pain. One night with her would never be enough.

Before he made a fatal mistake and temporarily assuaged his longing, only to find out there would never be another time, they had more talking to do. With a mixture of elation and terror, he left the church and joined her in the car. She didn't look at him as he started the engine.

Once they were on the road, he glanced at her profile. "To answer your question, I want you a hundred times more now than I did on our wedding night. If I haven't touched you, you know the reason why."

"That's all I need to hear."

"Kellie—you could have no comprehension of how I felt in the church just now when you let me know you wanted me. Those are the words I've dreamed of hearing you say, but never expected the moment to happen. You've changed from your former self into a woman I hardly recognize."

That brought her head around, causing the golden strands to swish against her shoulders. "I'm sorry you've had to wait so long for me to say the words in my heart," she said with tears in her voice.

"I'm not," he replied. "The wait has made them all the sweeter. Your bravery has emboldened me to ask the one question still unanswered for me. Do you want to call off the divorce? I never wanted it. When you told me you were leaving me…" He gripped the steering wheel harder.

She reached over to touch his arm. "It sounds like

you expect me to spell it out, so I will. I don't want a divorce."

"Thank God."

"Deep inside, whether I was consciously aware of it or not, I know I flew to Athens to get my marriage back. Our precious babies were an excuse to face you after all the terrible things I'd done to you. But that version of me is gone, Leandros. You're beholding the new me, who's ready to love you like you've never been loved before. How am I doing on answering your question so far?"

He could hardly breathe. "Just keep talking until we reach the villa."

"I adore you, Leandros. I always have. You're my whole world, my whole life! I couldn't bear that we were having problems."

"Tell me about it." He half groaned the words.

"It didn't seem possible to me that you could be such a loving husband, and yet be carrying on behind my back with your sister-in-law. Nothing made sense, but I didn't know how to deal with it."

"You weren't alone."

"I have something else to tell you. I spoke with my aunt and uncle for a long time last night."

The information was coming at him like a meteor shower. He could scarcely take it all in.

"The bottom line is, they're going to move into your uncle Manny's villa just as soon as we can arrange it. As you know, Aunt Sybil was always against relocating to Greece because of her worries for Uncle Jim's health. But I got them both on the phone so she couldn't answer for him.

"It would have warmed your heart to hear him tell

us how much he loves you and how crazy he is about the idea of a new adventure. After I explained that your dad would love a fishing partner to go out with every morning, my uncle got excited. He told my aunt he didn't want to miss out on one day of watching their grandchildren grow up. My aunt broke down in tears of happiness. I think we can get Frank to help them here until we find a permanent replacement for him."

Speechless, Leandros grasped her hand and clung to it.

"I wonder what Olympia will say at our next session."

The blood pounded in his ears. "She'll tell us to go slowly."

"I know. And she'll ask questions we haven't thought of."

"That's good. She's been pivotal in helping us see into ourselves. I'd like to keep going to her so we'll stay on track."

Kellie squeezed Leandros's fingers. "So would I. Later on we'll have to send her the right gift to show our gratitude. I'm going to have to think about it for a while, but I can't think while I'm sitting next to you, dying to be in your arms.

"When we get back home, I want to go out on our cabin cruiser. I'll pack the food we love. We're going to need a couple of days and nights to get reacquainted, without anyone else around."

Leandros was already thinking a month at least.

"Be warned, I plan to ravish you before I grow as big as a house!"

He laughed with joyous abandon.

"Then I plan to love you to death and never let you go back to work, but that would make you unhappy."

"You don't really think that—"

"I really do. So in a few days you should fly to Athens and do what you do best, by running the Petralia Corporation. Frato is trying to pull his weight, bless his heart, but I happen to know every man and woman in the company is holding their collective breath until you're back at the helm."

His natural impulse was to speed the rest of the way home so he could crush her in his arms, but the instinct to protect his family was stronger and had come out in full force. His wife had finally come back to him, and their babies were growing inside her. What more could a man ask for?

The second he pulled up to the villa, he hurried around to Kellie's side of the car. She already had the door open and flew into his arms, almost knocking him over. "Kiss me, darling," she cried, lifting her mouth to find his. "Don't ever stop."

There was no space between them as they tried to assuage their great longing for each other. His wife was vibrantly alive, kissing away the shadows. Every touch and caress, every breath filled his mind and body with indescribable ecstasy.

He carried her into the house and followed her down on the bed with his body. But he was careful with her as they found old ways and new to bring each other the pleasure denied them for so long, while they'd been sorting out their lives.

It was evening before they lay sated for a while, their legs entwined, simply enjoying the luxury of looking at each other and being at peace. "The first time we swam together and made love, you reminded me of a painting of the famous Spanish artist Luis Falero. It was called *A Sea Nymph*. She's appearing above the waves with her body submerged. Very enticing. I was taken with it at first glance."

Her smile lit up his insides. "Why didn't you ever tell me?"

"Because you'd never been intimate with a man before and you were easily embarrassed."

She kissed his lips. "But now that I'm with children—*yours*, as a matter of fact—you think I can handle it."

"I think if you saw it, you'd blush, as you do so charmingly. But that was over two years ago and pregnancy has changed you."

"Is that right."

"In the most incredibly gorgeous ways." He pressed a long, hard kiss to her tempting mouth. "Falero did another painting called *The Planet Venus*. The centerpiece is a goddess with flowing gold tresses, very much like you, in fact. After studying you now, I believe his model was in the early stages of her pregnancy. I was always drawn to it."

"I had no idea you were such a lover of nudes."

"Admirer of many, lover of *one*," he corrected, provoking a gentle laugh from her.

"Well…" she eyed him playfully "…since this is confession time, while you were lounging on the sand after we'd made love, it was like the *Reclining Dionysos* on the Parthenon had come to life before my eyes. He's quite spectacular."

Leandros laughed again. "That's not fair. He's missing some of his parts."

She brushed her hand across his well-defined chest.

"Everything important is still there." Suddenly the teasing was gone. She leaned over him. "I love you so much, Leandros. Make love to me again. I'm on fire for you and am feeling insatiable."

"That makes two of us, *agapa mou.*"

CHAPTER TEN

"Congratulations, Mrs. Petralia. You've reached your thirty-fifth week and all is well with your little boys. Most patients with twins deliver between now and thirty-seven weeks. Since I can predict your babies are going to come earlier than the desired forty weeks for a single baby, I want you to be especially observant of what's going on with your body."

"What *isn't* going on?" she exclaimed. "Last week, when we told our marriage therapist we wanted another appointment with her, to talk about how to be parents to twins, I told her I was as big as a house. I don't think she believed me until she saw me. Secretly, I'm afraid Leandros compares me to a giant walrus." Dr. Hanno burst into laughter. "It's true. That's exactly how I feel."

"It won't be long now. Those menstrual-like cramps you've experienced are normal. So is the lower back pain and uterine pressure. Sometimes you can't tell if you're having contractions. You'll need to listen to your body very carefully from here on out. My advice is to stay off your feet for a few hours every day to avoid that pressure."

"You mean my swollen stumps?" she quipped. "I can't even bend over to see them."

"Be sure you're still getting the equivalent of four glasses of milk a day. Any questions before you leave?"

"Yes. How do I help my husband to calm down? He's known for being a tour de force in the corporate world, but you wouldn't know it if you lived with him."

The doctor grinned. "There's no cure for what he's got except to have those babies."

"I realize that. Half the time he watches me like a hawk. If I yawn or sigh, he asks me what's wrong. When I get up in the night lately to go to the bathroom, he's pacing on the patio off our bedroom. I'm glad he has to go to work! But throughout his day, he phones every few hours. His parents and my aunt and uncle are a stone's throw away from our villa, but nothing seems to ease his mind. Every night he comes home from work with a new toy or outfit. At this rate we're not going to have room for the babies."

Dr. Hanno eyed her speculatively. "I'm sure you know how lucky you are. Too many women don't have a husband, and even if they do, he's not like yours."

Tears filled her eyes. "I know. I'm very blessed. The hardest thing about the end of this pregnancy is trying to help him not get too worried. His first wife was killed in a plane crash, and she was pregnant. I'm sure those demons are haunting him right now."

"What about your marriage counselor? Maybe the two of you should ask her."

"That's a brilliant idea, but I don't think he'd want to. I'm afraid I'm going to have to talk to him and get him to admit what's driving his heightened anxiety. I'll have to find a creative way to reach him. Thanks for everything, Dr. Hanno."

"I'll see you in three days."

"If not before?" She was so tired of being pregnant, it would be wonderful for it to all be over.

"Maybe."

That *maybe* gave her hope. She left his examination room and walked out to the reception area mentally revitalized.

Her aunt had been reading a magazine. When she saw Kellie, she put it down and got to her feet. "How are you doing?"

"Just great. He wants to see me in three days."

"You'll probably be going into labor soon."

"I think so, too."

"Let's get you back to the hotel and order a meal. Before long Leandros will be through with work and we'll fly back to Andros."

"He'll be waiting to hear how my appointment went. I'll call him from the limo."

When they left the building, the temperature outside was 56 degrees, typical for February. Kellie had been hot for months and loved the cool air. There'd been a little rain on their way to the doctor's office, but it had stopped.

As soon as she got in the back of the car with her aunt, she phoned Leandros. He picked up after the first ring. "Kellie?" On a scale of one to ten, his anxiety was a hundred.

"Hi, darling. The doctor said everything looks great. I have to keep my legs up for a few hours a day, but otherwise we're ready to go."

"That's the news I've been waiting for. I'll be leaving the office in twenty minutes. Where are you right now?"

"In the limo."

"You're going straight to the hotel, right?"

"Yes. We'll be there in a few minutes."

"I love you." The tone of his deep voice permeated to her insides, thrilling her.

"I love you, too."

"I've decided this is going to be my last day of work." *Oh, help!* "I've had Frato here in the office. He's going to take over for me starting tomorrow morning. I can't concentrate anymore. Mrs. Kostas told me to go home and not come back."

No doubt he'd been driving her crazy, too. Kellie laughed, resigned to the fact that she was going to have her nervous husband around day and night until the big event. "That's marvelous news. I'll see you shortly." She hung up.

Her aunt smiled. "What was that laugh about?"

"Leandros informed me he won't be going to work anymore until after the babies are born."

"Oh, dear."

They both laughed. "I've got to come up with a project for him that will keep him busy for hours at a time."

"I know just the thing. I want to have some window boxes built on the east side of the house."

"Perfect! I'll send him with you to pick things out. With Uncle Jim directing traffic, it ought to keep his mind occupied for one day, anyway." More laughter ensued.

The limo pulled to a stop in front of the Cassandra. Kellie thanked the driver and they both got out. She took two steps on the pavement and felt her sandal slide in a tiny pool of water. The next thing she knew, she was sitting on the ground, having landed with a hard thud. Talk about a beached walrus that wasn't going anywhere.

"Are you all right, honey?" her aunt cried.

"I think so. I feel like an idiot, but I'm thankful I didn't take you down with me."

"You're not in pain?"

"No." She started to get up.

"Let me help."

"Thanks," she whispered. But the moment she stood, she felt moisture run down her legs in a gush. It wasn't from the pool. "Aunt Sybil? My water just broke."

"Hang on to me, honey. I'll call the driver and tell him to come back."

Within a minute, the limo returned. Kellie climbed in while her aunt told the driver they needed to get straight to the hospital.

"Tell him not to phone Leandros. I'll do it or he'll freak out completely."

"Agreed."

She was starting to have pains that were different than what she'd experienced now and then. Her stomach grew rock-hard. The contractions were starting. While they drove to the hospital, she reached in her purse for her cell and phoned Leandros.

"Kellie?"

"Hi, darling. There's been a change in plans. My water just broke and I'm in the limo on the way to the hospital. Our babies are coming." Her voice wobbled. "I'll meet you at the hospital."

"I'll be there in five minutes." His line went dead.

* * *

Leandros, masked and gowned, sat next to Kellie while he watched the miracle of their firstborn son's birth. The baby had a tuft of black hair, and according to the pediatrician attending him, he weighed in at six pounds two ounces and was twenty-one inches long.

The excitement in the birthing room was palpable. Leandros didn't know he could be this happy.

"Here comes number two, slick as a whistle." The doctor lifted their second son by the ankles. Again they all heard the healthy infant cry announcing his arrival in the world. Leandros felt pure joy in every atom of his body. "You've got yourselves another beautiful boy. How are you doing, Mom?"

Tears streamed down Kellie's face as she beamed at Leandros. "I'm afraid I might die from so much happiness. Are our babies really all right?"

"They're perfect," he whispered before leaning over to kiss her lips gently.

An army of staff filled the birthing room. The other pediatrician turned his head toward them. "Baby number two weighs in at five pounds fourteen ounces and measures twenty and a half inches. You've given birth to healthy fraternal twins. Congratulations."

In a few minutes they'd been washed and wrapped so Kellie could hold them in her arms. "Oh, darling," she wept. "Our babies…" She kissed their heads. "They're gorgeous, just like you."

Leandros was so full of emotion, he had to wipe his eyes to get a good look. "I can see your beautiful features in both of them. Just think. You and I grew up as only children. They'll always have each other."

"I know. Isn't it wonderful?" But her eyes had closed.

Alarmed, Leandros looked at the doctor. "Is she all right?"

"I've given her a hypo. She'll sleep for several hours. Why don't you go down to the nursery with your sons and get acquainted with them."

After kissing his wife's flushed cheek, he watched the nurses put the babies in carts, and followed them down the hall to the newborn unit. For the next half hour he had the time of his life, examining every finger and toenail. Their sons had made it. His wife had made it. A wave of love for her, for their offspring, swept through him, shaking him to the very foundations.

When he finally went out into the hall, he saw everyone standing at the glass—his parents, her aunt and uncle, Fran and Nik. The celebration could probably be heard throughout the wing. His mother flung herself into his arms and sobbed. As for his father, he was so choked up he couldn't talk.

Leandros leaned down to give Jim a hug, then swept Sybil into his arms. All everyone did was cry. Fran was no different. She gave him a giant hug. "Hallelujah this day has come," she whispered.

Then it was Nik's turn to give him the mother of bear hugs. "Sybil told us you're on vacation now. Believe me, you're going to need it with all those two o'clock feedings. I couldn't be happier for you, Leandros."

"I feel like *I've* given birth. I can't even imagine what Kellie's feeling like."

"She's blissfully knocked out."

"You're right." He chuckled. "Thanks for being here."

"We wouldn't be anywhere else. Have you decided on names?"

"We did as soon as we found out we were having boys. We decided the first one to come out would be Nikolas Vlassius Petralia."

Nik's eyes grew suspiciously bright. "You're kidding me."

"I swear I'm not. Kellie was adamant about it. She loves you like a brother. I think you know that by now."

"I'm honored," he said in a croaky voice. "What will you call your other son?"

"Dimitri Milo Petralia in honor of her uncle Jim, who was the perfect father to her all her life, and of course her birth father."

"Does Jim know that yet?"

"We had dinner for everyone last week and told them."

"The Petralia brothers, Nik and Dimitri. That has a definite ring."

Leandros had to admit that it did. After they were born, he'd told Kellie what it meant to him to have sons. She'd kissed him and said, "Don't you think I know that? Don't you know how I watched you suffer each time we knew we weren't pregnant? It almost killed me to see your pain. After all, you're a proud Greek male. I'm just thankful you finally got your heart's desire."

"One day our children will be playing with your Demi."

"They grow up fast. You've done great work, Leandros."

"I give all the credit to my angel wife. She's the one who got us into counseling and saved our marriage."

Nik shook his head. "I'm convinced you would have made your way back to each other no matter what. I shudder to think that if she hadn't phoned Fran to come to Greece..."

Leandros patted his good friend on the shoulder. "You would have met Fran at a later date. When you consider the if's, it makes you realize it was all meant to be."

At 6:00 p.m. Kellie tiptoed into the nursery to check on the babies one more time. They'd both been fed and burped. Now they were sound asleep. She got a swelling in her chest. They were the dearest babies on earth, and that wasn't just because she was their mother. Their Petralia genes made them beautiful.

She looked down at each one, feasting her eyes on their darling faces and bodies. The sky-blue of their little sleepers with feet brought out their dark hair and olive skin, just a few of Leandros's striking assets. They bore a strong resemblance to each other, but there were distinct differences she was happy about.

Kellie wanted them each to grow up being their own person. Leandros felt the same way. It would be fun to play up the twin thing once in a while, but it was important they had their own identities.

They were seven weeks old today. She remembered back to the time when Dr. Creer had told her she was pregnant and seven weeks along. "Big as blueberries," he'd said. Children had brought a whole new meaning to her life.

Lately she'd found herself thinking a lot about her

parents. Unquestionably, they would have loved Kellie the same way. What a lucky girl she'd been to be raised by her aunt and uncle, whom she looked upon as her heroes. They'd not only raised her, they were now helping her and Leandros raise the children.

With everyone in both families pitching in, the exciting, chaotic and exhausting experience of having twins hadn't been quite as overwhelming as she would have imagined. Fran and Nik had spent several weekends with them. With their precious Demi walking around, getting into everything she could touch, while the babies lay on the floor watching her, they had hilarious times.

"Good night, my darlings," she whispered. "Forgive me if I don't see you for the next twenty-four hours, but I've got special plans for your father he doesn't know about. All these weeks he's been waiting on you and me. Now he needs some personal attention. Both your grandmas will be taking care of you until we come back tomorrow night. Be good for them. I'll miss you." She kissed each one and tiptoed out of the nursery.

Thea and Sybil were settled in the living room watching television. Kellie walked over to give them each a hug. "I'm leaving now. Call us if there's an emergency."

Her aunt nodded. "Of course. Now you go on. If you don't come back for a week, we won't mind, will we, Thea?"

"We wish you *would* stay away more than twenty-four hours."

"I couldn't bear to be separated from them that long. And you know Leandros. He's so crazy about them, I'm not sure he'll last until tomorrow night."

The two women gave each other a knowing smile, causing Kellie's cheeks to go warm. "Thank you from the bottom of my heart." She blew them a kiss, then let herself out the front door into the April evening. The helicopter would be bringing him home from work any minute. Her plan was to be there the moment he jumped out.

She was wearing a new pair of jeans and a short-sleeved, oatmeal-colored cotton sweater he'd never seen before. Though she still had ten pounds to lose, she'd gone down enough sizes to fit into non-maternity clothes. To her satisfaction, she could tuck in the sweater. She wanted to make sure he knew she was getting her shape back. He liked her hair long, so she'd left it loose after blow drying it. A little perfume, lipstick and makeup did wonders for her spirits.

When she heard the helicopter coming, she began to tremble, anticipating the night to come. Two weeks ago she'd had a checkup. The doctor told her she could have relations with her husband at seven weeks. Tonight was the night, only Leandros didn't know it yet.

She hid behind a tree until the helicopter touched down and Leandros got out. He spoke with the pilot for a few minutes, then started down the path to their villa, throwing his suit coat over his shoulder. She sneaked up behind him and wrapped her arms around his waist, clutching him tightly against her.

"Don't turn around if you know what's good for you. Do everything I say, and you won't get hurt."

His shoulders started to shake with silent laughter. "Don't I even get a peek?"

"You talk too much, Mr. Petralia. Just keep walking down to the pier. I'm right behind you."

He went along with her little game and began walking. "What do I do when I get there?"

"We're going sailing. Just you and me."

"It'll be dark soon."

"We don't have to set sail tonight. We can wait until morning."

"That's good, because I'm starving."

"I plan to feed you."

"I'll need a shower first."

"That's all been arranged."

They reached the dock where her sailboat was tied up. She'd spent part of the afternoon making the bed and getting things ready belowdecks. After going to the store, she'd stocked the fridge with his favorite goodies. On her final trip, she'd brought down his toiletries and laid out a new robe for him. He wouldn't want for a thing.

"How soon can I turn around?"

"After you go below."

He stepped into the boat. She stepped where he stepped and trailed him down the stairs.

The lights of several dozen votive candles placed around the ledge beckoned him from the small bedroom. He stopped in place when he saw what she'd created. Suddenly he swung around. His eyes blazed as he took in the sight of her. She felt his desire reach out to her like a living thing.

"Kellie—"

"The doctor gave me the seal of approval. I thought it was about time the man who holds my heart was paid a little attention for a change. Tonight there's no one but you and me. I'm dying to make love to you, Leandros."

"You look so beautiful, I'm staggered."

"Good. Now you know how I feel every time I get near you. What would you like to do first?"

"I want to devour you over and over again," he said in a husky voice. "Come here to me, darling."

Kellie didn't need those words to reach for him. His mouth was life to her. The touch of his hands on her body was a revelation to her. They fell on the bed, desperate for the closeness after having to wait the last two months for this moment.

Hours later they surfaced long enough to eat, then they went back to bed. During the night he pulled her into him. "I think I love you too much," he whispered into her hair. "You have no idea how divine you are."

"You took the words out of my mouth." She kissed his hard jaw. "I got so excited waiting for the helicopter to arrive, I almost had a heart attack."

"I would have come home sooner, but I had three unexpected visitors in my office before I left."

She cupped his face in her hands. "Who?"

"The Paulos family. Karmela has been in therapy for months. She came to apologize."

Kellie sat all the way up. "It must have been so hard for her to face you."

"I'm sure it was, but she did it."

"How is she, darling?"

"There's a definite change in her. She's not on the attack anymore. How much medication plays a role in this new behavior, I don't know, but it's welcome. The day you went to the hospital, she saw the news about our twins on TV. She wanted me to tell you she's very happy for us and sorry for any pain she's caused."

"That's a huge step in the right direction."

"I think so, too."

Kellie nestled against him again. "I'm glad you told me. We can finally leave all that in the past where it belongs, and concentrate on our new lives. I love our boys so much. I love you so much."

"Show me again how much, *agapi mou*. Show me again and again."

* * * * *

He forced himself to ignore the hurt in her tone. He needed to build the distance between them back up. But when she turned those big blue eyes on him something long buried inside him cracked.

"Lainey—"

She gave a little shake of her head as she reached her car. "Thanks again."

To hell with it.

Ben turned her around as she fumbled in her pocket for her keys. Her eyes widened and her lips parted, but before she could say anything he dipped his head and covered her mouth with his.

After a heartbeat, her cold mouth opened and let him into her warmth. It had been so long since he'd felt anything, *anything,* and she was warm and soft and so, so sweet. He fisted his hand in her hair to angle her head, so he could go deeper, and her moan lit fires inside him that had long been dormant.

For a reason.

He broke the kiss and stepped back, his ragged breath catching in his chest. God, what had he done?

She blinked up at him, her gaze smoky and slightly confused. Then her eyes cleared and a look of pure horror crossed her face.

"I've got to go," she said, yanking her keys out of her pocket.

"Lainey, I'm sorry."

As soon as the words were out he knew they were the wrong thing to say.

Dear Reader,

You are holding in your hands my very first published book! It's been quite a ride—it's been a 2012 RWA® Golden Heart® Finalist and a 2011 Mills & Boon New Voices Top 21 Finalist, both of which opened doors I couldn't even imagine. Now, I'm writing this letter for you before you read Lainey and Ben's story. I'm still pinching myself!

Lainey's struggling—she's trying so hard to get her life going the way she thinks it's supposed to be, but she just keeps getting curve after curve pitched her way. Ben is struggling too, but with inner demons that keep him from reaching for what he really wants. Together, the two of them learn that age-old lesson about best-laid plans and that, really, sometimes you've got to take a leap of faith to find your way home.

Please visit me at amiweaver.com and say hello!

All my best,

Ami Weaver

AN ACCIDENTAL FAMILY

BY
AMI WEAVER

First published in Great Britain 2013
by Mills & Boon, an imprint of Harlequin (UK) Limited,
Eton House, 18-24 Paradise Road, Richmond, Surrey TW9 1SR

© Ami Weaver 2013

ISBN: 978 0 263 90107 8
ebook ISBN: 978 1 472 00476 5

23-0513

Harlequin (UK) policy is to use papers that are natural, renewable and recyclable products and made from wood grown in sustainable forests. The logging and manufacturing processes conform to the legal environmental regulations of the country of origin.

Printed and bound in Spain
by Blackprint CPI, Barcelona

Two-time Golden Heart® finalist **Ami Weaver** has been reading romance since she was a teen and writing for even longer, so it was only natural she would put the two together. Now she can be found drinking gallons of iced tea at her local coffee shop while doing one of her very favourite things—convincing two characters they deserve their happy-ever-after. When she's not writing she enjoys time spent at the lake, hanging out with her family and reading. Ami lives in Michigan with her four kids, three cats, and her very supportive husband.

*This is Ami Weaver's fabulous first book
for Mills & Boon!*

For the Wicked Muses: Chelle, Jodie, Marcy and Rae.
Thank you for all your help. I love you all.
And for Dale, who believed. xo

CHAPTER ONE

THE STICK WAS pink.

Lainey Keeler squeezed her eyes shut, lifted the test with one trembling hand, then peeked with her right eye only.

Yup. Definitely a pink line. Maybe she needed to check the instructions to be sure....

Oh, God. How had this happened?

Okay, so she knew the technicalities of the how. In fact, she knew the when. Lord help her, that was the kicker.

Her eyes swam and her stomach rolled as she reached for the test box anyway, knowing what she'd see there. Knowing the result would read the same as the four other sticks—all different brands—in the garbage.

Knowing she'd been screwed in more ways than one.

So this was the price she paid for one night of lust infused with a heavy dose of stupidity. She slumped on the cold tile of the bathroom floor and let her head thunk on the vanity door. Hysterical laughter bubbled in her throat and she pressed her fingertips to her temples. Did it count, fifteen years after graduation, that she'd finally bedded the star quarterback? The same one she'd nurtured a killer crush on all through high school?

And managed to conceive his baby?

"And here I thought I had the flu," she said to her calico

cat, who observed her from the doorway. Panda's squinty blink in response could have meant anything. "Why didn't being pregnant occur to me?"

Single and pregnant. Right when she was starting a new business and her life couldn't be more unstable.

What would her parents say? She winced at the thought. At thirty-three, she was supposed to be burning up the career ladder. Instead, much to her family's chagrin, she burned *through* careers.

Chewing her lower lip, she took a last look at the pink line, then tossed the test stick in the trash with the others. Five pregnancy tests couldn't be wrong, no matter how much she wished it. She needed a plan.

"A plan is good," she said to the cat in the doorway. Panda meowed in response. Shoot, what was she going to do? She stepped over the cat and hurried into the small hallway, facing straight into her pocket-sized bedroom. Panic kicked up a two-step in her belly. She'd need a bigger place. The cozy one-bedroom apartment above her shop, The Lily Pad, worked beautifully for one person and an overweight cat. But adding a baby to the mix...? Babies needed so much *stuff.* She laid her hand on her still-flat belly. *A baby.*

Good God, she was going to be a mother.

She clenched her eyes shut and willed the tears away. What kind of mother would she be? Her ex and her family told her over and over she tended to be flighty and irresponsible. A baby meant responsibility, stability.

What if it turned out they were right? She certainly hadn't demonstrated good judgment on the night of her reunion.

The thought sliced her to the core and she took a deep breath. No time to cry. Not when she had a shop to open in a few minutes. Beth Gatica, her friend and employee, was already downstairs. She swiped at her eyes, tried to think.

"Where do I start?" she wondered aloud, trying to get her head clear enough to think.

A doctor. She'd need a doctor. Her usual doctor happened to be a friend of her family's, so she'd definitely have to head over to Traverse City. Since she felt better with something to do, she reached for the phone book.

"Lainey?" Beth's voice came through the door connecting the apartment to the shop. "Are you okay?"

Lainey fumbled the phone book and caught sight of herself in the small mirror next to the door. Dark blond hair already escaping from her ponytail? Check. Dark circles under her eyes? Check. Pasty skin? *Yikes.* Wasn't there supposed to be some kind of pregnancy glow? "I'm fine," she called. "Be right there."

"Okay, good. Because we've got a problem."

Well, of course they did. Lainey marched over and yanked open the door, almost grateful for the distraction. "What kind of problem?"

"Come see." Beth turned and hurried down the stairs, long dark curls bouncing. The fresh, cool scent of flowers hit Lainey as they entered the workroom. Beth tipped her head toward the older of the two walk-in coolers. "It's not cold enough, Laine. It's set where it's supposed to be, but it's nearly twelve degrees warmer in there."

"Oh, no." *No.* She needed the cooler to last another year—like she needed the van with its iffy transmission to last another six months. Preferably twelve. A headache began to pulse at the edges of her brain at the thought of her nearly empty bank account. Using only one cooler would mean reducing inventory, which meant possibly not being able to meet the needs of her customers. Which meant less income. And she couldn't afford to lose a single cent at this point.

To say The Lily Pad operated on a shoestring budget was to put it optimistically.

She pulled open the door, even though she didn't doubt Beth. She could feel the difference as soon as she walked in. She tapped the thermostat with her finger. Maybe it was stuck somewhere? She should be so lucky.

"Call Gary at General Repair," she said to Beth. "See if he can get us in today."

"On it." Beth hurried to the phone.

Lainey headed to the working cooler to do some rearranging. Some of the more delicate flowers would have to be moved over.

She tamped down the spurt of fear and worry that threatened to explode. No point inviting trouble, and Lainey figured she had enough to fill her personal quota. She closed her eyes and inhaled the fresh, green scent of the flowers, with their overtones of sweet and tangy and spicy. It always, always relaxed her just to breathe in the flowers.

But not enough, today, to rid her of her worries. About choking coolers. About babies. Lainey smothered a sigh. If she'd stayed home two months ago part of her predicament wouldn't be here. She'd invited trouble. Or, more accurately, trouble had invited her.

Of course she hadn't turned him down.

"Gary will be here at eleven," Beth said from behind her. "Want me to help move things?"

Lainey glanced at her watch. An hour and a half. "Sure. We'll just move a few for now. Let's group them by the door so we can open it a minimum of times." The colder it stayed in there, the better for her bottom line. She couldn't afford to lose a cooler full of flowers.

"Are you okay, Laine? You're awfully pale," Beth commented as she lifted a bucket of carnations out of the way.

Lainey sucked in a breath. Should she tell Beth? They'd been friends for years. Beth wouldn't ridicule her for her mistake with Jon. It would feel so good to tell someone….

"Lainey?" Beth's head was cocked, her brown gaze worried. "What's going on?"

"I'm pregnant," she blurted, and burst into tears. Beth hurried over to her, nearly knocking a bucket over in the process.

"Honey, are you sure?"

Lainey nodded and swiped at the tears. "Pretty sure." Five separate pink lines couldn't be wrong. Could they? "I'll have to go to a doctor to confirm it, though."

"Oh, Laine." Beth hugged her, stepped back. "How far along? I didn't know you were seeing someone."

Lainey closed her eyes. *Here we go.* "Well, I'm actually not. I'm about eight weeks along." She'd let Beth do the math.

"So that's—oh." Beth drew out the word and her eyes rounded. "Your class reunion."

"Yeah." Lainey couldn't meet her friend's gaze. Her poor baby. How could she ever explain the circumstances of his or her conception?

"So who's the daddy?"

"Jon Meier." Lainey could barely say his name. "We…ah…hit it off pretty well."

Beth gave a wry chuckle and opened the cooler door, a load of calla lilies in her hands. "So it seems."

"I have to tell him, Beth, but he lives so far away. Plus the whole thing was pretty forgettable, if you know what I mean. We used protection, but obviously…" She shrugged and swiped at her leaking eyes again. "It didn't work." An understatement if she'd ever heard one.

"He's not father material?"

"I don't know." It wasn't as if they'd discussed things like personal lives. "Plus he lives in LA. He's in some kind of entertainment industry work. He's not going to pull up and move back to Northern Michigan." He'd made his contempt for the area crystal-clear.

"Sometimes having a kid changes that," Beth pointed out.

"True." Lainey didn't want to think about it. "But I think we were pretty much in agreement on how awkward the whole thing was." So much for sex with no strings attached. The baby in her belly was a pretty long string. The length of a lifetime, in fact.

She wanted to bang her head on the wall. What had she been thinking, leaving with Jon that night? Was her self-esteem so damaged by her divorce she had to jump on the first guy who smiled at her?

Best not to answer that.

"I think you'll be a wonderful mom," Beth said, and Lainey's throat tightened.

"Really?" She couldn't keep the wobble out of her voice. Beth's confidence touched her. Her family would look at her being single, pregnant and nearly broke and lose their collective minds. She shoved the thought aside.

"Of course. You're wonderful with my kids. Now, let's get this finished before Gary gets here."

"It could go at any time?" Lainey could not believe she'd heard the repairman correctly. A year—she only needed twelve measly months. Why, oh, why was that too much to ask? "Are you sure?"

"Yes. We can cobble this along for a few more months. But you are definitely going to need a new unit." Gary's lined face wasn't without sympathy.

She took a deep breath. "Do what you have to, Gary. I need it to last as long as possible."

The repairman nodded and returned to the cooling unit.

Beth stood at the counter, ringing up a large bouquet of brightly colored carnations. A great sale, but not nearly enough to buy a new cooler. Or even a used one.

"Thank you. Have a great day," Beth said to the customer as he exited the shop. To Lainey she said, "What's the news?"

"We're going to need a new cooler. Sooner rather than later, probably." Exhaustion washed over her and she sank down on the stool behind the counter. "Even used, that's not something I can swing yet." Or possibly ever. No cooler, no business. No business, no cooler.

No business, no way to provide for the baby.

A wave of nausea rolled through her at the thought. Another failure. This one could be huge.

"Oh, man." Beth leaned on the counter. "Well, let's see. We've got the Higgins wedding coming up. We need more weddings. The funeral business has been picking up. That's good. Maybe…."

She hesitated, and Lainey knew what her friend hadn't said.

"Maybe if my mother sent business my way we wouldn't be in this predicament," she finished. "I know. I agree. I've asked." The answer, while not in so many words, was that the florist her mother used had been around a lot longer and wasn't in danger of folding. The implication? Lainey would fail—again.

Beth winced. "I know you have. I just wish she'd support you. I'm sorry I brought it up."

"It's okay. It's the truth. I don't know what will change her mind." Lainey stood up. "Let's finish getting the deliveries ready."

As Lainey gathered flowers and greenery she wondered if she'd let her business go under rather than ask her parents for a loan. They'd give her one, with plenty of strings attached, and she'd have to crawl to get it. This was supposed to be her chance to prove she could make something of her life without advanced degrees or a rich husband.

Right about now it didn't seem to be working.

Gary came out of the cooler, toolbox in one hand, invoice in the other. "You're all fixed up, Ms. Keeler. Can't say how long it'll last. Could be one month. Could be six. I'm sorry I don't have better news."

"The fact it's running right now is wonderful," Lainey said. "Thank you. I appreciate you coming on such short notice."

"Anytime. Have a good day, ladies." He left the store and the bell above the door chimed, its cheerful sound mocking Lainey's mood. She looked at the amount on the invoice and sighed.

She'd known when she bought the shop nine months ago there were no guarantees on equipment. Even in her current financial bind she didn't regret taking the plunge. This shop felt right to her in a way none of her other jobs ever had. Right enough, in fact, that she hoped to someday buy the building outright.

Working steadily throughout the morning, they completed their orders. The repair seemed to be holding for now, thank goodness. Lainey slid the last of the arrangements into the back of the van and closed the door. "All set, Beth. Hopefully we'll get more this afternoon."

"Fingers crossed." Beth climbed in and turned the ignition. She leaned back out the window. "I'll stop at Dottie's Deli and grab lunch on the way back. I think we've each earned a cheesecake muffin after this morning."

"Mmm." Lainey perked up at the thought. Everyone

knew the calories in Dottie's heavenly muffins didn't count. "Sounds wonderful. Thanks."

She held her breath as Beth thunked the old van into gear and drove off. Relief washed over her. After this morning she'd half expected the thing to go belly-up out of spite.

"Don't borrow trouble," she reminded herself as she turned and went inside.

The chime of the door caught her attention and she hurried to greet the customer.

Fifteen minutes later she started on a new arrangement, this one for a new mom and baby at the hospital. They really needed more of this kind of business—more happy occasions like...

Babies.

Pregnant.

Lainey gulped and gripped the edge of the worktable, her eyes on the array of delicate pastel flowers she'd gathered. She only had about seven months to stabilize her shop and get ready to be a new mom herself. A *single* new mom.

Seven months.

No one could ever accuse her of doing things the easy way.

Ben Lawless pulled into the driveway of his grandmother's old farmhouse and stared. Same white paint, black shutters. The wide porch was missing its swing, but two rockers sat in its place. The two huge maples in the front yard had dropped most of their leaves. Funny, he'd been gone for so many years but this old house still felt like home.

He frowned at the strange car parked behind his grandmother's trusty Buick. Last thing he wanted was to talk to anyone other than his grandma, to deal with friendliness and well-meaning questions. Acting normal was exhausting.

He pushed open the truck door, stepped out and scanned the layout of the front yard. Plenty of room for a ramp, though some of the porch railing would have to be removed, and it would block one of the flowerbeds lining the house's foundation. He kicked at the leaves littering the cracked walkway. The uneven concrete posed a hazard even to an able-bodied person. Why couldn't Grandma admit she needed help?

Why did you assume she didn't need it?

His self-recrimination didn't get any farther as the front door opened and framed his beaming grandmother in her wheelchair. He tried not to wince at the sight. She'd always been so tough, strong and able, and now she looked so small. He moved up the walk and the stairs to the porch.

"Grandma." He bent down to give her an awkward hug in the chair, afraid to hold on too tight. "How are you?"

She hugged him back firmly and patted his face. "I'm good. Making the best of this, I hope." She studied his face for a moment, her clear blue eyes seeing too much. "I'm so glad you're here. Not sleeping well?"

He straightened, not surprised by the observation. "Good enough."

She gave him a look, but dropped the subject and rolled back into the house. "Where are my manners? Come in, come in. I want you to meet a very good friend of mine."

Ben braced himself as he followed her across the familiar living room to the kitchen. Hopefully this friend wasn't one of the mainstays of Holden's Crossing's gossip mill. Last thing he needed was word getting out and people asking him questions or making accusations. He stopped dead when he looked into the cool blue gaze of the gorgeous—and young—blond at the kitchen table.

"Ben Lawless, meet Lainey Keeler. Lainey, this is my grandson. The one who's a firefighter in Grand Rapids." The pride in Rose's voice made Ben's stomach twist. "Lainey was a few years behind you in school, Ben."

No way. *This* was his grandmother's friend? Long dark blond ponytail, a few strands loose around a heart-shaped face. Clear blue eyes, smooth creamy skin. Full breasts a snug pink tee didn't hide. He gave her a brief nod, forced the proper words out. "Nice to meet you."

Her smile curved, but didn't reach her eyes. "Same here. Rose has told me so much about you."

"Did she?" He tensed at her comment, then forced himself to relax. It didn't mean she actually knew anything. He rested his hand on his grandmother's thin shoulder. "Grandma, I'm going to bring in my things, okay?"

Lainey rose. "I'll walk you out." She leaned down to plant a kiss on his grandma's cheek and gave her a hug. "I'll see you in a couple of days, Rose."

"Don't work too hard, honey," Grandma said, and Ben nearly laughed. If he remembered correctly, none of the Keelers had to work. They'd been given anything and everything on the proverbial platter.

Ben caught a whiff of her scent, something floral, as she moved past him. Since he'd gotten boxed in, he followed her out into the cool early October night.

Once on the porch, she turned to him with a frown. "She's glad you're here."

"And you're not."

Those big blue eyes narrowed. "I'm not sure. She's been struggling for months now. Where were you then?"

Temper flared at the accusation in her tone. He'd felt bad enough once he'd realized how much help his grandma needed. He didn't need this chick sticking her nose in, too.

No matter how hot she was. "She isn't big on admitting she needs help." Seemed to run in the family.

Lainey gave him a look that said he was full of it and stomped off the porch. "She's in her eighties. How could you not come visit and check on her?"

Guilt lanced through him. "She always said she was fine, okay? I'm here now." Why did he care if this woman thought he was a total heel?

She shrugged. "You still should have checked on her. How far is it up here? She's so proud of you. But you never bothered to visit."

Even in the dim light he saw the sparks in her blue gaze, the anger on his grandmother's behalf. "I'm here now," he said, his own temper rising.

"Till you leave. Then where will she be?" She spun around and strode across the yard.

God help him, he couldn't pull his gaze off her tight little tush. She climbed in the little car and slammed the door. The spray of gravel that followed her out to the road said it all.

Well, great. He'd managed to tick off his grandmother's hot little friend.

Ben shook his head and stepped off the porch, walked to his truck to get his bags. He'd done something far worse than that. His best friend was dead, thanks to him, and any problems with Lainey Keeler were not even on his list of important things. It made no difference what she thought of him.

Back inside, his grandma frowned at him. "Why were you rude to Lainey?"

But of course it would matter to Grandma. He scrubbed a hand over his face. "I'm sorry. It's been a long day. I didn't know you two were friends."

"We are. We met awhile back when she volunteered

for Senior Services and just clicked, as you young people say. She comes out every Wednesday. More if she can. I didn't think you knew her." His grandmother's eyes were sharp on his face.

"I don't. Just knew *of* her. She was four years behind me in school, as you said. How are you feeling?"

She studied him for a second, then seemed to accept the change of topic. "Every day is a little harder. I'm so glad you're here and can make this old house a little easier to live in. I don't want to leave it."

These last words were spoken in a soft tone. Ben knew this was the only home she'd lived in with his grandfather, her husband of fifty years. Her best friend.

The kind of love and relationship he'd ended for Jason and Callie.

Pain pounded at his temples and he closed his eyes. He shoved it down, locked it back into the deepest part of him he could. Thing was, that place was nearly full these days.

"You won't have to leave, Grandma. You'll have to tell me what you'd like done besides the ramp. Even in the dark I noticed the walk out front has seen better days."

Her smile was rueful. "A lot around here has seen better days, Ben."

"We'll get it fixed up, Grandma. You won't have to leave," he repeated.

"I know. I'm very grateful to you." She maneuvered the chair toward the living room. "Let me show you to your room. Well, partway anyway."

Ben started to say he knew where it was, but of course she'd have taken over the downstairs bedroom after the arthritis in her hip got too bad. "Which one?" There were three upstairs.

She stopped at the base of the stairs and looked up, the sorrow and longing clear on her face. "The back bedroom.

It has the best view and is the biggest room. Lainey freshened it up for you. Dusted, clean sheets, the whole shebang. The bathroom is ready, too."

His grandparents' old room.

"Okay. Tell her thanks for me."

Grandma backed her chair up and gave him a little smile. "You can tell her yourself. Didn't I mention she visits a lot?"

He stared at her. *Uh-oh.* "Grandma. I'm not interested."

She slid him a look and her smile widened. "No one said you were."

He'd walked right into that one.

Smoke filled the room, smothering him, searing his lungs, his eyes, his skin. God, he couldn't see through the gray haze. A cough wracked him, tearing at his parched throat. He couldn't yell for his friend. Where was Jason? He couldn't reach him. Had to get him out before the house came down around them. A roar, a crack, and a fury of orange lit the room. The ceiling caved in a crash fueled by the roar of flames. He spun around, but the door was blocked by a flaming heap of debris. Under it, a boot. Jason. Coming to save him.

Ben woke with a start, his eyes watering and the breath heaving out of his lungs as if he'd been sprinting for his life. Where the hell was he? Moonlight slanted through the window, silver on the floor. The curtain stirred in the faint breeze. He sat up and pushed himself through the fog of sleep. Grandma Rose's house. Had he cried out? God, what if she'd heard him? Shame flowed over him like a lava river. He stepped out of bed, mindful of the creaky floor, and walked down the hall to the bathroom near the landing.

No sound came from downstairs.

He exhaled a shaky breath and went into the bathroom.

He'd been afraid of this—of the nightmare coming. He had no power over it—over what it was, what it did to him. No control.

He turned on the squeaky faucet with unsteady hands and splashed cold water on his face. There'd be no more sleep for him tonight.

CHAPTER TWO

LAINEY WALKED INTO Frank's Grocery after closing the shop and pulled out her mental shopping list. Nothing fancy. Just sauce, pasta, shrimp, some good cheese. If she had more energy she'd make the sauce from scratch, but not tonight. So far the hardest thing about being pregnant was being so tired at the end of the day. She grabbed a basket from the stack and headed for the first aisle.

She came to a dead stop when she spotted the tall, dark-haired man frowning at the pasta sauce display.

Oh, no. Ben Lawless.

She didn't want to chat with Rose's grumpy grandson. He'd made it pretty clear he wasn't interested in being friendly. Since he stood smack in front of the sauce she needed, though, she'd have to talk to him.

He glanced up as she approached. For a heartbeat she found herself caught by those amazing light green eyes, by the grief she saw searing through them.

What the heck? She cleared her throat. "How are you?"

He tipped his head in her direction, his expression now neutral. "Fine, thanks."

His uninterest couldn't have been clearer, though his tone was perfectly polite.

"I just need to get in here." She pointed to the shelves in front of him. He stepped back, hindered by a woman and cart behind him, and Lainey slipped in, bumping him in the process. A little shiver of heat ran through her. "Sorry," she muttered, and grabbed the jar with fingers that threatened to turn to butter.

She managed to wiggle back out, brushing him again, thanks to the oblivious woman behind him who kept him penned between them. She plopped the sauce into her basket and offered what she hoped passed for a smile. "Um, thanks."

"No problem," he murmured.

She turned around and hurried out of the aisle, unsettled by both the physical contact and his apparent loss. So Ben had a few secrets. That flash of grief, deep and wrenching, hit her again.

Rose had never mentioned anything. Then again, why would she? She'd respect her grandson's privacy. It was one of the things Lainey loved about her friend.

It only took a few more minutes to gather the rest of the ingredients. Her path didn't cross Ben's again, and she unloaded her few purchases at the checkout with relief.

Outside, she took a big breath of the cool night air, and some of the tension knotted inside her eased. Fall was her favorite time of year. A mom and small daughter examined a display of pumpkins outside Frank's and her thoughts shifted back to her baby. Next year she'd be carving a pumpkin for her five-month-old. Oh, sure, he or she would be too small to appreciate it, but despite the precariousness of her position the idea gave her a little thrill.

She deposited the bags in the trunk and slipped into the driver's seat to start the car.

Click. Then nothing.

Oh, no. Maybe if she tried it again....

Click.

She leaned forward, rested her head on the steering

wheel, and fought the urge to scream. Not owning any
jumper cables, she'd have to go back into Frank's and find
someone who did. While she was at it she'd hope like crazy
the problem was simply a dead battery, and not something expensive. She yanked the keys out of the ignition,
grabbed her purse and got out of the car. One thing was
for sure—she'd push the stupid car home before she'd ask
her parents for help.

She nearly collided with Ben coming out of the store.

"Whoa," he said, checking his cart before he ran her
down.

Before she could think, she blurted, "Can you help me?"
Her face heated as he stared at her. "Ah, never mind. I'll
find…" She gestured vaguely behind him but he shook
his head.

"What do you need?"

"My car won't start. I think the battery's dead. The
dome light's been staying on longer than it should and it
didn't go off at all this time. I don't have any jumper cables." Realizing she was babbling, she clamped her mouth
shut.

He nodded. "Where are you parked?"

She pointed. "There. The silver one." Which he no doubt
already knew, since he'd seen her in it the other night. "The
space in front of me is open."

"Okay. Give me a minute. I'll pull around."

He walked off and she stared after him. *Shoot.* Why
hadn't she found someone else? On the other hand, the
whole process wouldn't take very long. Then she could
be on her way back home to fix her dinner and curl up
in her bed.

The wind picked up, skittering dry leaves across the
parking lot, and she tucked her hands under her arms
to keep warm as she went back to her car. She propped

the hood open as a big black truck rumbled into the empty spot.

Ben got out, cables already in hand, and went to work on her battery. Even though she knew how to hook them up—her mother would be appalled—she let him do it, because it was easier than having his carefully bland gaze on her.

He glanced up. "Do you know how to do this?"

Something in his tone made her bristle. She lifted her chin just a bit. "Actually, I do. I can even change a tire."

His mouth twitched in what could have been a prequel to a smile. "Good for you."

Before she could reply, a voice shrilled nearby. "Lainey? Lainey Keeler, is that you?"

Ben returned to the battery and the fragile moment was shattered. Lainey internally groaned as she turned to see Martha Turner, one of her mother's best friends, hurrying toward her.

"Hi, Mrs. Turner."

"Goodness, what are you doing?" The woman peeked around Lainey and frowned. "Do your parents know you have car trouble? I just left your mother at the Club. Have you called her yet? I'll never understand why you traded in that cute little coupe your husband bought you for—for this." She fluttered her hands at the car.

Not offended, Lainey bit back a laugh. She had to be the only person who'd ever traded in a new car for a used one. "Of course I didn't bother either of them, Mrs. Turner. It's really not a big deal. Just a dead battery."

Behind her, Ben cleared his throat. "Sorry to interrupt, but I need to start the truck now. It's loud."

"Okay." She gave Mrs. Turner an apologetic smile. "It was nice to see you."

Mrs. Turner's gaze went to Ben, reaching into the cab of the truck, then back to Lainey. "You too, dear. Take care."

Lainey could almost see the wheels turning in the other woman's head and imagined her mother would get a phone call before Mrs. Turner even made it inside Frank's. She sighed. She'd get her own call in a matter of minutes after that, and spend a half an hour calming her mother all over nothing.

So much for a relaxing evening.

Ben came back around and stood, hands in pockets, staring at her engine. Finally he lifted his gaze. "What did you trade in?"

Not exactly sure how to interpret his tone, she spoke carefully. "A Mercedes. After my divorce."

She didn't mention the sleek little car had been a bribe—an attempt to keep her in the marriage. Getting rid of it had been a victory of sorts. One of the very few she'd managed.

She caught a glimmer of amusement in his eyes. "That's funny?"

He rocked back on his heels. "Not the divorce. The car. I wouldn't think—" He stopped and she frowned.

"Think what?"

He looked at her, amusement gone, and seemed actually to see straight into her. The full effect of his gaze caused a funny little hitch in her breath. "I think you can start the engine now," he said, and she swallowed a surge of disappointment.

Which was crazy. She didn't care what he thought of her.

She slid into the car and tried not to notice when he braced one arm on the roof of the car and the other on the top of the door. When he leaned down she got a tantalizing glimpse of the smooth, hard muscles of his chest through the gap in his partially unbuttoned shirt.

Her mouth went dry.

"Go ahead and see if it'll start."

His voice slid over her skin and she gave a little shiver. She caught a whiff of his scent—a yummy combination of soap and spice. A little curl of heat slipped through her belly. She reached for the ignition and hoped he didn't notice her shaking hand. The engine turned over on the first try.

"You should be all set now," he said, straightening up. "Drive it around a bit to let the battery charge up."

"I will. Thank you," she said, and meant it. "I appreciate it."

He shrugged and stepped back. "No problem. I'd have done it for anyone."

Her little hormonal buzz evaporated. Of course he would. After all, she'd practically attacked him when he came out of the store.

"Well, see you around," she said, and he gave her a nod and then disappeared around the front of her car.

She sat for a moment, waiting for him to unhook the cables, and gave herself a reality check. She was two months pregnant. Being attracted to a man right now couldn't be more foolish—and she'd learned the hard way what a poor judge of men she was. She'd paid dearly for that mistake. Her focus was her shop, her baby, and making her life work without her parents hovering over her, waiting for her to fail.

Clearly these pregnancy hormones threw her off balance.

The hood of the car dropped with a thud and the sudden glare of headlights made her blink. With a little wave, in case he could see, she put her car in gear and backed out of her spot, then drove the long way through town back to her apartment. Ben stayed a respectable distance behind, but the thoughtful gesture gave her an unwelcome frisson of warmth.

Under his gruff exterior, Ben Lawless was a gentleman. Somehow that made him more dangerous.

Lainey let herself in to her apartment, not allowing herself to glance after Ben's truck as he drove on by. Her phone rang. She dug it out of her bag and checked the display. Ah, here was the call she'd been dreading.

"Hi, Mother," she said into the phone, as a purring Panda wound between her feet.

"Hi, dear," Jacqui Keeler trilled. "I'm almost there. Let me in, love."

That hadn't taken long. Mrs. Turner must have really run up the alarm if she was getting a visit, too. Lainey dumped her bags on the counter with a little more force than necessary. "Here? Why?"

"Can't I simply visit with my daughter?"

Oh, if only. "Of course, Mother. I'll be down in a sec."

She dropped the phone back in her purse and glanced around her cozy space. Her apartment was neat, for all the good it did. It would never meet her mother's standards, no matter what. She'd learned that years ago.

She hurried down the front stairs to unlock the street-level door just as her mother walked up.

"Lainey." Jacqui kissed her cheek, her usual cloud of sweet perfume tickling Lainey's nose. "You look tired."

She bit back a laugh. If her mother only knew. "Thanks," she said dryly as the trim older woman swept past her up the stairs. Jacqui, as always, was impeccably groomed. She wore a pale pink suit and her smooth blond hair swung smartly at her chin. Lainey ran her hand down her pony-tail and tried not to feel inferior in her non-branded jeans and tee shirt.

Damn it. She'd given that life up. But, oh, sometimes she did miss designer clothes.

"Have a meeting tonight, Mother?"

"I did." Jacqui tucked her monster-sized bag securely under her arm, as if she expected to be robbed right there on the stairs. "For the Auxiliary at the hospital. The gala."

No surprise there. For all their differences, Lainey still admired her mother's energy. "When is it?"

"Two weeks. Don't forget you are expected to be there."

Right. Just what she wanted. "Who did the floral arrangements?"

"Gail, of course. She does a lovely job."

Implying that The Lily Pad didn't. Disappointment clogged her vision for a moment. Lainey opened her mouth, snapped it closed. Frustration rushed through her. She'd never get through to her mother until the woman took her seriously. When would that be? What would it take?

"You really should move back home, honey," Jacqui said, her gaze drifting around the living room. "We have plenty of space. You could have your old room back. We'd love to have you."

Lainey stifled a sigh. More like they'd love to micro-manage her life into one that met their standards. Been there, tried that, failed spectacularly.

"I know you would. I'm very happy here, though." Lainey saw her mother's hand twitch, as it did when she was stressed. "Can I get you something to drink?"

"No, thank you." Jacqui perched on the edge of the sofa, the monster bag set primly on her lap, and Lainey sank down on a nearby chair. "Now, I received a disturbing phone call from Martha this evening. You had car trouble? Why didn't you call?"

Lainey smoothed her hand on her jeans. "It was nothing. Really. A dead battery. Not worth bothering you over. Rose's grandson Ben helped me out."

Jacqui's tone turned chilly. "Yes, Martha said you were with a man."

Lainey nearly choked. "Standing in a parking lot while someone was kind enough to jump my battery is hardly being with a man." Though she'd certainly had visions of another kind of jumping, but those were best kept to herself.

"If you'd kept the car your husband bought you—"

"Ex-husband," Lainey said through clenched teeth.

Unperturbed, Jacqui continued on. "If you'd kept the car, and the husband, you wouldn't need strange men to help you in the parking lot. Men who may have less than honorable intentions toward you."

Lainey tried to count to ten and gave up at three. "Excuse me? How does being nice equal intentions of any kind?"

Jacqui glared at her. "Do I need to spell it out for you? Your father's political connections are extremely valuable. Some people will use you for them. You don't always have the best judgment, Lainey."

Ouch. Direct hit. "Like Daniel did?" Lainey shot back. "You weren't concerned then, about my judgment *or* my connections, since he came from the right family. I can't see what need Ben Lawless would have for political connections, or how he thinks he'd get them when we only had ten minutes together."

"Martha said you looked awful cozy."

"Martha was wrong," Lainey said flatly. "Trust me, Mother. Please."

Jacqui made a noise in her throat. "I talked to Daniel earlier."

Betrayal sliced through her, sharp and quick. "What?"

Jacqui sent Lainey a look full of reproach. "He said you never call him. Why ever not, Lainey? He's a good man."

Lainey sucked in a breath. She'd worked so hard to get free of her ex-husband. "I can't think of any reason I'd ever have to call him." Not even if hell froze over. Twice.

Her mother looked at her as if she were a bit daft. "He misses you, dear."

Not a chance. She knew Daniel. Her ex-husband missed the perceived gravy train.

Lainey had never filled her family in on all the reasons behind her divorce. She'd been afraid they would take his side—a fear only reinforced as she looked at her mother now. Her parents adored Daniel. She'd dated him in an effort to be the daughter they wanted. They'd been over the moon when she'd succumbed in a weak moment, perhaps blinded by the three-carat princess-cut ring, and agreed to marry him. She'd thought she could make it work and earn her parents' respect in one fell swoop.

She'd been wrong.

"Why would he miss me now? We've been divorced more than a year," she said, and wasn't totally successful at keeping the bitterness out of her voice. Jacqui didn't seem to notice.

"I gave him your cell phone number and I've got his for you," she said, fishing in her bag. "He said he'd give you a call."

Anger propelled Lainey to her feet. "What? Mother, how *could* you? I don't want to talk to him. Ever. My life is none of his business now." He'd never cared when they were married. Why would he now?

Surprise crossed her mother's face. "Lainey, you were married for seven years. Those feelings don't just go away. He can help you out of this mess you're in. You're barely hanging on. Everyone knows it. You need his help."

Nausea rolled over Lainey. There lay the crux of the matter for Jacqui—the possibility of another public shaming by her wayward daughter and the offer of salvation by a man deemed worthy, no matter the cost.

"I most certainly do not." Telling her parents the truth of her marriage to Daniel would only prove how good she was at failing. "I don't need him or anyone else to make this work. I'm doing perfectly fine on my own." Well, except for the fact her shop was in the red and she had a cooler and a van on the fritz. Oh, and she was about to become a single mom. Still… "I'm happy, Mother."

Jacqui sighed, shook her head, and gestured around the apartment. "Oh, honey. You can't possibly be happy living like this, after how you were raised and how well you married. Talk to him when he calls. Maybe you'll get lucky and he'll give you a second chance."

Lainey shuddered. God help her. "I'm not interested." Those years she'd spent with Daniel were ones she'd never get back. She wasn't going to repeat the mistake of chaining herself to a man. No matter what.

"You should be." Jacqui glanced at her watch. "I'd better get going. Lovely to see you, dear. Come visit us soon."

Lainey bit back a sigh. Typical. Her mother would act as if nothing had happened. "I'll walk you out."

The next evening Ben looked up at the crunch of tires on the gravel drive. He recognized the silver car, and he already knew Lainey Keeler was coming over to visit his grandmother.

He wondered again at her modest choice of car. Somehow that intrigued him. He'd bet there was more to that story than she'd let on.

It would be flat-out rude not to make sure the car was running okay after he'd helped her yesterday. He'd be polite, then get back to his prep for the wheelchair ramp. He leaned the piece of wood he'd been about to cut against the wall and walked out into the twilight.

As he approached the car the door opened and he watched as Lainey planted one slim denim-clad leg, ending in a high-heeled black boot, on the ground. He tried not to notice how long that leg was. She appeared to be struggling with something so he went over to help.

"Evening," he said. She jumped, yelped, and nearly lost her grip on what he could now see was a pizza box. Big blue eyes swung his way and a pretty pink stained her cheeks. Her lips parted slightly and his gaze zeroed in on her mouth. *Very nice.* He shoved the unwelcome thought away. "Can I get that for you?"

She shook her head and her long hair shifted silkily on her shoulders. "I've got it. Thanks."

He stepped back to let her exit the car. "Is it running okay?"

She glanced up at him. "Yes. Thank you again." Her tone was cool, polite. She bumped the door shut with her hip, but her keys fell to the ground. Ben bent and retrieved them for her, pressing them into her palm. A quick zing of heat flashed through him at the contact. He pulled back quickly. *Hell.*

"Um, thanks," she murmured.

"You're welcome." He turned toward the garage. He needed to get away from her before he started to *feel*.

"Ben." Her voice—hesitant, a little husky—flowed over him. He turned back and she tipped the pizza box slightly toward him. "There's plenty here if you want to join us."

"No, thanks." The words came swift, automatic, but he caught a flash of hurt in her eyes. *Damn it.* "I'm in the middle of a project," he amended. "I'll try and grab some in awhile." Why did he feel the need to soften the blow? Since when had big blue eyes affected him? Since last night, when she'd narrowed her eyes and told him she could change a tire.

She shrugged. "Good luck. Rose and I love our pizza."

He slid his hands in his front pockets. "I'll keep that in mind."

She turned to go and he couldn't tear his gaze off the sway of her hips as she walked up to the house.

Double hell. He couldn't risk forging any type of connection. No way would he allow himself the luxury. How could he, when he shouldn't be the one alive?

Turning, he headed back to his project, tried to ignore the feminine laughter floating through the kitchen's screen door. Lainey's throaty laugh carried, teasing at the edge of something he'd shut down after Jason's death.

His phone rang before he could start the saw. A glance at the display revealed the caller to be his boss. Nerves jolted through him, but he kept his voice steady as he answered.

"Hi, Captain."

"Ben." The concern in the older man's voice carried clearly and Ben shut his eyes against the guilt it stirred up. "How are you, son?"

"I'm getting by," he replied.

"Just getting by?"

"Pretty much." Ben paused. He didn't need to paint a rosy picture for his boss. He'd already been ordered to take leave due to the stress of Jason's death. It couldn't really get any worse than that.

"Still having the symptoms, I take it." Not a question.

"Yeah." When the dream stopped, would he be free of the pain? Did he want to be? Wouldn't that be disloyal to the friend he'd loved like a brother?

After all, Ben was alive. Jason wasn't.

The Captain sighed. "It won't do any good for me to tell you again that it was an accident and not your fault, right?"

"With all due respect, sir, you're wrong." The words caught in Ben's throat. "It was my call. I made a bad one, and a good man—a family man—died because of me."

"That's not what the investigation found," the Captain reminded him softly.

It didn't matter. The investigators hadn't been there—in the inferno, in the moment. "I don't give a damn." Ben shut his eyes against the waves of guilt and pain that buffeted his soul, tried not to see Callie's grief-ravaged face. "I know what happened."

"Ben—"

"Please, don't."

There was a pause, then another sigh. "Then I won't. This time. Son, when you heal, come back and see us. There will always be room for fine firefighters such as yourself and I'd be honored to have you."

Heal. Ben swallowed a lump in his throat. He didn't know if it was possible. "Thank you, sir. I'll keep it in mind."

He disconnected the call and the emptiness he'd been battling for the past six months constricted his chest. He could never work as a firefighter again. He no longer trusted his judgment, his ability to read a situation and respond appropriately.

Without those skills he was nothing.

"Ben?"

He looked up sharply, feeling exposed. Lainey stood in the open door with a plate, uncertainty on her beautiful face. He cursed silently. How much had she overheard?

"Rose thought you might be hungry." She lifted the plate slightly.

He rubbed his hand over his face, afraid the rawness of

his emotions showed too clearly. He needed to get them back under control—fast. "Thanks." He shoved the phone in his pocket and walked over, not wanting to look at her and see pity. Or disgust. He'd seen plenty of both over the past couple of months. She handed him the plate wordlessly, then laid her hand on his forearm before he could move away.

His muscles turned to stone even as the heat from her simple touch sought the frozen place inside him. His gaze landed on hers, despite his best intent. He saw no pity, only questions, and he couldn't take the chance of her asking them. Not now, with everything so close to the surface.

He cleared his throat and she stepped back quickly, taking her warmth with her when she removed her hand. It was a much sharper loss than he'd like. "Thanks for the pizza."

"Sure." She hesitated and he held his breath, afraid she'd ask. Perversely, he was almost afraid she wouldn't. She gave him a small smile. "Eat it before it gets cold."

Then she turned and walked into the night before he could tell her how very familiar he was with cold.

And what a lonely place it was.

CHAPTER THREE

AN IMPERIAL SUMMONS was never a good thing.

Lainey had long thought of her mother's invitations to dinner as such a summons—and more often than not they included some well-meaning but completely off-base idea of her parents' to "improve her life."

She'd met her ex at such a dinner. And apparently she was the only one who saw it for the farce it had turned out to be.

Now, if Daniel had been a man like Ben maybe things would have been different. The thought wasn't as shocking as it might have been, considering she'd been unable to get Ben and the haunted look on his face out of her mind for the past two days. She hadn't overheard enough of his conversation to find out what was eating him alive, but she'd heard the pain layering his voice, each word laced with more than the last.

Still, Ben struck her as a fundamentally honorable man, not one who would marry for money without dumping his long-time girlfriend first. Like, say, her ex-husband. The good thing was her heart hadn't been involved—but her pride and self-worth had taken a beating.

Lainey sighed and turned through the thick stone columns into her parents' driveway. Since her parents were expecting her, the black iron gate stood open. She wound her way up the drive and parked in front of the massive log house that managed to be both rustic and majestic.

Lainey turned the car off and got out. On the plus side Grace, the cook, always put together fabulous meals, so she'd make sure she enjoyed that even while avoiding the bombs that were likely to be lobbed over the table. The front door opened even before she made it all the way up the carefully landscaped walkway.

"Lainey!" her father greeted her in his big voice.

"Hi, Dad." She allowed herself to be drawn into a hug. Tall and trim, Greg Keeler cut a handsome picture with his dark, youthful looks, a perfect foil to Jacqui's petite blond paleness. Even in their late fifties, they looked every inch the power couple they'd been for as long as she could remember.

"Come on in. We're in the family room."

He turned and Lainey followed him into the large room off the foyer, with its high ceilings, thick carpet and fire-place. While the outside screamed North Woods, inside the only concession to the house's rustic roots were the thick beams soaring overhead.

Lainey walked across the luxurious carpet, its velvety pile the color of cream, with nary a stain in sight. She tried to picture a baby crawling around in here and failed. Nothing about this room said *family*—even with the pro-fessionally shot family photos on the mantel. She vowed to make sure she raised her baby in an environment that was warm and welcoming, not precious and impersonal.

Her mother perched on the edge of a chair near the fire. A manila folder lay on an end table next to her.

"Hello, dear." Jacqui rose and offered her cheek to Lainey, who came around the end of the sofa to place the obligatory kiss.

"Hi, Mother."

"Have a seat." Her dad gestured toward the sofa and turned to the mini-wet-bar. "Can I get you anything to drink?"

Well, no. I'm pregnant. She swallowed the words. That would get this little pow-wow off to a roaring start. In fact it might create stains on the carpet from dropped or flying liquor. "No, thanks."

He raised an eyebrow but said nothing as he mixed his drink quickly and took the seat opposite Jacqui.

Lainey flicked her gaze between both of them. There was no reading her parents. Whatever they'd done, they wouldn't be smug, since they'd consider it a necessary move. She might as well get it over with. "What's going on?"

Jacqui frowned a little. "Wouldn't you rather eat first? Grace has a lovely roast chicken prepared."

Lainey's shoulders tensed at the deflection. "I'd like to know what's going on." She looked at her father but his expression was unreadable. "Dad? Please?"

He down set his drink—a screwdriver, no doubt. "Might as well cut to the chase. Lainey, we want to help you."

Oh, no. Her stomach lurched. She threaded her fingers together in her lap to keep from shaking. She kept her tone measured. "Help me how?"

"With your little shop, honey." Jacqui reached for the folder and the hairs went up on the back of Lainey's neck.

"My little shop? What have you done, Mother? Dad?" She heard the note of panic in her voice. She'd been safe, had rented the business from Esther Browning, what could they possibly—?

Jacqui beamed. "We thought you'd be pleased to know we bought your building."

The room tilted a little and Lainey gripped the arm of the chair, struggling to focus on her mother's clueless face. She couldn't have heard correctly. "I'm sorry—what? Why?"

"You're having such a hard time getting this going, and Esther was worried about making ends meet. You know she needs the rent to live on, dear."

My parents are now my landlords. The realization swept through her, followed closely by rage. "I've never paid late. Not one single payment." She bit off each word. If nothing else, she prided herself on that. She knew her elderly landlord depended on that income, and made absolutely sure those payments went out on time.

Her father cut in. "Of course not. But there's reason to believe you might have a hard time making them, so we thought this would help both of you out."

Lainey sucked in a breath. Poor Esther. The prospect of having the building all paid for, most likely in cash, must have been powerful. She'd done what was best for her, and Lainey refused to fault her for that.

Keeping her voice even, she asked, "But you didn't think maybe you should ask me? See how I'm doing?" Of course the documents would have been anything but reassuring, but still… Betrayal rose in her throat, the taste bitter, and she swallowed hard. Why was it too much for them to think to include her in the decision making?

Jacqui looked surprised. Or would have if the Botox hadn't been working so well. "Well, we already know how you're doing. The whole town does. We've got your best interests at heart, dear. Always."

Lainey shut her eyes. How often had she heard that little line? When would it actually prove to be true? "How exactly does this help me?" She braced herself for the kicker.

"Well, you won't have the monthly payment anymore. We won't make you pay rent. And you can live here now. We'll rent out that little apartment." Her mother sounded pleased, as if she'd truly solved a problem. Her father nodded in agreement as they exchanged a look.

She sucked in a sharp breath. "No. I can't live here." *How am I supposed to puke in private every morning? Hide my rounding belly? Raise my child here?* Panic seized her and she jumped up as her father's phone rang. He checked it, and rose.

"I've got to run. Lainey, we'll talk more later. But for now we feel this is the best thing for you."

He kissed her cheek and strode out of the room. Lainey stared after him, floored because both of her parents seemed to think this was a done deal and hadn't bothered to truly consider *her*. "Why did no one ask me? Has no one noticed I'm an adult? I'm not moving back home." Where she'd go, she didn't know. But it wouldn't be here.

Jacqui set her snifter on the table. "Of course you are, dear. That little place isn't good for you. We've got plenty of room. We can remodel your suite if you'd like. Daniel agrees you should be here."

Lainey whipped around so fast she nearly got dizzy. "He has no say in my life. None. We're divorced, remember?"

Jacqui leaned forward, her gaze earnest. "You were wrong, Lainey. He loves you and he's willing to give you a second chance. What is so bad about that? Now you don't have to struggle anymore. We've taken care of it."

Lainey stared back. Her mother really believed it. She could see the sincerity in the other woman's gaze, hear it in her voice. They didn't understand it was Lainey's problem and she wanted to be the one to solve it—or not. That had been the whole point of taking over the shop—to make it work by herself. Now the choice was gone.

She lifted her chin and met her mother's expectant gaze. "I'm not coming home." Each word came out crystal-clear and Jacqui's eyes widened. "I'm happy where I am. I love my job, my shop. My apartment. I'm not going to give it up, give you control of my life, because you can't accept I'm an adult and haven't chosen the path or the man you wanted for me."

Jacqui frowned. "Lainey, please be reasonable. You needed help. We gave it to you."

"Yes, but at what cost to *me*?" Despair rose and Lainey fought it back, preferring anger. There was really only one option here, since she wasn't going to walk away from the shop she loved. "What do I have to do to get it back?"

Jacqui sat back. "Pardon?"

"I want it back," she repeated. "I'll buy the building flat out from you. And you'll have to completely butt out of my life."

Jacqui frowned, as if this wasn't going the way she'd planned. "I don't think—"

Lainey stood up, the words she should have said years ago boiling out of her. "I'm not letting you force me into this. And there's no hope for Daniel. You have no idea what my marriage was like. *None*. I'd hope you'd want better for me, even if it's not what you would have chosen." She picked up her purse with shaking hands. "I'm going, Mother. I'll find somewhere else to live. And don't worry. I will make those rent payments on my shop. They will be on time. I'm never late."

Pulse roaring in her ears, she walked away before Jacqui could say anything else.

The nerve. Lainey pulled over a couple of miles past the house and sat for a minute, tears of rage pouring down her face. *The nerve.*

Poor Esther. Lainey hoped they'd at least given the woman a fair price. But while apparently not above blackmail, her parents weren't cheats. One small thing in this whole mess to take comfort in.

What she needed was a plan. One that could get her the money, and the time, to solve this herself—which was all she wanted. Just to prove she could do it—run a business, be successful on her own terms without any help from her family.

To show them she wasn't a screw-up, but just as worthy of being a Keeler as they were.

She fished a napkin out of the glove box and wiped her face. Crying wasn't going to solve anything. She put the car back in gear and headed for the public park at the lake. She'd spent many hours here as a kid, and later as a teen when she'd needed space. Sure, there was a private beach at her parents' home, but the park had swings and a playground, now upgraded to a fancy plastic playscape. They'd kept the old metal merry-go-round, her favorite thing in the park.

The gathering twilight and chilly breeze off the water ensured the park itself was empty, though a couple cars parked nearby indicated joggers still out on the loop that ran next to the water.

Lainey pulled the hood of her jacket up and settled on a swing. She scuffed her feet in the wood chips, then backed up, ready to swing. Back and forth she went, pumping her legs, stretching out in the swing until her hood slid off and her hair fell in her face when she leaned forward. The moon hung over the quiet lake, full and incandescent, a bright star to its left. *Star light, star bright, first star I see tonight.* A small laugh escaped her, followed by more tears. She'd gone way beyond childish wishes, even if as a kid she'd believed in the power of the first star. The tensions of her parents' betrayal slid away in the stinging wind, into the encroaching darkness. Finally she stopped pumping, let herself glide through the cool evening air, slowly coming to a stop.

A motion to her left caught her eye and she turned her head.

Ben Lawless sat on the merry-go-round, watching her. Her belly clutched. Oh, no. What was he doing here?

"Did it work?" Despite his low tone, she heard him clearly.

Caught, Lainey forced herself to meet his gaze. "Did what work?"

"The swinging. The tears. You looked like you were trying to get rid of something."

She tilted her head so it rested on the chain. No point in denying it. She didn't want to. "For the moment, maybe." Though the ache under her heart hadn't gone away.

Her parents had bought her building. She squeezed her eyes shut as another wave of betrayal washed over her. How had she not seen it coming?

When she looked back over at Ben he stood up from the merry-go-round, gave it a small shove with his hand. It wobbled in a slow circle. "For the moment?"

Lainey scuffed her foot in the wood chips. Was that an opening for her to talk, no matter how reluctantly issued? She almost laughed. Where would she start? With her parents? With her baby? With her ex-husband? With the father of said baby? "I don't know. Can we not talk about it?" The very thought of trying to explain the twisted mess her life had become exhausted her.

Ben laughed—a quick deep flash that sent tingles though her body. "As long as we don't talk about me."

His grief-stricken face flashed across her memory. "Deal." She hopped out of the swing and her balance shifted a bit. No doubt an effect of her pregnancy. She started toward the water, simply needing to move.

She was surprised when Ben caught up to her. He walked beside her, his arm almost brushing hers. Even without the contact she could feel the heat from his big body as hers seemed to be *way* too tuned in to him.

This was bad.

Distracted, she stumbled a bit on the uneven sand. He caught her arm—pure reflex, she was sure—especially because he let go of her almost as soon as he touched her, as though she'd burned him somehow.

"Careful," he said, his voice low.

"Thanks," she murmured, keeping her eyes on the ground. His scent, a yummy mix of soap and fresh air, drifted over to her. She curled her fingers into fists and shoved them in her pockets so she didn't do something stupid—like reach for him and bury her face in his chest.

Even as the urge confused and scared her she knew Ben wouldn't lie to her, use her, or treat her like a wayward child. Even with his secrets, he came across as sincere in a way she so wanted to believe in.

Except she was done with believing.

They stopped when they reached the lake. The water was almost mirror-still. Perfect for skipping rocks. When was the last time she'd done that? The moon was bright enough that she could see pretty well, so she started to hunt for flat stones. She didn't look at Ben, but could feel him watching her.

Strangely, not talking felt right. She didn't feel she needed to fill the night with chatter—after the bombshell her parents had laid on her that was a good thing—and he seemed to be quiet because he was more comfortable without words.

She picked up a rock—a flat disk, smooth and cold in her hand. She lined up and let it fly over the still water, counting twelve skips. She couldn't resist a little fist pump. She still had it after all these years.

"Not bad." Ben fingered his own rock. "My turn."

"Good luck," she said politely. She'd always been a top-notch rock-skipper. One of her many under-appreciated talents. She couldn't smother a small sigh. No doubt her mother would be appalled.

His rock flew over the water. Thirteen skips.

"Hmm." Glad for the distraction, Lainey narrowed her eyes when he turned to her, eyebrow raised. "I can beat that."

A small laugh escaped him and he looked surprised at the sound. Her heart tugged. Had he really gone so long in sorrow he'd lost laughter?

He leaned toward her, not close enough to touch, but close enough to see the challenge in his eyes. "You're on."

His warm breath feathered over her cheek and her little shiver had nothing to do with the chill in the air. "Good luck," she said again. The words came out a little husky, and she turned away quickly to look for more rocks. What was wrong with her? What was it about Ben Lawless that drew her in? It was wrong on so many levels. She was pregnant, for God's sake. And her life was a mess. There was no room for a man. Especially one with issues of his own.

It took everything Ben had not to ask why she'd been crying. The tracks from her tears were dry now, but even in the light of the moon he could see her beautiful blue eyes were red-rimmed. An unwelcome protective surge caught him off-guard and left a sour feeling in his stomach.

He couldn't protect anyone. He knew that. But tonight he'd been drawn in by her obvious distress. Since she was a friend of his grandma's it had seemed wrong just to walk away until he knew she was okay.

Yeah, that was all it was. A favor to Grandma.

Riiiight...

Choosing to ignore his inner voice, he let his gaze follow her as she searched for rocks along the water's edge. The moon's light turned her hair to silver as she lifted potential candidates, weighed them in her hand, then discarded some and slipped others into her pockets. That unfamiliar smile tugged at his mouth. She took this seriously. He'd do the same.

He picked up a few rocks of his own and was ready when she came back. Determination sparked in her eyes. He swallowed hard. "You ready?" If she noticed the rasp in his voice she didn't show it.

"I'm ready. I'll go first."

She stepped forward to the edge of the water and Ben allowed himself to admire her slender figure as she let the rock fly and stood, as if she were holding her breath, until it sank, leaving an expanding ring of ripples on the water's surface.

"Ten skips."

"Not bad." He moved up next to her. "But let me show you how it's done."

He was rewarded with an eye-roll. He bit back another grin.

He took his turn and after nine skips she turned to him, her glee barely contained. "*That's* how it's done?"

In spite of himself he laughed again, the feeling foreign after so many months of not being able to. It felt—good. But scary, too. Here in the moonlight, with a beautiful woman who wanted nothing from him, playing a silly game, he was almost relaxed.

Back and forth they went, and after six stones each Ben sent her a look. "This is it. Winner takes all."

She arched a brow and pulled out her final stone. "Really? What does the winner get?"

"Bragging rights."

"Good enough." She pulled out her final stone and readied herself. She let it fly and Ben watched it, counting the skips until it sank.

"Fifteen skips." Triumph filled her voice. "Beat that, Ben."

He took his turn and they both watched as his rock sank after twelve. "You win."

She did another fist-pump. "Yay. I like to win." Then frowned. "No offense."

He shook his head. "None taken." He hesitated. "Better?"

She nodded, but he saw the shadow that fell over her features. "Yes. Thank you for staying."

He turned with her to walk back. "No problem. You're my grandma's friend."

There was the tiniest of hitches in her step. "Right. Of course."

He forced himself to ignore the hurt in her tone. He needed to build the distance between them back up. But when she turned those big blue eyes on him something long buried inside him cracked. "Lainey—"

She gave a little shake of her head as she reached her car. "Thanks again."

To hell with it.

Ben turned her around as she fumbled in her pocket for her keys. Her eyes widened and her lips parted, but before she could say anything he dipped his head and covered her mouth with his.

After a heartbeat her cold mouth opened and let him into her warmth. God, it had been so long since he'd felt anything, *anything*, and she was warm and soft and so, so sweet. He fisted his hand in her hair, to angle her head so he could go deeper, and her moan lit fires inside him that had long been dormant.

For a reason.

He broke the kiss and stepped back, his ragged breath catching in his chest. God, what had he done?

She blinked up at him, her gaze smoky and slightly confused. Then her eyes cleared and a look of pure horror crossed her face.

"I've got to go," she said, yanking her keys out of her pocket.

"Lainey, I'm sorry." As soon as the words were out he knew they were the wrong thing to say.

Her back stiffened as she unlocked the car. "It's forgotten." She got in the car and slammed the door.

He stood in the cold and cursed as her taillights disappeared out of the park. Hell. He'd just made a huge mess of something he had no right even to start.

And he had no idea how to fix it.

CHAPTER FOUR

"THEY DID WHAT?" Beth's words ended on a small shriek. The look on her face would have been comical if Lainey could muster the energy to laugh. "No way. Is that even legal?"

"Unfortunately," Lainey said as she selected a few silk 'mums for the centerpiece she was working on.

"They're kicking you out," Beth breathed. "I never thought—"

"It's not technically a kick out," Lainey corrected her. "It's a very strong suggestion I move in with them." And a heck of a way to do it, too. Though where in the budget she'd find the money to rent a place plus continue to pay her parents she didn't know.

How had it not occurred to her parents that their "helping" would put her in this kind of bind?

Beth frowned. "Are you going to? How would that work with the baby?"

A chill ran through Lainey. "I can't think of anything I want less than to live there. Especially since my mother is apparently in cahoots with Daniel. I'm going to ask Rose if she knows of any rental houses. I know she owns a couple."

Maybe she'd get lucky and one would be open. On the other hand, that would make Rose her landlord, and she wasn't sure she wanted to risk extra contact with Ben.

The kiss flashed through her mind and a delicious little shiver ran through her. It had been a mistake, which he'd acknowledged. She had to agree. But a small part of her was hurt. She'd spent much of her adult life being made to feel everything she did was a mistake. To hear it after something as sweet as that kiss, on top of her parents' antics, had cut deep.

"Wow." Beth shook her head and cut a length of ribbon. "I'm just floored."

"Yeah, me too." Lainey fitted the 'mums into the floral foam and stepped back. "These look nice. Let's get them in the window."

It took a nice chunk of time to redo the front windows with a fall theme geared toward Halloween. Lainey was pleased with the result. She glanced at the clock. Almost noon. "I need to call Jon and tell him."

Beth came around the counter. "Do you need me there?"

Lainey gave her friend a hug. "Thanks, but, no. I'll be fine. I just need to get it over with."

She climbed the stairs to her apartment with butterflies roiling in her stomach. She and Jon hadn't even bothered to exchange contact info. It had been pretty clear how forgettable the whole thing was—or would have been except for the baby.

Her hands shook as she sat down at the computer and pulled up the website she'd found for Jon's company. Since California was three hours behind Michigan it was early morning there, so she hoped she had a chance of catching him at his office.

It took two tries to dial the number correctly, but amazingly she got through. His assistant sounded about twenty and possessive, and Lainey bet Jon valued looks over work ethic. How could she have such poor judgment when it came to men?

"Jon Meier." His crisp voice sent a chill over her skin.

"It's Lainey Keeler. We—ah—met at the reunion." She stumbled a bit over the words. How exactly did one phrase *one-night stand* for polite company?

A pause. "Lainey. What's going on?" His tone was wary.

Lainey stared at the ceiling of her living room. It seemed there was only one thing to say and one way to say it. "I'm pregnant."

The silence roared in her ears. She gripped the small phone tighter.

"Jon?" she ventured after a few seconds.

"I'm here," he said, sounding slightly strangled. "Are you sure it's mine?"

Indignation spiked. "Of course it's yours. Who else's would it be?" Like she was some slut.

He said a clear and succinct curse word and Lainey winced.

"I'm sorry," he said, his voice low. "But there's something you should know."

Her heart kicked up in a pattern of dread. Those words never meant anything good. "What's that?"

She heard him exhale roughly. "I'm married."

Nausea hit Lainey like a freight train. Oh, God. *Married?* How had she not known? He was just like her ex-husband. Her stomach rolled and she sank down on the floor, hand pressed over her mouth. *Oh, no. No, no.*

"Lainey? Are you still there?"

I'm married. The words almost physically crawled over her skin. She'd played a role in the betrayal of a marriage. *What Daniel did to me.* "Oh, my God. How could you? You cheated on your wife." She couldn't keep the horror and disgust out of her voice.

There was a rustle of paper. "Well, in my admittedly weak defense, we were going through a rough patch. She doesn't—she doesn't know. I can't have her know. I can pay to take care of it, though, if you'd rather not have it."

It took her a second to sort through the numerous atrocities in those sentences. "Are you—are you offering to pay for an abortion?"

"You're what? Eight weeks? Early enough. Listen, Lainey—"

"No." The word came out furious and flat. Temper rose like bile in her throat, a sharp burn.

"I can't be a father to that baby, Lainey. My wife—she's pregnant, too. I can't risk—"

"Can't risk what? Her finding out what a slime you are?" She couldn't help the angry words. Not because she wanted him in her life, or the baby's, but because she'd given her child this kind of man for a father. The same kind of man her ex was. She pressed her hand over her eyes, willing the tears of anger and frustration away.

He let out a sigh. "Something like that. Listen, I haven't been the best husband, okay? I get that. But we are finally getting on the right track again. I can't—I just can't risk it."

Lainey sucked in a breath. The depth of his deception hit her hard. She couldn't get involved in his mess, though. She and her baby would stay above this.

She couldn't keep the disgust out of her voice. "I want you to sign off on all parental rights. I don't want you in my child's life."

"I'll talk to my lawyers," he said after a moment, and she allowed herself to breathe again. "I don't see how I could be involved even if I wanted to be. My wife…" His voice trailed off. Then, "I'm sorry, Lainey. I really am. But—you understand?"

Your poor wife. Lainey truly felt for her. She could see her own ex-husband pulling this exact same stunt. For all she knew he had. The thought made her even angrier.

"What I understand is you are a cheating, lying bastard. When will I hear from you?"

"End of the week," he said, apparently unfazed by her description of him. "I'll need your contact info. I'd prefer to communicate through email, if we need to discuss anything further."

"Fine with me." She gave him the relevant information and hung up, mind whirling. The sick feeling wouldn't recede. Most likely she'd get what she wanted, but at what cost? What could she tell her baby? The loss here was truly Jon's, but her baby deserved a father.

She dropped her face into her hands. Given her track record with men who seemed great on the surface but were total losers, she wasn't sure she could trust herself to know a good man when she met him. She pushed herself off the floor and went to get a glass of water.

Ben flashed across her mind. He was a good man. His kiss. His quiet playfulness last night. Even though it had seemed as if he was coming out of a deep shell, for that scant hour she'd spent with him he'd been more real than her husband or Jon had ever been. Maybe it was because he hadn't wanted anything from her. Maybe it had to do with the other two men being cheaters. Another wave of nausea flowed over her and she put her head back in her hands. She'd been with a married man. How had she not known? How could she know, with no ring and no mention of a wife?

She went back downstairs. A couple of months ago her life had been pretty simple. Keep her shop open and stay out of her parents' line of fire. Period. Now she was looking at single motherhood and her parents buying their way into her life and pulling her ex along—not to mention her odd connection to Ben.

Maybe one of these days she'd do something the easy way, instead of somehow making everything as difficult as possible.

* * *

Lainey called Rose that evening and at her friend's invitation went over to her house. She didn't want to see Ben, seeing as how the awkwardness level there would be epic, but she wasn't going to avoid her friend. Plus, being with someone who didn't want to manipulate her sounded wonderful.

She didn't see Ben's truck, which was both a relief and an unexpected disappointment. Ignoring the disappointment part, she saw he'd been busy. The framework for the ramp was already in place. It touched a little sweet spot in her that he took his grandma's issues so seriously.

Rose opened the kitchen door with a concerned look. "Hi, honey. Come on in. Everything okay?"

She stepped in with a smile. "Yes. Just a little tired." She didn't ask where Ben was as she slipped her jacket off. She told herself she didn't care. Not to mention it was very important that Rose did not realize Lainey's conflicted emotions regarding Ben. She didn't want any matchmaking attempts, and she doubted Ben would appreciate it, either. Possibly less than she did, if his aloof manner was any indication.

But, oh, the man could kiss.

"Dear, you look a little flushed. Are you sure you're okay?" Rose wheeled over to the table.

Her face heated even more. She couldn't very well tell the older woman she'd kissed her grandson, so she took a seat at the table and filled Rose in on her parents' bombshell.

Rose frowned when she'd finished. "I'm sorry, Lainey. I understand they mean well, or think they do, but they really don't take you into consideration, do they?"

Lainey stared at the table, a small knot in her throat. It was the truth. "Not really."

Rose reached over and squeezed her hand. "Well, as it happens I've got a little place you can rent." Her surprise must have shown on her face because Rose chuckled. "I do. I've got a little rental house over by the lake. The same couple has rented it for—oh, goodness—decades. Thirty years or so? Anyway, they moved out a couple weeks ago. Decided to retire in Florida."

Lainey opened her mouth, then closed it. Hope surged through her. "I—wow. Really?"

"Of course. Two bedrooms. Nice backyard. It's a little Cape Cod. Not real large, but plenty big for you and your cat."

Relief rushed through her. "It sounds wonderful."

Rose reached for the phone. "It needs a little work. Nothing major. Just some freshening up and some minor repairs. Why don't you go take a look? Ben's over there now, assessing what all needs to be done. He seemed to think it could be ready in around a week or so. You can even pick your paint colors."

Ben was there. Anticipation zipped through her, too quick for her to stifle. She didn't see a way to refuse without raising Rose's suspicions. "All right. I'd love to see it, if you're sure?"

Rose waved a hand. "Of course I'm sure. I can't think of anyone I'd like more to have for a tenant than you. Let me call him real quick and you can head over."

Lainey followed Rose's directions to the house, which was on the other side of the lake from her parents' place, a block from the water. The little white house was charming, from what she could see as she pulled in the driveway behind Ben's truck. It had a garage, a front porch, and the backyard was fenced. A little shiver of excitement ran though her.

"It's very cute," she said aloud as she walked up to the front porch. The light was on. She knocked, then stuck her head in. "Hello?"

She'd been hoping somehow that Ben wouldn't be here, or that someone else would be here, too. Anything but just the two of them. Not that she couldn't control herself—of course she could—it was just the last thing she needed was another complication in her life. As Ben appeared in the living room archway she couldn't help but wish all complications could be so hot.

"Lainey?" Ben said, looking behind her. "I'm sorry. Grandma said there was a potential tenant coming to check the place out."

In spite of her nerves, Lainey laughed. *Oh, Rose.* "It's me. I'm the tenant."

"You?" His brow shot up. "I thought you lived above your shop."

Lainey closed the door behind her and unzipped her jacket. She couldn't quite keep her voice steady. "Not for long."

She saw understanding dawn in his eyes, but all he said was, "I see."

Awareness sparked between them, hot and deep, and she knew while he didn't mention it he was thinking about *the kiss.* Lainey pulled her gaze off him and focused on the wall behind him. He looked so good, even with the wary expression he seemed to wear perpetually. Except the other night, when he'd actually laughed. And kissed her.

Darn it. She shut her eyes. *Not helpful.*

"You okay?"

She opened them again and gave him a small smile. "Peachy." She gestured with her hand. "Can I look around?"

Ben stepped back out of the doorway. "Sure. Kitchen—

dining room through there—" he pointed to his right "—bedrooms. Bathroom that way. I'll be in the kitchen if you need anything." Then he disappeared.

She took a minute to wander around the room she stood in—a good-sized living room, with two large windows and a fireplace, flanked by two smaller, higher windows over built-in bookcases. The former tenants' drapes remained, but otherwise the room was bare. The floor was hardwood, scuffed and worn and in need of being redone. She rubbed the toe of her shoe on it. How would a hard floor be with a baby? Maybe she could get some thick rugs. The paint color was an odd shade of pinkish tan, but maybe that was the light from the overhead fixture, which was a little harsh. Still, it had charm and lots of potential.

She walked across the floor and it creaked under her feet. She heard banging and swearing from the direction of the kitchen, so she detoured that way down the short hall.

Ben was on his knees, bent over, half in the cabinet under the sink, and her gaze locked on his very fine butt and flexed thigh muscles. The back of his shirt had ridden up, exposing an inch or so of an equally nice back. She blinked and forced herself to refocus.

"Is there a problem?" she asked.

He scrambled back out from the cabinet, whacked his head and muttered another choice word. She winced.

"Sorry," she said. "Are you okay?"

"Fine." He stood up and rubbed the back of his head. "Need something?"

"Um…no. I heard some noise and thought I'd see what was going on in here." She looked at the array of tools and wet towels on the floor. "Maybe you need a plumber?"

Ben stared at her, then let out a sharp bark of laughter. "What I need is another wrench." He bent over and she tried very hard to keep her eyes off his butt and failed. She very much wanted to chalk it up to pregnancy hormones, except for the little fact she wasn't attracted to any other man but this one. He pulled out two pieces of what had been a wrench and held them up.

"Oh. That's not good."

"No kidding. Are you parked behind me?"

He was going right now? The little stab she felt couldn't be disappointment. It had to be relief. "Yes. I'll move my car."

He turned away to wipe his hands on the towel lying on the counter. She glanced around the room, noting the old but serviceable appliances, the Formica counters that were a bit worn, the old linoleum on the floor. The cabinets were in good condition. It was a nice size. It would work well for her.

"Not what you're used to, I'm sure," Ben said and she blinked at him.

"What isn't?"

He swept his hand out, indicating the room. "This."

It took her a second, then anger spiked. "Oh, for God's sake. Why would you think that?"

He just looked at her and she shook her head, sadness chasing the anger away. Just because she'd been raised in a wealthy household it didn't mean those things mattered to her. "You don't know me. At all. I'd appreciate it if you'd keep your judgments to yourself. I'll go move my car to the street."

Ben shut his eyes as she stomped off. He'd achieved his goal, which had been to drive her away, but he felt no sense of victory. Only shame. She'd looked way too hot, standing there in her jeans, boots and sweatshirt, with her hair up in a ponytail. None of it was even particularly form-fitting, but it was enough. Worse, he'd wanted to touch her, to feel her hot, responsive mouth under his again. That was dangerous. *Wanting* was something he tried to keep a lid on, along with feeling. He saw her headlights flash across the wall as she backed out of the driveway.

Now he needed to apologize. Whatever had prompted last night's crying jag had brought her here today, and it wasn't right for him to make it harder for her just because he was attracted to her. Or to lose a tenant for his grandmother.

So he went into the living room and didn't back down under the cold glare she leveled at him when she came through the door. "I'm sorry. I was out of line."

She considered him, her blue eyes cool. Finally she nodded. "You were. But I accept your apology. Next time don't assume you know anything about me."

I know how you kiss, he wanted to tell her. *I know how you feel in my arms, how soft your skin is under my hand. I know how your breasts feel against me.*

She must have read his thoughts on his face because her gaze skittered off his and she jingled her keys in her hand. He cleared his throat, trying to bring his thoughts back around.

"Okay, then. I'm going to go. If you leave before I get back you can lock the door behind you. Also, if you're considering renting this place, start thinking of paint colors. The sooner you can get them to me, the better. I can get started as soon as I finish a few repairs."

She nodded. "I will. I like it. So far I think it'll suit us just fine."

"Let me know." As he escaped out into the night, he wondered, *Who's us?*

CHAPTER FIVE

LAINEY SHUDDERED OUT a deep breath when the door closed behind him. There had been no mistaking the look on his face when she'd said he didn't know her. Odd that he could know her a little physically but not at all as a person.

It seemed to be a pattern. Her ex-husband had never attempted to really get to know her. He'd had his secretary take care of gifts and things. She'd allowed herself to pretend it was because he was busy, but she knew it had been because he'd never cared enough to find out.

Lesson learned.

She shoved all the thoughts away and walked down the hall to the bedrooms. Two of them, both of which were bigger than her bedroom at the apartment, plus a decent-sized bathroom. Another door led to an open and clean attic.

She went back to the kitchen, where she found a small pantry, an entryway by the back door with hooks for coats, and stairs to the basement. A quick scout revealed it to be clean and apparently dry, and she found the laundry hookups. At some point the space might make a good play area, if there was a way to cover the cement with carpet.

Back upstairs, she mused over paint colors as she went back to the bedrooms. She hadn't decided yet if she wanted to know if she was having a boy or a girl. Then she frowned. Either way, probably better to go neutral. That way she could forestall any questions for longer.

With a groan, she rested her head on the doorjamb. It wouldn't matter. Her little secret would out itself in a matter of weeks. Her pants were already feeling a little snug, and she had taken to wearing slightly baggy tops to cover up.

That wouldn't work much longer.

Her phone rang and she fished it out of her pocket. Seeing Rose's number, she answered.

"What do you think?" There was excitement in Rose's voice and Lainey had to smile.

"I love it."

"I knew it." The smugness in her friend's tone made Lainey laugh. "Come on back tomorrow and we'll sign a lease."

Lainey hesitated. "How much are you asking?" She'd told her parents she'd make rent payments anyway, and to add house rent on top of it would seriously stretch her already tight budget even more.

Rose named an amount that Lainey knew had to be way low, considering the size of the house and the location. "Rose, are you sure? That's not much."

"The house is paid for," her friend said, then added impishly, "And don't you dare argue with your elders."

Lainey laughed and flicked the light switch off in what would be the baby's room. "Well, when you put it like that…"

"You can help do some of the work if you want," Rose said. "Painting and such."

"Sure," Lainey said. How would that work with being pregnant? She'd have to make sure it was safe before she cracked open a paint can.

They talked a few more minutes, then Lainey hung up.

She locked the door behind her after one last look around. She would make a home here, for herself and her baby. But to get it she'd have to work with Ben.

Ignoring the little thrill that gave her, she started her car. She needed to remember Ben would leave. She was going to be a single mother. He was clearly struggling with some kind of issues of his own. None of that held hope for any kind of relationship.

And the very fact she'd even thought the word *relationship* in regard to Ben was troubling.

"So, I've found a place to live," Lainey told Beth as she carefully unpacked the latest shipment of flowers the next morning.

"Really? That was fast."

"Yep. It was perfect timing. Rose has an empty rental house."

Beth snipped the ends off a handful of lilies before plunging them in the water bucket. "Hmm. Will this put you in contact with her very appealing grandson?"

Lainey's face heated. Of course Beth *would* make that connection. "I wouldn't call him appealing," she hedged. *Liar.* "She wants me to help with the cleaning and painting and stuff. Which Ben is doing."

Beth set her scissors down, arched her brow. "Hmm. Is there something you're not telling me, Lainey?"

Lainey busied herself breaking down an empty box. Then she gave up. Her friend would figure it out anyway. "He kissed me."

Beth's mouth dropped open. "Holy cow! When? Was it amazing?"

Amazing? Lainey recalled the tender yet hot way his mouth had moved over hers and her whole body buzzed.

"Um... After the thing with my parents. And, yes, I guess it was."

"You *guess*?" Beth's eyes bugged out. "He doesn't look like the type to rate 'I guess' on the kissing scale."

She had a point. "Okay, yeah, it was amazing."

Beth grinned. "I knew it. So. Spill. What happened?"

Lainey filled her in on her visit to the park and finding Ben there. She finished with, "But it was a mistake. It won't happen again."

Beth shook her head. "Why not?" The front doorbell jingled and she pointed a finger at Lainey. "Don't go anywhere. We're not done here." Then she hurried out front and Lainey heard her greet the customer.

Lainey's phone buzzed in her pocket and she pulled it out. She didn't recognize the number, but answered anyway, tucking it under her chin as she reached for the next box of flowers. "Hello?"

"Lainey?"

Her blood froze. She'd recognize that smooth voice on the other end of the line anywhere. Flowers forgotten, she gripped the phone so hard it hurt.

"Daniel." His name fell like a razor off her tongue. "What do you want?"

He chuckled—a low sound that sent chills up her spine. How had it ever thrilled her? "Why, to talk to you, baby. It's been a long time. Can't I talk to my wife?"

"Ex-wife," she corrected, because it had been hard-won and it mattered.

"Whatever," he said, and she pictured him waving away her words with a sweep of his hand, like so many pesky flies. "It's just details. Can we get together soon? I'd love to see you."

She nearly dropped the phone as rage rolled through

her. "No. Way. I've got nothing left to say to you." As if he'd ever listened, ever heard her.

"Laine. It's been so long. I miss you. I made a mistake." The seductive tone of his voice made her skin crawl and she shivered.

"Yeah, so did I," she muttered. Her marriage had been one big fat mistake from start to finish.

"Lainey, please." Now he sounded almost pleading.

"No." Oh, it felt so good to tell him that. "I can't talk right now, Daniel. I'm at work."

He sighed. "So I've heard. Some little flower shop, right? It's not going well. Your mother said you're having some problems—"

"Having some problems?" she sputtered. His condescending tone had her teeth grinding together. This was the Daniel she knew. "It's a new business. I'm still getting it off the ground."

"Yes, but it's been—what?—nine months? It was an honest try but it's not getting better, Lainey. You need to face reality."

Hearing him voice her own fears made her stomach churn.

His tone turned slightly wheedling. "I'd love to help. I think we could make it work this time."

"Did she dump you?"

A beat, then, "I'm sorry? Who?"

"You don't want me, Daniel. You never did. You want what you think I stand for. Calling me and belittling my shop and the life I've built without you is not going to change my mind. Nothing will," she qualified. Fueled by her chat with Jon, she added, "You cheated. You used me. Don't call me again."

"Lainey, for God's sake, just listen. You can't do this."

His anger snapped through the connection and for a heart-beat she froze.

"I am doing it. Goodbye, Daniel." She clicked the little phone shut as hard as she could. Oh, for the days when a phone could be slammed in a cradle.

She dropped the poor phone on the worktable and leaned forward on her palms, head down, tried to settle. He was right. It had been nine months and she was still struggling. Hearing him voice her fears, in that awful tone, had tears burning her eyes. What if the scumbag was right?

More than that, couldn't he see if he'd really loved her he'd want her to succeed? Couldn't he see she knew what he really was?

More than all that, though, *what if he was right?*

Beth came in and started toward her in alarm.

"Lainey! Are you okay?"

"I'm fine," she said, and wished she meant it. "Daniel just called."

Beth sucked in a breath. "What? Wow, he's got some nerve."

She gave a sharp laugh. "Daniel's got nothing *but* nerve."

Her feelings must have shown on her face because Beth leaned in. "Listen to me. Don't you dare let him get to you. Look at what you've done here. It took a lot of guts to divorce him and buy this place. To keep your parents at arm's length despite their meddling. It hasn't been easy but you're doing it. Don't let them derail you now."

Lainey stared at her friend. "I never—you see it that way?"

Beth leaned over and gave her a one-armed hug. "Of course. And you should, too."

Lainey had never thought of it that way. Oh, she did what needed to be done, but usually well after it should have been done to begin with. Long after she'd been taken for a fool. It didn't strike her as something to be proud of.

The chime of the front door saved her from answering. "I'll get that," she said, and slipped past Beth.

Her friend's words were kind, but Lainey could only hope she was right. There was too much riding on her being able to make this work.

Ben wouldn't admit it to anyone, but he'd been listening for her car.

When he saw her park at the curb he tried to squelch a completely inappropriate spurt of anticipation. He told himself he didn't want this, didn't want her, but every time he saw her it got a little harder to believe it. So he'd rather be anywhere than here, having her help him paint. Just having her in the same house made his skin feel too tight.

Before, he would have asked her out. Seen where it went. But that was—before.

Now he needed to keep his distance—something he wasn't doing very well at.

He heard her come in the front door and turned his attention to finishing taping the bedroom so she could paint. Heard her quick, light steps coming down the hall. He tensed even more as she came in the room.

"Hi." Her voice was slightly tentative, as if she expected to be shot down.

He turned and simply took in the sight of her in old jeans, an oversize sweatshirt, her hair pulled up in a ponytail. She plucked at the sweatshirt uncertainly and he realized he was just standing there, gaping at her like a fool.

He cleared his throat. "Hi. You ready?"

She moved into the room a little farther. So as not to spook her, and to give himself some space, he busied himself popping the top off the paint can.

She came to stand beside him. "I can't wait to see this."

She'd gone to the hardware store on her lunch hour to pick the colors. He'd gone in later to pick them up. Efficient.

She made a little humming noise in her throat. "That's a little pinker than I thought."

"It'll look different once you get it on the wall. It will dry darker. They all do." He set the can off to the side. "You know how to do this?"

He looked up in time to see her shake her head.

He stood up. "You can change a tire, but have never painted a room?"

She looked a little sheepish. "Ah. No. My skills are a bit scattered, I'm afraid."

He didn't want to find that sweet. Or charming. *Damn it.* He turned back to the paint cans and cleared his throat. "Lucky for you, it's easier than changing a tire."

She laughed. "I hope so."

He stirred it and tipped the can to pour into a paint tray. He handed her a paintbrush. "This is pretty simple. You'll do around the trim first. I taped in here already."

He explained the method and showed her how to make small, careful strokes, taking care not to touch her. But she seemed to take equal care not to touch him. She smelled so good it was hard not to give in to temptation.

"When that's done you can do the rest. The roller's pretty simple. Just don't get too much paint on it. You'll be okay in here? I've got some other things to finish up."

Translation: he needed some space. Quickly.

She gave him a small smile and moved the ladder over by the open window. "I'll be fine. I'll call you if I need you."

Dismissed. He walked down the hall toward the kitchen, rubbing his hand over his face. He needed to get this house finished quickly, before the woman in the bedroom back there drove him out of his mind.

When Ben returned to check on Lainey it had only been a half-hour. He'd stayed away as long as he could, which was pitiful. He found her on the ladder by the window, carefully painting under the crown molding. He took a moment to admire the long, lean lines of her legs and the curve of her ass, which was hugged nicely by her soft jeans. Her sweatshirt lifted when she extended her arms up to paint, but not quite enough to give him more than a small but tantalizing glimpse of skin. He tried to shut the feelings down—kissing her had been a mistake because it had unleashed a whole torrent of feelings he didn't want. Couldn't afford. And he was now swamped with them.

This was bad.

She shifted then and he stepped fully into the room. The last thing he wanted was to get caught staring and make things even more weird. "Lainey—"

She turned quickly on the ladder and upset it enough to lose her balance. With a little cry, she fell awkwardly on her rear on the hard floor.

He crossed the room in about two strides. "Lainey! Are you okay?"

She twisted to sit up, wincing. The floor was hard and he imagined it had been quite a landing. She grabbed her ankle with a sharp hiss.

He knelt beside her, worry clouding his vision. "Honey. Are you okay?" When she shook her head he pulled up her jeans leg to see her ankle starting to swell. "We'd better get that checked out. You might need an X-ray."

Her gaze swung to his and he saw the horror and worry there. She shook her head. "No. No X-rays." She gave a forced little laugh. "I'm just clumsy."

"Your ankle—"

"No."

He sat back. "Lainey, listen—"

"I'm pregnant," she whispered and he drew back to stare at her.

The word rang in his head. *Pregnant.* And he'd been kissing her and wanting her—someone else's woman.

She must have seen the expression change on his face because she grabbed his arm. "The father—he's not in the picture. I'm in this alone. My balance is off. That's why I fell. And X-rays might be bad for the baby."

"What kind of man walks out on his responsibility?" he said, not really expecting an answer, but outraged on her behalf.

She gave a humorless little laugh. "One who misrepresented himself. I'll be fine." She tugged her pant leg back down. "I have to ask—no one but my friend Beth knows this yet… Please—don't say anything to Rose. I'll tell her, but…" She hesitated. "I didn't mean to tell you."

"I understand. I won't. But the father—" For some reason he seemed to be stuck on that fact more than anything.

She cut him off with a slash of her hand. "He knows. He's not on board, so to speak."

A surge of anger welled in Ben. A baby should have a father. And here was a man, apparently alive and well, not willing to take on the responsibility for the little life that he'd created. A responsibility that a good man, like Jason, hadn't been able to keep even though he'd wanted to. "His loss."

Her gaze shot to his and she grimaced slightly. "Damn straight. Can you help me stand?"

"Let me check that ankle first." At her confused expression, he added, "I'm a firefighter and an EMT. I'm not a substitute for a doctor or an X-ray, but I may be able to tell if it's broken."

"Oh." She extended her leg slowly and inched up her jeans.

He removed her shoe carefully but didn't miss her wince. With careful fingers he probed her slim ankle. Her skin was smooth and soft and he was a total heel for his completely unprofessional physical response to touching her.

"I don't feel anything broken," he said. "Let me help you stand."

He got to his feet and took both of her hands in his, trying not to feel the heat her soft touch generated in him. He gave a gentle pull and she hopped up on one foot, overbalanced, and landed on his chest. His arms went around her before he could stop them and he looked down into her beautiful, upturned face. There was confusion and pain and heat and wanting in her blue gaze, and his groin tightened at the press of her breasts against his chest.

He cleared his throat. Kissing her was *not an option. Not an option, not an option,* chanted the loop in his brain, but he wanted so badly to lose himself in it, in her, in this—

Pregnant woman.

He cleared his throat and loosened his hold but didn't let her go fully. "So...um...how's the ankle?" His voice was a little rough.

She rested it on the floor and pulled back a bit, putting a little weight on it. Her wince spoke volumes and he steadied her with his hands on her waist. "Lainey. Please. I know I didn't feel anything broken but some types of breaks I wouldn't necessarily feel. Do you need to go to the hospital?"

She gave a little hopping motion and moved backwards.

"No. I'm okay. It's sore, but I can take acetaminophen for it. I want to finish this."

Somehow she hadn't upended the paint when she fell off the ladder, even though she'd dropped the brush on the drop cloth. He took the tray off and poured the paint back in the can so he wouldn't reach for her again. She'd felt far too good in his arms.

But she was pregnant. And even with the father out of the picture he couldn't risk a relationship with her or her baby. He wasn't that kind of guy. Not anymore.

"We'll finish tomorrow. Right now you need to get that ankle up with ice on it. Don't argue," he added when she opened her sexy little mouth to do just that. "And I want you to promise me you'll go in tomorrow if it's worse or not getting better."

She pressed her lips together, then nodded. "Okay. You're right."

"I'll drive you home. You'll need help up to your apartment, right?" He'd get her home, get her settled. It was the least he could do for her, for his grandma's friend. "Tomorrow I'll bring you your car. Leave me your key."

He saw all the arguments cross her face. "I don't want you to go to any trouble—"

"No trouble." He caught her chin, unable to stop the action. The surprise in her eyes licked him like fire. "Lainey. You need a little help. You need to be careful so you don't hurt the baby."

That got her attention and she nodded. "Right. Okay. Thank you."

He swung her into his arms. She let out a little, "Eeep!" and her arms went around his neck.

He gave a little chuckle, surprised by the sound. "Relax. I've got you."

The scary part was how damn good she felt in his arms.

How right. How oddly protective he felt of the baby. He hadn't seen the swell of her belly, but her sweatshirt prevented that.

He cut his thoughts off right there. There was nowhere for this to go that could end well. He would be leaving as soon as he had his grandma squared away and his confidence back. He'd only hurt Lainey and he couldn't bring himself to risk it.

CHAPTER SIX

WHAT WAS SHE thinking?

Lainey winced as she buckled her seat belt and Ben walked around the truck to get in. Holy cow. She'd just blurted out her secret to this man, and she hadn't even told his grandma—her friend—yet. Somehow her filter kept shutting off and then her mouth took over.

"I'm not the type who sleeps around," she blurted as soon as he got in the truck. *Ack!* There went the filter again. Maybe it was the pain in her ankle? Yet for some reason it was very important he understand.

He fitted the key in the ignition. His jaw was tense. "I didn't say you were. Things happen."

Yes, they did. She was living proof that *things* tended to happen to some people more than others. She stared out the window, not wanting to see him even in profile, lit by the dash lights. It wasn't his fault he kept showing up when she was falling apart, though it had happened with alarming frequency since she'd met him.

The drive home was tense but Lainey had no desire to talk. Her ankle throbbed and she tried to focus on that rather than the fact she'd told Ben about the baby. Told an almost perfect stranger who'd kissed her, for God's sake. There was a kind of intimacy that they were both pretty good at ignoring. And she'd just added to it by blurting out that she was pregnant. A little panic raised its head. It had been far, far easier to tell him than it should have been. What was it about him that made her spill her secrets? Was it because he was so different from her ex-husband? She frowned. Even that didn't fully make sense, since she barely knew him. But something about him spoke to her, soothed her. Almost as if she recognized him somehow, on a deeper level.

She gave herself a mental shake. Wow. That really didn't make sense. Maybe she'd somehow managed to hit her head when she fell. Or the pain in her ankle was making her a little crazy.

Ben pulled in front of the shop and she reached down to unbuckle the seat belt. "Well. Thanks for the ride," she said brightly. "Sorry to put you out."

He caught her hand. In the dim glow of the streetlights, he looked as surprised as she was at the contact. "You could never put me out. Stay there. Please. Let me help you down."

"I can—"

"Of course you can," he interrupted. "But you don't want to risk a fall that might hurt the baby or further damage the ankle. And you might need some help navigating those stairs."

Darn it. He was right. "Okay."

He gave her a small smile before he slipped out of the truck. "It's okay to need help, Lainey."

She watched him walk in front of the truck through the wash of the headlights and couldn't help but think he wasn't totally correct. Needing help didn't make her weak, but it left her open to people like her parents and their manipulations. It was safer to rely on herself than sort through the motivations of others.

He opened the door and reached for her. It was a little

awkward to slide out into his arms, and she was surprised when he didn't put her down, instead settled her into his arms. She didn't want to admit how good the hardness of his chest felt against her side, how incredibly good he smelled.

"This is easier if you relax a little," he said close to her ear.

She looked up to see humor spark in his eyes. The humor died, though, when his gaze fell to her mouth and his arms tightened perceptibly around her.

She caught her breath at the dark heat she saw there and an answering one rose in her. It wouldn't take much, just a slight shift…

A car drove by and the spell was snapped. He cleared his throat and started for the door.

Her face burned. Good Lord, what *was* this?

She forced herself to relax into his solid chest. Weird moments aside, it felt good to lean on someone. Just for a minute. His heart beat faster against her ribs. Its rhythm matched that of her own and she wondered if it was from the moment they'd shared or the exertion of carrying her. The coolness of the evening did nothing to counteract the warmth he generated in her.

He got her upstairs and she unlocked her door.

"Sit," he said as he steered her gently toward the couch, and she sank down gratefully.

He put a pillow under the ankle. She couldn't help but notice how he sucked all the air out of the room and made her small space seem even tinier.

"I'll get you ice and some acetaminophen. Where do you keep it?"

"Bathroom, in the medicine cabinet," she said, adjusting the pillow. Not because it needed it but because then she didn't have to look at him and see—what? Or maybe, more accurately, he wouldn't see what kind of effect he had on her.

"All right." He went in the kitchen. "Hey, kitty," she heard him say, and her heart tilted just a bit. Then, in a louder voice, "Where are the glasses? And do I need to feed the cat? She's looking at me like she expects something."

She swallowed a laugh. "She does. There's a can of food in the fridge. You can put the rest of it in her dish. And glasses are in the cupboard to the right of the sink."

She listened to the sounds in the kitchen, the low murmur of his voice as he talked to the cat, the opening and closing of the cupboard, the rattling of ice. She rested her head on the back of the couch and shut her eyes. No one had ever taken care of her before. Such a little thing—ice for her ankle, feeding the cat, water for the pills. Not earth-shattering. Yet it was somehow.

He appeared with the items and placed ice, wrapped in a towel, over her ankle. "That okay?"

The gentleness of the action nearly undid her. She swallowed hard. "Yes. Thanks."

"Here's the water. Hold on while I get the pills."

He headed down the hall, looking first to the left—her bedroom—then to the right—her bathroom. Where she'd thrown bras she'd hand-washed over the shower rod. She shut her eyes in mortification. There was a brief pause as he entered the bathroom—no doubt he'd gotten an eye-ful—then the rattling of the pill bottle. When he came back down the hall he didn't actually make eye contact. Then again, neither did she.

"Here you go." He plopped the pills in her palm. Was it just her, or were his fingers slightly unsteady? "Can I call anyone for you?"

She almost laughed. "No. I'm all set, thanks."

He cleared his throat. "All right, then. I'll bring you

your car tomorrow. If you need anything, call me. Where's your phone?"

She tugged her purse over and pulled the phone out. He took it from her and added his number. "Now you have no excuse. I'm serious. Especially if you need help with those stairs in the morning." He handed the phone back and this time their fingers lingered for a heartbeat.

Breathless, she tried to smile. "I will. Um…thank you. For everything."

He stepped back. "No problem."

When the door shut behind him she flopped back on the cushions and pressed both hands over her eyes, unsure if she should laugh or scream.

She was in way deeper trouble than she'd thought.

Ben stared at the game on the TV above the bar. He couldn't have told anyone who was playing, much less the score, and he was only vaguely aware it was a hockey game. All he could see was Lainey's perfect mouth forming the words *"I'm pregnant"*.

They still packed a punch. It wasn't even his kid, and he'd never meet the baby—no doubt he'd be long gone by the time Lainey gave birth. In fact, it was most likely he'd never talk to her again, unless they ran into each other though Rose somehow. So why the hell did it matter?

He shifted on the stool. Lainey was dangerous. The kind of dangerous that made him want what he couldn't have. It wasn't fair to Jason—or Callie, for that matter. What right did he have even to think about pursuing a woman—Lainey—when Callie's husband was gone?

He took a swallow of the beer he couldn't even taste. He was pretty sure the bitterness in his mouth came from his own feelings rather than the drink in his hand.

Pregnant.

He'd felt a stab of jealousy straight to his soul when she'd looked at him with those big blue eyes and whispered those words. No use passing it off as anything but that.

What could he offer her? He didn't even know if he could do his job anymore. That anxiety was ever-present, hovering in the back of his mind. Shading everything he did. It mixed with guilt into a potent brew of shame and sorrow.

So, no, he wasn't in any shape to pursue her. Therefore, being jealous was a complete waste of time and energy. Still, he'd felt a roaring protectiveness when she'd fallen. And far more than that when he'd walked in her bathroom and seen those lacy, sexy bras lined up on the shower rod.

God help him. He was getting in way over his head and all he'd done was help her. But something about her drew him in and he couldn't seem to walk away. All those feelings he'd walled off…? Yeah. He was in danger of drowning in them if he didn't get them under control fast.

It didn't matter. He set aside his half-empty beer, since he couldn't even taste it, and signaled for his bill. He wasn't getting anywhere having a pity party and it was a waste of time anyway. Might as well go home, where there were at least projects he could do to stay busy.

He entered the house quietly, but his sharp-eyed grandma was in the living room, knitting. He couldn't tell what it was but her hands flew and the needles clicked together sharply. She looked up when he came in.

"So. How was it?"

Ben sat down opposite her, since it seemed rude to stand and talk when she was all settled in. He outlined the progress he'd made on the house, then hesitated.

Rose arched a brow. "What?"

He debated how much he could say and keep Lainey's secret safe. "She twisted her ankle," he said finally. "Stepped wrong off the ladder."

Rose's hands stopped moving. "Is she okay?"

"I checked it out," he said. "She was adamant about not going to the hospital."

"She needs an X-ray," Rose muttered and Ben sighed.

"I suggested it but she shot me down." True enough.

Rose sighed and her needles started moving again. "I bet."

"I offered to call her mother, but she said no." He wasn't fishing, exactly, but he was curious as to why Lainey seemed to think she was on her own when she had family nearby.

Rose snorted. "That woman doesn't have a maternal bone in her body. And that ex of hers—" She pressed her lips together tightly. "Well. Anyway. I'd better call her—make sure she's okay. I wish you'd brought her back here."

Ben was pretty sure Lainey didn't want Rose to figure out about the pregnancy. As Rose dialed Lainey's number he took a good look at the knitting project on her lap. The soft colors and small size looked an awful lot like a baby blanket. But he wasn't going to ask any questions.

They'd each keep Lainey's secret.

He hung around, fixing himself something to eat he really didn't want in the kitchen, but he wasn't going to admit that. When he went back in the living room Rose was hanging up and frowning.

That protective instinct reared back up and he forced himself to keep his voice level. "Is she okay?"

Rose's gaze flicked to his. "She's hurting."

Ben started to stand. "I can go—"

Rose shook her head. "She won't come. Thinks she has to be strong." She gave him a pointed look. "Like someone else I know."

He opted not to touch that comment. "I've got to get her car to her tomorrow."

"That's good. Then you can see if she's okay in person. She's likely to not admit it over the phone."

She had a point.

He cleared his throat. "Sounds good. You need anything before I go take a shower?"

Rose shook her head, her hands flying once more over the blanket. "Thank God for DVR. Got one more show to watch. I'm all set, thanks."

He chuckled and walked toward the stairs. She said his name softly. When he turned, she looked at him, her faded blue gaze serious.

"She needs someone like you."

Ben froze as the words pinged around in his heart. "No. No, I'm not what she needs."

"Ben." Her voice was sharp. "You are exactly what she needs. Don't sell yourself short."

He had nothing to say to that. As he went up the stairs his heart was heavy. He wasn't what Lainey needed. He was too damaged to be enough for anyone.

Still. He regretted not being able to have the chance.

Where there's smoke, there's fire.

Ben could see the black plume of smoke the next morning from the front porch of his grandma's house, where he'd been working on the ramp. It was coming from the other side of town. *Lainey's side.*

That thought bumped him into action. He'd go check on her, make sure—just make sure. Since he had to take her car back anyway, this gave him the excuse. And she wouldn't be moving real fast after that fall, so no one would think twice if he checked on her.

"I'm going to take Lainey's car back," he told his

grandma, who was in the kitchen with her Sudoku book. "You need anything while I'm out?"

She tipped her glasses down her nose. "Everything okay?"

He hesitated. "There's a fire."

She gave a small nod. "We've got good people here, Ben. Maybe you should be one of them?"

He opened his mouth, then shut it again. He shook his head, grabbed his jacket from by the back door and hurried to his truck.

It only took a few minutes to drive to the other house. From this angle it was hard to tell precisely where the fire was, but he could smell the smoke. He flexed his hands on the wheel as he turned onto the street and pulled into the rental house's driveway. He started Lainey's car and headed for downtown.

He whipped the car into a spot down the block from Lainey's shop and jogged across the street toward the smoke. He needed to see, to know if he could handle it. Now he could see ash floating in the air, and he heard the wail of sirens. Tension built in his shoulders and he rolled them in an effort to release it.

He took a deep breath of the smoky air and coughed as he turned down a side street to see a fully engulfed building. He stayed well back from the cordoned-off area. Fire didn't fascinate him the way it did other people. It was an enemy, a force, a beast to be tamed and conquered. Seeing it lick gleefully at the building gave him no thrill.

He watched the firefighters doing their job—*his* job— and swallowed hard. This was what he was born to do, but he wasn't sure he could ever go back. God, but he missed it. He missed it like he'd miss his arm if he'd lost it. Missed the adrenaline, the teamwork. The battle. It could be grim work—messy, and damn hard—but, hell, there wasn't anything else he'd rather do.

When the roof caved in with a shower of sparks and the flames leapt higher he shut his eyes as nausea rolled over him. For a second he couldn't breathe. Finally he turned and walked away, disappointment lodging in his gut like a rock. He'd wondered—now he knew. He wasn't ready. Would he ever be?

He stopped in front of The Lily Pad, its bright windows and festive decor drawing him like a beacon through the cool, smoky air. He didn't want to examine his relief at finding her shop okay or his anger at himself for his reaction to the fire. Or the real reason the shop pulled him: the woman inside.

Every step closer tangled everything tighter inside him. He pushed it all away and walked through the door.

Lainey looked up and gave him a small, startled smile. He didn't miss the flash of pleasure that crossed her beautiful face.

"Ben."

He tamped down his own reaction and pulled her key out of his pocket. "Thought I'd stop by and give you this." He moved forward and shook his head when she started to get up. "No, sit. How's the ankle?"

"Better today." She held out her hand and he pressed the key into her palm. Her skin was warm under his cool fingers. Her eyes widened slightly at the contact and he wondered if she felt it, too. The heat, the spark.

Sparks.

"Did you see the fire?" She shook her head as she slipped the key into her pocket. "Of course you must have. I can smell the smoke on your jacket. You said you're a firefighter, right?"

He cleared his throat, suddenly having trouble breathing. "Yeah. I did. I was." *Was.* His voice stuck a little on the word. Was he or wasn't he? Could he ever go back? What if he couldn't?

"Ben?" The concern in her voice made him wince. "Are you okay? You looked a little lost there for a moment."

Lost. That was a good word for him. "I'm fine. Sorry."

She studied him, and for a second he thought she'd ask him more questions. But her phone rang. She glanced at it, then at him.

"I'll get out of here." So he wouldn't touch her, he put his hands in his pockets. "Your car's down about half a block."

"Thank you," she murmured as the phone rang. "I appreciate it."

He didn't hang around as she answered the phone, but he did pause at the door and look back. Her eyes were on him and she blushed just a little as her gaze caught his. He swallowed hard and walked out into the smoky fall air.

Lainey let out a shuddering breath as she hung up the phone from an order. She'd managed to get all the information, but it had been hard, seeing Ben through the windows as he'd walked, slightly hunched against the wind, past the windows of her shop. She'd hoped—foolishly— he'd look back at her one more time. *Silly.*

She entered the last of the order information into the computer and stretched. While her ankle needed to be propped up, the position was uncomfortable for her back.

Beth breezed back in, to-go bag from the café in hand. She shook her head as she placed it on the counter. "Was that Ben I saw walking by? Was he here?"

Lainey took the offered sandwich and set it carefully on a napkin. "Just for a minute. He brought my car up here."

Beth waggled her eyebrows. "Is that all?"

Lainey sighed. His face—so closed up today, after how sweet he'd been last night. He'd shut down even farther when, in her apparently misguided quest to make conversation, she'd asked him about being a firefighter. Clearly a sore spot. "Yeah. That's all."

Beth clucked her tongue. "Too bad. He's hot. And the two of you would be so cute together."

She thought of how easily she'd fit in his arms last night, and the heat in his eyes, and a little shiver passed through her. "That's silly."

Beth shrugged and snagged a French fry. "Maybe. Maybe not. But you have to start somewhere, Laine."

She stared at her sandwich. No, she didn't. Not really. And Ben wasn't interested in her. Well, actually, that wasn't true. He was clearly interested in her. But he wasn't willing or able to take it anywhere.

And neither was she.

CHAPTER SEVEN

THE DOOR CHIMED and Lainey walked carefully out of the back room, not wanting to admit the little skip in her pulse was the hope it was Ben coming back, no matter how unlikely that was. She'd decided to ask him to her mother's gala, and didn't want to lose her nerve.

It was a complete surprise to see her brother. "Kevin?"

"Hey, little sis," Kevin greeted her with a smile. "What's going on? Mom said you're moving."

Lainey looked at her brother, still in his scrubs. He looked tired, and there were definite lines around his blue eyes, but his smile was warm.

She gestured to him. "Come on back. You stopped in to ask me that?"

"Well, I was on my way to Mel's Café for lunch and thought I'd stop in." When Lainey opened her mouth, he held up his hands. "No, I'm not here to convince you of anything. I'm just asking."

Lainey moved to the worktable and pulled out a length of pumpkin-colored ribbon she was using for a silk centerpiece. Kevin had rarely, if ever, been on the receiving end of their parents' ire. He was a surgeon, lived in an appropriate condo, and drove a nice car. No wife yet, but that wasn't held against him. "Did they tell you what happened?"

Kevin leaned on the table. Now his expression was concerned. "No."

She took a deep breath. "They bought this building."

Kevin cocked his head. "Doesn't it help you out?"

She stabbed a floral pin in with a little more force than necessary. "Kevin. They didn't ask me. They showed me the deed and said I had to move back home."

Kevin swore softly under his breath. "I'm sorry, Laine. Did they say why?"

"Of course. I'm not doing well here. Yet. It's been a struggle. And I guess they don't think that reflects well on them." She didn't mention Daniel. No point in muddying the waters.

"Are you?"

"Am I what?"

"Moving back home?"

She gave a sharp little bark of laughter. "God, no. I found a nice little house a friend of mine owns. I'm moving there—this weekend, in fact."

He chucked her under the chin, a gentle and brotherly gesture. "Good for you. I'm glad you stood up to them."

Emotion flooded her. She'd never really expected him to watch her back. "Thank you."

He stepped back. "Do you need help? I'm on call this weekend, but I can come over if I'm around."

She hesitated. Why not? Beth and her husband were helping, but she could use the extra pair of hands. "Sure. That'd be great."

"All right." He turned to go. "I'll be here at nine unless otherwise noted. That okay?"

"See you then," she said, and watched as he disappeared through the workroom door. Strange to have him in her corner. Maybe she'd walled herself off from her brother with her own feelings of inadequacy and inferiority. If so, shame on her. It seemed Kevin might actually be an ally.

God knew she could use one.

That evening, Ben looked up from the whine of the saw to see Lainey standing there, her eyes hooded in the dim light of the rental house's garage, her hands twisted into knots in front of her. He hit the switch on the saw and silenced it.

"Hey."

She swallowed hard. "Hey."

He came toward her and she tipped her head back to look at him. He saw anxiety swimming in her eyes and he closed his hand into a fist to keep from stroking her face.

"Let's go outside—out of the dust." He took her elbow and lightly steered her toward the porch.

"What are you doing in there?"

"Repairing one of the cabinet doors. Do you need some help with the painting?"

She shook her head and her hair bounced lightly on her shoulders. He caught a hint of a lightly fruity shampoo. "Actually, I need you."

The words stopped him cold, even as a spear of heat shot through his belly. It would be no hardship to have her need him, but of course she hadn't meant it that way. He cleared his throat. "For what?"

She paced across the front lawn, kicking at the leaves. "I feel so stupid. I wouldn't ask you if I wasn't desperate."

Ben was pretty sure that was his ego, flying away in shreds. "Desperate?"

"Oh!" She spun back around and her cheeks were bright pink—a huge improvement over the paleness they'd held a few minutes ago. "I didn't mean— I just meant—"

"It's fine," he interrupted. "What do you need?"

She stared at the sky for a minute and he wondered if she was looking for a lightning bolt.

"A date."

He couldn't have heard her right. A date? He didn't date—even casually. If he did date, it definitely wouldn't be a woman who was in danger of making him feel things again. He opened his mouth to tell her so but she rushed on.

"My mother hosts this fundraiser gala thing at the hospital every year. I need to go, and I don't have a date. I was hoping maybe you'd come with me."

"When is it?" God, was he actually considering it? He'd meant to say *no way*.

"Next Thursday." When he said nothing she turned even pinker and turned to walk away. "You know…this was a bad idea. I'm sorry. I'll just go alone."

He crossed to her in two steps. "Black tie?" Hell, he hated black tie.

She swallowed. "Yes."

"I'll go." Holy hell, what was he thinking?

"It's okay—" she started, then stopped as his words sank in. Her eyes widened. "You will?"

He nodded.

"Oh, thank you," she breathed, and flung her arms around him for a brief, tight hug. "Thank you."

He couldn't resist teasing a little. "Only because you're desperate." Hell. He was getting soft. He couldn't possibly be letting her get to him. Right?

She pulled away, but he looped his arms around her back and held her against him, wanting to feel her for a moment. Her gaze caught his and the world fell away for a minute. Heat wove around them, lazy and slow, and his gaze dropped to her mouth. The memory of that kiss in the park hung between them—her warm, sweet mouth and hungry response. He wanted it. Especially now, with her pink cheeks and slightly parted lips tempting him to claim them.

She made a little sound in her throat and he let her go, setting her away from him. Her gaze refocused, then bounced away, landing anywhere but on him.

"So…ah…I'll get going," she said, edging toward her car. "I'll see you later."

"Yeah." He marshaled his thoughts away from kissing her. It took way more effort than he wanted to admit. "What time for the gala?"

"It starts at seven—so say, six-thirty?"

"All right," he said, and she hurried to her car and hopped in. As he watched her drive down the road he wondered where the hell he'd find a tux by next Thursday night.

He strode back to the garage. Then he fished his cell out of his pocket. First things first. He wouldn't let Lainey down.

It seemed the harder Ben tried to keep his distance, the more he was drawn to Lainey.

It wasn't good.

He locked the little house up behind him. Lainey had gone home after painting. They'd managed to avoid any more awkward moments like they'd had outside. It seemed the best thing he could do was bump up his timetable. He'd finished the ramp for his grandma just today, and he was nearly done with this rental house. So there weren't any real reasons to stick around once he'd gotten his grandma squared away. It would be best to get away from Lainey before he got any more involved with her.

Which was why it had floored him when he said he'd go with her to that party. That wasn't the way to keep his distance.

He scrubbed a hand over his face with a sigh. While he wasn't ready to go back to firefighting yet, there was really no reason not to go back to Grand Rapids.

Well, there was Callie and her broken family. He blew out a breath. He couldn't go back yet. He wasn't ready. He couldn't even return Callie's phone calls. Eventually she'd quit trying. One more thing to add to the morass of guilt.

He'd finish up the house, go to the gala, and that would be the end of the contact he had with Lainey. He'd make excuses and leave when she came to visit. It would be easier on both of them. She wanted to see his grandma, anyway, not him.

He cleaned up his mess and drove back to his grandma's house. As he got out of his truck a car turned in the driveway behind him. Grandma—coming home from her knitting group, he thought. She had a very full social calendar, which amused him no end. And pleased him, too.

He walked up to the car and opened her door. She beamed up at him. "Hello, Ben."

"Hi, Grandma."

He went around back when the driver popped the trunk and pulled the wheelchair out. Then he held it steady as his grandma moved from the car to the chair. As much as he hated to see her like this, he had to admit she handled it with grace and humor.

"Thank you," she said, and waved at her friend. Ben helped her wheel up the ramp into the house.

"This ramp is wonderful," she said as they came in the door. "I can't tell you how much easier it is going to make my life. I appreciate it so much."

Ben shut the door behind them, uncomfortable with her gratitude. He didn't deserve it. He'd been gone for too long, and she'd needed him. Lainey had been right about that when they'd first met. "I'm glad," was all he said.

She wheeled around to face him, a frown on her face as she put her knitting bag on the floor by her favorite chair. "It was an honest compliment," she said quietly. "It's okay to accept it."

He shoved his hands in his pockets. "I know. I just feel like I should have been here long before now."

She sighed. "I could have let you know, Ben. I was very clear that I didn't want to worry you. This isn't all on you. As you can see, I've got a very solid support system. I've been managing. And I am very grateful you took this time to help me out. That is all I meant."

He knew that, but it was hard to let go of the self-recrimination. He'd held on to it like a shield for the past week or so, using it to keep his distance.

"So," she said. "Is the house ready for Lainey?"

Grateful for the topic-change, he said, "Pretty much. I'm still working on some minor repairs. But, yes, it's otherwise ready."

She gave a little nod. "Excellent. She's moving this weekend, then?"

"Far as I know." He opted not to mention yet that she'd asked him to the gala. That might put ideas in Grandma's head he didn't want her to have. She liked Lainey, and he didn't want to get her hopes up.

Or your own?

Choosing to ignore that particular thought, he shoved his hands in his pockets. "It'll be all ready for her. You can call her and firm up the date and time."

Rose cocked her head. "You've got a truck," she said thoughtfully. "It might go faster if you offered to help."

Ben swallowed hard. Of course it would. Lainey's car wasn't nearly big enough to haul furniture. And he wasn't going to *not* help her because he was so damn terrified of her. "When you call her, tell her I offered."

She didn't push. "I will. Thank you, Ben."

"Sure," he said, not adding, *I'd do it for anyone.* Because he was afraid that wasn't true.

Lainey's cell buzzed. The number was the same area code as she'd dialed for Jon. Her stomach instantly fell. Beth had left for deliveries so she was alone. She took a deep breath and answered.

"Hello?"

"Lainey. It's Jon." His voice was crisp. "Wanted to let you know we've drawn up the paperwork to begin the process for me to terminate my rights. It's been overnighted to you."

Lainey froze for a moment. This was what she wanted, but somehow saying *thank you* seemed both wrong and inadequate. "I—okay. I'll look out for it."

There was the slightest of pauses, then he cleared his throat. "Best of luck to you, Lainey."

She turned and stared out the window at the cars passing by. "You too. You're going to need it far more than I will."

He barked a laugh, even though she hadn't been trying to be funny. "Don't I know it? From here on out if you have any questions refer them to my lawyer."

"I can't imagine I'd have any need," she said. "But okay."

She clicked the phone shut in her hand. Slowly the import of the conversation began to sink in. She was well and truly a single mother now. Relief mixed with sorrow that it had gone this way. That she'd given her baby a man like Jon for a father. A man who would sign his rights away rather than tell his wife. Instead of a man like Ben.

She sighed and slipped the phone in her pocket. Ben would leave, too. He'd been clear that he was only here for a short time, and even more telling, that his attraction to her was reluctant at best. Something he couldn't help rather than something he actually wanted.

She'd do well to keep that in mind.

"Geez, sis, what do you have in these boxes?"

Kevin's grumbled question on Saturday morning made Lainey smile.

"Rocks—just for you," she teased, and saw Kevin frown out the window. "What?"

"You expecting someone? Big truck. Tall guy. Wait—is that Ben Lawless?"

Lainey's heart skipped. "Yes." It was a good thing he could help, since Beth and her husband hadn't been able to come after all.

"Our job just got easier. He's got a lot of room in that truckbed. Let's get these boxes out of the way so we can move the furniture."

Ben came up the stairs and Lainey tried very hard not to flush or otherwise react in case her brother picked up on anything. As it was, she'd taken care to dress in clothes that hid her slightly rounded midsection, without being obvious about it. She couldn't take the chance that Kevin's doctor eye would spot what she wasn't ready for him to see.

Ben's greeting was a nod, before he turned his attention to Kevin and they launched into a moving strategy discussion. Feeling oddly left out, Lainey slipped into her bedroom, where she'd left a couple boxes of fragile items she didn't want mixed in with the rest of her things.

It only took a few trips. It was a little depressing that her life had been reduced to a couple of car and truckloads, including the furniture. Now it was all in her new house, somewhat willy-nilly, though the guys *had* asked her where she wanted things. Kevin had left after the last trip, and Ben was coming back with a few miscellaneous items.

Lainey went in the kitchen. If she started in there she would be able to at least eat a bowl of cereal or soup. When the front door opened her pulse kicked up. She'd managed to keep Kevin between them. Not too hard, considering they were the ones doing the heavy lifting. But now she and Ben were alone.

She ripped open the box closest to her and found her dishes. She heard Ben's steps in the hall and rose from the floor to greet him. He leaned on the wall and surveyed the mess.

"You've got your work cut out for you," he observed, and she took the opportunity to turn and examine the chaos.

"Yep. It will take me a couple days, but I'll get it all done." Not sure what to do now, she hesitated, then stuck out her hand. "Thank you. I appreciate your help."

He paused just a heartbeat before he took her hand in response. His palm, warm and rough, sent shivers up her arm. What would it feel like on her skin?

She released his hand and stepped back, willing the thoughts away. He shoved his hands in his pockets. She didn't know how to make the awkwardness stop—wasn't even sure it was the best thing to do.

He cleared his throat. "Grandma's invited you to lunch at Mel's Café. She'll be there—" he glanced at his watch "—in about fifteen minutes."

"Oh. That's wonderful, but I think I need to get cracking on this." Practically on cue, her stomach growled loudly and he arched a brow.

"What are you going to eat? One of these boxes?"

Humor glimmered in his eyes and it took her breath away because she knew how rare it was to see it.

"I—well, yeah. Maybe with peanut butter?" She grinned at him and was rewarded with a small smile. Which for him was an ear-to-ear grin.

"We can do better than that," he said dryly. "Come on. I'll drive you."

Unable to think of a suitable excuse—and really she didn't want one, she was hungry—she grabbed her purse and followed him out the door, which she locked with her new key. He opened the passenger door and she climbed in.

"How is Rose getting there?" she asked when he got in the other side.

"A friend took her to get her hair and nails done this morning. She'll drop Grandma off."

Lainey frowned. "How will she get home? This truck is awful high." His expression was shuttered and she realized he'd taken it as a criticism. "I didn't mean that as anything other than a statement of fact," she added stiffly.

He didn't touch her comment. "She's got something else going on after lunch."

"Oh." Lainey stared out the window, mentally kicking herself for her thoughtlessness. It seemed every step they took forward was quickly followed by three back. Such an awkward dance they were doing—trying to be ultra-polite while pretending there was nothing between them.

It was exhausting.

She unbuckled when he'd parked at the café, just down from her shop and her now-former apartment. Once they entered the café she saw Rose at a table by the window. The older woman waved and Lainey waved back. She slid into the seat across from Rose and was surprised when Ben sat next to her. Until she realized Rose had taken over the second seat with her coat and purse. In spite of herself, she wondered if it had been intentional. Was Rose match-making? She wouldn't put it past her friend.

"Love your hair," Lainey said, admiring the soft curls, and Rose patted it.

"She did a good job, didn't she? Makes me look good."

Lainey laughed and caught Rose's hand. "What color is this?" It was a deep pink, a perfect shade for her skin and her silver hair. It occurred to her *she* hadn't had a manicure since she'd divorced Daniel. Not that it mattered, but was one more sign of how much her life had changed.

"I can't remember exactly. It had peony in the name."

"Did you order?" Lainey asked, and Rose shook her head.

"Not yet. But I know what I'm getting."

The waitress came over and Rose ordered a club sandwich, Lainey a turkey sandwich, and Ben something big with roast beef.

Rose sat back. "So. Did you get it all moved?"

She glanced at Ben. "Yes. Ben and Kevin made it look easy. I guess it helped I didn't have that much stuff."

Ben stretched his legs out in front of him and bumped her thigh in the process. She sucked in a breath.

"Sure seemed like a lot for one woman and a cat."

His low, teasing tone gave her goosebumps. She smacked him lightly on the arm, trying desperately not to respond to him. *Rose is here.* The mental reminder didn't work.

"Not that much," she said with a laugh, and saw Rose watching them with an expression that could only be described as thoughtful. Lainey sighed inwardly. The undercurrents between them were on full display.

So much for not feeding the matchmaking fire.

CHAPTER EIGHT

LAINEY'S WEEKEND PASSED in a flurry of unpacking. While the end result was a little sparse, she wasn't worried. One thing she'd always loved was finding treasures at places like thrift shops and garage sales. One more thing her mother had never understood. So she'd keep an eye out for what she might need.

Well, after baby needs, of course. That was her next project. Setting up the nursery.

In fact she stood in the room in question right now. Nothing was in here yet. She'd left it empty on purpose. She needed a crib, a changing table... Maybe she could find a dresser that could do double duty. A rocker for the corner. A bookcase for toys and such. She left the room, a smile on her face, and walked back though the house. Being here felt right. Panda sat in a spot of sunlight on the kitchen floor. While the cat hadn't been pleased about the car ride, she'd settled in once she'd found her food and water bowls, as well as her litter box. Lainey was hopeful come spring she could let the cat out into the fenced-in backyard.

She padded into her bedroom to get dressed. And frowned when her low-rise jeans didn't snap. Yesterday they'd fit—albeit a bit snug. Today, no dice. That meant two things.

One: full-time maternity clothes.

Two: telling her family.

Lainey shut her eyes. The moment of truth was here. Her father was out of town, so she'd have to tell her mother alone. She'd do it after work, when she returned the apartment keys.

She left the house with a little fizzle of joy as she used her new key to lock it up behind her, and drove to the shop. As was her habit now, she checked the cooler temperature first thing. It was running a tick above where she wanted it, but it had been holding fairly steady.

Beth walked in a few minutes later. "Hey, Laine. How was the move?"

"Pretty smooth," she answered.

"Was it just you and Kevin? Aw, Laine. I'm so sorry we couldn't be there. We should have—"

"You should have gone to visit your father-in-law, just like you did. It all worked out. Ben helped, too," Lainey said quickly. "I think Rose asked him to."

A small smile tugged at the corners of Beth's mouth. "Really?" she said, drawing out the word. "How was that?"

Lainey rolled her eyes and stomped over to open the cash register, pretending not to catch her friend's meaning. "A lot of work—what else?"

Beth's low laugh followed her across the room. "Mmm-hmm. Do you think Kevin noticed anything? Lainey, it's pretty obvious there's chemistry with you guys."

Oh, she hoped not. "I don't think so. He's a guy, so he can be pretty oblivious. Plus, I really didn't see Ben that much. They just loaded and unloaded. They were together more than we were." Then she realized what she'd just admitted. "Oh—"

Beth wrapped an arm around Lainey's shoulders and

squeezed. "Now all you have to do is stop fighting it. Let yourself just give in."

She stepped away, her point clearly made, and Lainey busied herself with the cash drawer. It wasn't as easy as *just giving in*. There was too much at stake to *just give in*. Why couldn't Beth see that? She wasn't sure she could give in if she wanted to. She was aware of how quickly things could go wrong. Once you'd had your wings clipped, it made it awful hard to get off the ground.

And she was scared to try and fly again.

Lainey turned down her parents' street and her stomach fluttered. Silly, really, since she was an adult. But those old habits of wanting to be a good daughter were hard to break. She'd decided to go in quick, say her piece, and get out. She'd send for the housekeeper if her mother passed out.

The thought made her giggle just a little hysterically. The unflappable Jacqui—completely flapped.

Her mother's car was parked by the garage—a sure sign she'd be heading back out later. Lainey parked in the circle and took a second to brace herself. While it was time, it would be nice if she had someone to back her up, and she almost wished she'd asked Kevin to come along. He'd know how to manage their mother.

She rang the bell and waited. Jacqui answered after a minute, brow arched high. "Lainey. This is a nice surprise. What brings you here?"

She stepped aside and Lainey entered the foyer.

"I need to talk to you for a minute." Her voice was calm, not betraying her nerves. Good.

"Of course. I've got a meeting in a half-hour. Will this take long?"

"I don't think so," Lainey said.

She followed her mother's trim form into the living

room and took a deep breath. Once again she tried to imagine a baby on the floor, or pulling itself up on the velvet-covered furniture. She couldn't picture it. Was that because she was afraid her parents wouldn't want her and the baby in their lives? Wasn't that part of what had made her so reluctant to tell them?

It didn't matter now. She took a deep breath. "I have something important to tell you."

"I see." Jacqui crossed to the mini-wet bar. "Well, then. Something to drink? Will you be joining me for dinner?"

Not likely. "No, Mother."

Jacqui turned, a can of ginger ale in her hand, an expectant look on her face. "Well, then, what do you need to tell me, dear?"

There was no point in beating around the bush. "I'm pregnant."

Jacqui gasped, and the color leached from her face as the pop can slid from her hand and landed on the carpet with a fizzy hiss. The golden liquid splashed all over her legs and feet. Frozen for a heartbeat, Lainey leapt up and grabbed a handful of paper towels from the wet bar, almost grateful for the distraction.

"Are you sure?" Jacqui's voice was faint.

Lainey didn't look up from blotting at the mess. She wasn't sure she could look at her mother just yet. "Positive. I'm a little more than two months along." Her hands shook as she dropped the first mass of sopping towels in the garbage under the bar.

Jacqui let out a long exhale. "Good God."

That about sums it up.

"Are you getting married? Who's the father?"

Lainey winced. "No. And the father is no one you know." True enough. Jon wouldn't have been on her parents' radar.

"Ben Lawless?" Her mother nearly spat Ben's name.

Lainey bobbled the paper towel roll. What did her mother have against Ben? "No. Of course not. He'd *want* to be involved in the baby's life." The truth of those words batted against her heart.

"And the father doesn't?"

Lainey couldn't speak over the wave of shame that rose in her. She pressed her lips together instead and shook her head.

Jacqui sighed and stepped out of her sticky heels. "Oh, Lainey. You need to get married, pronto. I wonder if Daniel would be willing to marry you with you carrying someone else's baby? Lainey, *damn it*. I think you just ruined any chance you had with that man!"

Lainey sat back on her heels, temper snapping at her throat. "I already told you I don't care, Mother. I'm not getting married. I will be a single parent. I don't give a damn what Daniel thinks. I'm sure he has kids somewhere. He did enough sowing of the seed, as they say."

Jacqui gasped. "Lainey!"

"Well, he did. If it wore heels, he chased it. He almost never slept with *me*, thank God—who knows what I could have come down with?—but he did with other women. At the end he was bringing them into our home, did you know that?" The humiliation burned though her all over again. "I'd be gone, or maybe not. The basement was his little playboy cave. He could have cared less about me— about our marriage. He married me for you and Dad— for your money, for where your name could take him. So when I grew a spine and divorced him it really threw him. He's not back here for *me*, Mother. He wants to get back in your lives."

Jacqui stared at her, jaw dropped. "Lainey—" she said finally, then lapsed into silence.

"But you knew, didn't you?" Lainey said softly. "Some of it, anyway. And it was okay, because he had the right connections, the right amount of money. You were willing to look the other way, like you've done with Dad." The truth arced through her, sharp and hot.

Jacqui stood very still. "Be very careful, young lady. You're on dangerous ground now."

Lainey couldn't stop. It was too important. "He's always been very discreet—unlike Daniel. I'd have thought you'd want better for me than you had. I know I do."

The truth hurt. She loved her father, but she knew his weaknesses. Daniel was just like him, only without the intelligence or compassion. She also knew her father loved her mother, despite his failings. And that was between them. Not her business.

She stood up and threw away the last of the paper towels. "I'm going to go now," she said quietly. There was nothing more to say. It wasn't as if her mother was going to embrace her and squeal with joy at the thought of grandchildren. So the lump of disappointment in her throat was useless. She turned and walked toward the door.

"Lainey—wait."

She paused and turned.

Jacqui asked, "Who else knows about this?"

Lainey laid her hand on her belly and saw Jacqui flinch. "Only Beth knows about your grandchild." There wasn't any reason to tell her Ben knew as well. It would only make things worse.

"Okay, good. We need to make this spin positive somehow. I'll get on it and let you know the plan." Jacqui, clearly perked by the thought of something to do, padded across the carpet on sticky feet.

"No."

Jacqui stopped. "Excuse me?"

Lainey shook her head. "You can plan all you want, but it's not going to make it go away. Not going to make it any more or less than it is. I'm not going to go along with any plan. My baby. My life."

Jacqui's mouth flattened. "Your store—"

"I know. It's at your mercy." Lainey grabbed her purse. "You keep telling me. Now you know why I won't let it go under. I need to succeed so I can support myself and my child. Can I call anyone for you before I go?"

Jacqui shook her head. "No. I don't—I need to talk to your father first. He's going to be so disappointed," she added, more to herself than to Lainey. "Plus it's an election year."

Lainey stared at her. "Mom, I'm thirty-three. Not a teenager. Not even close. So what if I have a baby on my own?" She nearly laughed. As if it was such an easy thing to do. Maybe she was crazy. "Women do it all the time."

"But not women in *your* position," Jacqui said.

She kept her voice steady with effort. "And what position would that be?"

"Women whose lives are under scrutiny," she said, and Lainey's jaw nearly dropped.

"I'm hardly under any kind of scrutiny. Besides, I don't think this is any worse than my divorce," she said dryly. "And it's a much happier occasion."

Jacqui shook her head. "Don't make a joke of it. You don't understand. You never have."

Lainey hesitated, then simply turned and walked toward the door. There wasn't anything else to say. Behind her, she heard her mother on the phone with the housekeeper, telling her to come clean up the mess.

Outside, she took a deep breath as she got in her car and drove out of the driveway. Then she pulled over. She reached for her cell and called her brother.

Amazingly, Kevin answered.

"You're not in surgery today?"

"Nope. Office visits all day. I've only got a few minutes, though. What's up?"

Lainey fiddled with the steering wheel. "I just came from home."

"Oh? How's Mom?"

Lainey stared out the window, not seeing the rain on the windshield. "I kind of shocked her, Kev. She's not happy."

"You told her you're pregnant?"

Tears stung her eyes. Even though she'd suspected he knew. "How did you know?"

He sighed. "I can just tell. Where are you going for your OB?"

Lainey filled him in on the details.

"Is Lawless the father?"

Oh, she wished. Of the few men she'd been involved with, he was the most honorable, hands down. "No," she whispered.

He made a noise that could have been anything. "I caught him looking at you a couple times on Saturday. Really looking. Not how a brother wants a guy to look at his kid sister."

She nearly laughed, and tried to ignore the spurt of pleasure and pain his words caused. "Wow. I'm pretty sure you're wrong. And don't ask me any more about the father, okay? It's not—he's not interested in being a father."

"That's too damn bad," he growled. "Do you need me to hunt him down?"

Now she *did* laugh, at the vision of her respectable surgeon older brother beating the hell out of Jon. It would be quite a match, but her money would be on Kevin. "No. But, thanks."

A pause. "That's not right, Lainey. He shouldn't leave you—"

"It's okay," she interrupted him. "We're better off without him."

Kevin sighed. "All right. And, little sis? You'll be a hell of a mother."

His words and his faith in her warmed her. It was so nice to have him stand up for her. But still… "I don't want to be like our mother," she whispered. There it was…her deepest fear.

Kevin snorted. "You won't be. She somehow flat-out missed the maternal gene. You've got it in spades. You feeling okay?"

"Yeah. Just a little tired. Thankfully I don't have much nausea."

"Okay, good. I've got to run. I'll stop by and see Mom after I get out of here. Let me know if I can help, okay? You don't have to do this alone."

His words brought tears to her eyes. "Thanks, Kev. I will," she promised, and disconnected, feeling a little better. Kevin would smooth out what Lainey couldn't, but she doubted either of them could make Jacqui see this as a good thing.

She tucked the phone back into her purse and sat for another few moments. Her mother's reaction hadn't really shocked her. Jacqui would spin and spin, but in the end it was what Lainey did that mattered, and she'd make it work on her own. Again, if things were different— But they weren't. Whatever was going on with Ben, it had him clearly reluctant to make even the slightest commitment. She needed someone reliable.

So far the only reliable one was herself. The irony of that wasn't lost on her.

* * *

Lainey stood in her new backyard the next day after work and stared up into the nearly empty oak tree, then down at the ground where she stood ankle deep in yellow-brown leaves. Yesterday they'd all been on the tree. Today they were all on the ground. Clearly it was time for a trip to the hardware store to buy a rake.

She trudged through the leaves, hearing the crunch under her feet, on her way out front to her car. Her trip to the hardware store, where she purchased a rake, leaf bags, and a pair of work gloves, took less than half an hour.

She went out back, rake in hand, and tilted her face to the sun. She had a couple of hours before it would be too dark. Might as well make the most of it.

She hadn't been going for more than ten minutes when Ben's big truck pulled in the driveway. Her pulse kicked up and she gripped the rake a little harder. She walked over to the gate to greet him.

"Hi," she said, when he emerged from the truck and turned her way. She tried not to devour him with her eyes. She wanted to curl herself into his embrace, feel his warmth through the black fleece jacket he wore—

Wait. No, she didn't.

"Hey," he said, coming closer, his expression neutral. His gaze dropped to her belly. "Is this okay, in your condition?"

"Of course. I'm not doing any heavy lifting, so I'm fine," she said. "I can do pretty much anything as long as I don't overdo it."

He lifted his gaze to hers. "I can see you overdoing it."

She smiled and shook her head. "I'm very careful. I'm not going to put the baby in any danger."

"Of course you won't. I'll help."

She tried not to stare at the rear view as he walked to the

bed of his truck. How could she not notice how those worn jeans hugged his rear and thighs just right? She cleared her throat. "Do you just carry a rake in the back of your truck for emergencies?"

"I was here earlier and saw what had happened," he answered as she stepped aside for him to come through the gate. Before she could ask, he nodded to the garage. "The light in there was out. I put in a new bulb."

"I'm going to get spoiled—all this personal landlord service," she teased, and saw his back stiffen. "Not to worry. I can change my own lightbulbs."

He sent her a grin. "Does your mother know?"

"Shh," she murmured. "She'll hear you."

He laughed and started raking.

They worked in relative silence for a bit. Lainey kept sneaking glances at him. He'd unzipped his jacket and, while the tee shirt he wore underneath wasn't exactly skintight, she could still see the play of muscles underneath it when he raked.

She exhaled. It had certainly gotten hotter out here since he had shown up.

They raked a big pile over the next little while, and a slight breeze stirred the remaining leaves on the tree and several came floating down. He reached out and plucked a piece of one out of her hair, his fingers lingering on the strands. Her mouth went dry at the intense heat in his gaze and her pulse kicked up when he dropped his gaze to her mouth. Lainey stopped herself from leaning forward, from pressing her mouth to his. He stepped back and offered her the leaf with a small smile.

She took it and twirled the stem in her fingers. "Wow, thanks." She held it up, looking at the red and green threaded in with the yellow. "Pretty, isn't it?"

He closed his hand over hers. She looked up into his gaze.

"Gorgeous," he murmured, drawing her closer and she knew, with a flutter deep inside, that he wasn't talking about the leaf anymore.

He settled his mouth over hers. With a sigh, she melted into him, opening, letting his tongue slip in. When the kiss became deeper, hotter, she fisted the front of his jacket and he gripped her hips, drawing her closer, before plunging one hand into her hair, angling her head to thrust his tongue even deeper.

Fire skipped through her veins, burned along her nerve-endings, sent heat arrowing into the depth of her belly. She pressed closer, feeling his hardness against her and the an-swering heat of her response.

Suddenly he broke the kiss, though he didn't pull away from her, but rested his forehead on hers. Their breath mingled as she tried to calm her breathing. Every time he touched her she craved more. It wasn't enough. But it was all there was. Frustration welled and she squeezed her eyes shut.

"Lainey," he murmured, his voice raw and rough. "I told myself I'd stay away, but…" His voice trailed off as he stepped back, and she shivered from the loss of his heat. "We'd better get to work."

Shaking, Lainey bent to retrieve her discarded rake. She needed to pull back, keep this kind of thing from happening.

But the real question was, did she want to? In her heart, she feared the answer was no.

CHAPTER NINE

IT DIDN'T TAKE all that long to make a huge pile. Ben pulled some sticks out. "When was the last time you jumped in a leaf pile?"

Shame flushed Lainey's cheeks. "Well, never."

He stared at her. "No way? All those trees on your parents' land and you never played in a leaf pile?"

"No. My mother—you'd have to know my mother. She's not big on dirt." That sounded sad, but it was the truth.

"Oh." There was a wealth of understanding in the word. "I see."

She looked at him in surprise. "You do?"

He nodded. "You need to experience it before the baby gets here. Let me make sure all the sticks are out."

He poked in the pile and she watched with a combination of amusement and exasperation. After extracting a few more sticks, he fluffed the pile with his rake and turned, the satisfaction on his face making her laugh.

"Does it pass muster?" she teased gently.

He nodded. "You're not too far along for this, are you?"

On impulse, Lainey unzipped her vest and ran her hand over her very slight baby bump. The tenderness in his eyes as he watched made her breath catch. "Am I jumping out of a tree?"

His gaze jerked up. "Of course not."

"Then I'll be fine." She leapt lightly into the pile, landing on her knees. The crackle of the leaves and their fresh scent invigorated her. She laughed and threw an armful of leaves in the air, then tried to cover her head when they came raining back down.

"Incoming!" Ben called, and before she could scramble too far over he came crashing into the pile with her. He gave her a big grin—the first she'd seen with no shadows, no pain in his eyes—and tossed a handful of leaves at her. "So, what do you think?"

She threw some back at him. "It was worth the wait."

He laughed. "Yeah? Awesome." He turned and flopped back, folding his hands under his head. "I'm guessing you never looked at cloud shapes either?"

"Stop reminding me how deprived my childhood was," she scolded him with a laugh, and he snaked out a hand and pulled her head down to his. The sweetness of this kiss after the passion of the earlier one threw her.

When she pulled back, searching his face with her gaze, he touched her cheek, twining his fingers in her hair. "I'm sorry," he said.

She arched a brow. "For what?"

"For all you missed. I assumed, growing up as you did, you had everything."

She shrugged and pulled a leaf out of his hair. "I had everything material you could want. Only I didn't actually want it. I didn't get time with my parents. But I see now my mom didn't know how to raise us. She was so caught up in perceptions that just letting me be a kid wasn't possible. She meant well, but…" She sat up in the leaves. "We turned out okay, Kevin and I. Him more than me," she added with a little sigh, thinking of her struggling shop, her pregnancy and her money woes.

Ben frowned. "Don't do that."

Startled, she looked at him. "Do what?"

"Put yourself down like that. You're living life on your terms. How is that not okay?"

"Oh." She nibbled on her lip while she thought. "You're right. I hadn't thought of it like that. I guess I just want to prove I can do it."

"You are. You will." He stood up and extended a hand to her.

His quiet confidence warmed her down to her toes and her heart tipped dangerously.

"Let's get this done."

She grasped his warm, callused palm and let him draw her to her feet. "Okay."

They managed to load about half the leaves into bags before it got too dark. Lainey's arms and back were screaming, and it was with an incredible sense of relief that she dropped her rake on the ground to stretch her back.

"Did you overdo it?" The concern in his voice made her smile.

"According to my back and arms, yes. But none of that will hurt the baby."

"Go on in," he told her. "I'll put these things in the garage. I'll finish tomorrow."

She hesitated before starting toward the house. "Do you—do you want to come in? For coffee or something?"

"I'd like that," he said softly. "If you think you aren't too tired?"

"No, I'm fine. Come in when you're done."

She hurried into the house and started the coffee maker. A quick trip to the bathroom revealed wild hair and a nose bright red from the cold.

Oooh. Sexy.

Though Ben clearly hadn't minded. He'd kissed her. Twice.

Would there be a third time?

She shook her head at her reflection. *Stop it.* She detoured to the living room to switch on the fire. While the walls were bare in here, as she hadn't had a chance yet to deal with artwork, she'd gotten the furniture arranged like she wanted and unpacked pillows and a couple throws. It was comfy enough for the moment. Ben would understand.

When she got back to the kitchen she caught a glimpse of him coming out of the garage. For just a heartbeat she was a wife and a mom, waiting for her man to come in.

The thought threw her. She'd been a wife, and had given up waiting for her man to come in pretty quickly. She was going to be a mom—and that terrified her. But she'd never felt for her ex-husband what she felt for Ben—and she wasn't even in love with Ben.

Not yet.

Reeling from that thought, she opened the cupboard to take out coffee mugs as Ben came in through the back door. She gave him a bright smile. "It's decaf. That okay?"

"Sure," he said, and shrugged out of his jacket.

She poured his and handed it to him. "Let's go in here," she said and led the way to the living room. She settled on the couch with him across from her.

"Something wrong? You look a little pale."

Ben's casual comment threw her. She certainly couldn't tell him *he* was part of what was worrying her. "I'm not ready to be a mother," she blurted. "But I'm committed now."

He looked genuinely surprised. "Why do you think you're not ready?"

"I'm still getting my shop off the ground. I'm not in the best place financially." He just looked at her and she shut her eyes. "I'm not. My parents are wealthy, yes, but there was no trust fund or anything. It was kind of understood

I'd either get a fantastic career or a loaded husband. Or both." She stared at his shoulder, unable to meet his eyes. "I managed to do neither."

"You say that like it's a bad thing," he said softly.

She looked at him and the misery in her eyes nearly had him reaching for her. He wanted to tuck her under his arm and hold her against his chest, where he already knew she fit perfectly.

"I know it shouldn't be. And my ex-husband is a real doozy. Seven years of my life I'll never get back. But somehow it is—in my family. I'm happy where I am. I'm just—"

She stopped and he saw the sheen of tears. "Just what?"

"So worried. Because I don't want to be a bad mother," Lainey blurted, and covered her face with her hands.

Now he did reach for her, and caught her wrists and gently pulled her hands away. "Why would you think you would be?"

She gave a harsh little laugh and looked down in her lap. "My mother has no maternal genes. None. Zero. We aren't close, even though it seems like I see her all the time. I don't want my baby to feel like he or she doesn't matter."

Anger washed through him. "You feel like you don't matter?"

She stood up and walked over to the fireplace. She stared into the dancing flames. "I— Yes. I've never really been a part of the family. I always felt like just a prop, I guess. The black sheep."

He came up behind her and slid his hands down her arms. "You are going to be a wonderful mother, Lainey." When she shook her head, he leaned down and pressed his cheek to hers, inhaled her sweet scent. "Listen to me. I haven't known you long, but what I see is a warm, compassionate, giving woman who cares deeply about those who matter to her. You're strong. You're sweet. You're funny. All of that is going to translate naturally to motherhood."

She turned in his arms and looked up at him, her eyes huge in the soft light of the lamp and the fire. The uncertainty in her eyes killed him.

"You think so?"

He'd meant every word. He touched her face, unable to stop himself from feeling her soft skin. She leaned into him just slightly, eyes closed, and he swallowed hard but couldn't step away even if he wanted to. Which, God help him, he didn't.

"No. I know so."

Her eyes fluttered open and he gave in, lowering his mouth to hers, hearing her sharp inhale. He hesitated at the last second. Her breath feathered over his and she closed the gap, coming up to meet him. He slipped his hands in her hair, even though they really wanted to roam farther south. All he wanted to do right now was feel.

Lainey. Only Lainey.

The kiss grew more urgent quickly, and she opened to him with a little growl in her throat that only served to fuel his internal fire. When her arms went around his neck and she pressed her length against him he was lost.

No. He was found. He hadn't wanted to be, and he wouldn't be able to stay. But she'd managed to lay waste to all his defenses.

He broke the kiss before he accidentally toppled her into the fireplace and rested his forehead on hers. She didn't move away, though he felt the tension return to her body. "I didn't want you to end up in the fire."

She blinked at him, then a small smile curved her mouth. "Thoughtful of you."

"Isn't it, though? Gentleman through and through." He savored her laugh as he took her hand and led her to the couch. If she knew how badly he wanted to take her to bed, to feel her move beneath him, to make love to her, she'd know he wasn't any kind of gentleman.

And those thoughts weren't helpful.

Trying to bring them back around, he asked, "How are your shoulders?"

She rolled them and winced. "I'll be feeling this for a couple days, I think."

He pulled her down on the couch and sat so he was behind her. He began to knead her shoulders gently. "Wow. You *are* tight. Relax and let me see if I can help with that."

She let her head fall forward. "Mmm. That feels wonderful."

Yeah. It did. But touching her like this, on top of the kisses earlier, was sending all his blood south. And when she moaned his breath shortened. He leaned forward and kissed her neck, still massaging, but letting his hands slip over her shoulders to brush the tops of her breasts through her shirt, then moving them back up to her shoulders. Her little inhale prompted him to do it again, this time slipping his hands under her breasts to cup them in his hands, brush his thumbs over her nipples. Was this one of the lacy, sexy bras he'd seen that day in her bathroom?

"Lainey…" he murmured against her neck, and she tilted her head to the side, her breathing shallow. He kissed her neck one more time and she shifted out of his arms. He let her go, instantly feeling her loss, but she just turned around and settled on his lap, wrapped her arms around his neck.

"Stay," she whispered. "Please."

"Lainey." He rested his forehead on hers, struggling for some semblance of control. "Are you sure?"

She slid off his lap and held out her hand. It was trembling slightly and he could see uncertainty warring with desire in her eyes. She was offering him a gift and she was afraid he wouldn't take it.

This might be his only chance. A few hours of heaven he knew he didn't deserve.

But Lainey did.

He took her hand without ever breaking eye contact and stood.

Smoke filled the room, smothering him, searing his lungs, his eyes, his skin. God, he couldn't see through the gray haze. A cough racked him, tearing at his parched throat. He couldn't yell for his friend. Where was Jason? He couldn't reach him—had to get him out before the house came down around him. A roar and a crack, and orange lit the room. The ceiling caved in on a crash fueled by the roar of flames. He spun around, but the door was blocked by a flaming heap of debris. Under it was a boot. Jason coming to save him.

Ben woke up, gasping, to find Lainey's terrified face over him.

"Ben?"

The concern, the worry, was too much for him, and he clamped both hands over his face so she couldn't see the pain, the anger, the shame seeping from him like tears.

Her hand was soft on his arm. "Ben?"

He shook her off. "Lainey—don't. God. I—it's just a dream." He sat up, cursing himself for falling asleep, for allowing the intimacy at all, for thinking maybe it would be okay.

She drew back, a sheet pulled up over those glorious breasts, her gaze steady and worried. "If it's just a dream why are you so rattled?"

She saw too much. Too damn much. He was stripped

emotionally bare after their wonderful night together—all that emotion which he hadn't expected.

"I can't explain it now," he said, weary. "Go back to sleep. I'll see myself out."

Her quick intake of breath lanced him. No point in telling her he wouldn't sleep anymore, anyway. Better she knew as little as possible. Better he didn't give her the chance to soothe him, to connect, while he was vulnerable.

She said nothing as he pulled on his pants in the dark, fumbled with his wallet.

"What ever it is, running isn't going to make it go away."

Her words, though soft, hit him as hard as if she'd shouted or thrown glass shards at him.

"It's not going to make it stop."

"I'm sorry," was all he could say, while he thought, *Yeah, but all I can do is run.* If she knew what he'd done she'd never speak to him again. Bad enough now she'd see him as weak.

He paused in the doorway, looked back. She'd lain down again, her back to the door, covers pulled all the way up. He ached to go back to her, but he knew it was for the best.

"Go if you're going to," she said, her voice raw, and he did, leaving her in her warm bed and slipping into the chilly night.

Beth stopped in her tracks as soon as she entered the shop the next morning. "Wow. You look tired. What happened?"

Lainey winced, then sighed. It was true. Between Ben keeping her awake and then leaving after the nightmare she'd gotten pretty much no sleep. "Ben happened."

Beth cocked her head. "If you were glowing, I'd guess the lack of sleep was due to happy times with Ben," she said. "But I'm guessing not so much?"

"It ended badly," Lainey said finally. "I'm not sure what happened. We were—well, we…" She paused as her cheeks heated and Beth's brow rose as a grin stole across her face. "I guess I don't have to explain it to you. But he just left." She shrugged as if it hadn't hurt. After how wonderful everything had been, she couldn't *help* but be hurt.

It infuriated her.

"Just walked out as in thanks and bye?" Beth's tone was incredulous.

"Not quite that crass, but, yeah." Lainey couldn't tell Beth about Ben's nightmare. He seemed to be ashamed of it, and it wasn't her place to tell anyone. "I really don't want to talk about it."

Beth sent her a sympathetic look. "Love is messy."

Lainey nearly dropped the bucket she held. No one had said anything about love. Especially not with a man who was clearly keeping something from her. "We've just got really good chemistry."

"Chemistry is good," Beth said cheerfully. "And, all told, this is a huge improvement over last week, when I told you to go for it and you looked like I'd kicked a puppy." Her voice sobered and she threw an arm around Lainey's shoulders. "Seriously, though, I see more than just chemistry. The way you say his name—"

"Oh, Beth." Lainey interrupted before this got any worse. "I do *not*. Obviously I like him a lot but that's all. There's no more than that."

Except the slight twist in her belly told a different story. The way he'd loved her, cherished her. The way he made her feel important. The way he stood up for her, even to herself. How crushed she'd been when he shut her out last night.

Oh, no.

Beth looked at her steadily. "If you say so."

Lainey forced a smile. "I do say so." As she forced herself to walk casually to the back room, gripping the bucket handle so hard it hurt, she was afraid Beth was right. This whole thing, at least for her, had tipped well past mutual chemistry and into dangerous emotional territory.

Clearly she'd learned nothing from her past.

But Ben wasn't Daniel or Jon. And, really, how would she know love? She'd never been in love before. It most certainly couldn't happen this quickly.

Could it?

Ben sat at the Rusty Hammer bar, a burger with all the trimmings before him. Best damn burgers anywhere, but it could be cardboard for all he could taste it. Still, the owner was looking at him, so he gave it a shot.

Someone settled on the bar stool next to him. A quick glance revealed Kevin Keeler. The other man nodded in acknowledgement and Ben did the same. Fantastic. Just what he needed.

"What can I get you?" The owner had come to stand in front of Kevin.

Kevin inclined his head toward Ben's plate. "One of those and a beer, please."

"On the way." He drew the beer, placed it in front of Kevin and headed for the kitchen.

Kevin took a long draw. He set the glass down with a thunk and half turned to Ben, who braced himself.

"So. What are your intentions toward my sister?"

Ben nearly choked on his burger. Kevin thumped him on the back. "It's probably a good idea to do that in front of a doctor," he observed dryly.

Ben shook his head and grabbed his beer. Was this a trick question? Did Kevin know he'd slept with her? He doubted it. Lainey would never kiss and tell to Kevin. Besides, big brothers weren't inclined to be friendly when you messed with their little sisters.

"Nothing. No intentions. She needed a date and invited me to the gala. That's all." His words were hollow but he hoped Kevin wouldn't pick up on it. He'd never intended anything to go as far as it had, physically or otherwise. She'd filled holes in him that had desperately needed filling, as hard as he'd tried to avoid it.

Kevin tapped his glass. "It doesn't look like *all*," he said. "You were looking at her pretty seriously. With her being pregnant, I need to know what your intentions are."

Ben picked up his beer and took a deliberate swallow. "Like I said—"

Kevin leaned in. "She deserves better than a guy with *no intentions*. A hell of a lot better. She's been through hell and back with that idiot of an ex-husband, not to mention our selfish, clueless parents."

Ben met the other man's serious gaze. "I completely agree. That's why I have no intention of getting tangled up in her life." *Anymore than I already am.* "She asked for a favor. I agreed. She's an amazing woman and I wish her all the best."

Kevin sat back with a frown. "She's got feelings for you."

"I hope not," he said quietly, but he knew Kevin was right. The hell of it was, he had powerful feelings for her, too. "Like I said, I can't give her what she needs." The truth was painful and he gripped the bottle tighter. "So. My intentions are to walk away and let her live her life." The words were like ash in his mouth.

Kevin nodded at the owner, who'd delivered his burger. "I'm not sure if you're smart or a coward."

Ben barked out a laugh. "Truthfully? Me either."

Actually, that wasn't true. He did know. He was keeping Lainey safe, and that wasn't a cowardly move.

Was it?

For all his not wanting to be part of a family, for not wanting home and hearth and kids and a wife, he knew underneath it all he was a sham. He wanted all of it. He wanted what Jason and Callie had had. He didn't know how to open himself up to have it. But if he could— Lainey was a good woman. She'd be a wonderful mother and wife to the right man.

Just not for him.

CHAPTER TEN

LAINEY HURRIED HOME after work on the day of the gala. Of course her mother *would* schedule this party on a Thursday. And, being only her and Beth at the shop, Lainey couldn't exactly take the afternoon off. So she was left with an hour to do all the primping required for a black tie affair.

Her nerves wouldn't settle. She hadn't seen Ben since he'd left that night. She took a deep breath and tried to focus on her hair and make-up, which were thankfully simple. Even with a redo of eyeliner due to her shaking hand. She got the dress on and tried to suck in her belly as she turned to study herself in the full-length mirror. Then she relaxed. The black fabric draped low over her breasts and gathered gently at her stomach, so the pregnancy wasn't obvious.

She eyed the black heels lying on the floor of her room. Sparkly and sexy, they absolutely killed her feet.

She'd make the sacrifice.

The doorbell rang and she scooped up the shoes and made a quick stop in the bathroom. She tried to examine her make-up in the mirror, but all she could see was flushed cheeks and sparkling eyes. She'd piled her hair on her head in an elaborate updo the likes of which she didn't have a reason for too often anymore.

For someone who'd insisted repeatedly this night meant nothing, she'd sure spent a lot of energy stressing over it.

Hearing the bell again, she took a deep breath and hurried over to open the door.

She simply lost her breath.

The tux emphasized Ben's broad shoulders and slim hips. His hair curled a little over the collar, and she took a step back so she didn't reach out to run her fingers through it.

His gaze swept over her in the way a man's did when he appreciated a woman he was interested in. Her nerve-endings sizzled, as if he'd actually caressed her. Heat ran down her spine and he gave her a rare, slow smile.

"You're gorgeous." The words were simple, heartfelt, and she felt her heart stutter at the raw edge in his tone. Daniel had never looked at her like that or said anything so simple—and meant it. Something inside her shifted.

"Thank you," she managed. "So are you."

She stepped aside to let him in. The butterflies in her stomach had grown into bats.

She cleared her throat. "I've just got to get my shoes on."

"All right." He studied her while she sat down and buckled them on her feet. When she stood he must have noticed her wince. "Why do you wear them if they hurt?"

No point in being cagey. "They look great." She lifted the hem of her dress over her ankle so he could see. "See?"

He lifted his gaze from her ankle to her face and she felt the heat of it. She was very glad she'd decided to paint her toenails a sexy red.

An answering sizzle ran through her as he cleared his throat. "Lovely." His voice was still a bit hoarse.

A visceral shudder ran through her at the memory of his hands on her the other night. How wonderful they'd been together. Until he'd left.

She swallowed and grabbed her clutch. "I'm ready."

He rested his hand on the small of her back as they went out her door. The touch was familiar and intimate. "What do women carry in those things anyway?"

"This?" Lainey held up the silver clutch. At his nod she continued. "Well, I've got keys, phone, lipstick, a couple of tissues. A couple of make-up things. The usual girl stuff, I guess." Other than things like tampons, of course. Pregnant girls didn't need those.

"Keys? In there?" He stepped aside so she could lock the door.

"Well, off the ring. Just for the door— Oh!" She turned around and stared at the black coupe, an exact replica of the one she'd owned a year ago. Daniel's gift to her. Recovering before he could notice her shock, she added, "Nice ride."

"Thanks." He opened the door for her and held it while she got in. The rich scent of the buttery leather and the new carpet hit her. A few seconds later he was sliding in the driver's seat. "I didn't think my usual ride was appropriate for tonight. I figured you'd be in a fancy dress and it might be hard to climb in and out of the truck."

Her heart caught. He'd done it for her. Even though she'd ambushed him with it less than two weeks ago, he'd come through. "Thank you," she said after she got her voice back. "It was very thoughtful of you."

"More what you're used to," he said, without looking at her.

Oh, so *that* was how it was. "Ben, you see what I drive now."

He said nothing and she sighed. "It's in my past. And I'm happier without it." The full truth there. That car had symbolized her ultimate failure and catalyzed her ability to do something about it. She gave the dashboard an affectionate little pat and heard Ben's low chuckle.

The full moon hung huge and silver in the obsidian sky as they drove to the Lakeside Country Club. As she looked at it, shining over the lake, she couldn't help but wonder if her mother had managed to call in a favor from somewhere to arrange for the moon.

The club, of course, was gorgeous. What had to be miles of twinkle lights outlined the building, luminaries lined the walkways, and through the wide glass doors she could see a roaring fire in the fireplace. Ben pulled up to the port-cochere and a valet glided forward to open the door. "Good evening, sir and madam," he said as Ben held his hand out and helped Lainey out of the car. She was perfectly capable of exiting on her own, but with Ben it didn't feel like a grand gesture for the sake of it but more as if he wanted to touch her any way he could.

So she let him.

The valet closed the door and took Ben's keys. He cocked his arm at her. "Shall we?"

She tucked her hand in the warm crook of his arm and enjoyed the little fizzy feeling touching him gave her. She took a deep breath and had to keep herself from turning into him to just breathe him in. "Yes. Let's."

After stepping inside and taking care of her wrap, Lainey proceeded with Ben to the hall where the gala was being held. It was early, so the room was little more than half full, and they perused the tables until they found theirs. With her parents, of course. And Kevin.

"Lot of people here already," Ben commented, looking around.

"Yes," Lainey agreed. "Mother does a wonderful job with this." Credit where it was due. Her mother knew how to throw a party.

Lainey spotted her mother heading toward them, a vision in designer gold. On anyone else the form-fitting gown would be tacky. On Jacqui it was perfect.

"Lainey." She offered her cheek and Lainey dutifully kissed her, then offered her own.

"Hi, Mother." She laid a hand on Ben's arm, felt the heat of him through his sleeve. "This is Ben Lawless. Ben, this is my mother—Jacqui Keeler."

Jacqui gave Ben an obvious once-over. He held out his hand with a smile and she took it.

"Nice to meet you," he said.

"Likewise," she said, and turned to Lainey. "Now, honey, you two mingle for a bit before you take your seats. And no leaving until ten o'clock." Someone must have signaled her mother, because Jacqui turned abruptly to leave before Lainey could say a word. "I'll see you at dinner." And she was gone.

"Sorry," Lainey said immediately. "My mom's a little intense. Don't take it personally." What Jacqui could find lacking in the smoking hot package that was Ben, Lainey couldn't fathom. Because he wasn't Daniel? Couldn't give her what her mother deemed most important—money?

"I see that," Ben said as he steered her toward a buffet table piled high with sinful goodies. "And I'm not offended. Let's get something to drink."

Along the way they got pulled into several conversations—people who knew Lainey, or thought they did. The whole process was as exhausting as it always had been to smile for her mother or stump for her father. Tonight was a bit of both.

"Here." Ben pushed a golden flute into her hand. "I know your…situation. But I think you need this. Just carry it if nothing else."

The champagne bubbled in the flute and Lainey took

a tiny sip. It fizzed in her mouth and slid down her throat. Ben was right. Just having it in her hand was enough. She didn't need anyone questioning why she refused to drink. "Thank you. It hits the spot."

Ben bent so his mouth was next to her ear. She could hear him over the band, which had just started up. "You're welcome."

Lainey hoped he didn't notice the little shiver that skittered down her spine at his warm breath on her skin. She was so, so lost to this man. And he didn't even know it.

He moved away slightly and she felt the immediate loss of contact. She chided herself for letting herself get caught up in this even for a moment. Despite her decision to enjoy tonight, it wasn't real. It didn't change anything.

"So, what's good here?" Ben asked her as they surveyed the table loaded with *hors d'oeuvres* of every persuasion. There were tiny *petit-fours*, as well as fancy little things that looked like shrimp, mushrooms, cheese. All high end. No mini hot dogs for this party.

"I'd say all of it," she said. "My mother doesn't skimp on this stuff."

He smiled and handed her a plate. "Not surprised."

Lainey took a few small things and put them on her plate, and Ben did the same. Her brother approached them and Lainey braced herself.

"Laine," Kevin greeted her. She noticed he was dateless, and frowned.

"Kev, where's your date? How did *you* get away with coming stag?" Realizing how her words sounded, she quickly turned to Ben.

He just nodded at Kevin and said, "I see someone I need to talk to. I'll catch up with you in a bit, okay?"

"Um, okay," Lainey said, feeling like a total heel.

"Nice job," Kevin commented, lifting a flute of champagne from a passing waiter. "You've got a way with men, sis."

Lainey sent him a sour look, even though he was right. "I didn't mean it how it sounded." Still, she'd hurt Ben with her thoughtless comment. And after he'd gone to such trouble for her tonight. She tracked him with her eyes and noticed he'd stopped next to a tall, gorgeous, slender blond. Who couldn't possibly have natural boobs. Lainey frowned.

"And you're not listening to anything I say," Kevin said, amusement in his tone. "You can't take your eyes off the guy, can you? Does Mother know?"

"Does Mother know what?" Jacqui materialized next to them and peered critically at Lainey's plate. "Be careful, dear. I know you're—" she glanced around and lowered her voice "—pregnant, but you don't want to gain a lot of weight."

Lainey looked at her and for the first time saw an unhappy, brittle woman whose need to control everything had nearly estranged her from her children and whose marriage had taken a serious toll on her self-worth. Instead of being insulted by her thoughtless words, Lainey felt only pity.

"No worries, Mother," she said smoothly, and selected a prosciutto something from her plate. She was eating for two, right? Might as well do it tonight. "Lovely party, by the way."

Effectively sidetracked, Jacqui glowed. "It is, isn't it? Almost time to get seated for dinner. Lainey, get your date. Kevin, thanks for coming. I know you have to get back later."

Lainey's gaze lasered to Ben as her mother hurried off. Now he was laughing with the blond, his dark head near her golden one. Something sour curled in her belly. Couldn't be jealousy, could it? Despite their night together, and all her feelings for him, she had no actual claim on him. None at all.

So it was silly and petty to be jealous.

As if he'd felt her watching him, he lifted his head and locked on her gaze. The sour feeling was replaced by something much, much sweeter.

Kevin stepped closer, into her line of sight, his gaze intense and knowing. Her stomach sank.

"Anything you want to tell me, sis?"

Lainey stared up at him. *Oh, no.* She swallowed hard. "No. Nothing."

He gave a little nod and stepped back. He looked as if he wanted to say something, then thought better of it and turned and walked away.

Ben made his way through the crowd to Lainey. Her gaze snapped to his and relief lit her big blue eyes just for a moment. Then it was gone.

"Sorry about that," Ben said, coming up next to her. She smelled so good. Like vanilla and something sinful. Sweet and sinful. That was Lainey, all wrapped up in one sexy package.

Sexy *pregnant* package, that was.

God, he was in trouble.

"It's okay." Her voice was a little remote. "Of course you know people here."

"Megan is an old friend, but not *that* kind of friend." Ben surprised himself by how important it was that she understand. "I was surprised to see her here."

She gave him a sideways look. "I get it."

He caught her hand and twined his fingers with hers. She looked down, clearly startled, then up to his face.

"Lainey. You are the only woman I can see." The words were rough in his throat, but true in every sense. There was no one but her. If things were different there would never be anyone but her. All he could give her was tonight. It had to be enough.

Her gaze stayed on his, her blue eyes wide and hopeful, fearful. He wanted to drown in them, in her. Instead he gave her fingers a squeeze and stepped back. "I take it we're supposed to sit down?"

A shadow passed over her face quickly, then she smiled. "Shall we?"

They made their way to the table. He noted she kept an eye on her parents, who were still mingling and mixing and chatting up the guests. The table was set for eight and Kevin was already there, his gaze firmly on Ben.

His words from the other night hit him hard. *No intentions.* Yeah, he was a liar. He wanted so much more than he could give her—wanted to give her what she deserved—and Kevin's hard stare said he knew it. Not only that, he knew Ben was going to walk. Ben met the other man's gaze squarely. They both knew she deserved better.

Dinner went fairly quickly. Prime rib, decadent desserts, rich sides all filled the plates. Ben hadn't eaten so well in ages. Lainey, he noted, only picked at her food.

"Not hungry?"

She looked up and flushed. "Not really. These things— it's not my cup of tea." She slid her plate toward him. "Here. Help yourself if you want."

He did fork up a couple of pieces of her prime rib, because it *was* prime rib and he was a guy. He caught Jacqui's fierce frown at her daughter as she got up and he wondered at it.

Jacqui walked to the microphone at the front of the room. After a little speech of welcome and thanks, she added, "Dancing will begin as soon as the last of the plates are cleared. Don't forget the silent auction—there's still time to place your bids."

"I'm going to hit the ladies' room," Lainey murmured to him. She stood and picked up her little silver purse. "Back in a few."

"So. Ben." Her father leaned forward across the table as soon as Lainey had left. "How do you know my daughter?"

Wow, was he sixteen again, or what? He kept his tone level. "Through my grandmother. Lainey's been helping her out at her place."

The man looked surprised. "Really?"

Ben nodded. "I think her visits are the highlight of Grandma's week." How could this guy not know the kind of person his daughter was?

"What do you do for a living?"

Ben tensed just slightly. This man could and would ferret out the truth, and Ben would bet he wanted to know. "I'm a firefighter."

Greg Keeler arched a brow. "Really? Where?"

"City of Grand Rapids." He hesitated for a beat as he met the other man's gaze. "I'm on medical leave right now." Better just to say it than have it found out and used against Lainey somehow.

The very fact he was even concerned was a problem.

The older man's gaze sharpened. It was no doubt only a matter of time before the man looked him up if he thought Ben was interested in his daughter. "I hope your recovery is going well."

Ben managed a smile. "Well enough." Actually, there was some truth to that. Being around Lainey had helped him. Better than any therapy.

Greg leaned across the table. "While being a firefighter is a very important job, you need to realize you're not what we have in mind for Lainey," he said, almost apologetically. "Her ex-husband is a partner in a very prestigious law firm. I understand they're considering reconciliation."

Ben's brow shot up, as did his pulse. He sure as hell hadn't seen any indication that Lainey was interested in her ex-husband. In fact, if memory served him, she was no fan of his. "Is that so? Then why isn't he here with her?"

"Because I didn't invite him." Lainey's voice was cold as she stood behind Ben and regarded her father with sharp eyes. "He's my ex-husband for a lot of very good reasons."

Her father sat back and shook his head. "Lainey—"

She shot him a hard look and turned to Ben as the band struck up. "Want to dance?"

"Of course." He pushed back from the table and inclined his head to Greg. The older man crossed his arms and frowned as he led Lainey away.

"How about a walk instead?" he asked. The band was playing, but it was too early to dance. They'd be the only ones on the floor, and possibly the center of attention. He doubted Lainey wanted that.

She nodded. "I'd like that."

He put his hand at the small of her back, because he couldn't not touch her, and they made their way to the glass doors at the other end of the room. They opened out to a sheltered patio that overlooked the water. It was chilly, but he figured he'd keep her warm.

As soon as they were outside she took an audible breath. Sympathy filled him. "Is that the first time you've breathed all evening?"

She gave him a rueful smile. "Seems like it. Old habits. I never wanted to do anything that might draw attention to myself. I always wanted to be anywhere but here."

"I can understand that." Seeing her interact with her family—except for her brother—was eye-opening.

"Can you?" She leaned on the railing and the position

allowed him a fantastic view of her breasts. He shifted position slightly so he could see better—if he chose to look—and so no one coming up next to them would get the same treat.

"You don't think I can?"

"I don't know. My childhood was so lonely. I didn't have a Rose. As you can see, I didn't even have normal parents." She didn't look at him. "What was yours like?"

He rested a hip on the railing. "Normal, I guess. Both parents—though they got divorced when I was twelve. My brother and sister. All of them live downstate, around Detroit. After the divorce things changed, but our parents took a lot of trouble to make sure we knew we were loved." Really, they'd been lucky. He could see that now, in Lainey's wistful expression.

She was quiet for a moment. "I'm sorry about my dad. I'm not sure what got into him."

"He wants what's best for you." The words caused an ache in his chest. It wasn't him. But part of him—a huge part—wished it was.

Her laugh was low and sad. "If that's true, they should know Daniel's not what's best. The man's a snake." She turned and looked up into his eyes. "There's no chance of reconciliation, by the way."

While he truly hadn't thought so, relief still trickled through him. "You definitely deserve better than a snake."

A smile tugged at the corners of her mouth. "Aw. That's so sweet."

He touched her chin. *You are the sweet one,* he wanted to say. Actually, he wanted to say much more than that, and it worried him. The band struck up a slower tune and he held out a hand. "Dance with me?"

She looked up, startled. "Out here?"

"We can go inside if you'd rather. But there are more eyes."

"Good point." She turned to face him and he pulled her into his arms, then steered her away from the railing into the deeper shadows caused by the overhang of the roof.

She felt so good in his arms. She fit so well. He tried not to think of the other night, when they'd moved together in perfect sync. He pulled her closer and felt her stiffen slightly. It shouldn't matter, but it did.

He lowered his head to her ear. "You can relax. I don't bite."

She gave a half-giggle, half-sigh, and he was pleased to feel her body relax a little. "I know. I'm sorry. Just trying to get through this…" Her voice trailed off as he tugged her a little closer, so her breasts touched his chest. Her breath hitched just a bit and she shivered.

"Cold?" His voice was low, and he pulled her in even closer. She'd be able to feel, now, just how affected he was by her. What he couldn't tell her was how right she felt in his arms, how much he felt as if he'd finally come home.

"Not at all," she breathed, and tipped her face up to his.

Unable to help himself, he pressed a kiss on her soft mouth. Two things crossed his mind.

He was in trouble.

And, after all she'd done for him, she deserved to know the truth.

CHAPTER ELEVEN

THE MOMENTS SPENT in Ben's arms were magical. Almost as magical as the other night. Lainey hadn't thought dancing could be so intimate, but somehow they were in their own little world of two. She didn't want it to end, and that was a first. But, since the band had taken a break for her mother to announce the winners of the silent auction, maybe it was time to take their own personal party elsewhere.

"Do you want to leave?"

Ben's arm was draped across the back of her chair and he brushed his fingers over her bare shoulder. "This is your shindig, Laine. You know the protocol better than I do."

She leaned forward to pick up her clutch from the table. "Then let's go. My feet are killing me."

His low chuckle warmed her. "Sacrifice over?"

"Something like that." She scanned the crowd. "I'll have to say goodnight to my mother. Give me a minute to track her down."

"I'll go with you." He unfolded himself from his chair and offered her his arm. She took it. All the vibes he gave off were those of a man who liked her, desired her—yet there was a layer underneath she couldn't quite get to…a place he kept away from her. It contrasted sharply with the intimacy of the evening. With how badly she wanted to open her heart to him.

How afraid she was, after tonight, that she already had.

Lainey found her mother near the auction exhibits. "We're heading out. It was a lovely party, Mother."

"You're leaving?" Jacqui's gaze darted from Lainey to Ben and back again. "So soon?"

Lainey kept her gaze steady on her mother's. "Yes. I'm tired and my feet hurt."

"Of course. I guess in your—" she lowered her voice "—condition that's to be expected." Someone called out to Jacqui then, and she offered her cheek to Lainey, who dropped the expected kiss. "Go straight home," she instructed, and hurried off.

Lainey sighed at the words and turned to Ben. "Shall we?"

"Absolutely." He put his hand on her back again—a gesture that Lainey was starting to love for its quiet possessiveness. It didn't take long for them to get the car and head toward home.

"Will you—will you come in?" she asked when he pulled in her driveway. The bold words startled her, especially in light of how their night together had ended before. Was she really willing to have him run away again?

He turned to her, and by the light of the dash she could see the pain in his eyes. "I'm not sure that's a good idea."

She sucked in a breath, the shininess of the evening tarnished. "Of course. Well. Thank you for everything." For the dances. For the kisses. For the feeling that this was actually going to be able to go somewhere when he must not feel the same. How could she have read it all so wrong?

He reached over the console and caught her hand as she fumbled for the door handle. "No. Lainey. Wait. I just don't want to hurt you."

She stared at him. They were in this far too deep for that. "We're adults. I know you're leaving, Ben. I know this isn't forever." But given the chance she'd take forever. The thought rocked her.

He rubbed his thumb over her lower lip and she closed her eyes.

"I can't stay the night."

The hesitation in his voice made her open them again. "All I was going to offer was coffee."

He laughed and rested his forehead on hers. "Lainey... God. I don't deserve you."

He got out of the car, and as he walked around to her door she whispered, "Yes, you do."

"Did you tell her yet?"

Ben put the leftover roast back in the fridge. For two people, they had enough to feed them for a week. Maybe two. "Tell who what?"

Rose wheeled around and he saw her frown. "Don't play games with me, Benjamin. When are you going to tell Lainey about Jason?"

He shut the fridge and stared at the sandwich he no longer had an appetite for. He was tired, he wanted to get out of the tux, and he had no idea why his grandmother had waited up for him. "I'm not, Grandma. She doesn't need to know." He didn't want her to think less of him.

Her gaze went to slits. "Oh, yes, she does. You are in love with that girl—"

Panic sliced through him. "She's hardly a girl—" *That* was what he protested? He'd meant to say no way was he in love with Lainey. Sure, she'd helped him open up in ways he hadn't thought were possible, but that didn't mean he was in love with her.

His grandma waved his words away impatiently. "Semantics. When you're my age a thirty-something woman is a girl. You love her—even if you aren't willing to admit it yet. She's got it equally bad for you. I would have thought going with her tonight would help you see that. You don't have forever, Ben. Ask Callie."

Her voice was quiet, and Ben sank down in a chair as if she'd taken an axe to his knees. "Geez, Grandma, how can you say that?"

She wheeled closer, her gaze intense. "Do you think Jason wasted one single minute when he first spotted that girl? No, he didn't. He had some good years with her, loved her fully. And he—he alone—was reckless and lost it all. How do you think Callie would feel, knowing you are throwing your own chance at love away because her husband is gone? Is that going to make her feel better? Bring Jason back?"

Her words pinged around in him, echoing in his head. "I— No, of course not."

She poked him in the chest. "Listen to me. I know a thing or two about love, having been married to your grandpa Harry for fifty-odd years. You've found a woman who'd give you everything. You're walking away because Jason isn't here. Ask yourself—would he divorce Callie if the roles were reversed?"

He shook his head and stood up. "Of course he wouldn't. But it's not that easy, Grandma. He went in that building after me. I shouldn't have been there to begin with. It was my job to keep him safe." *I failed him.*

"It was a miscommunication that was out of your control and not your personal responsibility," she said simply. "He made a choice. He knew the risks. You both did. It's part of the job. You weren't his babysitter. You need to go see Callie. But first you need to accept that it's time to move on."

He went cold. See Callie? See first hand the destruction he'd caused? He hadn't even been able to face returning

her calls. He wasn't sure he'd be welcome, that she'd want
to see him. He didn't want to make things worse for her,
for her kids. For Jason's sake. For her own.

For his.

But this wasn't about him.

Rose laid a hand on his arm. "You need to accept that
it's okay to move on," she said quietly. "You're a good man.
You deserve Lainey, and Lord knows both of you deserve
to be happy. Even beyond that, she needs you and you need
her. Don't let it slip away."

Her words rang true. But he didn't know if he was capable of being the man Lainey and her baby deserved. The
risk of failing them was far too great. He'd failed Jason,
and by extension Callie.

When he closed his eyes all he saw was Lainey. All he
heard was her laugh, her voice. He could still feel her in
his arms. But he couldn't be in love with her. He'd shut
that part of himself down for good.

Hadn't he?

It was time to sign the paperwork.

Lainey'd read over the pages from Jon and asked Beth's
husband, who was a lawyer, to look over them as well.
While technically she'd need to take him to court to fi-
nalize the custody transfer, it should be able to be handled
with lawyers only. This was the necessary first step to
being well and truly free of her baby's father. She signed
them and put them away, both relieved and a little sad.

She went into the kitchen and had just started a pot of
coffee—decaf, of course—when there was a knock on
the front door. She padded over that way and took a look
through the peephole.

Daniel stood on the front step.

Lainey inhaled sharply and leaned her head on the door.

She'd love to ignore him, but her car was in the driveway instead of the garage. And she knew he wouldn't go away.

She opened the door. "This is a bad time, Daniel. I'm really tired."

He looked her over, his gaze both hot and contemptuous, and she gripped the door tighter.

"I just want to talk."

He tried the old charming smile, but it did nothing but annoy her. She crossed her arms. "Try again. We've got nothing left to say to each other. Why are you really here, Daniel?"

He dropped all pretense. "You're pregnant." He nearly spat the words.

Her pulse picked up in warning. "Yes, I am."

"How are you going to raise it by yourself?" He stepped a little closer and she forced herself to hold her ground. "You'll be a single mother. Who's going to raise it with you?"

Ben. Oh, if only. "I'm going to be a single mother, yes. Did you need something? Because I've got things to do—"

He interrupted her. "You're making a mistake, Lainey. Your parents have opened their house to you. They're trying to help you. We all are. Don't you see? I can take care of the money problems you have. You won't have to do anything you don't want to do."

Anger spiked. "I won't have to do what? Work at a job I love? Something that has meaning to me? That I get up each morning and *want* to do? Why do you want to take that from me?"

He blinked at her. "No one's taking anything from you. We're offering solutions so you don't have to struggle anymore. Especially now that you are pregnant."

"What I need is to make my own solutions," she said simply. "Not have yours forced on me. And the fact you can't see that means you don't know me at all. You never did."

He frowned and put his hands in his pockets. "Of course I knew you. You were my wife for seven years."

And in all that time you never picked out one birthday gift. She shook her head. "I was a tool. I was the means to an end—which was my father." Funny how she couldn't muster up any fire. She truly didn't care. He was so far behind her now he'd never catch up.

His expression radiated sincerity, but she knew better than to believe it. "I'm sorry you felt that way, Lainey. I cleaned some things up before I came here. I've changed. I made a mistake or two. You of all people know what it's like to make mistakes."

The words hit home. Still. "Yes. I do. But my baby isn't one of them. Also, I never hurt anyone or deceived anyone like you did. You made a mockery of our marriage. Of me. And that's why, even if I'd ever loved you, I wouldn't get back with you. *That* would be the biggest mistake of my life." She stepped back. "Now, if you'll excuse me, my coffee is ready."

Daniel crowded closer and stepped inside the door. His tone was wheedling. "No, wait. It was good with us, Lainey. It's better for a baby to have a father. We can have some of our own."

"No." She'd never inflict a man like Daniel on a poor kid. No child deserved that. "You need to leave. Now."

Daniel grabbed her by the upper arms, and when she tried to pull away he dug in harder. She swallowed a yelp of pain. "Lainey. This is what works best for me. For both of us. You—"

The door banged open and Daniel let go of her in surprise. Ben stood there, and the smoldering anger on his face took Lainey's breath away.

"Get away from her." The words were a low growl.

Daniel reached for her again. "Lainey, listen—"

"Get out," she hissed. "Don't come back."

Ben took a menacing step toward Daniel and he took a step in the right direction. "She asked you to leave."

Daniel scowled, cursed, and slammed out the door.

She turned to Ben, willing her heart to return to normal, unsure if it was pumping so hard from the encounter with her idiot ex or Ben's very intoxicating nearness. "Why are you here?"

"I was in the neighborhood and saw him through the door." He shoved his hands in his pockets. "I thought you could use backup."

She pressed her hands to her face. "I wish everyone would stop trying to help me. I had it under control."

"Of course," he murmured. "I saw him handling you and jumped to conclusions."

She laid her hand on his arm as he turned to go. "No. Please. I'm sorry. I'm just so sick of my family interfering. You did me a favor by showing up here. It's not the first time he's handled me roughly."

His eyes went to slits. "He abused you?"

"No." She shook her head. "He'd grab me, like you saw tonight, but he almost never touched me. In any manner." Then she blushed as it hit her what she'd admitted.

Ben touched her face and the delicious roughness of his fingers on her skin caused a little shiver to run down her back. "Lainey. How could he be married to you and not see what he had?"

Her gaze pinged to his at his words and the rawness in his voice and she barely dared to breathe. The reverence she saw there made her want to cry. Daniel had never looked at her like that. Ever.

She clasped his wrist and turned into his touch. "I don't think he ever saw me, Ben. That's not what he wanted."

Ben didn't get that. He looked at her and wanted everything. Wanted the whole package. Wanted the baby, the chance to be a father. It was killing him. He didn't know how to reconcile things so he could have it. *Jason, dead. Lainey, pregnant. Baby, not his.* They all bothered him and worried him and he didn't know how to move forward. She looked at him with those big eyes and he wanted to take her in his arms, into his bed, and let her soothe away the pain. Only letting go of it all seemed like a betrayal to Jason. And dumping it on her was more than he could ask of her.

Would she think less of him? He couldn't deny it mattered, even though he wished it didn't.

"Ben?"

He looked into her worried face and couldn't help the question. He needed to know. "So he's not the father?"

Her head snapped up and she laughed—a sharp bark. "God, no." She stepped away and shut the door. "Can I get you something? A drink?"

He smelled coffee. "Coffee's fine."

He followed her to the kitchen, trying and failing to keep his gaze off her perfect ass in those clingy black pants. He leaned in the doorway while she opened cupboards and lifted slightly on her toes to get mugs. The movement pulled her shirt snug across her breasts and the slight swell of her belly. He wanted nothing more than to pull her against him, hold her tiny bump in his hands. The longing nearly brought him to his knees.

She poured the coffee with a slightly shaking hand, and he accepted his. She got out milk, sugar and spoons, and led him to the small table in the dining room. He sat opposite her and watched as she doctored her coffee.

"Let me tell you about my baby's father. This is not

a story I'm proud of," she said quietly, and took a deep breath. Then she poured out the whole thing, without meeting his gaze.

Ben cursed. "He didn't tell you he was married?"

She stirred her coffee without taking her eyes off the mug. "Nope. And I didn't figure it out. Pathetic, I know."

"He is. You're not." When her head came up and she opened her mouth he held up a hand. "Let me see if I've got this right. You were recovering from a marriage that was completely loveless and lacking in affection or respect of any kind. This guy showed up and took advantage of that. How is that *you* being pathetic?"

She stared into her mug. "I just should have known better."

"Oh, honey." The endearment startled him, but he meant it. "No. He took advantage of you. That's not on you."

"I could have said no." She shut her eyes. "It wasn't like I really wanted him. It was just the idea of someone actually wanting me."

"Yeah." He pulled her to her feet. "But if you had said no, you wouldn't have this." He laid his hand on her belly and her eyes went wide. She laid her hand on top of his. "Would you wish this away?"

"Never," she said quietly. She took a deep breath. "The only thing I'd wish for is a better father for him or her. Someone like you." The words were nearly a whisper, and her soft gaze caught his.

He froze as if ice had formed in his muscles. "No, Lainey, not like me. I'm no good for you, for a baby." He wasn't what she needed. Not anymore.

She saw the shields come down and all but heard the resounding clang as they locked into place. She forced herself to hold his gaze and pressed his trembling hand against her belly. He wanted this, wanted her. She knew it—could see it. Had been seeing it as they'd gone through the past couple weeks. She wanted him too, even knowing how impossible the situation was.

"Why not?"

He slid his hand out from under hers and stepped away. The coldness she felt was as much at the loss of contact as it was for his emotional shutdown. "I can't talk about it."

She gave a little laugh and fought against the burn of tears. "Oh? But it's okay for me to spill my shames to you? It's a one-way street?"

"It's not that simple." His voice was low.

She lifted her chin. "My problems aren't simple."

"No. No, they're not," he agreed. "I meant it's not—it's not something I can talk about."

That destroyed look was back, and her heart ached. She was falling in love with this man, and he would never let her close enough to help. To love him as he deserved. As he needed.

She thought of the nightmare but didn't bring it up. The fact he chose to shut her out hurt, but what claim did she have to him? They'd been physical, she was emotionally invested, but there was no actual commitment—nothing that would mean he should tell her what had happened.

Still. She had to try. "You don't have to carry this alone," she said quietly. "Whatever it is."

He stared at a spot on the wall, but she doubted he was seeing anything in the room. "Some things have to be," he said finally, and the pain in his voice burned in her heart. He shoved a hand through his hair. "I'm sorry, Lainey. It's just so damn hard to talk about."

She got out of her chair and moved to kneel next to him. He wouldn't look at her. "Why?" she asked, and held her breath.

His jaw worked. "I killed my best friend, okay?" At her

sharp whimper he looked her in the eye. "I made a stupid mistake and a great guy died. A family man. He left his wife and two little kids. Sons who will never know their daddy now because of a mistake *I* made."

Pain washed through her—for him, for the man's family. She wanted to climb in his lap and hold him, but settled for touching his face, feeling the roughness of stubble under her hand. "Oh, Ben. I'm so sorry."

His eyes glittered with unshed tears as he looked at her. "Not as sorry as I am. I'm not the man you want, Lainey."

"Don't you think I get to decide that?" she asked, and tugged him to his feet. He let her, and she slid her arms around him, rested her head on his chest and squeezed her eyes shut as she listened to the pounding of his heart beneath her cheek. The warmth of him seeped into her pores and pooled in her heart. He stood very still for a moment, then wrapped his arms around her, too. She hoped he would allow himself to take comfort from it, from her.

They stood that way for a few minutes, then Lainey heard her phone ring. Ben stepped back, the moment broken. "I'd better get going. You okay?"

She looked at him and saw the careful remoteness back in his gaze. Her heart ached as she nodded and followed him through the living room to the door. "Fine."

He turned around and lifted her chin, his fingers lingering. The look in his eyes was a strange mixture of regret and affection. He leaned down and planted a hard kiss on her mouth. "You're not any kind of damaged goods, Lainey. Don't let anyone make you feel otherwise. Ever. You're an incredible woman." Then he left.

Lainey pressed her fingertips to her tingling mouth, her heart heavy as the front door clicked shut behind him. The tears she'd been fighting finally broke loose, and as she sank back down at the table, head on her arms, she had another thought.

His parting words had sounded an awful lot like good-bye.

CHAPTER TWELVE

AT THE END of the next day Lainey went into the little office area in the back of the store and checked her books. The familiar feeling of dread pooled as she added up the numbers. Better, but not good enough. She could chart steady progress upward, though, so that was hopeful. But was it enough?

"What's the verdict?" Beth walked over.

Lainey leaned back so her friend could see the screen and rested her hands on her belly. "Better. Definitely better. But not there. Yet."

Beth hesitated. "Mark and I were talking. If you're interested, we can probably swing me buying in if you want a partner."

Stunned, Lainey stared at her friend. "I— Beth, I hadn't—"

Beth held up a hand. "I know you want to do this all on your own. But you can be a success even with a partner. It doesn't make it less because you have help." She smiled and touched Lainey's shoulder. "Think about it, okay?"

"I will," she promised.

After Beth left, she stared at the numbers on the screen. Beth buying in would mean a new cooler. Repairs on the van, which even today had given her fits about going into gear. Bigger payments to her parents and therefore being out from under their thumb earlier.

Excitement and hope flared.

It was tempting. But was it the right decision?

She stood and paced out into the shop. She took in the silk flowers, the cheery Halloween-themed window. Sure, the carpet was worn, and the cash register was old but completely reliable. The fresh scent of the flowers overlaid everything and made it feel almost homey. This place was more than just a business. She loved it—loved all of it. It suited her to a T. Because of that, she couldn't let it go under. What good was it to be determined to prove herself if ultimately it sank her? That would only prove her parents right and she'd be back where she started.

She'd gone too far to let it all go under now.

She took a deep breath and walked into the backroom. Beth was right. She just needed to make sure the numbers were stable enough for her friend to take the risk. And then she and Beth and Mark would look them over together. She wouldn't let them buy in if it turned out to be too risky. She wanted to succeed, but she was pragmatic enough to realize she wasn't out of the woods just yet.

A lightness she hadn't felt in a very long time crept into her heart. This was the right thing to do. Too bad she'd been so damn blind she hadn't been able to see it. Or maybe she hadn't been *ready* to see it. She owed Beth for putting it all into perspective.

After leaving work, Lainey pulled into Rose's driveway. She'd promised to take her friend to bingo. Ben's truck sat there, and she tried to quash the silly little spurt of anticipation. She'd stop in and say hello. Sort of face the elephant in the room head-on—see if his confession to her had done any good for him.

The light in the garage indicated he was in there, even though the big door was shut. She opened up the side door and stepped inside, almost holding her breath. How this went depended on how he looked at her when he saw her.

Her heart sank when he turned. His face was the polite mask he'd worn when she'd first met him. "Lainey."

"Hello, Ben." She kept her voice steady with effort. Two could play this game. He just looked at her and waited. "I just—wanted to see how you were. After last night." Darn it, she sounded tentative. But his impassive expression wasn't helping.

"How should I be?" He kept his gaze on her. Completely shuttered. "Nothing's changed, Lainey, if that's what you're asking."

Well, that was to the point. "Okay, then," she said stiffly. "See you around."

And she left the garage, slamming the door behind her. Not the most mature of moves, but the man frustrated her no end.

On the short walk to the house she took a couple of deep breaths, hoping Rose wouldn't notice her mood. She didn't want to be quizzed—just wanted to lick her wounds in peace.

No such luck. Rose took one look at her as soon as she entered the kitchen and frowned. "Okay. First Ben, now you. That boy's been in a serious funk all day. What happened? He won't tell me."

Lainey blanched but managed a small smile. "Nothing happened."

Rose shook her head. "Oh, no. I may be old, but I'm neither blind nor stupid. There's much more than that, isn't there?" She sat back and examined Lainey. "Did he tell you about Jason?"

She gave a little nod. "I don't know what to tell him, Rose."

Her friend gave a little sigh. "There's really not much to say. He's got a lot to work out. On top of that, nothing ties a man up in knots more than when a relationship that was supposed to be casual turns out not to be."

Lainey gave a little shrug that she hoped was casual, even though she felt anything but. "It's the wrong time."

Rose gave a decidedly unladylike snort. "It's always the wrong time. You don't get to pick when or who you'll fall in love with, child. I see how that boy looks at you. Does he know you're pregnant?"

Despite Rose's gentle tone, the words might as well have been a shout. Lainey winced. "Yes. How did *you* know?" Had Ben told Rose after she'd asked him not to?

"Not from him," Rose assured her. "I can just tell. You've changed physically. And the fact you told him should tell you something, honey."

Startled, Lainey met her friend's gaze. "Tell me what?"

"You told him before you told me," she said gently, and raised a hand when Lainey opened her mouth to protest. "No—no, wait. I'm not saying you should have told me first. But think about it. Why did you tell Ben?"

"I had to tell him why I couldn't go to the hospital for an X-ray," Lainey pointed out, but in retrospect she could see the holes in that theory. Why *had* she blurted it out?

Rose nodded. "But there were other reasons you could have given. Or, for that matter, no reason at all. He didn't need an explanation. A simple no thanks would have sufficed. He wouldn't have pushed. But you felt safe enough to tell him. Am I right?"

That was true. She hadn't needed to tell him. But feeling safe? With Ben? He made her feel anything *but* safe.

Well, that wasn't entirely true. He'd made her feel safe

and cherished the night they'd spent together. The danger from Ben wasn't that he'd take her for granted, or treat her like her ex had. It was that he made her want things she couldn't have, that he couldn't give. And she wasn't willing to open herself to any more emotional destruction.

"Lainey." Rose leaned forward. "I know you've been through an awful lot. You have very little reason to trust people. The fact you told him is significant. The fact he went to that party with you is significant. He hasn't done anything social in months."

"The timing is all wrong," Lainey said again, because it was true. "He's not in any place for a relationship, and I— Well, I really need to do this on my own." Actually, she was starting to rethink that statement. If Beth bought in to her shop what counted was making it a success. The same idea applied to her personal life. Having a partner in life would be wonderful—but only if it was the right man.

Was Ben that man?

Rose sat back. "I understand. I do. I just want to see both of you happy. And if the two of you could be happy together—well, that would do my heart good."

"I'll be fine," Lainey assured her. Fine wasn't the same as happy, of course, and she doubted very much the distinction would be wasted on Rose.

Rose studied her for a long moment, then nodded. "I'm glad to hear it," she said. "We should get going. Don't want to be late for bingo."

Grateful to be off the hook, Lainey stood up and gathered her purse and keys.

As she wheeled her friend down the ramp Ben came out of the garage. Her heart gave a little leap and she was glad she was behind Rose, so her sharp-eyed friend didn't read anything that might be on her face. He gave Lainey a nod and she managed to smile back. As he came closer she could see the stress lines bracketing his mouth. She wanted nothing more in that moment than to go to him and smooth them away, to hold him and be held.

She looked away instead.

Ben helped Rose into the car and took care of the chair while Lainey slid behind the wheel. As they backed out of the driveway Rose narrowed her gaze on Ben, who stood watching them, hands in pockets. She muttered something that sounded like, "Foolish boy."

No, Lainey wanted to tell her. He's smart enough to know his limits.

And so was she.

"So, we've got a Friday wedding this week," Lainey noted. The flowers were simple and seasonal, fitting for a second wedding for both the bride and groom. They were starting on the bouquets today. "And a big order for a baptism on Sunday."

"Isn't it great?" Beth asked as she cut open a flower box. "Word is getting out. We're doing good."

Lainey agreed. Part of her was a little sad, though, that her personal life seemed to be one-hundred-eighty degrees away from her growing professional life. But to dwell on it wouldn't do her any good.

"Speaking of weddings," Beth said casually, "how's Ben?"

Lainey sent her a warning look. "Beth—"

"What?" Her friend's innocent look didn't fool Lainey. She shook her head and Beth sighed. "Okay. I heard at the café that you and Ben were super cozy at the hospital gala." She plopped a box on the worktable and sent Lainey a mock glare. "Of course I didn't hear that from *you*. My supposed best friend and subject of such hot gossip."

Super-cozy. Well, she supposed they *had* been all

wrapped up in each other and the spell of the evening. Dancing and kissing in the shadows. His car in front of her house for hours.

"I— Well, yeah. I guess it would look that way." She winced. "Don't people have anything else to talk about? Surely there were more interesting couples than Ben and I?"

Beth gave her a pitying look. "Lainey, I think the interesting part was the chemistry the two of you have. I heard that you were so hot together people were concerned you'd combust. Or maybe get down right there," she added thoughtfully, earning a playful smack from Lainey.

"Well, it doesn't matter now," she said, thinking of last night and how he'd been completely shut down. Pain lanced through her. She'd give anything to have this work out, to make it so they could be a couple.

But that wasn't an option. It was silly even to think it was.

"How is that?" Beth asked. "The guy kissed you. At least that much. But from how red you just turned I'm guessing it's much more than that. He helped you move. He took you to a formal party on short notice. Guys don't just do that for women they aren't interested in."

"His grandma sent him to help me," Lainey muttered. Beth didn't know how far things had gone with them, but they must have been giving off some pretty serious vibes at the gala. "And that first kiss was a pity kiss."

"Pity kiss?" Beth raised her brow. "Oh, come on, Laine. Ben doesn't seem like that type. He's so reserved. He's not going to go around kissing women because he thinks it will make them feel better."

Beth had a point. Still… "I meant it was just the moment." They'd had a lot of wonderful moments that she held on to tightly. Privately.

"Moment or not—and I think you are withholding key information from me, but I'll let it go this time—there's clearly something between you. The question is, what are you going to do about it?"

A little shiver ran through Lainey. That was the question. What *was* she going to do? She knew what she wanted, but not what he wanted. She stuffed a 'mum in florist foam with a little more force than was necessary and nearly bent it. "I'm not going there, Beth."

Beth touched her arm. "All kidding aside, why not?"

She widened her eyes. "You know why, Beth. Look at my marriage. Look at how I got in this situation. I'm doing this alone. I'm barely hanging on. There's no way he and I could make it work, even if I wanted it to. I need to keep him at a distance." She wouldn't tell Beth about Jason. It wasn't her story to tell.

"So you'll shut him down?" Beth said quietly.

She winced. Actually, he'd shut *her* down. More or less.

Beth continued. "But you don't *have* to do this alone. That's the whole point. Okay, so maybe Ben's not the guy for you. I don't know one way or the other. Chemistry is wonderful, but definitely not the only thing to base a relationship on. But don't shut yourself off all the way. Single parenting is hard. You might want someone to share it with."

"I—" She'd love to share it with Ben. She didn't see another man coming into her life whom she'd want more. But it didn't look as if that was to be. Unable to finish her sentence, she cleared her throat and changed the subject. "Well, we've got a lot to do here. Let's get these done so the bride can relax."

Beth looked as if she wanted to say something, but simply shook her head instead.

Lainey knew she was a coward. But it seemed like the only way to protect herself.

That night, Lainey had just propped her feet on the coffee table and turned the TV on when a knock sounded at the door. She padded over and peeked through the peephole to see her parents standing there. It wasn't like them to drop by unannounced. She frowned as she opened the door.

"Is everything okay?"

"Of course. Do you have a minute?" Her father's voice was strangely formal. "We won't stay long."

"I—yes, I do." She stepped aside to let them in and tried to tamp down a little surge of nerves. There could be no good reason for this visit.

Jacqui looked around the room as she slipped off her shoes. Lainey looked too—she was proud of the home she had created. A fire crackled in the hearth, and the low light of the lamps cast a warm glow over the space. She took a seat on the slip-covered couch. Panda was draped across the back. The cat didn't even crack an eye open.

Her parents sat in the chairs while Lainey muted the TV. Frankly, *Survivor* was a great backdrop for her wranglings with her parents. She set the remote carefully on the end table, dismayed to note her hand shook slightly.

"Can I get you anything?" she asked, and they both shook their heads.

"This is certainly—cozy," Jacqui said carefully, and Lainey sighed. In this case, "cozy" wasn't a compliment.

"I think so," she said, choosing to ignore her mother's meaning. "I love it."

"Well." Always one to cut to the chase, her father leaned forward. "We've got some information you might find interesting."

Her heart kicked up a bit. "Information? About what?"

Her parents exchanged a look. "About Ben Lawless, dear," her mother said.

Lainey tensed. Oh, God. They'd dug into his past. She kept her voice level as she said, "Really?"

"Yes." Jacqui pulled some papers out of her monster bag and held them out. Lainey took them reluctantly. "I think you'll find it interesting reading."

Lainey laid the pages on the couch next to her. She couldn't bring herself to look too closely at them. *Local Firefighter Under Fire* was the heading on the first page. Poor Ben.

"Why are you doing this?" She tried to keep her voice steady but failed.

"So you can see once and for all why it's a bad idea to get mixed up with him. Lainey, he's directly responsible for the death of a fellow firefighter. Ben went in after being told not to. The other man went after him. As a result, a young family man is dead. Ben's been removed from the squad. He's had some mental health issues as well. He's not stable. It's in your best interests to stay away from him." She nodded at the papers. "It's all there."

Lainey sucked in a breath. "Oh, Mother. How could you? This is beneath you."

Jacqui recoiled and flushed slightly, and looked at her husband. Greg cleared his throat. "You don't want to get mixed up with an unstable man, honey. You deserve better."

Lainey stared. Surely they couldn't mean Daniel. "A lying, cheating man who threatens me is a better choice?"

Greg winced slightly. "No. Of course not. But if Ben isn't stable you could be hurt. And you've got a child to think about. You're going to be a mother. It's time you were responsible and made better choices."

Lainey's mouth fell open. She snapped it shut. "While

I appreciate you looking out for me, I'm perfectly capable of making decisions for myself. You don't know Ben. I do. He's a far better man than Daniel. Than most men. He's got honor, integrity and loyalty in spades. Not to mention he actually *listens* to what I say and doesn't make any attempt to manipulate me. He's a good man, and I never thought I'd find one like him. As for this—he's told me himself."

She stomped over to the fireplace and placed the papers on the flames. They went up with a *whoosh*. If only it were that easy to help Ben be free of his demons. When she spun back around she saw her parents staring at her and realized with a sinking feeling she'd said far, far too much.

"You're in love with him." Jacqui's tone was shocked. "What do you think he can possibly give you?"

Her mother's words stymied her. *In love with Ben?* She couldn't be. Could she? She'd been trying so hard not to be, teetering on the edge but holding her heart in reserve.

She swallowed and tried to focus. "He can't give me anything right now," she said, and heard the sorrow in her voice. "But then again he never said he could." *And I've never asked.* She'd been afraid of the answer. Just as she'd been afraid to admit she was flat-out in love with the man.

Jacqui simply stared at her, her throat working. Greg stood and pulled his wife to her feet. "Lainey, for your sake I hope this infatuation passes quickly. You've got a lot going on, trying to keep your shop going and getting ready for the baby. If you have a prayer of making this work you need to let Ben go. He's not the man for you."

"You're wrong," Lainey said, her voice quiet. She met her parents' gazes squarely. "He *is* the man for me." She knew it with all her heart. What she didn't know was how to make him understand it.

Greg herded a sputtering Jacqui out the door and Lainey sank back on the couch. In love with Ben.

She squeezed her eyes shut tightly. She'd been doing her best to ignore the truth, but there it was. She was in love with him—in all likelihood had been since they'd skipped stones at the lake. When he'd been so gentle with her. When he'd kissed her the first time.

Tears burned at the back of her throat. It was no good to love someone who had no idea how to accept it. Who was held up by the past, by something he couldn't let go.

She had to hope he loved her too, and would be willing to work through his past to give them a future. But what if he wasn't?

CHAPTER THIRTEEN

"Lainey." Her mother stood in the doorway of The Lily Pad, clearly agitated. "We need to talk. Can you take a break right now?"

Startled, Lainey took a few steps toward her mother. She hadn't thought she'd see her parents for a while after last night's little ambush had been thwarted. She'd never seen the older woman so distraught. "Mom? Are you all right?"

Jacqui shook her head. "I just—we really need to sit down and discuss this."

Beth hurried over to Lainey. "I can cover this right now. Why don't the two of you go ahead?"

Her eyes searched Lainey's face, and Lainey saw the concern there. If she disagreed, and opted to stay instead of talking to her mother, Beth would back her up. In light of last night's conversation with her parents, her mother's arrival this morning was a bit of a surprise.

She squeezed her friend's hand. To her mother she said, "Okay. How about Mel's?" It wasn't fully private, but this time of day—mid-morning—business at the café should be a little slower.

Jacqui nodded. "That's fine."

Surprised, Lainey grabbed her coat and followed her

mother out the door. She didn't think she'd ever seen Jacqui go to Mel's.

They walked in silence though the October chill. Halloween was only a couple days away, and November apparently had chosen to make an early appearance this year. Inside the warm café, Lainey led Jacqui to a corner table in the hopes they'd be undisturbed. They ordered hot drinks and sat in silence until the steaming mugs were delivered. Jacqui tapped her nails on the table relentlessly, a show of nerves Lainey didn't think she'd ever seen before.

Not wanting to wait any longer, Lainey reached over and touched her mother's hand. Jacqui looked more haggard, more tired, than Lainey could ever remember seeing her. "Mom, what's this about?"

Jacqui fussed with her coffee, then lifted her gaze to meet Lainey's. "I need you to explain how things got this way. How you could be so careless…" Her words trailed off.

"Careless as in getting pregnant? Or about Ben?" She hadn't been careless either way.

Jacqui nodded. "Either. Both. And you won't tell anyone who the father is!"

Lainey sat back. She had to choose her words carefully. "Mom, I wouldn't say I was careless. No, it wasn't planned. But it's not a mistake. As for the father…" She hesitated. She clearly had to say something, but what? She settled for an abridged version of the truth. "Well, he's not interested in being in our lives. He's got his reasons, and none of them are anything I want my child associated with." She hesitated just for a second before adding, "Why do you keep pushing Daniel on me?"

Jacqui looked her straight in the eye. "Because he can take care of you. And now the baby, too. It's going to be so hard for you to raise the child and run that shop. I'm sure he'd let you keep the store, and you can work when you want. But you wouldn't have to worry about money. Are you *sure* the baby's father is out of the picture?"

Lainey thought of the papers she'd signed with a little pang of sorrow mixed with relief. "Yes." She crossed her arms on the table and leaned forward. "Mom. I understand you want me to be taken care of. I do. And I appreciate your concern. But Daniel's not the way to do it. I'm managing—working things out. It won't be easy, but I'm going to make it work. You and Dad need to just let me do it."

Jacqui was silent for a long moment, fiddling with her untouched coffee mug. Then she said, "I just don't understand why you'd want to struggle when you don't have to. When there are people who can give you so much."

Lainey saw the puzzlement on her mother's face and knew she truly *didn't* understand. "It's not that I want to struggle. It's that I want to do something on my own. When you guys step in and try to take over you attach strings and conditions and you take the power away from me. It's not mine, then. Being a single mother isn't ideal. It will make everything a lot harder, to be sure. But that's how it's going to be, Mom. I can't change that." She took a deep breath and thought of Ben with a sharp pang. "If I ever get married it will be because I love the man, and because he loves and respects me for who I am—not who I come from or what I can do for him. Does that make sense?"

Jacqui clasped her hands tightly in front of her for a moment. Finally she lifted her chin. "Yes," she said quietly. "It does. Does Ben know how you feel?"

Lainey dropped her gaze to her mug of tea. Her heart squeezed. "I don't think so."

Her mother pushed her mug out of the way and leaned toward her. "Then you need to tell him. Sooner rather than later. Why would you let him walk away?"

Lainey's jaw actually dropped. "Mother…" she managed. "I— Whoa. I thought you were against Ben?"

Jacqui reached over and covered Lainey's hand with her own. "We don't want you to have to struggle when you have the opportunity to avoid it. But you need to be happy, too. It's been so long—" She stopped for a moment, then sighed. "I love your father, even with all his faults. When you talk about Ben you light up. The way you defended him last night—well, you should have the chance to see where that leads you. I'm sorry for making it so difficult for you."

It was quite possibly the first time her mother had ever really listened and actually heard what Lainey was saying. She got up and pulled her mother into an awkward hug, right there in Mel's. Her mother's quiet words were as good as Jacqui could do, and Lainey was willing to accept them as a start.

Her mother patted her awkwardly on the back. "Go get him," she said, and Lainey's eyes got damp. "And, please, if we can help let us know. I'll try not to shove myself where I've got no business being."

Lainey stepped back and laughed even as she swiped at her eyes. "Thank you." Jacqui wouldn't understand, but that was the nicest thing her mother had ever said to her.

"All right, then." Her mother gathered her bag and her coat. "I mean it. If we can help with the shop and the baby let us know."

"I will," Lainey murmured. She didn't want their help, if at all possible, but having it offered rather than rammed down her throat was a huge improvement. She tried and failed to picture her parents babysitting. The thought almost made her giggle. Maybe they'd come around.

She hurried back to work. Beth was ringing up a sale,

but by the time Lainey got her coat off and went back out front was already heading for her. "How did it go?"

Lainey reached for the watering can. "It was fine, actually. She made an effort to listen to me. I'm not sure she understands why I feel the way I do, but she seems willing to accept it. It's some small steps in the right direction." She'd take the olive branch and hope it held. To have her parents work with her rather than at cross-purposes would make everything so much easier.

That evening was pizza night with Rose. Lainey was half tempted to cancel. She was so tired, and the thought of seeing Ben and simply exchanging polite words, pretending there'd never been more between them, was just too hard.

But she picked up the usual pizza and headed out. She'd do her best to put on a happy face.

Ben was nowhere to be found when she pulled in, and relief tempered with a good dose of disappointment flooded through her. She tried to push it all away. She was here for Rose only, and had been long before he'd come back. She would be long after he'd left again.

"Come on in!" Rose called when Lainey knocked.

She pushed the door open and fixed a smile on her face which faltered when she spotted Ben's jacket draped over a chair. How far gone was she when the sight of a fleece could almost reduce her to tears? She busied herself putting the box on the counter and removing her own coat while making small talk. She thought she'd actually done pretty well until she sat across from Rose and looked at her sympathetic face.

"Oh, dear. You've got it that bad, huh?" Rose's question was gentle.

Lainey couldn't meet her friend's eyes so she looked down at the slice of pizza she had zero interest in eating.

Her answer stuck in her throat as if the words were glued there, and she was afraid if she tried to speak all her carefully rigged control would go right out the window.

The back door opened then, and Ben came in. Her gaze flew to his and Lainey would swear time stopped. Her breath caught at the pain and the longing she saw, which he quickly dropped behind the mask she was all-too-familiar with. She looked away. She should have stayed home tonight. Rose would have understood.

"Pizza, Ben?" Rose's voice was overly bright, and it seemed to bounce off the tension that filled the room.

"No, thanks."

The deep rumble of his voice resonated deep in Lainey's soul. Oh, did she have it bad. Rose didn't know the half of it.

"I need this."

The jacket whooshed off the chair next to her and Lainey squeezed her eyes shut tight when she caught a bit of his scent mixed with the fresh air notes that came from spending a lot of time outside. She didn't dare look up until the door shut behind him.

Rose made a little noise of frustration in her throat. "Oh, my goodness, I'm not sure I've ever seen a couple so right for each other work so hard to avoid it! Talk to him, Lainey. Please. Don't let this get away. From either of you. You don't want to regret it later."

It wasn't quite that simple. "Rose—"

Her friend leveled her with a gentle look. "Do you love him?"

Lainey sucked in a breath. "Yes. Yes, I do." The answer was oh-so-easy, but not simple.

"He went back into the garage. Go to him. Please." Rose looked at her with shrewd eyes. "Don't waste anymore time. That little baby needs a daddy and Ben would be a wonderful one. Plus, not only does he need you—you need him."

He needs you. Lainey didn't know if that was true or not. If he needed her, how could he shut her out and hold her at arm's length? Still, she found her feet carrying her out the door to the garage. Her heartbeat picked up the closer she got to the building. Was she crazy to lay it all on the line? She hadn't come here intending to do so. Even though Rose was right. It *was* time. She couldn't go on in this half-life. She had to know.

Ben looked up when she came in, and she caught the longing in his eyes before he shuttered it. "Hi."

"Hey. How are you feeling?"

His voice was perfectly polite. She could almost see the force fields around him, trying to keep her at a safe distance. It hurt that after all they'd shared he could just lock her out.

"Okay." It wasn't a lie. Pregnancy-wise, she was. Otherwise, not so much.

He nodded, then met her gaze. "What do you need, Lainey?"

You. She took a deep breath and jumped in. "Can you tell me the rest of the story, Ben? About Jason?" Since everything seemed to hinge on his friend's death, she needed to know.

He set down the tool he'd been holding. His hands were shaking slightly. "I told you the gist of it."

"Yes, you did. But I don't know what actually happened." She moved a little closer. Her hands shook so badly she shoved them in the pockets of her coat. "I don't know exactly why you blame yourself, because from what I've seen you aren't so careless as to knowingly or intentionally lead another person into danger."

He winced, raked a hand through his hair. "Lainey—"

She kept her gaze on him steady. Kept her voice calm and didn't move any closer, so she wouldn't spook him. "Ben, please. Let me in. We've got the potential here for something wonderful, and I'd love the chance at a future with you. But with this between us we can't." She couldn't bring herself to ask if he wanted it, too. The very real chance of him saying no would destroy her.

"Don't make me a better man than I am." His words were harsh and he moved toward her, his gaze hard on hers.

She stood her ground as he stalked closer.

"I didn't get the order. Somehow there was a breakdown in the chain and I didn't get the order that the building was clear. As far as I knew there was one occupant left." He stopped, took a shuddering breath. "I went in. Jason came in after me because he recognized the signs that the situation was deteriorating rapidly. He'd gotten the order. He knew he wasn't supposed to go in." He shut his eyes. "He came in anyway. For me. When he had so much to lose. He had everything to lose. His wife—Callie. Those kids."

Lainey's eyes burned at the bleakness in his voice and she didn't even try to stop the tears. Now she got it. He blamed himself for living when his friend was dead. She came a little closer and rested her hand on his arm, feeling the tightness of the muscles beneath. He blinked at her, as if he'd forgotten she was there for a few moments, lost in his own private hell. "How can you blame yourself for Jason's choice? What does his wife say?"

He froze and then looked away, his jaw working.

Her heart sank. "Oh, no. Ben. How can she blame you?"

Misery was etched on his face. "I don't know if she does. I haven't seen her or talked to her since—since the funeral. She's called, but I haven't called her back."

Lainey inhaled sharply. "Ben, why not?"

He moved away from her, his movements agitated and

jerky. "I can't, okay? What if it's the wrong thing to do?" He paused and drew in a ragged breath. "You didn't see her at the funeral. She was so—lost. She's been through so much already. I can't make it worse for her. I can't take that chance."

She shook her head. "Okay, but who are you to decide what makes it worse for her? Ben, how can you possibly know? You're a living link to Jason for her, for her kids. That's so important. How can you leave them like that? Is that what he'd want?"

He turned around, propped his hands on his hips. "Lainey—"

She was too far in to back out now. "Go. Talk to her. See what she has to say so you can get some closure. If you can't do that we don't have a future. *You* don't have a future as a firefighter, much less as a husband. You can't punish yourself forever. You need to forgive yourself, and Jason as well. He didn't give up his life so you could spend yours all alone."

He opened his mouth, but snapped it shut when she steamrollered right over him.

"I love you. But if you can't choose me—choose a life with me over your past—then we've got nowhere to go."

She barely breathed as he stood in the middle of the garage and stared at her.

Finally he said in a low tone, "I can't risk it, Lainey."

Her heart shattered, the razor sharp edges of pain nearly bringing her to her knees. "Then you're not the man I thought you were."

It took everything she had to turn and walk away from the man she loved.

Ben stood frozen in the garage after Lainey had left. She had simply sailed out, her chin high, tear-tracks fresh on her beautiful face. He heard her car start, then the crunch of tires on the driveway.

The loss of her ripped through him. God, how could he be so damn stupid? He wanted nothing more than to go after her, tell her how much he loved her. But he couldn't.

Because he was an idiot. What kind of man let the woman he loved walk away?

One whose past held him firmly in its snare. He knew that. He'd allowed it because it meant he was able to hide, somehow thinking that would make up for the loss of his friend. Worse, he'd used it as an excuse to cement the belief he was better off alone. That was inexcusable. Even though over the past few weeks he'd been busy falling for Lainey. She'd burst right through his defenses, made him feel, made him want, and while he'd convinced himself those were the last things he wanted she'd gotten in his heart anyway.

But if you can't choose me—choose a life with me over your past—then we've got nowhere to go.

Her words echoed in his head. What kind of man chose to live in the past when the future hovered so brightly in front of him? Lainey wasn't wrong. It was past time he paid Callie a visit. Set some things right and got closure. Maybe Jason's widow needed it, too. And choosing to live his life and love Lainey seemed like a far better tribute to his friend's memory than staying in the shadows for the rest of his days.

Then he'd see if he could have a true future with Lainey. She deserved all of him—not some damaged shell. He'd prove he could move on. He pulled his phone out of his pocket, took a deep breath, and dialed a familiar number.

Beth came in and plunked down a small bakery bag. "Cheesecake muffin. Because I'm pretty sure you haven't eaten yet."

Lainey winced. "I'm trying, Beth. I'm just not very hungry."

Her friend nudged the bag closer. "I know, honey. But you've got to feed that baby."

Lainey managed a smile. "I know that. And I am." *Mostly.* Lainey opened the bag. Her appetite hadn't been stellar since her first conversation with Ben about Jason, and had virtually disappeared after their confrontation in the garage two days ago. He'd made his choice. It wasn't her.

So it was over before it really had a chance to begin.

The pain broke over her again. Every time the wave wore her down a little more. She took a shaky breath and took the bag from Beth.

"I know this is so hard for you. Can I do anything, Laine? I know I keep asking, but—" Beth broke off. "It's so awful to see you like this. Can you call him? See if you can work it out?"

Lainey managed a little smile. She knew she didn't need to pretend around Beth, but she was hoping to fool herself into thinking it wasn't as painful as she thought. "It didn't end in a way I can actually fix. He's got—he's got issues that only he can resolve. And he has to be ready to do that. I can't make him ready." And there was also the simple but excruciating fact she didn't actually know if he loved her.

Beth leaned forward. "I've seen him look at you, Laine. That man is in love with you."

"Maybe. But he never said the words, Beth." Her eyes burned with tears she did not want to shed in public. "I *think* he'd love me, if he could. But I don't really *know*. He knows how I feel." She took a shaky breath and tried to smile, even though it failed to actually form. "So I'm going to try to move on."

If only it was that easy.

"Oh, honey. I'm so sorry." Beth glanced back as the back doorbell buzzed. "Eat that. I'll get the delivery."

She left and Lainey opened the bag and removed the muffin, centering it on a napkin. She'd been through the whole thing over and over. No use going over it all for the umpteenth time. The story of a broken heart was as old as time. She'd manage to survive.

But it was a huge hole in her heart. She missed him. Missed what they'd never really had a chance to have. Missed what might have been.

That was almost as dangerous.

She broke off a small bite of muffin. Normally it was one of her favorite treats. It would take her all morning to eat it, because today she could probably eat the bag it came in and not notice any difference in taste. But Beth was right. She needed to feed the baby.

The front door chimed and Lainey's idiotically optimistic heart kicked, then crashed. It hadn't been Ben yet, and this time was no different. A smiling man approached the counter, wanting a dozen roses for his wife. Lainey put them together with a smile, but her heart ached.

"Thank you," he said as she handed him the roses wrapped in green and pink paper. "She's worth every rose you've got in your store. But I can only afford a dozen today."

Lainey gave a little laugh, but a little spear of sorrow pierced her heart. If things had been different would Ben have said the same about her? "She's a lucky woman."

He winked as he slid his wallet in his pocket. "Nah. I'm the lucky one."

Whistling, he walked out, and Lainey watched him go

with a heavy heart. People clearly could make love work. Some of them overcame crazy stuff to be together.

And some of them couldn't.

CHAPTER FOURTEEN

BEN STOOD IN front of the little white bungalow, with its cozy front porch and dormant rose bushes. A house not too different from the one Lainey lived in. Pumpkins on the front steps. Fake spiderweb on the porch. Like almost every other house on the block.

But this one belonged to Callie and Jason. Well, just Callie now. He swallowed hard at the thought.

He'd come to finally make amends—something he should have done months ago.

The front door flew open and Callie stood there, the baby—who wasn't really a baby anymore—on her hip. She looked at him steadily and his heart thumped in his chest as he started up the walk towards her.

"Callie." He swallowed, the words suddenly seeming inadequate. "I'm—"

"If you say you're sorry, Ben Lawless, you cannot take another step and come in this house." Eyes blazing, Callie stepped out on the porch.

Confusion stopped him in his tracks more than her threat. "What?"

"You heard me." She jerked her head toward the door and her coppery curls bounced on her shoulders. "Come in. We need to talk and it's cold out here."

He followed her into the house, the reminder of Jason

not as physical a punch as it would have been a few weeks ago. The oldest boy, Eli, who was three, looked at him out of his father's eyes and smiled his father's smile.

"Hey, buddy." Ben bent down and accepted the hug the little boy offered. His heart squeezed. He'd do better by Jason's kids if Callie would let him. He'd love to see them grow up—maybe play with Lainey's baby if she would forgive him.

"Have a seat." Callie nodded at the table which held a basket of crayons and a stack of coloring books. "Let me get them set up for a little while." To the kids she said, "How about *Bob the Builder*?" A chorus of yeses followed her words and soon cheery music wafted from the living room. She returned to stand across from him, her posture stiff.

"They'll be good for a bit now. Can I get you a drink?"

He shook his head. "Ah, no. Thanks. Callie—"

"No." She gave a sharp shake of her head, splayed her hands on the table and leaned forward. "You listen to me first—okay, Ben? I can't believe you stayed away for so long. It wasn't your fault. Jason did *not* die because of you."

Ben closed his eyes. While rationally he knew she was right that Jason had not died because of him—and a hard-won victory *that* was—being here, with Jason's young widow, he could still smell the smoke, hear the roar of the flames crackling in the back of his mind. It gave him a bad moment.

"I know that. It took me far too long to figure it out. I want to apologize for staying away so long. I never meant to. And I am terribly sorry for the loss of your husband and my friend."

"Thank you. That's an apology I will accept," Callie whispered. She threaded her fingers together. "While I know Jason for the most part followed the rules—he didn't want to be careless—he was at heart a risk-taker. Once he realized what had happened to you there was no stopping him." She took a shaky breath and Ben met her gaze, seeing the sadness in her green eyes. "He didn't think, Ben. That's the thing. He just acted. They told me—after—they told me they couldn't stop him. Nothing could have. He loved you like a brother."

"It was mutual." It was true. And he knew Callie was right about her husband. In a potential do-or-die situation there wasn't time to stand around and waffle about what action to take. He and Jason had both done the only thing they could do in the moment. If the situation had been reversed he would have done the same thing.

So many people said they'd walk through fire for their loved ones. Jason had actually done it.

The kids' laughter caused Callie to turn her head in their direction. She pulled out a chair and sank down into it. "I've been mad as hell," she said quietly. "But not at you. Or at least not about this. For staying away—that's something else entirely. Jason loved risk. I knew when I married him—well, I knew. I never thought it'd end like this, but it did." She tipped her head toward the living room. "And now they don't have a daddy. Jason didn't leave us on purpose. He wouldn't let you accept responsibility for his choices any more than you would have let him."

"I know that now," he said. "It took me a while to get there—longer than it should have. Callie—again, I am sorry. Sorrier than you know for your loss, for the boys' loss. Someone helped me see how blind I've been. It's been at your expense. I'm sorry." Lainey had been right when she'd said Jason hadn't given up his life so Ben could ignore his own.

Callie reached over and squeezed his hand, the sheen of tears in her green eyes. "Thank you for that. Please, don't be a stranger in our lives. You are such a valuable link to Jason, and I'd like the boys to know you. You can help them understand what their daddy was like as a fire-fighter."

"I will," he promised, relieved that the thought didn't fill him with the kind of pain he'd been accustomed to. The lightening of the load was an amazing thing, and while the apology he'd made had helped, it was Lainey who'd shown him the way.

He pulled Callie in for a hug. She hugged him back, then patted his chest.

"Who's the someone? She must be awfully special if you finally came to see me."

"Ah…" Uncomfortable, he looked into the living room, where the boys played with trucks and watched the movie. "She pointed out a few things to me that I'd been missing."

Callie gave a little laugh. "Well, I like her already. When can I meet her?"

He met her gaze. "Well, about that…"

Her eyes went to slits. "Oh, no. What did you do?"

Was he so transparent? He scrubbed his hand over his face, then gave her an abridged version of events and didn't cut himself any slack.

"Do you love her?"

"I do." There was no hesitation.

She gave him a small shove toward the door. "Then why are you still here? What you need to do is go back and see if she'll still have you." She gave him another little shove, her voice urgent. "Ben. You've got to go see if you can make it work. Don't waste any more time. You never know how much of it you have."

"I know. It's where I'm going next. Now I know—" He stopped, about to add, *what you and Jason had.* It seemed somehow cruel to bring it up.

But Callie nodded and smiled—a small smile, with tears in her eyes. "Yes. Now you know."

"I've got to go," he said. "I had to be sure you were okay."

"I'm hanging in there," she said softly. "It hasn't been easy, but I'm doing my best. I'll miss him every day for the rest of my life. But I knew my husband, Ben. I know how he was. I know *who* he was. And he's a hero."

"Yeah, he is." He drew her into another hug, rocked her back and forth. "Thanks, Callie."

She hugged him back tightly. "Go get her. Good luck."

"I will. And, God knows, I'll need it."

He left the house, with Callie standing on the porch, arms crossed against the cold, and drove away. He pointed the truck north, toward Holden's Crossing. Time to put the beginning of the rest of his life in motion. If Lainey would have him.

There was only one way to find out.

Lainey had shoved the last of the clothes in the dryer when she heard a knock on the kitchen door. It was seven-thirty on a rainy night. Who could possibly be stopping over this late? She trudged up the stairs and peeked out the peephole.

And gasped.

Ben stood there, rain glistening on his jacket. She blinked. Was it really him? Or was her mind playing tricks on her?

He knocked again and she jumped, her shaking hands making a fumbling hash of the lock and the knob. *Ben.* Why was he here? Could she take any more heartbreak? She was afraid the answer to that was no.

She swung the door open and simply drank him in. His intense gaze settled on her and she saw pain and longing there. Hope surged a little bit, but she tamped it down. He looked tired, and stress lines bracketed his mouth. Not for the first time she wanted to reach up and smooth them away.

"Lainey. Can I come in? I'll understand if you say no." His voice was a low rumble and she stepped to the side quickly, her heart hammering so hard she was afraid he'd hear it.

"Of course. I was just surprised." She shut the door behind him and turned to face him. As glad as she was to see him, a little anger flared. She welcomed it. She needed it to keep her distance from him until she knew why he was here. "Since you were pretty clear the other day that we weren't going to work out." She couldn't quite keep the bitterness out of her voice.

He let out a long exhale. The misery etched on his face echoed that in her heart. "I know. I'm sorry. I need to talk to you."

"I see. Well, come on in." Without waiting to see if he'd follow, she walked through the kitchen into the living room. She sat on a chair near the fireplace and wound her hands tightly together. The heat of the fire did nothing to soothe her nerves.

He didn't follow right away, but a thump from the kitchen area indicated he was probably removing his boots. A few seconds later he appeared and she had a hard time breathing. He seemed to fill the small space and absorb all the oxygen.

She gestured to the chair across from her. "Please sit."

He did, and she tried not to notice when he looked at her with a tenderness that nearly undid her. "Lainey. God, you're gorgeous."

She kept her gaze on his steady, even though she felt anything but steady inside. How could he say that? She'd barely slept and had no appetite. She was a mess, not to mention an emotional wreck. "Thank you." She didn't know what to say, what to ask. There was so much to say, really, she didn't know where to begin.

But, since he'd more or less rejected her, she'd let him talk first. He knew where she stood. She'd laid it out for him the other day in the garage. It was past time she could say the same about him.

He dropped his gaze, leaned forward and rested his forearms on his thighs. The awkwardness grew as he seemed to gather his thoughts. She watched the firelight dance on his dark hair. Finally, too tightly wound to wait, she gave in. She needed to know.

"Ben, why are you here?"

He looked up. "Should I be?"

The question threw her. "I don't know." Her voice dropped to a whisper. "You made it clear the other day you couldn't choose me." Despite her earlier flare of anger, she couldn't muster any heat in the words, only pain.

He took a deep breath and sat back. Her traitor cat came and wound around his ankles. She frowned at Panda, but of course the cat ignored her. Ben reached down to stroke his hand down Panda's back. "I was pretty screwed up, Lainey. In a lot of ways. I've still got work to do. I don't know when I'll be able to work again." He looked up and in his gaze she saw pain and something else. Her heart picked up. "You're going to be a mom. You need a guy who's stable. I can barely take care of myself. How could I take care of a family?"

"So you pushed me away," she said, unable to keep the hurt from her voice. She focused on the traitor cat at his feet.

He leaned forward and laid a hand on her arm, forcing her startled gaze to his. "I did. I thought it was better for you. I wanted to protect you," he admitted. "But you just kind of worked your way in and I started wanting more. A lot more. After you left the other day I realized how blind I'd been. I made an appointment with a counselor. And there was one last thing I needed to do."

"Callie?" she said softly.

He nodded. "I went and talked to Callie. Not for permission to move on, but because you were right. She was angry—but not for the reasons I thought. She was mad because she felt I'd abandoned her and the kids. She never blamed me. But even if I'd known that I'm not sure it would have made a difference."

His eyes were wet as he looked at Lainey and her heart broke for him.

"I blamed myself fully. But there were things that night that were out of my control, out of his control. I can't bring him back. But the way I've been living is no way to honor my best friend. Jason would kick my ass."

A surprised laugh bubbled out of her. "He sounds like a true friend."

Ben smiled. "He was. I wish you could have known him. He'd have liked you."

Tears stung her eyes. "I wish I could have, too. But—"

His smile turned sad. "But that's not how it is. I hope I can convince you to meet Callie, though. I think you'll like her. And the kids."

She circled back to the fact that had surprised her. "You saw a counselor?"

Ben nodded. "Well, not yet. The appointment is next week. Monday. One of the terms of coming off leave is I need to get a mental health exam, I guess you'd call it. I need to know—and my captain needs to know—I won't flashback and freeze the next time I go out on a call."

She swallowed hard. That didn't sound as if he was going to stay here. "Ah. Will it work?"

He gave her a crooked smile. "I don't know. I hope so. I'd like to be cleared in a month or so. I want to go back to work."

"That's great, Ben." She meant it. But, really, did the man have to drive all the way back here to tell her this? That he wouldn't be back, after all? A phone call would have given her a little more dignity. "Well, I'm sure they'll be thrilled to have you back."

Something in her tone must have given her away, because he looked at her quizzically. "They won't."

She stared at him for a moment, not comprehending. "But you just said—"

"I know," he interrupted her. "But you're jumping to conclusions. I won't be working in Grand Rapids. I'll be here. Or almost here. In Traverse City. Holden's Crossing is close enough I can live here. The job—it's time-consuming and there's always risk."

Her heart beat faster. Had he really just said what she thought she'd heard? "Oh," she said. "Here?"

Instead of answering right away, he came to his knees on the floor in front of her and cautiously laid his hand on her rounded belly. "I know it hasn't been that long," he murmured, "but I missed you. Both of you."

Lainey laid her hand on his and held her breath. She didn't trust herself to speak. She was afraid to ask the question, more afraid of the answer.

He slid a cold hand around the back of her neck and pulled her down toward him. "I love you," he whispered. "I love both of you. I missed you. So much." Then he kissed her, soft at first, then with more urgency.

"I love you, too," she whispered against his mouth. "Ben—"

He sat back and ran one hand down the side of her face. Her heart lifted at the reverence and love on his face. "So, to answer your question, yes. Here. In this house, if you want. I want to be your husband and a father to this baby. I know it's short notice, and I've been an idiot, and—damn it—I don't have a ring and you might not be ready—"

She laid her fingers on his lips, joy coursing through her. "I'm ready." Oh, was she ever? She'd been wrong about not needing a partner in her life—she needed Ben. She hadn't even known what she was missing until he'd come into her life. "There's no one I want to be with more than you."

His eyes widened and a slow smile spread across his face. "Are you sure?"

Her voice was strong and she was pretty sure she might burst with happiness. "Yes. I want forever. And I want it with you."

"Oh, thank God." He stood up and held out a hand, a wicked gleam in his eyes. "Then I say we go celebrate. Plus, I think we've got some making up to do." He gave her a little eyebrow-wiggle that made her laugh.

"Sounds good to me. We'd better get started." Lainey put her hand in his and smiled up at him, ready to embrace their future.

Ten months later

Lainey tugged at the bodice of her wedding dress for what had to be the fifteenth time in as many minutes. "Are you sure this looks secure?"

Beth, her matron of honor and business partner, laughed and pulled Lainey's hands down. "It looks great, Laine. No one can tell you've got nursing pads in the sexy bra under it. You are a gorgeous bride." She leaned over and plucked Lainey's bouquet from the box on the table, pressed it into Lainey's hands. "Here. Now, turn and look in the mirror."

Lainey did. The woman staring back at her barely re-sembled herself. Flushed cheeks, sparkling eyes, flowing off-white beaded simple strapless gown. The flowers, done by Lainey herself, were a perfect complement for a summer wedding in shades of pink and cream.

Beth touched the small veil that covered Lainey's head and shoulders. "See? Perfectly gorgeous. Are you ready?"

"Very." Lainey smiled at her friend. "I can't wait."

"Then let's go." Beth exited the small room, and with a deep breath Lainey followed.

As Beth took her place at the head of the aisle Lainey paused, out of sight of the guests in the sanctuary. A well of emotion threatened to break over her as her father and brother approached her. They were here to walk her down the aisle in this small church. Amazingly, her mother had exercised great restraint and hadn't interfered with the planning or the size of the wedding. Not too much, any-way. They'd made strides—especially after the birth of baby Lily.

Rose had her three-month-old great-granddaughter in the front pew. Lainey sincerely hoped she wouldn't have to take a break mid-ceremony and nurse her daughter.

Her heart was absolutely full.

"Honey, you look amazing," her father said, his voice rough with emotion, and Lainey blinked furiously.

"Don't make me cry," she managed on a laugh, and he squeezed her arm.

"No promises, there, my girl. It's your wedding. We may not have a choice."

She gave a little giggle as Kevin came to take his place at Lainey's side. He chucked her lightly under the chin. "Ready, little sis?"

She smiled up at him. Oh, was she ever? "Yes. Yes, I am."

The music swelled and Lainey moved to the head of the

aisle. She took the first few steps toward her future. Her gaze landed on Ben. Her steps nearly faltered as she took in how handsome he was in his tux and she couldn't take her eyes off him. He was hers.

Ben's gaze never left her, and she saw all the love, all the heat, all the joy in her own heart reflected on his face as she reached for his hands at the altar. Her heart swelled as she looked into his beautiful eyes.

"Hi," he whispered. "God, you're gorgeous."

She smiled back. "So are you."

Together they glanced at their daughter—the baby who was everything to Ben despite the fact she wasn't biologically his—then back at the minister, who now began the ceremony.

Somehow, despite everything, without even looking for it, they'd become a family.

Forever.

* * * * *

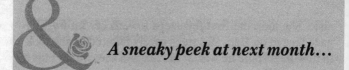

A sneaky peek at next month...

Cherish™

ROMANCE TO MELT THE HEART EVERY TIME

My wish list for next month's titles...

In stores from 17th May 2013:

☐ The Matchmaker's Happy Ending — Shirley Jump

& Second Chance with the Rebel — Cara Colter

☐ A Father for Her Triplets — Susan Meier

& First Comes Baby... — Michelle Douglas

In stores from 7th June 2013:

☐ From Neighbours...to Newlyweds? — Brenda Harlen

& The Texan's Future Bride — Sheri WhiteFeather

☐ Ten Years Later... — Marie Ferrarella

& Holding Out for Doctor Perfect — Teresa Southwick

Available at WHSmith, Tesco, Asda, Eason, Amazon and Apple

Just can't wait?

Special Offers

Every month we put together collections and longer reads written by your favourite authors.

Here are some of next month's highlights— and don't miss our fabulous discount online!

On sale 17th May

On sale 7th June

On sale 7th June

Save 20%
on all Special Releases